"She has been in a coma ever since...."

Piers Anthony responded to this mother's plea with a long letter, which did evoke a small response from the little girl when it was read to her in her hospital room. In that letter he promised to name a character after her in the next Xanth book he was working on.

But that letter was only the first of many. Anthony decided that he would write to Jenny every week, telling her of the progress of his writing. Jenny responded. Slowly at first, she began fighting back toward consciousness, and then health. First she managed to blink her eyes for "yes" and "no;" soon she could wiggle a toe, then a finger. And through it all, her favorite author sent her encouragement and sympathy and laughter and love.

Here are the first year's worth of letters to Jenny. These warm, compassionate and wise letters offer an unusual glimpse into the heart and mind of one of America's best-selling writers, and a look at the reasons behind his personal relationship with his legions of fans.

Tor Books by Piers Anthony

Alien Plot
Anthonology
But What of Earth?
Demons Don't Dream
Ghost
Hasan
Isle of Woman
Letters to Jenny
Prostho Plus
Race Against Time
Shade of the Tree
Steppe
Triple Detente

With Robert E. Margroff

Dragon's Gold
Serpent's Silver
Chimaera's Copper
Orc's Opal
Mouvar's Magic
The E.S.P. Worm
The Ring

With Frances Hall

Pretender

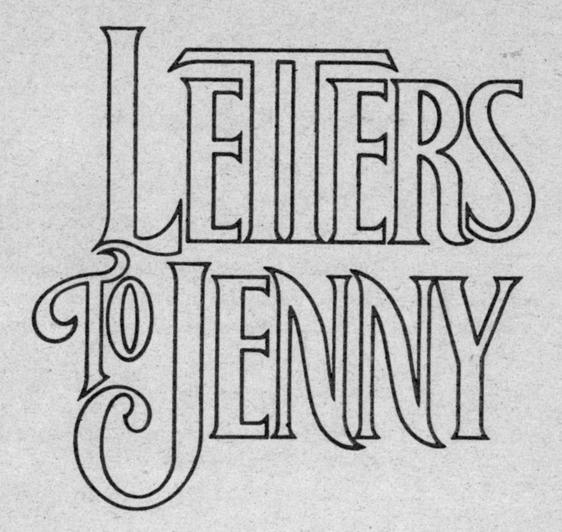

PIERS ANTHONY

A TOM DOHERTY ASSOCIATES BOOK
NEW YORK

LETTERS TO JENNY

Cover art by Jael

A Tor Book
Published by Tom Doherty Associates, Inc.
175 Fifth Avenue
New York, NY 10010

Tor® is a registered trademark of Tom Doherty Associates, Inc.

ISBN: 0-812-52282-6
Library of Congress Catalog Card Number: 93-19380

First edition: August 1993
First mass market edition: December 1994

Printed in the United States of America

0 9 8 7 6 5 4 3 2 1

Contents

Introduction

by Alan Riggs

A few words about the words that follow:

Whenever possible the letters in this volume have been preserved in their original form. The words have been altered only when necessary to preserve the privacy and peace of mind of the families involved. Where Piers felt that additional comments would help clarify the letters, he has added brief notes at the end of chapters.

A few words about the story that follows:

Do not be deceived. This is not just a collection of correspondence, of interest only to literati and biographers. Taken by itself, each letter is a brief glimpse into the thoughts of one man, a snapshot of the lives of two people, a few frames featuring the bit players in some vast motion picture. Taken as a whole, they become scenes in a touching and compelling story, a story which speaks softly and strongly to those well-guarded parts within us that still reach out in hope.

When I first reviewed these letters for Piers I was struck by the power and sensitivity of that story. More than once, I cried as the narrative unfolded. Months later, as I read through the letters again in preparing this volume, I was again surprised by the essential unity of this account. You see, I had begun with some idea that it was necessary to decide *which* story these letters should tell: "The Famous Author and the Adoring Fan"; "The Young Girl Struck Down Tragically and Fighting to Recover"; "The Old Man Trying to Help the Youth in Trouble"? But that decision was not mine to make. As with all the best stories, this one defined itself. The beginning is unadorned. The ending hasn't happened yet. And the story is the story of Piers and Jenny.

Consider yourself introduced.

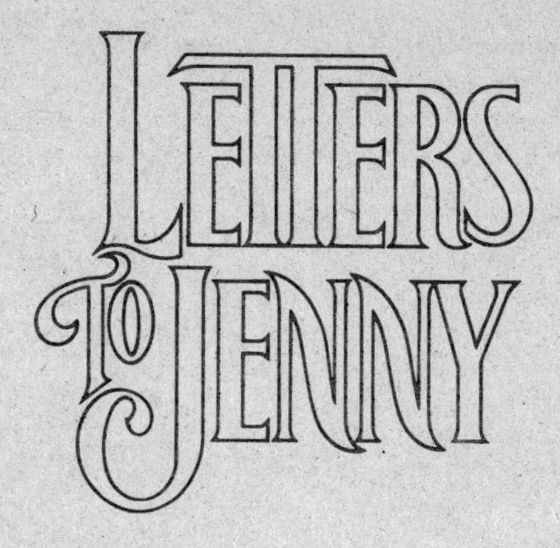
LETTERS TO JENNY

February 1989

A story begins.

Dear Mr. Anthony,

Let me get right to the point: I need your help.

I'm at my wit's end and am grabbing at straws, so decided to write to you in hopes that you might take a few moments of your time for my daughter Jennifer.

Jennifer is twelve years old, and, along with the rest of the family has very much enjoyed your Xanth series. Unfortunately, at the moment, she is in no condition to be able to enjoy your latest offering. On December 9th 1988 while walking home from school she was struck by a drunk driver, and she has been in a coma ever since.

She is responding to very little, although she will, occasionally and inconsistently, wiggle the big toe of her right foot, lift her head and/or track with her eyes, upon request. We've managed to elicit some minor response from her (a widening of the eyes and a heavy sigh) by showing her pictures of our cats and reading a note from one of her friends, but aside from that, she will more often than not merely lie in her bed, staring off into space, either refusing or unable to cooperate with us or her therapists. We know that she can hear us, but just how much she is able to perceive is in question. There is SOME perception there since she seems to remember her cats and her friends, as evidenced by her reactions to the photographs and the reading of the note from her friend, and by the movements performed, however sporadically, on request.

As I've already mentioned, she's read and enjoyed all but one of your Xanth books, and the rest of us, my brother and I in particular, have read them all with great relish. Some of your creatures and creations have even managed to insinuate themselves into our everyday conversation: "Mom, how do you spell [whatever]?" "Do I look like a spelling bee? Go look it up in the dictionary!" and "Jennifer, look at this plant! I just watered it yesterday, and yet it's wilted as if to die!" "Agent Orange must have done it, Mother . . ." (I later found out that our big orange cat, Peanut, decided that the planter remarkably resembled a kitty-litter pan and chose that spot to relieve himself! Agent Orange, indeed!) or "Mother, may I have a pair of those new shoes like Carrie's got?" "Not till pay day—if that's not soon enough for you, go pick them off the Lady Slipper bush in the back garden!" Of course, we have our own Gap Chasm (a drainage ditch that runs the length of our back property) and a Gap Dragon (a nasty stray tom who'll attack anything that moves) to inhabit it. And many's the time that I've sworn it must be a Forget Spell on Jenny's school books that caused her to forget just how much homework had been assigned, or a Forget Whorl that somehow got trapped in her room, since she just could never remember it long enough to keep it tidy. On the other hand, Jennifer maintains that the television is a hypnogourd because her daddy exhibits a vacant stare while gazing into it, and the only way to break his attention away from it is to step directly in front of the screen. The Bed Monster is blamed for anything that's gotten lost in her room ("He took it because he got jealous that I'm not spending enough time with him, Mother"), and I've been accused of taking lessons from Grundy Golem after having hurled a particularly nasty epithet at someone or something that's made me cross. There are many other examples, but I believe that these more than illustrate my point.

We've been trying everything imaginable to stir something within her, to help her come out of this coma. Anything that might elicit some response, however slight, would be a blessing. I believe that a letter or note from you, the author of her favorite books, just might get a reaction from Jennifer. Sayings and characters from your books have become familiar friends in our household, and to me it seems only logical that a word to Jenny from you would be something to which she could relate and possibly respond. Mr. Anthony, my gratitude would know no bounds if you could find it within your heart to write something to my daughter. I realize that your time is exceedingly limited, and I would not ask this of you if I did not believe that it just might make a difference.

Before undertaking the writing of this letter, I spoke with a friend of mine, another author (Andrea Alton, whose book *Demon of Undoing* was recently released by BAEN BOOKS), to get an author's perspective on the request I wished to make of you. She encouraged me not only to write you, but went so far as to suggest that I ask you to name a Xanth character after Jenny, telling me that naming a character after someone isn't difficult to do since the character itself does not have to resemble that person in the slightest. Just the fact that a character has been named after one would be honor enough. And the last thing she said was that the worst you could do would be to say, "No." I was hesitant at first to make so bold, but, as Andrea told me, there was no harm in asking, and should you decide to do Jennifer the honor, I'm certain that it would be one of the high points in her life.

The latter is purely secondary to my original request, however.

Jennifer is currently at Cumberland Hospital in their Acute Care section. If you are able to write to her, please send it to our home address. We will take it to the hospital, read it to her ourselves and reiterate just WHO the letter is from.

Thank you, Mr. Anthony, for having spent the time to read my letter, and I ask you, please, to give serious consideration to my request.

FeBlueberry 27, 1989

Dear Jenny,

Your mother told me that you were in an accident, and are in the hospital. She asked me to write to you, because though you and I have never met, you know of me and like my books. I am Piers Anthony, the author of the Xanth series of fantasy novels.

Let me tell you some things about myself that you may not know. I liked writing the Xanth novels, because they are really set in the state where I live, Florida, with some magic added. They became very popular, and the publisher paid me a lot of money, and I used it to buy a tree farm, because I like trees and want to have more of them in the world. We built a house on that tree farm, and now we live in it, and our horses graze among the pine trees. Today a man was mowing between the rows of pines, so that the grass can grow better for the horses. I went out to see how it was going, and I saw that some small wild trees were getting mowed down, because they don't belong among the pines. Even some small pine trees were crooked, and got pushed down too. I hate to see that, but there's not much way to run a tree farm except to keep the wrong trees out. There are blueberry bushes growing wild between the rows, and they will get mowed down too. I wish that didn't have to be, because I like blueberries. Your mother can tell you how much I like blueberries, because I named this month after them. I walked among the bushes this afternoon, and I thought of you, because I had just read your mother's letter. I think you were mowed down through no fault of your own, and I'm sorry that it happened. I like trees, but I also like people, and I don't like to see any of them hurt. I have two daughters, Penny and Cheryl; they are both in college now, as perhaps you will be some day. I remember how it was when they were babies, and when they were just starting school, and when they were your age, and when they grew up and became young ladies. Now they are away, and it is quiet here. It has been said that a child is someone who passes through your life and disappears into an adult. That is sad, in a way, because to my mind there is nothing more precious than a little girl; but also happy in a way, because it means they can finally make their own lives. But what is worst is when they don't make it through, because something terrible happens along the way.

You were struck by a car, and now you are in the hospital. I learned of a young man who liked my novels, just as you do, who was writing a novel of his own. He was struck by a car and killed, at the age of sixteen. His folks sent his partly-done novel to me, and I finished it, and this year it will be published. It is called *Through the Ice*. It was a terrible thing that happened to him, and a terrible thing that happened to you. But you are alive, and I hope you will get better. I hope that some day you will be able to read that novel, even though it will make you sad because of what happened to him.

I understand that you read the Xanths except for the last one, *Heaven Cent*. Let me tell about that one, because then I can tell you something that may interest you. In that novel, nine year old Prince Dolph sets out to find the Good Magician Humfrey, who disappeared in the last novel. His parents say he has to travel with an adult—you know how parents are!—so he goes with Marrow Bones, the walking skeleton. He has many adventures, and meets two nice girls. He agrees to marry both of them, when he grows up in seven years. For some reason his parents don't understand about that; they think he should marry only one of them. (I told you how parents are!) So they ground him until he decides between the girls. But it is even more complicated than that, because the girl he really likes, Nada Naga, who can turn into a snake, is not the child of eight he thought, but a young woman of fourteen. What a disaster! That's the same age as his big sister Ivy. The other girl, Electra, is your age, twelve; she was put to sleep for most of a thousand years when she took a bite of the wrong apple, until Prince Dolph woke her, and now she will die if she doesn't marry him. What is he to do? I think you will like Electra, and understand her problem.

Well, the next novel, *Man From Mundania*, which will be published this OctOgre, doesn't answer that question, because it's about Ivy when she is seventeen, and shows how she shocks everybody by wanting to marry a man from—no, it's too horrible, so I won't say more about that. Oh, he's a nice young man, but I mean who in her right mind would get serious about a Mundanian? But the novel after that, Xanth #13, will be *Isle of View*, and in that one Prince Dolph will come of age and have to make his choice. Nada is the one he likes, despite her age, but he doesn't want Electra to die. So the two girls, who are now young women, try to settle it on their own by going on a quest. Maybe something will happen to one of them, and then Dolph can marry the other. But they are both nice girls, and they like each other, so they really don't want anything bad to happen. They encounter Che, a little winged centaur who is lost, and try to help him find his mother, who is Chex Centaur, whom you may remember. I'm sure there will be many adventures, but I don't know what they are because I haven't written that novel yet. I should be working on it in a couple of months, though.

Now here is where you come in. I realize that this is a long letter, and you probably fell asleep after the first paragraph, but now you have to wake up, because I'm going to put you in that story. Well, not you exactly, but your name. I'll have a girl your age named Jenny. She probably won't look anything like you, and she may not be human; she may be an elf girl. Do you read ELFQUEST? Then you know about elves. Someone like that, maybe. I'll find out when I get there. I suppose she could be an ogre girl—oh, all right, not that, if you feel that way. Anyway, if you would like to have some say in the matter, tell your mother, and she will write to me. But don't worry, she'll be a nice girl. Maybe some day you will get to read about her, and you'll tell everyone "She's named after me!" and no one will believe you. Then you can turn to the Author's Note at the end, where it will tell who Jenny is named after, and show them, and then they'll say "Who cares?" which will mean they are secretly jealous.

All right, now you can sleep, after you pet the Monster Under the Bed. I'll bet you didn't know he got lonely, and moved under your hospital bed. No, don't ask the nurses; they're grown up, and can't see him. If they did see him, they'd probably just give him a loathsome shot in the rump. He wouldn't like that. Maybe Mare Imbri will bring you a sweet dream, and you'll have a harpy night.

But puns aside, my best to you, honey. Get well soon. Here's a Harpy Holiday card for you, a bit out of season, but you know how harpies are.

Dear Mr. Anthony,

Thank you so very much!!! We received your card and letter to Jennifer on March 2nd, though today was the first time since its arrival that we've had the opportunity to travel the 53 miles to go see her (a blizzard, then freezing rain, icy roads and all that sort of wretchedness), so it wasn't until this afternoon that we read to her your words.

I wish I could give you news of a miraculous spontaneous recovery; however, I CAN give a report of the next best thing: your letter brought a great widening of her eyes and a smile to her lips (a first since the accident), and when asked how she'd like to be represented in your story it was VERY clear that she greatly preferred an Elven persona to all others. The "Harpy Holidays" card is very beautiful, and I believe that Jennifer was able to at least partially perceive it when we held it up in front of her eyes. We hung it in a prominent position on the wall of her hospital room where she would be able to readily view it whenever she should so desire.

You appear to have a great deal of insight, and on many levels, Mr. Anthony. Yes, Jenny does very much like ELFQUEST, and has worn those books dog-eared from all the reading and rereading of them. And, I also thought that it was clever of you to include the portion reading, in part: ". . . if you would like to have some say in the matter, tell your mother, and she will write to me . . ." It gives her a bit of incentive to try to communicate more, as well as imbuing her with a sense of having a bit of control over her own circumstances.

We've made "flash cards" for her with the words "YES" and "NO" printed on them in LARGE letters, and she differentiated between the two today (another first!). When she gets worked up and excited she begins to perspire and to shake with what appears to be a form of sensory overload, whereupon she becomes totally confused, and we have to give her a breather to let her get a grip on the situation and to be able to make the connection between what we're asking her to do and how to respond. She did respond consistently (four times in a row) to the questions, "Would you like to be an Elf in Mr. Anthony's book?" (she glanced to the "YES" card) and "Would you rather be something other than an Elf in Mr. Anthony's book?" (she glanced toward the "NO" card). After doing that four times she started to shake and perspire, so I told her that it was time for her to take a little break, and that I was going to the cafeteria to grab a cup of tea while she recovered somewhat, and would be back shortly.

The rest of the afternoon spent with Jenny was a pure delight. She wriggled her right big toe for us so much that I thought it was going to fly right off her little foot, and as I'd mentioned earlier, she did several things today that she's never done before, one of the most impressive being that she actually squeezed my fingers, and then let go on request. This she did four times before I called her daddy in to see it, then she did again while he watched, whereupon we called for the nurse to witness this minor miracle, and she not only squeezed my fingers in front of the nurse, and let go on request, but she squeezed the nurse's fingers, too. The nurse was singularly impressed with Jenny's "showing off"! She was one happy and responsive little pumpkin today, and I firmly believe that your letter had a great deal to do with it. I certainly hope and pray that her progress continues in this vein, and I've left a request for the nurses to read your letter to her periodically, and to question her on her preferences whenever they think it would benefit her mood or willingness to work on coming up out of the fog.

You told Jennifer a few things about yourself, so I'd like to tell you a few things about Jenny. Though academically a bit on the stubborn side, she is extremely talented in the area of art. She is rather accomplished for a child of twelve, and her drawings are alive with movement and wordless poetry of the kind rarely found in what passes nowadays for art. She attended a school for gifted and talented children, and while her math grades left quite a bit to be desired, her reading and her art classes were A+ work. My daughter's art teacher told me candidly that Jenny was by far one of the most creative art students she'd ever had the occasion to teach, and strongly recommended that should she express the desire to do so, we allow her to attend art classes in addition to the ones at school.

Jenny's art reflected her strong love of fantasy and nature (which from my point of view are by no means mutually exclusive), her main subjects being princesses and unicorns. Now I've heard all the psychological arguments surrounding girl-children and their equine interests, but be that as it may, Jennifer's art bespoke of a love of magic and sweetness and nature that belies any psychobabble. Just as you paint a picture with words, Jennifer authored entire stories with one drawing.

As for Jennifer's physical characteristics, she's slightly chubby (as her mother I tend to think of it as "cherubic" rather than "Chubby"!), with a turned up nose, a few freckles spattered across her cheeks, and chestnut brown hair that streaks almost butter blond with the coming of the summer sun. Her hands are deft, her fingers long and slender; strong enough to pull a recalcitrant weed from her rose garden, gentle enough to quiet a trembling rabbit ousted from his hutch while his straw is changed. Her brown eyes, though quite myopic without her spectacles, are quick enough to pick up a change in the gait of one of our eleven cats ("Mother, I think Smokey's got his old kidney problem again—see, he's walking with a bit more waddle than usual . . .").

She has a magnificent ear for music, and, when she believes herself to be alone, sings her little heart out, sometimes one of the medieval ballads we all know, occasionally something she's heard on the radio, but more often than not, she makes up her melody and lyrics as she goes along, singing to her rabbit, her roses, one of the cats, a stray dog, or just to herself as she does her chores or draws a picture. Her songs, though simple, are strangely beautiful, being comprised of what she's feeling at the moment, or things she sees that strike her fancy. She's exceedingly bashful about her singing, though, and while we've countless times tried to coax her into singing with us during a musical session, she's always been more comfortable beating the drum or filling in on the keyboard than giving voice to the music within her while in the presence of any but herself, her flowers, or the animals.

If there is any such thing as magic in this world, I believe that it would be found in Jenny's singing and her artwork. When she sings, sketches, works in the garden, or keeps company with the animals, she's transported to a world of her own making, one in which magic is the essence of life, people are good, elves inhabit the nooks and crannies (you need only look a bit further than the end of your nose to find them), all animals are friendly, and monsters just need to be shown a little kindness and love to enable them to comport themselves with some modicum of decency. And sometimes, when I listen to my daughter sing, or watch her draw, I'm transported with her, and often I find myself quite reticent to drag myself back to the real world of deadlines, dirty dishes, crashed computers and skinned knees.

I am unable to adequately express my gratitude, Mr. Anthony. Your letter means so much to Jennifer, and it means just as much to me. To see my daughter smile after three months of non-responsiveness is to me the greatest gift in the world. I agree wholeheartedly with your words, ". . . to my mind there is nothing more precious than a little girl. . . ." But to me, it's MY little girl who is the most precious in the world (as I'm certain yours are to you), and the gift you gave her of your time and the thoughtfulness you exhibited in the writing of your letter to her is helping to bring my Little Gift back to me again.

I will write and keep you informed of Jenny's progress, and will keep you up to date on anything she communicates to me regarding her, ". . . say in the matter . . ." of preference in characterization.

Again let me express a resounding "Thank You" for having written to my daughter.

---

*Author's Note:

On occasion there are references that need to be clarified, so I will do so by means of asterisk footnotes like this. Though Jenny's mother had told me much about Jenny, I knew there was much I did not know, so I was careful. I addressed my comments to what I assumed would be of interest to any twelve-year-old girl in Jenny's situation, and when in doubt, I made sure to explain things carefully. As time passed, and I got to know Jenny better, and as she got older, I spoke more specifically, and sometimes more intimately. But at this stage I did not know that Jenny was to become my major correspondent, with hundreds of letters.

March 1989

An alphabet board spells its first word, "CAT," and begins its second, "XAN. . . ." Some letters arrive addressed to an elf named Jenny c/o the Monster Under the Bed in A Cute Care Section of a Cumbersome Hospital. Eleven cats vie for a maiden's favor. And a little girl laughs again for the first time.

Marsh 10, 1989

Dear Jenny,

Remember me? I'm the author of the Xanth novels. I wrote to you in FeBlueberry, the day I received your mother's letter. I said I was going to put a Jenny in my next Xanth novel, *Isle of View.* You don't remember? I thought maybe I'd make her an ogre girl, and—oh, you *do* remember! You were just teasing me. And you say you want her to be an elf girl. Okay, elf she is. It's been a long time since there's been a lady elf as a character in Xanth, about 400 years, when Bluebell Elf had something to do with Jordan the Barbarian. Never mind what; the Adult Conspiracy forbids me from discussing anything like that with you. Today Rapunzel is their distant descendent. So it's about time that a full elf made the scene again. I will be starting to work on that novel about the time this letter reaches you, but it will be the end of Mayhem by the time it is finished, because even with magic these things take time.

Then it will be late 1990 before it is published, because there isn't much magic in Mundania, and things take much longer there.

Your mother says that Fracto, the evil cloud, tried to stop her from bringing my letter to you at the hospital; he blew up a real blizzard and spread ice on the roads. Yes, he does that. But she finally did get through. She says when you heard the letter, you smiled, for the first time in the three centuries since you had the accident. Well, maybe it wasn't quite that long, but it seemed like it, didn't it? Thank you; I'm glad you were listening. She says you managed to wiggle a toe and squeeze her fingers and move your eyes around, and that you could indicate Yes or No. Just now, while typing this letter, I called the hospital and asked the nurse at the Acute Care Section how you were doing, and she said you are improving. That's the way! I guess it's no secret that you have a long way to go. It's like falling into a deep pit, and having to climb your way out inch by inch, and it's hard, and your folks are sort of peeking over the edge, far above, and calling to you, but they can't climb for you. You have to do it yourself, and maybe you get very tired, and maybe you slide back down sometimes, and that's very frustrating. But you're in a good place, the A-cute section; you should see the ones at the A-ugly section! The point is to make a bit of progress when you can, no matter how slow it seems. Remember what I said: things take time, in Mundania, because there is hardly any magic there.

The nurse said you hadn't regained consciousness yet. That's all she knows! She must think that if you don't sit up and scream, you're not awake. Actually, your mind is going at a mile a minute, but your body is stuck in slow-sand and doesn't respond. Nerves take a long time to heal; you just have to be maddeningly patient. Maybe that's why they call the folk in hospitals "patients." They're really "impatients" because they want to get out of there fast.

Well, you're stuck there for a while. At least they can't stop you from dreaming. You can dream about being in Xanth. I haven't figured out yet what Jenny is doing in Xanth; I think she's lost, at first. So is Che, the winged centaur foal. I think she has one of her cats with her, which is odd, because there aren't many elf-cats in Xanth. Well, we'll see.

Remember, don't let any night mares in. Only Mare Imbri, the day mare, with her sweet dreams. And smile for your mother; it makes her so happy. She wrote me a four page letter, when you smiled.

Marsh 18, 1989

Dear Jenny,

I think you had a better day than I did, today! This is Saturday, and I was trying to edit and print out a piece I wrote for a writer's magazine. I mention you in that piece, though I don't give your name; I just said that even funny fantasy can relate to serious life, and told how a twelve year old girl perked up when I wrote to her, after being pretty much out of it for months. You see, some folk think that fantasy is stupid and that writers should stick to serious things, like international politics, instead of wasting their time with puns and goblins and all. I get annoyed by that attitude, for some reason, and when I get annoyed I can become most expressive. So I wrote that article, and I suspect it will be published eventually. Anyway, everything went wrong. Do you know about computers? Not yet? Well, here is all you need to know: when you sit down at a computer, it is out to get you. It will pretend to behave, but the moment you aren't watching, it will do something to you. You have to be paranoid to stay ahead of a computer. So when I went to print out my article, I thought things were fine. I have a nice laser printer whose print looks just like this: [tell the one who is reading this letter to you to hold it up for you]. See? Usually for letters I use the dot-matrix printer, while I save this one for my novels. So the first copy I printed had the wrong heading on it: it said ISLE OF VIEW, which is the title of the novel Jenny Elf will be in, any day now when I catch up with a pile of letters. All right, my fault; I forgot to tell it this was a separate article. So I typed in Anthony instead, and printed those 8 pages again. This time it didn't have any page numbers. Somehow they had gotten erased when I changed the heading. So I remade it to get it right, and ran off a third copy, and this one had the "Anthony" and the page number—but it had changed it to justify on the right margin. That is, it made the words line up evenly on the right side, just as they do on the left side. Growl! I didn't want that! So I remade the heading once more, and ran off the fourth copy, and it finally was right. My afternoon was gone, too. So you see, you were doing better than I was, because you smiled and laughed today. I wasn't laughing, I was saying #$%&*!! [no, don't translate that!] because of all the time and paper I wasted today. Just to top it off, I shoveled some horse manure for my wife's bulbs she's planting—yes, our horse Blue is the model for Mare Imbri the Night Mare, and she's a wonderful horse, though she is 31 years old now, which is pretty old for a person, let alone a horse, as your mother will tell you—and it was full of ants and a red ant bit me. Now I don't like to hurt other creatures, but when that red ant bit me I squished it, and I feel sort of bad about the whole thing.

So I decided to do something nice with what remained of my day, and write to you. Your mother called me last Monday, and said your father read my second letter to you, and that you really liked it. She was very pleased. Apparently you had had nothing better to do than watch the hypnogourd—oh, in Mundania that's called the TV set—and that my letter snapped you out of that. I'm glad to know you enjoyed the letter. So as I set up to type this letter, I phoned the Cumbersome Hospital and asked about you. But when the aide found out who I was, she freaked out and refused to tell me anything. So I called your mother, and if you think my day was bad, you should hear about hers! That ear ache, you know. She said she was in the perfect mood for a good fight. She's another person who can get most expressive when annoyed. I guess you know that. At any rate, she called the hospital and got it straightened out. We figured out what happened: the aide thought I was someone else. But I did learn about your good day, and that's what counted.

So I'm sorry about boring you with all this business—oh, you're not bored yet? Or maybe you're just too polite to say so. Okay, stop me when you do get bored. You know, I hate to waste time. I mean I have things to do, like writing *Isle of View*, so I can't afford to waste time in mundane things. But last month one of my readers asked me to come see a play his group was doing. So I went, and I happened to be in a bad place in the auditorium, and all the sound was garbled, so for two hours I was stuck not being able to hear the play. I talked with the man afterward, and he said they had a catalog, and I could order a video tape of that play. So I did that, and also ordered some music from that catalog. You know about music? I love it. Actually, I love all the arts, but I was able to get good in only one of them, writing. I had thought of being an artist, but though I did have talent, it wasn't enough. I took a semester of piano in college, and the teacher said I could become a decent pianist if I worked at it, but I'm not a piano man. I like the recorder. You know, that's like a wooden flute. I have a nice tenor recorder, but twenty years ago when I picked it up to play, a roach fell out of the mouthpiece and I lost my interest in playing for a decade or two. Anyway, I was never much good at it, and I don't read music, so mostly I just listen to it. When you get older and start reading my Adept and Incarnations series you'll see how I build music in to those novels. The right music just does something to you that can't quite be described—yes, I see you do understand. When I was your age I used to sing folk songs to myself; I memorized about fifty of them, which was something, because I hate to memorize. But I wouldn't sing when anybody else was around, because they didn't understand. When I got to college I sang folk songs with other students, and took a semester of chorus. Some of those songs are really great when you have all the harmonies. But mostly music has just been my secret. Anyway, when the order arrived I looked at the cover on a record called "Heartdance," and that picture fascinates me. I have it propped up where I can see it while I work. It shows huge old stone musical instruments—a violin, a special kind of guitar, and something called a hammered dulcimer—I mean, these things are about fifty feet tall, and cracking apart, and the grass is starting to grow over them. But at the top a young woman in a red dress is dancing, and in the background there are stone walls, and green pastures, and on a mountain way in back what may be a castle. I haven't even listened to the record yet—I have to take time to get my record player set up—but I just keep looking at it, with the girl dancing to hidden music, and who knows what fantasy in the background. So I did what comes naturally: I'll make that scene part of a future novel. No, not a Xanth novel; this really isn't that kind of picture. This will be one titled *Fractal Mode*. By the time I write it, and you read it, you'll be fifteen or sixteen, just about like that girl in the picture, and then you can dance to the hidden music too.

Are you bored yet? No? Then why are you snoring? Oh—it's the Bed Monster snoring. Yes, he does that. He's not interested in music or pictures, just ankles. Okay, I'm running out of time, so I'll tell you about one more thing. It's a secret, so don't tell your folks, because they might get the wrong idea about Xanth. Or, worse, the right idea! One of the things in *Heaven Cent* is when Prince Dolph watches a mer-woman change her fishtail into legs. They can do that, you know; they make legs when they need to walk on land. Dolph is worried, because his mother Irene was very strict about boys not being allowed to see girls' panties. I mean, wouldn't you die of embarrassment if you were walking along, and a gust of wind blew up your skirt, and some stupid boy saw your panties? But then Dolph relaxes, because he realizes he isn't seeing any panties—because the mer-woman isn't wearing any. He won't be in trouble after all! That's the part you mustn't let your folks know about, because they might not think it is funny. But Dolph is incorrigible; he keeps trying to see someone's panties, and he does get in trouble for it, as boys do. We tackle this issue head-on in Xanth #15, which is to be titled *The Color of Her Panties*. That's the mer-woman's panties, of course. You see in #14, *Question Quest*, the Good Magician Humfrey searches for the one question he can't answer, and that question turns out to be "What is the color of the mer-woman's panties?" He can't answer because she doesn't wear any. It's a real problem. But remember, don't tell anyone about all this; I don't want to get in trouble. Anyway, I still have to write #13 and figure out what Jenny Elf is doing there.

Keep getting better, Jenny; you're making everyone very happy. Except maybe King Fracto Cumulo Nimbus, the evil cloud, who hates to see anyone being happy.

Marsh 26, 1989

Dear Jenny,

I have a whole lot of news this time, so you won't have to sleep through this letter. I wrote you a three page letter a week ago, and it probably bored you, but this one will be more interesting.

You see, I have just finished writing the first draft of

the first chapter of *Isle of View*, and have just introduced Jenny Elf—and the second chapter will be all about her. But before I tell you about that, I have to tell you some other things. Yes, I know I promised this wouldn't be boring, but such a promise is almost impossible for an adult to keep. I was delayed for several days because I had to proofread the galleys for another one of my novels, *And Eternity*, which will be published early next year. If I don't read the galleys carefully—they are an early printout of the novel—and catch the errors, it will be published all wrong. But at least I had figured out the chapters for *View*. They are all alliterative—that is, the first letters match—and they sort of hint at what's going on. Here, I have printed out a copy for you. The first chapter is "Chex's Challenge." Do you remember Chex from *Vale of the Vole?* The winged centaur filly? She got married in the next novel, and now she has a foal, Che, and someone has kidnapped him. So her challenge is to find him before anything bad happens to him. She's pretty desperate, the way mothers are. At the end of the chapter she encounters an elf girl with a cat.

I paused here to phone the Cumbersome Hospital and inquire how you were doing. (I had to wait until my daughter Cheryl got off the phone; she's home from college, and she's my Elfquest expert. Yes, I know I have written a story for Elfquest—it's in *Blood of Ten Chiefs*—but my daughter is the elf freak in this family.) The lady took a while to answer, because she was with you. I didn't mean to interrupt that! She said you had a good day and were smiling a lot, and that you sat in the sunshine for a while. That's nice. I told her to tell you I'd called. You do remember who I am? Don't give me that perplexed look! I see that smirk hiding. You're trying to pretend you don't remember, and it won't work. Not this time. I think.

Where was I? Oh, yes—the elf girl and her cat. That's Jenny Elf, and her cat can find anything—except home. So she has to chase after him (maybe it's a her—your mother described your eleven cats and one rabbit to me, but didn't say which one of them finds things, so I don't have a name or description yet. When you hear this letter, you can let me know exactly which cat it is) so she can bring him back home when he gets lost. This time he was looking for a centaur feather, and he found it, but by the time he did, he was lost and so was Jenny Elf. *Really* lost. Because, you see, she's not from Xanth. Xanth elves are associated with Elf Elms, and the farther from the elms they get, the weaker they are. Jenny is from the World of Two Moons, and she doesn't know anything about elms or centaurs. That's right—she's an Elfquest elf, and oh, boy is she lost! She was so busy chasing after the cat, just trying to keep him in sight, that she paid no attention to the route they took, and made a journey no one else ever made before, from Elfquest to Xanth. The second chapter will be all about her. See, it's titled "Jenny's Journey." Now I'll have to bore you with some technical stuff again. You see, I can't just take an Elfquest elf without asking. But as it happens, I know Richard Pini, who publishes Elfquest; his wife Wendy draws the pictures. So I'll make sure it's okay with him. I'm sure it will be. Some day they may make Xanth into one of their comics, so we have to get along. When we met, Cheryl just about freaked out, meeting someone that famous. She was trying to drink a milkshake, as I recall, and each time she took a mouthful he would say something funny so that she had to laugh. We have a picture of her trying not to laugh in the middle of a mouthful; her cheeks are bulging and she looks desperate. I'm the only other one I know who is mean enough to do that to a fan. Anyway, it should be all right, and this will be something unique: Elfquest in Xanth. If folk hate it, it's all your fault.

Okay, you can wake up now, the boring part is over. Chex mentions that she's looking for Che, and Jenny's cat takes off, and Jenny runs after him because she knows she'll never find him if she doesn't keep him in sight. He's not running away from her, understand; he just gets so excited with the chase after something that he forgets. He really does want to come home, once he finds what he's after. Chex tries to follow, but they disappear into the thick jungle where she can't follow and are lost. That's why the second chapter is from Jenny's view. The cat finds Che—but the goblins have him. That's bad, and Jenny knows she has to do something to get him away. She does, but then the goblins chase her too. She finds a raft and takes Che on it on the With-a-Cookee river where they can't go. (Oddest coincidence: near here we have the Withlacoochee River that flows the same way.)

Well, there's a whole lot of adventure I won't bore you with, because I haven't figured it out yet. But near the end they learn why the goblins grabbed Che: the granddaughter of their chief is a very nice girl—goblin men are all ugly and mean, but their girls are pretty and nice—but she's lame and just can't get around very well. So they wanted to get a good steed for her, so she can ride places. Of course Che is too young to ride, let alone fly, but the goblins didn't know that. The goblin girl is Gwendolyn, Gwenny for short, and Jenny likes her a lot. It's really too bad she can't have a centaur to ride. No need to spoil the ending for you—what? But—well, if you feel that way, okay, I'll spoil it. They finally take Gwenny to live with the centaurs, and Jenny stays with them too, because no one knows how to get back to the World of Two Moons. Not in this novel, anyway.

There's more to the novel, about Dolph and which of his two betrothees he chooses, but you have the idea about Jenny Elf. She wraps up in Chapter 14, and then we go to Dolph and the girls for what turns out to be a really difficult decision. I wonder if the Elfquest folk will want to take Jenny back to their world and have her in a comic? You never can tell what will happen. Anyway, you now know more about it than anyone else does, and I hope you're satisfied. You aren't? You what? Oh, yes, Jenny Elf does look a bit like you, in her elfin way. I thought you understood about that.

Odds & ends: remember when you smiled for the first time, and your mother was so excited she wrote me a four page letter? Well, then you laughed, and she wrote six pages. You had better slow down, because you don't want her to write even more! I managed to make her laugh, when I told her on the phone about the key I have on my computer; when I touch it, it flashes DON'T TOUCH THIS KEY AGAIN!. Another says HELP! I'M BEING HELD CAPTIVE IN THIS COMPUTER. It's a strange thing: your mother started smiling and laughing again just about the time you did. Isn't that a coincidence? Or maybe it was magic.

I meant to explain about something that happened way back at the beginning of time, when you listened to my first letter. (When folk are my age, it can be easier to remember the distant past than what happened five minutes ago.) Your mother asked you whether you'd like to have a Jenny Elf or a Jenny Ogress in the novel, and you indicated that you wanted the elf. She asked you again, and you indicated the elf again. She asked you the same question yet again, and you began to get a bit impatient, because you'd already answered it twice, and wondered why she wasn't paying attention. Then she asked still another time, and you got sort of frustrated. WHAT DO I HAVE TO DO TO GET YOUR ATTENTION—HIT YOU OVER THE HEAD WITH A TANGLE TREE?! I SAID ELF! At which point she began to get overexcited, and had to leave for a while. Well, I wanted to explain her side of it. At first she could hardly believe that you had answered, because the truth is, you hadn't answered many questions before. So she asked you again. Then she was afraid it was just chance; maybe your eyes were moving around randomly and she was just seeing what she so much wanted to see. So she asked again, and you answered again. Then she thought, suppose she tells the nurses, and they say impossible, that child's in a coma, you imagined it, so she might bring them in to see for themselves—and you'd be in a coma, not answering anything. So she asked again; she didn't mean to upset you. It can be very difficult to function smoothly when someone you love is in trouble, and it's very exciting when things start to get better. I guess you figured that out, because when she got hold of herself and brought a nurse in, you showed them that yes, you did know what you were doing, and the one who maybe thought it was impossible had to eat her thought. Now you know the whole story. Don't tell your mother I told.

Each time, I learn something new. In your mother's last letter she mentioned that you and she are vegetarians, because you love animals too much to hurt them by eating them. Would you believe, I am a vegetarian for the same reason. Well, there were other reasons too, but once I left high school back in 1952 I sorted things out in my mind and decided not to eat any more meat. So for 37 years it's been that way. My wife is a vegetarian because I am, and my daughters are too, though I told them they should make up their own minds about a thing as important as that. None of us like to hurt animals. My older daughter Penny has pet mice, because someone at college got a white mouse to feed to his snake, and when the snake wasn't hungry he let the mouse go outside his door in the hall. Penny was appalled; she knew that a tame white mouse couldn't survive in the wild, let alone the college dormitory hall. So she took it in and got another mouse as a companion for it, because mice don't like to be alone any more than people do. The oddest thing was that the mouse she saved wasn't grateful; it tried to bite her finger every time she fed it. We helped her buy a three story mouse cage for them. Penny has parakeets, too, adopted from folk who didn't want them. One was for sale at a flea market, and the poor thing was so downtrodden that it just hunched on the floor of the cage. But once it had company of its own kind, and decent care, it perked up and used the perches. We like to have a cage big enough so the birds can fly, you see. I think she has about five birds now, and they all look happy.

Are you asleep yet? Not quite yet? Okay, a little more. We have little spiders around our house, because we don't like to hurt them either, and they mostly mind their own business. We figure that if they can find enough bugs to eat, they must be doing us a favor. Sometimes one will come across my keyboard when I'm typing, and I wait and watch it till it's clear. Meanwhile we've had a minor adventure with a cow. Our neighbors have cows they raise for—well, we don't like to think about that. This is a brown cow who somehow got out of their pasture and into our forest, this past week. Last night she even found her way from our drive into our pasture, but she must have left again, because I spent twenty minutes looking for her this morning but all I found was some footprints, cowflops, and the white skull of a goat. Hm. Well, if that cow comes back, she's welcome to some of our hay, and the company of our horses. I wouldn't mind if the owner never got around to fetching her back. I'm calling her Elsie, the Bored Cow.

Keep getting better, Jenny; you're doing great.

April 1989

A communications board provides helpful messages: "My ——— hurts." A girl is moved to Ward 7. A nerve is blocked. A companion is chosen. A support brace to therapists becomes elven armor in a girl's imagination. Someone moves her left hand for the first time. A letter appears with a mysterious signature. A whistle sounds. And the first word is spoken, "Hi."

Apull 3, 1989

Dear Jenny,

What's that? Why didn't I send this letter in care of the Monster Under the Bed in the Cute Care section of Cumbersome Hospital, as I have before? Well, it's a long story. You see I have a feature of my computer program that will put on a whole address when I type one word. That way I can type "Jenny" and it puts it all there in half an eyeblink. I use it mostly for business letters, but since I've been writing fairly often to you, I decided to put you in too. Then when I print out the letter, I can copy that address for the envelope. But if I set it up with the Bed Monster and all, I might accidentally type that onto the envelope, and then I'm not sure exactly where the letter would go, but I'm afraid it would not reach you as quickly. So give the Bed Monster my regrets; this letter is in care of someone else.

I was going to write to you yesterday, Sunday, and phone the hospital to learn how you were doing, but things happened. My day started well, because when I rode my bicycle out to pick up the newspapers (we're so deep in the forest that our mail box is three quarters of a mile away) I saw a cloud sitting on the ground. It had come down to rest for the night, where it thought no one would see, but it overslept and I saw it resting about three feet above the ground, and the tops of the trees showing above it. It's a rare thing to catch a cloud napping like that; mostly they stay way up high and pretend that they never sleep at all.

I decided it was time to listen to that record with the beautiful picture on the album, the one with the huge stone musical instruments and the castle in the background, and the girl in the red dress dancing—well, maybe she's just standing there enjoying it, with the wind blowing her hair off to the side, just the way you're going to, one of these days, after you get better—but to do that I had to put together the record player, after postponing that chore for about a year. So I got it set up, and the tape player too—what a mass of wires and connections and things, all threaded through impossible-to-reach little holes in the back! That's almost as bad as combing the tangles out of your hair after you've been through a windstorm. That used up my morning, but I did listen to the record. That hammer dulcimer actually sounds delicate, not at all like a carpenter's hammer on metal. Oh I knew better, but somehow that's how I thought of it. It's nice enough music, and it does sound as if there's a heartbeat in it. Maybe I'll get one of those dulcimers, though I have no hope of playing it decently. If you and I ever meet, *you* can play it decently. My daughter Cheryl was home from college this week, and she's taking a class in the recorder, and she was practicing on it, tootling away at all hours of the day and night. My parents used to play the recorder, and I think it's great if my daughter does too. The more music the better. This morning on the radio I heard *Jesu, Joy of Man's Desiring*, and that's one of the loveliest pieces I've heard. I was trying to read the newspaper, but I just had to stop and listen. Oh, I know, that sounds like a cumbersome title, but believe me, the music is beautiful, and if you ever get a chance to listen to it, do so. For that matter, if you ever have a chance to listen to Grieg's *Peer Gynt*—I'm not sure I've spelled that right, but it's such wonderful music that it almost gives me hope for the world.

Anyway, that's how my morning went. Then the phone rang: two of my readers were in town and wanted to visit. Okay, I meant to talk with them for an hour, but I always talk three times as much as is good for me—it's a trait I share with your mother, I think—and it was close to three hours before they left. Then I had to mow our lawn. We're deep in the forest, but we do have a little lawn around the house, in patches; it was even, but the horses grazed parts down to bare dirt, until we confined them to the pasture. That finished my afternoon. Then I had to finish Chapter Three of *Isle of View*, and that was only 500 words but I kept running into things I had to figure out, so it took time. So I never got to this letter, and never called the hospital. I hope you didn't miss me. So now I'm doing it first thing this morning.

Yes, I wrote Chapter Two, with Jenny Elf. She managed to scare off the goblins by picking cherry bombs from a nearby cherry tree and tossing them behind the goblins, who fled. Then she untied Che Centaur and told the cat to find a safe place, and then the two of them followed the cat. Your folks were going to ask you about the name of that cat, but you had such a big day that day, with everyone visiting (and listening to my last letter? Ouch—I hope I didn't say anything naughty!) that there wasn't time for that. I understand you are doing so well that they may move you out of Cute Care. All those nurses there will be so lonely when you go! Anyway, Jenny and

Che and the cat do make it to the raft on the With-a-Cookee River, but mean Fracto drives them back to shore and the goblins capture them. Tune in next week, when maybe I will have written the next Jenny chapter and saved her from a fate worse than a flu shot.

I'm enclosing a comic strip, "Curtis." I don't read comics much these days, except for "Calvin and Hobbes," but the newspaper is just now starting this one up, so that they can have a black comic to go with all the white comics they have. I think I'm going to like it, and you can see why. We vegetarians can get obnoxious when we try.

Last night I looked out back, and there were dozens of fireflies flashing green. That's the first time I've seen them here. Maybe the freshly mowed lawn attracted them. Folk who hate bugs should try watching fireflies some time.

Remember Elsie the Bored Cow? Then I saw another one, Hownow Brown, and my wife saw a third, and we realized that there must be a hole in the fence. Those cows belong to the sheriff, and he checked and found that the air-boats had shoved a hole in his fence where it's at the pond, and the cows were getting through. So they weren't lost, they were just heading for the farthest and greenest pastures.

Tell your mother that I got her letter of Marsh 29 and I hope she's well enough this week to come in and see you. Maybe she'll be able to read this letter to you. Of course that means I can't say things about her, the way I have in other letters; she might be listening. She asked about the article I wrote for THE WRITER that mentioned you, so I'm enclosing one of the messed-up copies my computer ran off. You are mentioned on page 7; tell her she doesn't need to bother reading the rest of it, which is mostly about technicalities of writing. I don't know when it will be published, but at least this will let you folk know what I said.

Keep getting better, Jenny! I understand you even

waved to your daddy the other day. I guess that's better than wiggling a toe at him.

Apull 9, 1989

[This letter was addressed to Jenny at Warp 7-A, Sick Bay, Enterprise.]

Dear Jenny,

What's that? You don't recognize the pun? It relates to Star Trek, where they are always zooming into space at Warp Factor 7 or something. When I heard you had moved to—oh, *Ward?* Sorry, I misheard. And they have a barrier up to block off the nerds—what? Oh, *nerves*. I thought you said—well, never mind.

I have some good news, which you may already have heard. I wrote to Richard Pini, and he phoned me and said it was fine to use an Elfquest elf in Xanth. In fact, he said they would send you a note. I gave him your address; I thought it was all right. So if the one thing you wanted more than a note from Xanth was one from Elfquest, now maybe you have it.

Remember how your mother wrote me a four page letter when you smiled, and six pages when you laughed? When you got better enough to leave Cute Care, she called me and talked for seven pages. I think she's having trouble keeping up with you.

I'm still working on *Isle of View*. I am now in Chapter 5, "Chex's Checks," and right now Chex is trying to get past the evil cloud Fracto, who naturally wants to stop her from getting wherever she's going. Grundy Golem is with her, yelling insults at Fracto, so it's getting pretty stormy. I'll be back with Jenny Elf in the next chapter, but first I have to get through this one. Writing a novel can be almost as much work as recovering from a coma, I think. Well, maybe not that much. Some day maybe you'll write a novel, and you can let me know then. Chex is going to fly so high, trying to get over Fracto, that she winds up on the moon, and not the honey side of it either. Did you ever get all four feet mired in green cheese? Even Grundy's big mouth isn't going to be much help there!

Remember when I told you about our rows of pine trees, and the blueberries that were getting mowed down? Well, a lot of blueberry bushes did get flattened, but a number survived because they were between the trees where the mower couldn't reach. Now they have berries, and we'll be able to pick them before long. Spring comes early to Florida, you see. You know, as I look at those pine trees, and see all the rows, it's as though each row is a life, going straight through to the other side, with the trees alongside marking off the years. Some go a long way, and some only a short way. Each seems unique, yet if you step into the next row, there it is with its own life, just as nice. I think that if we could step from one person's life to another, as we can between the rows, we would see how similar they are, even though each is the only one that seems real to it, and each probably believes that if it closed its eyes, all the others would have no existence. It's sort of funny and sort of sad and sort of awesome too.

We had a little bat visit. We found it on our garage door a few evenings ago, hanging from the top of the screen. It must have been too tired to make it home, so it stopped at our house. It turned its head and looked at us, but didn't fly away. We left the garage open, but it stayed where it was all night, and the next day. I'm afraid it's dead now. We would have helped it if we could, but we don't know much about bats except that they are good to have around. They're like flying mice, really. So I guess we'll have to bury it. Some don't make it out of the hospital, unfortunately. I considered calling it Brick Bat, after the one in *Heaven Cent*, but that might be unkind.

Remember all those fireflies that turned up in our

forest? They're still here; every night they flash all around our house. I woke up one night and there was one flashing in our bedroom. I thought about catching it in a glass and taking it out, but I was afraid that in the dark I'd hurt it, so I waited till morning—and then couldn't find it. I hope it found its own way out, because houses really aren't the place for fireflies. We have fireflies by night and dragonflies by day. I was talking with some folk outside, and a dragonfly came and perched on my shoulder. They're so pretty, with their four wings and their different colors! I saw six blue ones at once, one day. When we go out, they are always curious just what we're doing, and sometimes they will sit on our hands if we hold them up.

I'm enclosing a cartoon about the awful oil spill this past week in Alaska. Do you watch the news on TV? Maybe you should. Two recent headlines have been about the oil spill and nuclear fusion. Do you want a lecture on how they're connected? No? Too bad, because I'm going to give it anyway, and maybe you'll be interested when you see how it relates to you.

You see, our world needs a whole lot of energy, for everything from jet planes to hospitals. They get most of it from fossil fuels like oil, and when they ship that oil, accidents happen. You know how bad drunken drivers are? You would not be in that hospital now, if the driver who hit you hadn't been drinking. It's a mean, bad business, drinking and driving, and there's a group trying to stop it, called MADD. That stands for Mothers Against Drunk Driving. Well, the captain of that oil tanker was drunk, and his ship cracked up and leaked oil into the sea, and now thousands of innocent birds and seals and fish are dying because they got soaked in oil. So we need to stop the drunk drivers—but also to stop the shipment of oil, so it can't foul the ocean.

The trouble is, we *need* that oil, for a squintillion things. So what do we do? Well, another source of power is nuclear energy. But that can foul things up awfully too, when some drunk driver pulls the wrong switch, and radiation gets all over the place. But there is one kind of nuclear power, nuclear fusion—that's pronounced New-Clear Few-Shun—that hardly makes radiation at all, and could make enough energy to take care of all our needs for just about forever. It's what makes the sun shine, after all. The trouble is, it is very hard to make fusion work on Earth; it takes about a billion dollars worth of equipment, and they still don't have it working. Except that now these scientists have found a way to do it simply and cheaply at room temperature. Maybe. They have set up something a bit like a car battery, that makes so much heat it melts the equipment, and they think that only fusion could account for that. We can't be sure until other scientists duplicate the effect, to be sure it really works. But if it does work, it may mean that we won't need oil any more, and no more poor ducks will die in the spills. That's why, in the cartoon, the animals are hoping that fusion will work.

So there was the lecture. Now you know why you should be interested in nuclear fusion. Because you care about animals. Maybe you'll grow up to be a cartoonist like that, who helps folk understand what's at stake.

I understand you may have a roommate now. I hope you get along okay. My daughters have roommates at college. Anyway, keep getting better, Jenny!

Apull 14, 1989

Dear Jenny,

Ha: I finally got my new ribbon, so the letter will print out dark instead of light. See, look at it—isn't that nice? No, don't squinch your eyes shut! I'll hold my breath until you look. One, two, threemph, fourmth, gasp—ha, you looked! Now let me catch my breath.

I have several things, this time. First, I'm typing this

letter Friday instead of Sunday, so that I can mail it Saturday, and it will arrive Monday or Tuesday so your mother can have it in time to read to you on Wednesday. Last time it came too late for her, and she was miffed, and you know how bad that is.

She told me that you had decided on Sammy to be the cat that makes it into Xanth with Jenny Elf, and she sent three pictures of him in his speed-bump mode on the stairs. Okay, I am replacing [cat] with Sammy in the text; I haven't changed them all yet, but I will when I edit the novel. I did go over Jenny Elf's introduction in the novel, and I printed out those three pages for you. So you can make someone read that to you any time—no, don't throw away this letter yet! You can wait till the end of this paragraph, can't you? Because I need to tell you the background. Chex Centaur is searching for her foal Che, and has been checking with all the search parties, but no one has seen anything yet. Finally she comes back to her cottage in a clearing, with Grundy Golem, who is helping her search. That's when this text starts. Remember, I'll probably make small changes later, as my daughter Cheryl catches me on more errors. If you spy any, let me know; I may have forgotten more than I ever knew about Elfquest. Okay, now you can throw away this letter.

Now let me tell you about the way I feel about cats. I don't like them. No, wait, don't throw the bedpan at me yet. You see, cats do like me. And there was one I did like, and she's the one I want to tell you about. But it's a sad story, so don't listen too carefully.

It all started with Pandora. Pandora was the girl who opened a box she shouldn't have, because she was curious (girls are like that), and all the ills of the world flew out and we've been in trouble ever since. Well, this cat had kittens in our car, and we discovered this when we were about to drive somewhere. So we called her Pandora, because of all the mischief. The daddy-cat had skipped out—this has been known to happen with people, too—so we had to take care of her and them. She was a stray cat, you see. There were three kittens: two tiger-striped like their mother, and one black with a white face. All three were males. You know, I just discovered that the females of most species have different names, except for cats. A female goat is a doe, a female sheep is a ewe, a female horse is a mare, and so on. But a female cat is a what? Apparently there it is the other way around, and it's the male cat who has to take the other name: Tom. Anyway, when they were old enough we gave away the two tigers, but we kept the black and white one, whom we named Panda, because he was the son of Pandora, and his coloration fitted. Pandora we didn't keep, because she had bad manners. If you walked along a path, she would rush past you, get just ahead of you, then hiss and scratch you if you continued walking on *her* path, even if you had never seen her come. So we had her spayed and gave her to a cat shelter.

Well, Panda grew up with our dog Canute, who was a beautiful Dalmatian, also black and white. Canute's story is a sad one, so I'll skip that. Then, months later, a small midnight black cat appeared, evidently dumped by some tourist going north—they do that, and if I say any more about the practice of dumping, I will become uncharitable, which is a polite way of saying #$%&*f¢!!, so I won't. We didn't want another cat, so we ignored her. But she seemed to want to take up residence in our garage. So we shut her out. Then, when we went to open it, she appeared from nowhere and dashed in. Now this was really pushing it, so I went in with the dog to rout her out. She stood guard before a box, so I kicked over the box, trying to make the point that we didn't want her in there, where she was apt to get shut in by accident and starve. And a kitten fell out.

Oops. I investigated. There were five newborn kittens, which explained why she had been so desperate to get back in; we had shut her out from them, not knowing. One looked just like her, and one looked just like Panda, and the others were all shades in between. This was a perfect genetic pattern, solidly incriminating Panda as the father. So we were responsible. We brought her into the house and named her Pandora II. Panda didn't like that; he was jealous of his turf. Too bad; he should have thought of that before he—well, never mind, the Adult Conspiracy just invoked itself. She turned out to be a perfectly house-trained cat. We had a different dog then—no, don't ask about Canute, this history is sad enough without that. Let me just say that once we adopt an animal, that animal is ours for life; kittens are the only ones who have left. I usually think of dogs as honest and cats as dishonest—stop glaring at me, will you, just let me tell my story!—but the dog would sneak anything she could, including the cat's food, while the cat sneaked nothing. I mean she would not jump up on the table to go after food. That's a rigorous moral code, for a cat. When we went for a walk around the block, Pandora II would come with us. She liked people. She did not go out at night to prowl; she preferred to sleep on my daughter Penny's bed. Penny was then five. The only problem was that Penny was hyperactive—if you don't know about that or dyslexia, you're lucky—and when she wiggled her toes under the covers, Pandora would pounce on them, thinking they were edible. You see, Pandora had survived alone for a while; she was a huntress. She would never claw a person knowingly. In fact she had a thing about that: no person could do any wrong. If anything happened, such as someone stepping on her tail—I know it's mean to mention such a thing, but accidents do happen—it was the dog's fault. She would go and hiss at the dog, who like as not was sound asleep and was quite confused by it.

Well, we gave away the kittens again, and kept Pandora II. She was a wonder. One day an obnoxious neighbor's dachshund came charging in to chase Pandora. She fled; I saw them disappear around the house. Then the dog reappeared, yipping, with the cat hot in pursuit. My daughter had seen it happen: Pandora had retreated to the base of a big punk tree—no, you don't have that kind where you live—whirled, hissed, and given the dog a good swipe on the nose. He was far larger than she; I think she weighed only about three pounds. But she just didn't take any guff from dogs. So, in the course of such episodes, I came to like her; she had a lot of mettle. She was our cat.

Then one evening she did not come in. We were perplexed, because she had not done this before. But if she wanted to be outside, we wouldn't stop her. It would be no good hunting for a midnight black cat at night! But in the morning, as I went out to pick up the newspaper, I saw her lying there at the edge of the street. "Oh, no!" I said, dreading it. She was dead; she had evidently been hit by a car. I buried her behind the house. Telling Penny about it was almost as bad as finding Pandora dead; it tore us both up. That was sixteen years ago, and it still hurts. So that is the story of the only cat I ever really liked, and I just can't see my way clear to liking another. I guess I'm a one-cat man, and Pandora was that cat. Oh, Panda was all right—but several months later, he too was hit by a car. You might get the notion that I don't like what careless cars do to folk. Right.

You know, years later I was on a panel at a science fiction convention with Andre Norton. I don't know whether you read her books; she has had over a hundred published, and many are juveniles. She loves cats. So it was quite a panel when I said I didn't like them. But then I told of Pandora II, and Andre Norton and I are friends.

Now on to better things. Yesterday we had our first magnolia flower of the season. You see, when we built our house here on the tree farm last year, we had to make a half mile long drive to the house, which is hidden in the deepest jungle. We wouldn't let them doze out any magnolia trees, which were growing wild throughout the forest. So now they are tame trees along our drive, and one of them is flowering. Magnolias are big, lovely flowers. We have a dogwood, too. Actually, I've never seen an ugly flower; even so-called weeds can have wonderful little flowers, if you just look carefully at them. But you can see a magnolia flower for a hundred feet. We can't count the magnolia trees we have on the property, but there are at least thirteen along the drive—those I did count—and some in the forest are huge.

Look, I am running on too long—who else do you know who does that?—and must stop. Beware; some letter I may tell you about the beauty of math. No, don't turn your nose away in disgust; I can tell you something about math that will fascinate you. You see, when I was your age, math was my worst subject. Then I discovered how it can relate to art. I may also get on the subject of the creative mind in the prison of circumstance. But not this letter, so relax.

Let me just pass along to you a riddle that annoys me. It is this: take a cup of coffee—what? Well, I know you don't drink coffee, and neither do I, and I'll bet your mother doesn't either, but that isn't relevant. Pretend it's mudwater, okay? Take one teaspoonful of that coffee and stir it into a cup of tea—you don't drink that either? Neither do I. But your mother does? Pretend it's something awful, like tannic acid from boiled leaves. Okay; now take a spoonful of that mix from the tea cup and put it back into the coffee cup. Now the riddle: is there more coffee in the tea cup, or more tea in the coffee cup? No, I won't tease you about the answer. As I figure it, they are the same: just as much coffee in the tea as there is tea in the coffee. Having figured it out, I looked up the answer in the back of the magazine where I saw this problem. It said that some problems were almost too easy, and that there was more coffee in the tea cup. What? Either I missed something, or that's a wrong answer. Which is the problem I often have with tests of any kind: their answers don't match mine. When that happens, their answers are wrong, of course. But I remain annoyed.

Remind me next time to tell you about the Llano; that should interest you too. Now I really must go, because I have to write a letter to your mother, and she's jogging my elbow.

Oh, what's Jenny Elf doing right now? Well, I'm in Chapter 6, and she and Che Centaur are the captives of goblins who have a grotesque fate in mind for them. But Jenny's magic talent is about to be discovered. Yes, she has one, because she's from a magic land. You see, she—oops, I'm at the end of the letter. Meanwhile, don't let things like this frustrate you; just keep getting better.

Apull 21, 1989

Dear Jenny,

Guess what: I had a letter from Sue Benes, your Occupational Therapist! Aren't you jealous? No? You say *you* got one from Elfquest? Well, try this one: I also have one from Jenny. Oops—that's you! In your Elven Armor. Well, now; I wouldn't have thought of that. Thank you. Just don't get into any fights with the human folk. And one from your mother. You remember how many pages she wrote me when you smiled (4), laughed (6), and moved to Warp 7 (7, of course—oops, that was that phone call)? This time you Spoke—right, eight (8) pages. You know, I was going to call the hospital today to find out how you're doing, but there was so much information in those eight (8) pages that I can't think of anything about you I don't already know. Besides, I'm afraid to try; I don't know the Warp folk as well as I knew the ones in Cute Care. But about your letter: your mother said you still have a bit of trouble signing things, but that she could make out the J and Y. Well, I can also make out an N in the middle. But you have a way to go yet before your signature gets as indecipherable as mine. The more I sign it—and I have had to sign thousands of times—the worse it gets, until now all you can read is the P, but you know there's an I there somewhere because the dot is in the middle of the P. I read a book about grapho-analysis once, telling how to judge folks' character through their handwriting, and I resolved that no one was going to get at *my* inner secrets of character that way, so I set it up so that the I-dot was always inside the P. Let them try to analyze that! They'll think that I'm impossibly introspective, and, um, ouch, they might be right. Sigh.

I'm enclosing a couple of comic clippings from today's newspaper: one Family Circus about a vegetarian, and a Curtis, because it seems your local paper doesn't carry it. It's really just an ordinary comic, though today's strip is a bit painful in an unintended way: I'd hate to have that happen to a parakeet. We used to have parakeets, starting with Cinnamon, whom we inherited from my wife's sister when she got married and moved away. Naturally we named the next one Nutmeg, and went on through the spices from there. But all that was before we were adopted by a cat. I wrote a story about parakeets; it's in my volume *Anthonology*, which volume is unsuitable for the mothers of teenagers to read. Anyway, I hope your music playing doesn't sound like that of the comic.

I guess that's all—oh, what's that? You're reminding me to what? Oh, to tell you about the Llano. Yes. I think you haven't read my other fantasies, and they're really not intended for folk who aren't in on the Adult Conspiracy, but this much should be all right. You see, in that fantasy series there is the ultimate song. It's really the operating system of the universe—I'll wait while you make your mother tell you what a computer operating system is—in the form of music, and the lady who becomes Nature has a rare talent for music and learns how to sing it. But even the pieces of it, the little fragments that some folk learn, have rare power; when folk sing them, wonderful things happen. There's the Song of Morning, which makes the dawn come and flowers grow, even when it's the middle of the day on a pavement. There's the Song of Evening, which brings love. So keep your ear open; some day you may hear a piece of the Llano, and you want to be sure to remember it.

I was also going to tell you about how math could be beautiful. No, don't drum your fingers impatiently on the armrest; someone might see you, and then there would be a great hue and cry: "She can drum her fingers!" and your privacy will be gone. You see, I know about the deadly dullness of math. I mean, who can stand to memorize the Times Tables? I couldn't! I took an IQ test once, and the problem was all in words, but I immediately saw that it worked out to eight times twelve. Then I had to stop and figure out what that was, while the woman was timing me on the stopwatch. It turned out that that was supposed to be the easy part; most kids couldn't get that far, but when they did, they knew the answer instantly. Which sort of thing explains why folk never thought I was smart. That, and the way I took three years to master first grade. Yes, I really did! So maybe some day I'll succeed in memorizing eight times twelve. I wonder if it's close to the answer for twelve times eight? That would be a nice coincidence! Anyway, arithmetic was the bane of my existence, until about ninth grade, when it changed. I didn't change, *it* changed. It quit with the stupid Times Tables, which are called Rote Learning, which is the stuff of idiocy, and started with algebra, which is like a puzzle. If X plus 5 equals your age, what's X? I'll bet you can solve that one! You can even use it to solve one of the trickiest riddles ever, which your mother probably encountered generations ago: Mary is 24. Mary is twice as old as Ann was, when Mary was as old as Ann is now. How old is Ann? This is the stuff of fun, if you like brain-buster riddles, which I do.

You can make lines and circles and things on paper with the right X and Y formulae. This is because the answers change. Next year X will be larger than it is this year, because your age will be more. So you can plot a line of all the possible values of X, and you can even follow it back into the past: when you were 4, what was X? What number added to 5 equals your age of four? A minus number, that's what! Maybe that seems foolish in the real world, but math is a world of its own where strange things can happen. It can be fun making up equations and finding out what pictures they make.

But mainly, it is that math can become very like art, especially with the aid of a computer. You see, a few years ago a man tried plotting an equation—what? No, his name doesn't matter. He used a complex equation—no, I told you his name doesn't matter. He made a drawing of all the points that fell inside this equation; the ones that fell outside he ignored. So—oh, all right, his name was Mandelbrot. Now will you listen? He took this complicated formula and used the computer to figure out all the points—and it turned out to be a very strange figure indeed. The main part of it looked like a lady bug, but there were also little lady bugs near it, and they were all connected by curling patterns. When he used colors to mark these patterns, it became beautiful. In fact I would call it art. The patterns keep repeating on smaller and smaller scale, but never quite the same as before, so there's always something new to find. So this science of figuring out such pictures is called fractals, and this one figure is called the Mandelbrot set (I can't think why!) and it is considered to be the most complicated object in mathematics—and perhaps also the most beautiful and fascinating. I can look at it for hours, always being amazed. There are patterns like little shells in there, and others like sea-horses, and who knows what else. Maybe your folks have encountered this, and can show you one of those colored pictures in a book. If your mind is anything like mine, you won't find it very interesting at first glance, but the more you look at it the more fascinating it will become as you try to figure out just what's *with* this weird design. All from an obscure mathematical formula. So remember: there's a whole lot more to math than the awful stuff they teach in grade school, and the higher math resembles the lower math much the way a beautiful princess resembles a squalling baby. I'll be getting into this when I write *Fractal Mode*, the novel with that picture I described on the record album jacket—you know, with the huge stone dulcimer and the girl in the red dress. I don't know which fascinates me more, the dulcimer or the damsel or the Mandelbrot set imagery I'll draw on. So I will write to Mr. Mandelbrot, to make sure it's all right to do that.

Now let's see—now stop that snoring, I know you aren't asleep!—I was going to mention that I have put a scene in *Isle of View* with a princess and a unicorn. See, I knew you weren't asleep! Actually there's a dragon in it too; I hope you don't mind. It's a nice story that they make into a bad dream for Fracto (no relation to fractal!) the mean cloud. You see, Fracto hates nice things, so this really nice tale drives him to thunderation. But Jenny Elf picks up on it too, and for her it's a nice scene. So the novel is progressing, slowly because a lot of other stuff came in this week, but it is getting there, and Jenny Elf is—well, can you keep a secret? She turns out to have a magic talent. Mundanes don't, but she's from the World of Two Moons where there is magic. So she has magic. It's that when she sings, which she doesn't like to do in public—I mean, who does?—a fancy forms, sort of like a daydream of a really nice scene, like a sweet princess and a nice castle, and anyone who hears her sing but isn't paying attention enters the fancy too, and enjoys the scene. But anyone who is paying attention can't get into it. This makes it sort of hard to verify her magic, as you might think. But it's there, and it helps her stave off the awful fate the goblins are planning for her. Oh, I know it's not Magician class magic, but it's good enough.

Tell your mother thanks for the copy of Andrea Alton's novel she sent. I am buried in reading right now—I have to read a fantasy novel for a publisher, for a blurb—that's a comment they can run on the cover, to encourage others to buy it—and I'm a slow reader. But in due course I'll get to this one, so tell her not to get too impatient about getting it back. I see it has cat folk on the cover, which makes sense; anyone you folk know relates to cats, right?

I must stop; it's supper time. Keep getting better, Jenny—I know I've said that before, but you know, I wouldn't want you to change your mind and start getting worse. May you dream of elves and unicorns and fractals—oh, all right, you can leave out the last.

Apull 28, 1989

Dear Jenny,

I heard something about something—details are obscure, because nobody is talking, but I think it was a whistle. I had to piece it together from secret fragments, and parts of it may be missing, but here is the unauthorized version of the incident.

Things were quiet at the Cumbersome Hospital, and the folk there were going about their various businesses. The doctors were counting their money in the Doctors' Club, the nurses were running around with big needles to give patients shots, the patients were hiding under the sheets hoping the nurses wouldn't find them, and the cooks were preparing something horrendously awful for the next meal. In short, everything was routine.

Suddenly there was a piercing whistle. It reverberated through the halls and made every person stop. What was that? The sound was so compelling that all the doctors, nurses and cooks charged up to Warp 7 to find out where it came from. They traced it to Jenny's room, and they all arrived there at once and squeezed through the door together. But it happened that the staff had been waxing the floor that day, and the surface was just about one degree more slippery than a wet bar of soap on melting ice. The nurse in the lead took a phenomenal spill and landed on the floor, sliding right up to the edge of the bed. The doctor behind her landed on top, and the nurse behind him landed on top of him, until there was a pile like a crazy sandwich just about six nurses, two doctors, one cook and a cleaning woman high.

Now it just so happened, by the type of coincidence that occurs only in a story like this, that the nurse on the bottom of the pile was the very nurse who had once threatened to give the monster under this bed a loathsome shot in the rump. Now her face was right up close, and she couldn't move. Suddenly a huge hairy hand came out and tweaked her on the nose. She screamed. "EEEEEEEEKK!!" It was the most piercing eeek ever heard in Warp 7, almost as penetrating as the whistle had been. It shook the entire pile.

Then, slowly, the pile began to fall. The cleaning woman on top grabbed at her bucket of slop water, but all that accomplished was to dump the bucket on the rest of the pile, wetting six nurses, two doctors and one cook. They all screamed with outrage as they fell. After all, it was suspected that that water was supposed to be saved for the next day's soup. "Aaaaaahh!!" Then the pile crashed to the floor, scattering arms and legs and whatever everywhere.

At this point the therapist arrived. Her name was Sue. "What are you all doing here?" she demanded indignantly. "This is supposed to be a private session!" The others scrambled out, humiliated. They never were able to find out who had blown that whistle. It is a mystery that remains to this day, because nobody likes to talk about it. In fact the doctors claim that nothing happened, nothing at all.

But Sue was unable to do the therapy session, because Jenny was sound asleep, with nothing but the very faintest of smiles on her face. Clutched in her left hand, out of sight under the sheet, was a silver whistle. Could it be? Sue shook her head and tiptoed out, so as not to disturb Jenny from her nap.

Okay, that's all I have been able to piece together. I wonder how much of it is true? The folk at the hospital all deny that any such thing happened, of course, and there's a perfectly good explanation why their uniforms looked like tomorrow's soup, but there *is* that whistle, and the monster under the bed seems happier than he's been in a long time. Your mother said something, but it wasn't at all like this, so she may be in on the conspiracy of silence. We'll probably never know for sure. But you can tell me: were you *really* asleep?

I had an experience with my computers this week. You see, I made a lots of notes two years ago for my big novel *Tatham Mound*, which is about the American Indians who encountered Hernando de Soto, the Spanish conquistador who landed in Florida and discovered the Mississippi River. He was looking for gold, and he wasn't very nice to the Indians who told him they didn't have any. So this will be a savage novel, and I have over a hundred books I plan to use for research. But my early notes were in my former computer, and I needed to translate them to this computer. Computers don't necessarily talk to each other, you see; sometimes you have to use eye blinks or keyboards or whatever to find out what they're up to. The floppy drives were on the blink: they kept saying I had no disk there, when I did. So we were going to have to call the repairman. But I tried it once more, because you know how things play possum, then work perfectly when the repairman is watching. It still didn't work. I tried it again and again, and it didn't work. After about six times I tried something dirty: I took the disk out and told it to read the disk. That gave it a real error to chew on. And would you believe: after that, when I put in the disk, it decided to read it! So I quick translated my two disks of *Mound* notes to the new format and read them into my new system. Now I have my notes and four chapters in my new system, ready for me to write more. All because I faked out the computer. Maybe it thought I was the repairman when I gave it a real error to work on. So I'm happy; it isn't often a person can outsmart a dumb machine. Ask your mother.

But there's a moral. Yes, you knew I was going to get to that, didn't you. And you're going to pretend you're sound asleep, clutching your whistle, aren't you! But it won't work; here is the moral anyway. It is that if something doesn't work the first time, or the second, keep trying, because maybe after the sixth time it will. I remember when you were in that deep pit—it was more like a well, actually, dark and lonely and scary—and you finally started to climb out, an inch and a blink at a time. You struggled and struggled and at last you made it to the rim—only to find that that was only the first hurdle in a mountain of challenges. So you're still struggling to get back your own, one muscle at a time. You wish nature would just let you get it all back in one swell foop, but foops are hard to come by. So keep struggling, Jenny, and maybe one day you'll get to take a giant step instead of a finger step.

One of our magnolia trees had seven flowers one day. Did I tell you about the magnolias? No? When we were having our half-mile drive put in, I was showing the man where, and I saw a little magnolia tree right in the path of the dozer. "Go around that tree," I told him. Thus it was that that little tree was saved. But they cut the road so close to it that some of the roots were damaged, and the poor little thing's leaves were turning pale and yellow. We were afraid the tree wouldn't survive, after all; it was sort of in the Cute Care section. Then I had a bright idea. Maybe nitrogen would help it. Plants like nitrogen; it helps them grow. It happens that there is nitrogen in urine. So whenever I passed that tree, I—well, never mind the details. But soon its leaves were turning green again, and it was doing better. It's out of Cute Care now and will probably grow into a fine tree in due course.

Your mother says the flowers in her garden just aren't as pretty when you aren't there. They will surely perk up when you return. You say maybe they need nitrogen? Your mother says Absolutely Not!! (No, I don't know what set her off. Women are strange that way.)

I have just written a scene between Sammy Cat and Prince Dolph. You see, Jenny Elf told Sammy to find help, when the goblins were capturing her and Che the centaur foal, and he took off and found Dolph. Dolph can change forms, so he became another cat and talked with Sammy in feline language. But Sammy never says two words when one will do. "Where did you come from?" "Home." That sort of thing. It was frustrating. Finally Dolph got smart, and told Sammy to find the captives. Then Sammy took off, and Dolph followed. But there's a lot of adventure still to come.

The other day we saw strange bugs on the screen enclosure of our swimming pool. They looked like huge gray Assassin Bugs, but one was pink. Was it hatching from its old gray skin? Then a cardinal came by and snapped it up. We like birds and we don't like assassin bugs, but it was a bit of a shock to see nature so directly in action. Everything preys on something else. We love the pretty colored dragonflies, though they are predators too. The thing is, they prey on things like deerflies, and the deerflies bite our horses (we do have deer in the forest, but I guess the deerflies can't always find deer to bite), so we really appreciate the way the dragonflies keep them down. I found a dragonfly in the pool enclosure. We always try to get them out, because there's nothing in there for them to eat, and they can starve. But they think it's a game when we shoo them out, and gaily dodge around us. This one had evidently been in a couple of days, and was flying slowly. I opened the door, but it landed on the doorframe instead. I actually touched its wing, but it didn't move. Finally I managed to jog it loose, and it flew on outside. I hope it had the strength to catch a fly!

Yesterday when I rode my bicycle out to pick up the newspapers—they are three quarters of a mile from our house, you see—I discovered halfway there that my little basket was half full of leaves and moss and stuff. Something was trying to make a nest there! When I got back, two wrens flew from that region. So I took off the basket and set it up in the corner, with its leaves and things still there, so that next time I wouldn't ride off with their nest. But the wrens did not return; they didn't trust it after that. I can't blame them. I'm just sorry I didn't see the leaves before I rode out. We like wrens; they are gutsy little birds, and they keep bugs from the house.

So our life goes on from day to day in its petty pace, and I guess yours does too. But keep working at things, Jenny; even inchworm steps are better than none. And tell your mother I meant to write her a letter too, this time, because I have a whole lot to say, but I ran out of time. So in a few days I'll write her. You say all I have to do is tell you what I want to say to her, and you'll tell her? Well, thanks, but do you really want to tell her two pages? I thought not.

PS—Since I changed from the manual typewriter to

the computer, my I's don't capitalize; I think I take my finger off the capital key too fast. So I made a macro to capitalize them for me. It just capitalized 27 in this letter! And four more in this paragraph. Don't you try to miss I's like that—you'll get cross-eyed.

Oh, one more thing: your mother told me of a story you wrote once, about flowers and a blind princess. Is it all right if I put that in the novel? I think it's a lovely story, and it does explain why flowers have pretty smells. You have such a nice way of seeing things, sometimes, Jenny.

Ouch—and the printer messed up your letter; I'm printing it over. As I said before, the computer will get you if you don't watch out.

---

*Author's Note:

The comic strip I mention showed Curtis having lunch with his white friend Gunk, a vegetarian, whose sandwich had a whole carrot in it. Gunk is a friend to all living things, and his homeland of Flyspeck Island is a magical realm. Jenny and I just had to like Gunk.

The whistle story is based upon a development in Jenny's therapy program. Jenny had gotten a whistle, and was able to blow it. This was a significant accomplishment, considering the general paralysis of her face. So I made a story about it, poking fun at hospitals in general. But I have to say that Cumberland Hospital is a much nicer place than the ordinary hospital, being rather like a resort in appearance and attitude, and this story has no relation to reality there.

These letters contain several mentions of computers in conjunction with Jenny's mother. She earns her living by programming computers, thus is ripe for teasing. There will be more of it. It seems that Jenny laughs when her mother gets teased, and her mother loves to have Jenny laugh, so she enjoys getting teased. This is a positive attitude.

May 1989

A right big toe uses a right useful computer to right difficult communications. 24 − X = 12 + X. *One person gives a story to another, who may or may not have missed something. A realization of hair loss incurs a moment of sadness. And a happy reunion takes place.*

Mayhem 5, 1989

Dear Jenny,

I figured out what happened to the last letter: this word processor puts a "ruler" at the top of the file, setting the margins and things. When I set up a new file, for the Jenny letter, it put on its default ruler (yes, your mother will explain that in more detail than you care to hear; just ask her. She's eager to start in, if you just give her the teensiest bit of encouragement) at the top. Then I used my "letter" macro to put my letter format on, forgetting the default format, which was now off the screen. So when I printed, it took the first ruler, which was the wrong one, and ignored the second. Then when I reset the paper, I put it in wrong. Growl!

I have things to tell you from the fun to the awful, and not enough time to tell it all, because I'm in a Jenny chapter of *Isle of View* now, with Jenny Elf and Che Centaur and Sammy Cat captives in the bottommost bowels of Goblin Mountain, and I want to get back and find out how they fare. Jenny is about to meet Gwendolyn Goblin—Um, I'd better check with you on this. She's lame; I always knew that. That's why the goblins wanted a horselike steed for her, so she could ride around instead of walking, and be princessly, or more properly chieftainessly because goblins have chiefs not kings, despite her handicap. But why foal-nap a centaur foal, instead of a mere regular horse or something? Because, I now realize, there is more than lameness wrong with Gwenny. She doesn't see well. If she rode a centaur, the centaur could see things and tell her, so that she would always know with whom she was dealing and what was going on, and never make embarrassing mistakes. But you see, this notion stems from your story about the blind princess, so it's not wholly mine. Your mother told me she would ask you if it's okay to tell that story here, and if you agree, Jenny Elf will tell it. But to have Gwenny Goblin with poor sight too—well, that fits so well that I think I'll do it, unless you scream blankety murder or blow the whistle on me. No, no, don't blow that whistle! The last time you did that—well, never mind.

Back to business: suppose I cut out the nice parts and cover the nasty parts instead, and—what? The other way around? Brother, you're fussy today! No, leave that whistle alone; I'll start with the nice.

Remember last time when I told you about the wrens in the bicycle bag? How they didn't come back? That was Thursday I found the nest being started. Well, Sunday morning when I returned with the bike, using a new bike bag, a wren flew out of the other one. So I went inside and opened the bathroom window right next to it, quietly, and watched. Sure enough, Carroll and Lina Wren (down here we have Carolina wrens, with reddish undersides) flew in immediately, perched on the bike and looked all around to make sure I was gone. They had returned to the nest! My daughter Penny happened to drive up from St. Pete that day—the nice thing about daughters is that they visit even after they grow up and move away—and I told her about it, and she said I hadn't looked closely enough. Her beady daughter eyes had spied an egg in that nest! A couple of days later there were two eggs there, and now there are three. So we have a family started here, and how glad I am that I took the trouble to set up that bike bag, though I thought they weren't using it. I'll report on developments as they occur. As I have said, wrens are good to have around the house; they are bold little birds who clean out the bugs that are trying to sneak into the house.

Now an ugly item. Ask your mother whether she should read it, as I happen to know she's already sneaked a peek at it. She'll skip it if you ask her to. This is from the news, and you may have picked it up already. A group of teenage boys in New York City went "wilding"—that's a new term—and ran through Central Park at night beating up anyone they could find. They found nine or ten people. One of them was a lady jogger. They hit her in the face with a brick and raped her and hurt her so badly that they left her for dead. Several hours later when help came she had lost three quarters of her blood. They put her right into Cute Care and managed to save her life. That was last month. Now she has come out of her coma and is able to squeeze someone's hand on command and move her eyes, and she evidently understands what is said to her, but they don't know yet whether she will ever recover completely. Her life will never be the same, regardless. I thought of you when I read about this, because though the circumstances of your injury were different, your situation is similar. I think you can understand how that woman is feeling. She is recovering faster than you, because (I think) she was hurt more in the body than the head, while you got bashed worse in the head. But none of it is any fun. I don't expect you to feel any better because someone else got hurt, but if you are the kind who prays, you might pray for her. You know what she needs.

Back to a nice item. Your mother sent me two of your

pictures—no, don't glare at her, she means well, honest she does, you just have to make allowance for mothers—of princesses—no, not the originals, she made copies, you don't think she'd risk the originals, do you? So stifle that glare—uh, where were we? Somewhere in that sentence I got lost! Also your story about the blind princess. So now you get my critique. Stop that! Come back from under that sheet! You're disturbing the Bed Monster! I told you this was a nice item, I think. Your spelling is like mine, which means you are a creative person. The only one in my family who could match my bad spelling was my dyslexic daughter Penny. Oh, I can spell now, of course; I learned it when I was an English teacher, and had to abandon my creativity. Sigh. I don't know whether I'll ever recover. But your pictures—what do you mean, what makes me think I'm an art critic? I took art classes for six years and once thought to be an artist, so there! Why didn't I become an artist? Let's change the subject. What? Look, we really don't need to go into that. Oh, all *right:* I realized that I was not good enough to make it as a commercial artist. Now are you satisfied? I feel your pictures are marvelously mature, considering your age, and expressive. Maybe you'll be able to do what I could not, and be an artist. But it's something else that brought me to this paragraph. One of your pictures is of a woman with her baby, and she is crying. I'm not sure what the story is there, but I don't think that's the blind princess, unless maybe there's a chapter I missed. But what I notice is her hair. It flows out and forms a kind of cape behind her, framing her upper body. I love that. I remember when—but no need to go into that.

Oops, you say you want to go into that? Sigh. All right. When I was eleven years old, I knew a girl who was twelve. No, I'm not making this up. She was everything desirable in a woman, as I saw her. I loved her. No, no one took it seriously, and certainly she didn't; what would this fine young woman want with a boy of eleven? But my mental picture of her remains to this day, and I think I still love her, over forty years later, in my way. I know it by the hair. Her hair was the length of that of the woman in your picture, and though it did not flare out like that—she wore it in two long braids, mostly—I like to think that maybe it could have, had she wanted it to. To this day the first thing I notice about a woman is her hair. Have you seen pictures of the singer Crystal Gayle? Right—she's my favorite singer. Because of that hair. Oh, she sings well, very well, but I really didn't notice her singing until I saw her hair. So when I see your picture, and that hair, oh Jenny, it touches me. Perhaps by no special coincidence, I have a lady goblin in *Isle of View* named Godiva, who has hair like that. And of course in a prior Xanth novel I had Rapunzel. Nada Naga, in *Heaven Cent*, has hair like that too, and younger Prince Dolph loves her. Now you know why.

And an in-between item. I understand they have to give you nerve blocks, because you get pain. I have half a notion how that is. Some years back, when I was doing more strenuous exercises than I do now, my right arm started hurting, especially when I moved it, and it got to the point where it was getting hard for me even to type on the computer keyboard. So I saw the doctor, and it turned out to be tenonitis, or inflammation of the nerve. Not a life-threatening ailment, and it doesn't sound like much, but if I moved my arm suddenly I could just about faint from the surge of pain. It was a job sleeping at night, because when I rolled over, the pain jerked me awake. Medicine didn't help. Finally the doctor gave me a shot of Novocain in the nerve. That wasn't a nerve block, and it didn't make the pain go away, but it did reverse its course, so that in the following months I was able, slowly, to reach farther before the pain started. About the time my right arm got better, it started in the left arm. This time medicine helped, but it still reversed grudgingly. All told, it was about two and a half years from start to finish, and it wiped out all my arm exercises. I had done as many as fifty chins on my study beam, and a lot of Japanese pushups, and I had muscles on my arms. All gone now. Running is the only exercise I maintained. But in the course of this, I learned that pain was not necessarily bad. I found that when I knew exactly what caused it, and how to avoid it, and could control it by reaching only as far as I cared to tolerate the level of pain, I could get along with it. I get the feeling that you suffer pain, and you don't want to make a scene about it and get everyone all up in a heaval, so you just tolerate it. Sometimes the pain is better than the shot in the nerve. Okay.

Your mother got tired of waiting for me to forward the "Curtis" comic strip, so had them run it in your local paper. Okay, I'll just enclose the ones I had already cut out, plus a cartoon about the unpleasantness of having a shot in a nerve or wherever. Tell her that Adept #6, *Unicorn Point*, is already out, in hardcover; if she makes the library ignore the bad reviews and stock it, she can read it. And I didn't mean to make trouble for you with that Mary and Ann problem; I can give you the formula to solve it, if—you say not to bother? Well, it's no trouble, really. Uh, okay, I'll drop it.

Mayhem 12, 1989

Dear Jenny,

Remember when I said I didn't think your picture illustrated the flower story? Ouch! Five lashes with a wet noodle. When I got into it to adapt it I saw my mistake: I was thinking of Lily, not her mother, and the picture was of her mother. Anyway, I did the scene, and have printed it out for you. But don't go straight to it; let me explain the background first.

Che Centaur, the winged foal, is captive in Goblin

Mountain. Jenny and Sammy go with him, voluntarily, because Jenny feels the foal needs company. They meet Gwendolyn Goblin, the daughter of Godiva Goblin, who turns out to be a rather nice twelve year old girl. The reason Godiva wanted a centaur companion for her was to help her get about and to see things, because she is a bit lame and so nearsighted that everything farther than a foot or two away is a blur. Jenny's problem was solved by her spectacles, but Gwenny's problem can't be solved that way, so she really does need help. She has a chance to be the first female chief of the goblins—a chiefess—who can make the goblins behave much better, but if any of them learn about her sight problem, they will kill her and put in a male instead, and things will be as brutish as they have always been with goblins. So Godiva really does have good reason for what she has done: only a centaur can work so well with Gwenny that the goblins will be fooled, and she can rule. That's part of the larger problem in this novel: Jenny and Che have agreed not to tell, because if they do, Gwenny will die, and she really doesn't deserve that. But can Che agree to be prisoner of the goblins for the rest of his life? So he hasn't made up his mind.

Jenny and Che and Gwenny get into a Tsoda fight, squirting bottles of the water of Lake Tsoda Popka at each other (we happen to live on Lake Tsala Apopka, here in Florida: another of those odd coincidences) and get drenched; it's great fun. Godiva doesn't quite approve of this, for some reason, but of course mothers don't have to have reasons for their objection to fun. So the kids clean up (Che has to face away and close his eyes so as not to see any Panties) and Jenny tells a story instead. She has to adapt it to Xanth terms, which is tricky, and it doesn't work perfectly, but the essence comes through. That's the excerpt I printed out for you. At the end, their shared dream is shaken apart when the mountain trembles: Cheiron Centaur is commencing the siege, by having rocs drop stones.

The battle has begun. Okay, now at last you can go to that scene. This is my first draft, so maybe there are typos, and I may change things later. If you see something that is fouled up, let me know and I'll fix it before sending the novel to the publisher. I'll also show a copy to the Elfquest folk.

Um, it occurs to me that you may feel that Gwenny is a name too close to Jenny. Well, I pondered this, but it just does seem the best way to simplify Gwendolyn. One letter of a word can make a big difference; I don't confuse you with my daughter Penny, for example. Penny is 21 now, in college, with a job, but she's still my little girl. So I think the name's all right.

On to other business. I'm enclosing a Sunday Curtis comic you may have missed, and a cartoon about the space shuttle launch; if you look at it twice you'll see what's funny. And two clippings about girls you may like: one saved her friend's mother's life, and the other sued her boyfriend when he stood her up for a prom. These are your type of girl, right? Plus an envelope with Polish stamps—oh, these'll never fit in the little envelope I typed! Well too bad, I'll type a bigger one. What do you care about Polish stamps? Well, they have pretty pictures of horses, penguins and dragonflies. The letter was sent to my old address, but managed to reach me anyway.

I understand you are using a computer now, to help communicate. I'm glad of that. Maybe they'll set you up with a paintbrush program, so you can paint pictures on the screen. We have Microsoft Paintbrush, which uses a mouse; you can paint good pictures with it, if you have the patience, and save them or print them out. If they haven't gotten something like that for you yet, blink your eyes and wiggle your toe until they do; I suspect you could have a lot of fun with the screen and that mouse control, and maybe turn out some great pictures.

I also understand you are back in Elven Armor again,

and casts on your arms. You put a good face on it, but I know that isn't much fun. I'd tell you to look on the positive side, but I know it's a pain, so might as well say so. One of the periodic debates I get into with those who believe in God is why God allows awful things to happen to folk who don't deserve it. Don't tell *me* you were a bad girl so you were punished by being almost killed. But of course I explain it all in my Incarnations series: Satan is doing it. Early next year the final novel, *And Eternity,* will tackle the matter of God and resolve it. You'll probably like that one, when you get old enough to sneak it past the Adult Conspiracy censors. Anyway, I understand also that you are getting a blazing fast red wheelchair, and that the nurses in the halls will be set spinning when you zoom by too fast to see. "What was that?" one will ask, "A bird? A plane?" and another will reply: "No, that's Spinning Jenny!" You know I joke about the doctors and nurses, and how they can get piled up ten deep, but I've actually had some experience with the real work that they do. I collaborated with a doctor on a book about kidney disease, dialysis and kidney transplants, and I interviewed doctors, nurses, and patients and learned a lot. The doctor changed his mind after I found a publisher for the book, and I had to drop the project, which I think was too bad; it was a good book. But by that avenue I got to know pretty well folk who were being saved from dying by the doctors and nurses, and what it took to keep them alive. If you want to know a lot about kidney dialysis, I can tell you, but not in this paragraph. I have also had some absolutely infuriating encounters with callous or incompetent doctors and nurses. So I have seen both sides. Just so you know that when I tease a person or a profession, that does not necessarily reflect my underlying opinion. Each profession seems to have its good examples and its bad ones, and this is true for writers as well as doctors and nurses.

Oh, I almost forgot: yes, the wrens are doing nicely.

The eggs are still there, and all seems well. Our magnolia trees continue to bloom. I see them when I ride the bicycle out to fetch the paper in the morning—it's a mile and a half round trip—and the bunnies along the drive. Also when I do my exercise run, which covers most of our tree farm. We have pretty big blue passion flowers now, too. And yes, I saw a dragonfly exactly like the one in the corner of the envelope, green and blue; it was probably the one who posed for that picture.

So have a harpy day, Jenny, and don't forget to ask about that paintbrush program. You don't have to wait to get all the way better, to draw again; you can do it now, if they have the setup.

Mayhem 19, 1989

Dear Jenny,

Yesterday I finished the novel proper, and this morning I finished the Author's Note for *Isle of View*; I'm sending a printout, which your mother may or may not read to you, as she sees fit. No, don't blink your eyes angrily at her; she has reason. Let me explain.

You may not remember much between when you were hit by that car, and the time my first letter helped bring you out of your long sleep. (I feel like a prince!) It was a bad time. The Author's Note describes it in fair detail. You walked through the valley of the shadow of death, and your family felt the terrible chill of it. That part of the experience is not fun reading. You may not care to listen to it now.

I have sent this because I want your folks to go over it and tell me where it is wrong and what parts should not be left in. I have named you only Jenny here, because I am afraid that folk could discover who you really are if I gave your full name, and there are some folk who shouldn't. But

I can change that if you wish. I will modify it as required, and ship the novel, Note and all, to the publisher. Along about OctOgre 1990 it will be published. By then I hope you are long out of the hospital and maybe out of your wheelchair, Jenny, and getting on with your life. I doubt you'll ever be a star Olympic athlete, but you can be a lot else, regardless. I hope you like the novel, when. There's a lot more than just Jenny Elf in it, of course, but Jenny is a major character.

I have tried to avoid subjects that I fear will bring you disquiet, but I seem to have been blundering into them anyway. I assumed that your mother's description of your present hair style was the way it's always been, and that you liked it that way. Now I learn that you had waist-length hair, before the accident. I'm sorry if I hurt you by my comments; it was the last thing I wanted to do. Let me tell you a bit more about hair, in my family. I wouldn't let my wife cut her hair, for the first ten years or so of our marriage, so she wore it waist length. But she complained that it was hot, especially here in Florida, and finally I realized that I did not have the right to make her uncomfortable. So she cut it, and has worn it short since. But our daughters—that's another story. The first one I claimed as mine; Penny was my little girl, and she never has cut her hair. She was hyperactive as well as dyslexic, and I told everyone that she had so much energy because her hair had never been cut. In the Bible Samson was the strongest of men while his hair was long, you see; when it was cut he became weak. Cheryl was our second daughter, and her mother claimed her. Penny's hair color matched mine, though I am dark and she is blond—you think that's crazy? No it isn't. When we checked we discovered that Penny's hair is the same shade as mine at the same length. If I wore mine waist length, it would bleach out blond. Anyway, Cheryl's hair was dark like her mother's, and she was good in school like her mother, while Penny's grades were like mine. Once Penny brought home a report card, and I lectured her: "Penny, I don't understand. This is not like you. I don't expect this sort of thing from you." It was all A's and B's, you see, instead of C's and D's. I suspect your dad would do the same with you, if you brought home an A math grade. Some folk don't understand the humor in a family where love is more important than success; too bad for those folk. Cheryl I teased the other way: that if she ever saw a grade below A+ she would be baffled, having never seen a B, and someone would have to explain what it was. Or even an A−. Cheryl was the one who made the highest SAT score in the history of her school. There weren't SAT tests in my day, but if there had been, no one knows what I would have done with it, but height would be the least likely course. Depth, maybe. No, I'm not stupid; the test makers are. They don't know the best answers to their questions. In fact they don't know the best questions. Anyway, Cheryl's hair was in the charge of her mother, who cut it short, until I remarked passingly how Cheryl looked like a little boy. About that time Cheryl, no dummy, began to take control of her life, and I don't think she has let her hair be cut since, and now her hair is well down her back. The two daughters together are a marvel, one blonde, the other brunette, a complementary set. My wife doesn't speak of the matter. So I'm glad to hear that you have the right attitude about hair; I understand you won't let your mother cut hers either. I guess we know who has the willpower in your family! I'm sure your mother looks much better with her hair long. There's a verse in a folk song that reminds me of: "Laura was a pretty girl, o-my-o!" Surely because she wore her hair long. Don't get me wrong: my wife is a fine woman. Just not perfect. She doesn't understand about hair. Anyway, go ahead and grow your hair long again, Jenny, and feel your strength returning with it.

There were other things I learned too late, such as about your getting beaten up by that bully of a boy last year. I might not have mentioned that business of the woman getting attacked if I'd realized. And you being dyslexic too. The first day in first grade, the teacher was yelling at my daughter, because of her handwriting and such. Um, you know what a pressure-cooker is? No? Ask your mother. Then picture the pressure rising toward the explosion point. That's me when someone starts yelling at my daughter. I was once a teacher myself, and I don't take any guff from teachers, many of whom are illiterate compared to me. But in Florida we were locked in, because of the system to prevent segregation. That is, if folk could choose their own schools, they'd be all black or all white, no mixing. We approve of integration, but this meant that we couldn't move our daughter out because they would think we were trying to get out of an integrated school. So we forced the issue on the basis of Penny's dyslexia: that school had no learning-disabled program, so we required that she be transferred to a school that did. That got her out of that class with the yelling teacher, and after that she did well in school, and learned to read, and has been reading at a great rate ever since. Her dyslexia doesn't affect input, just output. There were other battles to fight, and I fought them; I have been militant on behalf of my daughters throughout, right up into college. When Penny had trouble in college because of her vegetarianism, and they insisted she pay for the full schedule of college meals though she couldn't eat them, I showed her how to teach a college a lesson. I wrote to the college president approximately thus: "I will regard this meals charge as an involuntary contribution to the college. You may be sure I shall not make a voluntary one." That crossed in the mail with the college's appeal for contributions. What do you know: suddenly the unbendable rule was bent, and my daughter was free of college meals. So anyway, I hope that my references to things didn't disturb you too much. Just so you know I mean well.

Your mother says she's dyslexic too, and wonders whether it ties in with ambidexterity. That is, using either hand. I wonder too. As far as I know, I am not dyslexic, but it did take me three years to get out of first grade. The things I was taught to do, I do right handed; the things I taught myself, I do left handed. Some things I did both ways, just as a challenge. Today I write right handed (but I have written left-handed in the past; I quit because it's harder pushing the pencil into the paper than pulling it across) and eat left handed. My father thinks my absolute idiocy with respect to foreign languages derives from that; I mastered only one language, English, but I got pretty good at that, eventually. So I keep wondering about right and left handedness, and problems in learning, and male and female. You see, the brains of women may be wired differently from those of men; they have a larger corpus col—oh, I can't remember the term, but it's the cable that connects the halves of the brain, like the cable between the computer and the printer. A bigger cable makes for a better connection, and women often can see more sides to a situation than men can. But I'm strange; in ways I think like a woman, and I think it helps my writing. Left-handers may have a bigger cable too, to compensate. So I think I have more access to the parts of my brain than does the average man, and I can relate well to women, though I feel like a man. But you know, it's supposed to be mostly boys who are hyperactive and dyslexic, also they tend to be blond and blue-eyed. That's Penny. So maybe she's a girl who is wired in her brain like a boy. These crossovers are fascinating, but we really don't know anything for sure. Still, when something threatens you, how does your mother react: man-fashion or woman-fashion? Man-fashion is to bash that threat into oblivion; woman-fashion is to be understanding. Yes, I know: she reacts both ways. In short, ambidextrously.

And your mother says she copies all my letters, so

they can't get lost. Now that's flattering! But if one ever is lost, and you want it back, let me know; I keep copies of all my letters, and I can print one out again if necessary. Twelve letters—I've been writing to you pretty often, haven't I! I hope you aren't getting bored.

You know, I had some notes for this letter, and here I am over 1500 words into it, and I have used none of those notes. Sigh. Well, if you want to know what I would have said, had I stayed on track, tell me, and I'll say it next time. What? No I don't have room for it all this time; I'm already three pages along. STOP BLINKING AT ME! Okay, one item: back when you had the accident, I was working on *Total Recall*, a special project. A novelization. That is, they had the script for what will be a major science fiction adventure movie next year, and I turned it into a novel. So that novel will be published this SapTimber as a hardcover under my name, and then in paperback when the movie is released, starring muscle man Arnold Schwarzenegger. So if you like science fiction violence, you can watch it, and think of me, though I really had nothing to do with the movie. I just wondered what I was doing when the horror that was going to have the single nice effect of bringing you into my life occurred, and that was it.

And one other item, from those notes: I don't know whether you have gotten anyone to read *Heaven Cent* to you, but if you have the interest, I think you would like it. I had to check in it, because two major characters in *Isle of View* were introduced in that novel, and I saw things that I think would appeal to you and make you think. For one thing, twelve year old, freckled Electra. Now she's an old woman of eighteen, but then she was a girl of your generation, who slept long.

Well, this has been a sort of a serious letter. It happens. Maybe I'll get back to normal next time. Harpy thymes, Jenny!

PS (the morning after): I'm adding a clipping about a

British vegetarian girl who entered Oxford University at age 11 and is a math whiz. Both my parents graduated from Oxford, my mother the top in her class, my father almost, except his marriage to my mother distracted him. Everyone in my family was smart, except me.

Mayhem 26, 1989

Dear Jenny,

Your mother didn't write, and didn't write, and I knew what had happened: the doctor had finally caught her out of bed once too often and locked her in the hospital, where she was fretting about everything and sundry. There she was stuck, until her ulcers went down and her blood count went up. I thought of calling, to make sure, but I knew that if I did, she would turn out to be at home and would tell me in 9.35 pages exactly what a sad sod I was to ever believe that any thumping quack of a doctor could ever catch *her* out. So I took the cowardly way, and waited. Finally she got tired of that game, and got her computer in gear again, and I got letters today and yesterday, not necessarily in that order. She had lost a day's work by not saving her material, and naturally the computer had struck at the worst moment. Your mother is an idiot: tell her to get one of those programs that saves automatically every few seconds, so that her material can never again be lost. Every bloke but a Computer Systems Analyst knows that.

Just to get even, she says that you stuck your tongue out at me, because of that picture business. Oh you did, did you? Well, how would you like a pot of nitrogen on it? That'll teach you to keep a civil tongue in your head. A smelly one, maybe, but civil.

Let's see, where were we before we got into this quarrel? Your mother's browned off letters. She says you approved the Jenny Elf story, and that she has no keyboard with the pound symbol. Horrors; I'll lend her some of mine: £££££. It's just a matter of pounding them out. She says you're working on a letter to me. But I already have one from you, with your picture in Elven Armor, and about how your daddy fell out of his chair. And your signature, JNY. She also mentions your occupational therapy, where I gather you have arms and legs but not much middle. I wonder: would they ever let you try swimming? So the water would support you. It might be more comfortable exercise.

As of her last letter, you had not seen the Author's Note. I've made the corrections she gave, but you will have to say about some things, such as whether to call you just Jenny. Tell her that when I went over that Note, this morning, I also added in a reference to Andrea Alton, who suggested putting Jenny (Elf) in, and her novel. And I told other fans not to deluge me with requests for *their* names as characters. "If you aren't in a coma," I said, "don't ask."

She also sent pictures of your reunion with Sammy, and your cat sweater. I'm glad you two could get together again; it's been a long time. I see you have elven ears on, there, except that they aren't pointed. Ah, well, the Elfquest folk will no doubt survive.

Okay, I'll enclose some items for you. Gunk the vegetarian is back in the Curtis comic; he's an animal rights activist, of course. In that connection, there's a clipping about how they treat laboratory rats here in Florida: it's horrible. What they want to find out is how to stop the muscles of folk like you from wasting away while you're trying to get your head together, but the way they do it is sickening. However, we also have decent folk here, as the clipping about the veterinarian who takes in animals shows. I know you'd like him. I was raised on a goat farm, and little goats—those are the true kids—are the most wonderful pets. Little deer are a lot like that. We have families of deer living on our tree farm here; every blue moon or so we see them. Also possum, box turtles, snakes and whatnot; we value them all. The only thing we don't like is hunters, so we keep them off. I'm also enclosing a picture in an ad. It's not original with the ad; I first saw it over twenty years ago. Which face do you see: the young Jenny-girl, or your tired old mum? They are both there. No, keep looking; eventually you'll see them both. It took me forever to see the old one, way back when.

Meanwhile, what's new here? Well, remember that wren nest in my bicycle bag? The eggs hatched maybe a day after my last letter; I can see one of the chicks in there, though I don't dare look too closely, because Lina Wren has an attitude like that of your mother: Leave My Baby Alone. But little Wrenny is in there, and maybe two more.

Yesterday two significant things happened. I finally heard from your mother, and I had a letter from a video producer who would like to turn Xanth into a series of videos, using live actors mixed with computer animation. He sent some sample video cassettes of what he had done, and it looked pretty good. Of course there's a lot to check, yet; not everyone who wants to make a movie or video is capable of doing it right. But my agent is checking it out, and who knows: maybe some day there'll be a series of Xanth movies, including *Isle of View*, with Jenny Elf and Sammy Cat.

So I guess that wraps it up, and—what? You say I still have most of a page left over. Well, sure, but that doesn't mean I have to fill it. No, don't you dare stick your tongue out at me again! I'll blow a stink horn at you. That's the kind that makes a foul-smelling noise. So there. But okay, I'll fill in with a note or so.

One's about my Rapunzel doll. Yes, I do have one. STOP SNICKERING! Franklin Mint wanted to do some Xanth figurines, which they'll be promoting any year now; I even used their mountain setting in *Man From Mundania*, and you can only get onto that mountain by passing the Frankinmint plant. Then they pondered doing some Xanth dolls, and I said oh, you mean like Rapunzel? So they sent me their Rapunzel doll. She's about twenty inches tall, in a beautiful purple gown and robe, and her hair, oh, my, it reaches down below her feet. She's an expensive doll, about two hundred dollars, I think, but they sent her free. That's the advantage of being a successful writer. I have her standing on a file cabinet where I can see her as I type my novels. She reminds me of my daughter Penny; her face is similar.

Okay, now may I end this letter? I ran out of time last night (this is now the next morning), because I had an hourlong phone call from my agent in New York about a complicated contract. I could get a lot of things done, if it wasn't for the phone! You say one more note? All right, but this is the last one.

I may have mentioned that I answer over a hundred letters a month. Most of them I route through a secretary. I write my answers in pencil on the back of the envelopes as I read the letters, and once a week my wife takes the package of 20 or 25 letters to the secretary, who's about 10 miles away, and picks up the prior week's bunch. Some letters I do directly, like the ones to you. I have correspondents who are suicidal, or women who find me fascinating (stifle that snigger!), prisoners, bereaved families—I finished the novel of a young man who was killed by a car a year before you were hit—collaborators, and so on. After this letter I have to write to a murderer on Death Row, who brutally killed his girlfriend and their unborn baby. The funny thing is that in other respects he is ordinary and sensitive; when he learned I was writing to you he inquired, because he doesn't like crimes like that. He says "I know she/her family wouldn't appreciate me writing, but tell her I'm thinking of her and hope she has a full recovery."

*Author's Note:

When I referred to Jenny being injured mainly in the head, I was mistaken. Jenny was bashed badly in the body too; I just didn't know the full extent of it. I understand they use makeup to cover her facial scars, so that even when I met her, later, I didn't realize the extent of her injuries.

For those who like answers to their math problems: There are several ways to fathom this riddle, but perhaps the simplest is by using one unknown and solving it algebraically. Let X = the difference between their ages. Mary is 24. So Mary is twice as old as Ann was, which must have been 12, when Mary was as old as Ann is now. Mary's age minus the difference between them has to be Ann's age, and Ann's age plus the difference between them has to be Mary's age. So 24 − X is Ann's age now, and that's the same as Mary's age then, 12 + X. So the formula is 24 − X = 12 + X. Simplify that by moving 12 to the other side, and −X to the other side, changing the signs as you do. Thus 24 − 12 = X + X. Then 12 = 2X. Divide by two, and X = 6. So if the difference between their ages is 6, Ann must be 18. However, when I first encountered this problem, I just played with it in my head, and figured that the answer was probably somewhere around halfway between 24 and 12, and that worked. *Then* I proved it with the algebra. For me, the solution always was simpler than the math. Jenny did figure out Ann's age, probably the same way I did: by judgment rather than math. You might say that math is a tool for those who lack judgment.

The reference to a bully comes from an incident that Jenny's mother told me. The year before, Jenny, age eleven, had made a complaint about a fifteen-year-old bully, just standing her ground. Thereafter he ambushed her, beat her up, crushed her glasses (she was almost blind without them, having severe vision problems), and was stopped only by the intercession of a neighbor. All because she had tried to resist his bullying. This is a problem for women worldwide, in their dealings with men. Apparently this sort of thing will not be taken seriously as long as men govern the world.

June 1989

Abdominal muscles see their first use in months; will the elven armor be retired? A new chair is ordered. A new companion is gained. Some old stories are retold. An anniversary occurs. And a birthday occurs, maybe.

Jejune 2, 1989

Dear Jenny,

Well, it's a new month. I just finished last month, with a total of exactly 600 letters for the year to date—and this is the fourth letter this month. I—what? The last letter before this one? Oh, you wouldn't care about that; it was just to some dull old publisher. So let's—what do you mean, what publisher? Morrow, if you must know. Now let's get on to—will you stop interrupting me?! Morrow's a hardcover publisher, a major one. Now, as I was saying—good grief, girl, you're as bad as your mother! Once you latch on to something irrelevant, you never let go! All right, it was this: last month the editor at Morrow phoned me and asked whether I would start a story for a New York Book Fair story contest later this year, and be the judge of the winning entry. That is, I would write maybe the first thousand words, and then the contestants who picked that up at the Morrow booth at the fair would finish the story, and I'd decide who did the best job. Well, I was in the middle of writing *Isle of View* then, but I said I'd do it when I finished the novel. So now the novel is done, awaiting only your word on how your name should be in the Author's Note, so I wrote the story. It's titled "Baby," and it's about this newspaper reporter who does a feature on black-market baby adoptions, and discovers that no matter what race or sex the babies are, they are all the same age, weight and length, and look like twins. What could account for this? That's it—the contestants will finish the story, and I dare say some will have it turn out that the babies are really BEMs in disguise, waiting to take over the world. Oh, you don't know what a BEM is? It's a Bug-Eyed Monster, a standard item in cheap science fiction. BEMs are always chasing after femmes, which are—oh, you already know that. So my letter was to go with the story. Now aren't you sorry you were so curious? You should have taken my word that it was dull.

I'm enclosing a few things: last Sunday's Curtis comic, an item on saving a baby whale—you know, I just decided to join an organization called Greenpeace, that works to preserve aquatic creatures from extinction. Man does horrendous damage to the water folk, as he does to the air folk and the land folk, and if it doesn't stop soon, there'll be nothing much left on earth but man, and then man will set about exterminating himself too. I am disgusted. But I try to help save creatures in various ways, and this is one of them. I'm also joining an organization that fights censorship, because that's something I hate. But I'm wandering from the subject. I'm also enclosing a picture I don't like, which made me think of you—stop that, I didn't say I don't like you. It's a picture of about six girls seeing the body of a friend appear in the water, their horror manifest. I thought of your friends when that car hit you, and I think that's the way they looked. In this case, it was a drunken boat driver who ran over another boat and killed five young folk. Yes, they caught him. Our drunk drivers are just as bad as yours, more's the pity. There's also another letter enclosed for someone else; if your mother reads "Dear Andrea," tell her she's in the wrong letter, and to get on to this one. While you're telling her things, tell her to do what I do about saving computer files: to program one key for an instant save, and hit that key compulsively every time she pauses. I do that in addition to having an automatic save feature. I'm ornery about problems; I don't let the same one happen to me twice.

Your mother tells me about your days, which strike me as not much fun. I suspect you are a lot better patient than I would be. Are you able to read, if the book is in front of your face? I mean, I know you can't just pick it up and hold it there, or move your head around much, but if it were right, could you read, or do your eyes not focus well enough for the small print? I go crazy when I don't have my glasses on and then I have to read something; all I can see is the general shape of the words, like blocks lined up in rows. But if I wear the glasses, then I get seasick when I look beyond eighteen inches. So I'm forever putting them on and off, unless I'm wearing my half-glasses that I can peer over. A funny thing happened when the writer Jody Lynn Nye was here. I call Jody the Nymph, because she looks just like a nymph, only she wears clothes. She writes the Xanth Gamebooks, such as *Ghost of a Chance*; I don't know if you've read those. They are where all the puns of Xanth have gone. She and I collaborated on the *Visual Guide to Xanth*, which is to be published this NoRemember. So she was here, last OctOgre, along with her husband and the artist, and we were talking. Every time I looked at her and put my glasses on, she took hers off. When I took mine off, she put hers on. Hers were just like mine, too. It was weird. Finally I figured it out: she needs her glasses for distance, while I need mine for close work. So I put mine on to focus on her at close range, and she took hers off; then when we looked elsewhere, long range, we switched. I guess you keep yours on all the time, so that doesn't happen. Anyway, I was in the process of inquiring whether you can read, if the book is right. No, I realize that no one is going to stand there and hold the book in front of your face, and turn the pages when you blink; it would be hard to read, because the book would wobble and be at the wrong slant and all. They'd rather just read it aloud to you. But suppose the print were on a computer screen, and you could in effect turn the pages yourself, by pressing a button under your finger on the armrest? So you could sit there or lie there, with the screen just right, and read at your own pace or snooze in the middle without losing your place. Would you be able to read then, without getting a horrible headache? Because if you could, and would like to, they might be able to set it up that way. And if they could set up with an IBM AT-compatible system, which is what I use now, after four years on the DEC Rainbow, then I could send you a disk with *Isle of View* on it, and you could read the whole story of Jenny Elf in context. Because of course she's only part of the story, and there's a whole lot else going on, but she is intertwined with it throughout. This novel won't be published until OctOgre 1990, and I wouldn't want that disk to get into the wrong hands, but if this enabled you to read the novel yourself, even if it took you six months to get through it—well, first you have to decide whether you're interested, and then your mother has to find out whether it's possible.

Meanwhile, since your day isn't all that nice—by my definition, your day won't be nice enough until you are running through your yard and meeting the ducks who moved in during your absence—let me tell you about mine. I run through my yard—but my yard is an 87 acre tree farm. So my running route is 2.9 miles, from the house down along the forest path, beside the lake, through all the oak and magnolia and hickory trees, to the pump, where I prime it and pump the old bathtub full for the horses, then start my stopwatch again and run on through the slash pines, the dragonflies racing playfully with me and the blackflies trying to bite me, up to the gate at the north.

Then back down through pines and oaks, taking a shortcut I carved for the horses, to the other side of our house, by which time I'm close to half way through my run. Then up the paved drive to the little magnolia tree, where, you know, nitrogen—STOP LAUGHING! THE NURSES ARE STARING AT YOU—and on up to the main entrance, which is about the three-quarter mark of my run. Then around and back down that drive to the house. Today I ran that run in twenty-three minutes and forty-one seconds, which is okay for me. It's one sweat of a workout, I assure you, especially since the temperature was 90° F. But that's how I keep healthy. I'm in my fifties, you know. If my first child had lived, I could have had a grandchild your age by now. Have you ever noticed how the old and the young understand each other better than the folk in between do? I saw a cartoon once, showing three people emerging from a movie. The posters said "Great fun for young and old!" The old man and the boy were laughing their heads off, while the ordinary man in the middle was looking blank. So then I came in and took my shower and washed my hair, which is dull business, so I sing in the shower, trusting no one can hear. Those old folk songs I memorized when I was your age. "Nicodemus" and "Danny Boy" and funny sea-songs and love songs and such; I like everything if it's folk. I don't know if you know most of the songs I know. If we ever meet, and no one else is around, I'll sing some for you, but you'll have to promise no one else can overhear; you know how it is. One of the funny ones goes like this: "My sweetheart's the mule in the mine; I drive her without any lime; on the bumper I sit, and I chew and I spit, all over my sweetheart's behind." One of the serious ones is "The Ohio," pronounced O-hi-O, about a man who drowns his girlfriend because she refuses to be his bride. A song can be ugly but beautiful, as I guess you know. Then lunch and here to this letter. After this I'll have to proofread 27 fan letter answers the secretary typed and pack them off. Then, tomorrow, I can return to work on the story I have to do for someone else's anthology, and finally get to work on my real project, *Tatham Mound*, about the American Indians who encountered Hernando de Soto. No it's not fantasy, it's historical and archaeological. If you promise not to tell, I'll tell you a secret about that. Do you promise? No, I won't accept a stuck-out tongue as an answer; I demand a firm blink. Okay, the secret is this: I got interested in archaeology because my daughter Cheryl was getting into it, and the local folk discovered an untouched Indian burial mound right here in Citrus County, Florida. That's a rare thing; there are few if any left, and the culture of these Indians is unknown, because they all disappeared. What happened to them? Maybe this mound had the answer. What was needed was to excavate that mound scientifically, studying the placement of every bone and arrowhead and piece of crockery. But that would cost money, and there wasn't money. So I gave the University of Florida the money to do it, and my daughter Cheryl worked on it, and now we know much more about those Indians than before, and I will write a novel to bring them to life and show how they perished. It's a tragedy, all right; they were wiped out by plagues brought by the Spaniards. The evidence was in that mound. I expect this to be the most significant novel of my career, and tomorrow I get to work on it. But I don't want folk knowing about the money yet, because then everybody would be asking me for money, and I just wanted that mound to get done. Uh, no, it couldn't be left untouched, once discovered, because poachers would come and destroy it, as has been the case with most of the other mounds of Florida; that's why so little is known about the local Indians. So it was excavated with respect, and my novel will really make the case for those Indians. I know what their land was like, because I live in it, and I know how the white man treated them. Forget about cowboys and Indians; this is a serious novel.

Sigh; I have rambled on for three pages. Well, you're a good listener. Let me check your mother's last letter, which just arrived today. She says you haven't had a chance to answer about how you want your name in the Author's Note. Well, let me know, so I can do it right and ship the novel off to New York. There is one more thing you maybe should know: I'll be dedicating the novel to you, just to "Jenny," however it is in the Author's Note. Then folk can wonder who you are, until they find out at the end.

Your mother says they are setting up to rework your house, so that you can buzz around it in your blazing red wheelchair. She says she's trying to figure out how to fit twice as much computer into half the space, and asks "ten pounds of dung in a five pound bag?" Another term for that description is—oops, there's the Adult Conspiracy again. Well, I'll sneak it in in brackets, so no one knows about my violation of the Conspiracy. The term is [blivet]. Don't throw it around carelessly. Speaking of dirty things: she says that Ray's car is now called the "Nitrogen Pot." That must be some car! She also says she doesn't drive much now. But after your accident—well, I had a car accident, back in the first year I was married. I was looking for an address, and took my eye off the road at the wrong moment, as I hit a reverse-banked turn. I lost control and sailed off a six foot bank at 40 miles per hour. I didn't know whether I would wake after hitting ground. I remember the car going over and over. But I survived with only a bashed shoulder. I found my head in the back seat; this was before seat belts existed, and you bet I use them always now, as does every member of my family. The car was back on its feet and facing back the way it had come. So it was a complete rollover and turnabout. I never recovered my confidence in driving, and I do little driving today. I taught both my daughters to drive, as I have a better temperament for that than my wife does, and now I'm satisfied to ride with them or my wife. Once a person has been truly touched by the disaster that an automobile accident can be, he or she does not forget. That may have figured into my attitude when I completed the novel of the young man who was killed by a careless driver, and with you. It's one reason I don't like to travel. My daughter Penny had an accident in thick smoke, and now she's shy of foggy conditions.

Look, I have to stop; those fan letters are looming over me. Tell your mother I'll send her another copy of the Note once we have it straight, and we'll see how my family does on the "Choosing Sides" test she sent. My daughter Cheryl is home from college for the summer; she'll be working at the local newspaper, driving (ugh!) in each day.

Oh, I almost forgot: the wrens grew up and departed the nest, and I didn't get to see Wrenny go. Sigh; if you're not there right at the right time, they sneak out. So have as good a day as you can, Jenny, and no, you don't have to go over again the parts of this letter you slept through. I'll keep the next one shorter, I hope.

Jejune 9, 1989

Dear Jenny,

Ha—I finally heard from your mother, who says you suggest putting Jenny G. for your name. So G. it is. I'll set that up and run it off this weekend, so the publisher can finally see what it's paying for. Oops—revise this paragraph! I heard from your mother again, and she said no, you preferred Jenny Gildwarg. Okay, I'll do that, and if you change your mind later, the reference can be changed before publication.

Meanwhile, how are things here? Well, we have more magnolias blooming; all our trees above a certain size seem to intend to put out at least one flower this season, and there is one just off our property that has one tiny branch reaching across the fence onto our land—and that's the branch that does the blooming. I think those trees like us. We also have passion flowers and fruit all over the place. The flowers are lovely purple circles, and the fruit looks like limes, but we don't know whether it's edible. If it is, we could call it a passion fruit farm, because it grows everywhere, including our fences, and it tries to tie our gate shut. The wrens, having left the nest, don't visit or call, ungrateful birds. I found a pretty scarlet snake near our mailbox—that's a name, not a description. It looks like an imitation king snake, and the king snake looks like an imitation coral snake, and yes, we do have coral snakes here, and we like them. The poison is deadly, but they are harmless, because they're small and don't look for trouble. Spiders build webs across our drive and my running path, which is a problem. I don't like to mess up a spider web, but when I come running full speed around a corner, wham, I may be into it before I can stop.

Remember the prisoner on Death Row? I don't think you want to correspond with him, and I haven't given him your identity any more than I've given you his. But he has a message for you: "Atari was developing an eye-controlled joystick/games. Perhaps she could use it for communication. The address is Atari Corp. 1196 Borregas Ave., Sunnyvale, CA 94086, Tel: (408) 745-2367. I don't know if they still make it, or who they should talk to, but it would be worth the effort. Computer companies *like* to help (great PR), so if the situation was explained . . . And, given Atari's price—even if they had to pay $40 for a 2600 or $130 for a 130XE computer would be nothing compared to what she will get. (Incidentally, my computers were: Jenny, Jenny Jr., Son of Jenny. Yes they were!) I only wish I could present it myself. Give them my address. I'd like to write to her—if they don't mind. And, I don't like 'crimes like that'; I despise ALL crimes (DWI, robbery, white collar, political crime, discrimination/reverse discrimination.) To me crime is violence/violence is crime."

Okay, I have relayed his message, but not his address, because I don't think I would be doing you a favor. This person is seriously disturbed, and at present is asking me not to write to him again because he feels I'm too decent. He's not used to decent treatment, and has trouble relating to it. I can give his address if you want it, and you could write to him as you do to me, if your mother does not throw a fit, but I don't recommend it.

I understand that they are making you exercise to try to build up your middle muscles, so you can sit up better. That's probably a pain, but still worthwhile, because you need to be able to put it all together if you want to get walking sooner rather than later. I also understand that they want to change your red racer wheelchair to one with a seat/shoulder harness. That's probably so that you won't go flying out if you put on the brakes too quickly.

Stray thought, speaking of speed: did you notice how you moved to Warp 7, and then you heard from WaRP, the Elfquest folk? Cause and effect; what else? I'm going to ask them if they would like to do the cover for the novel, if the publisher agrees. I feel they could do Jenny Elf best. The picture probably wouldn't look too much like you, but that might be best, because you wouldn't want to pass people on the street and have them keep stopping and staring and saying "Hey! Aren't you that elf who helped the centaur foal?"

Meanwhile, having completed the Xanth novel, I'm into my next, *Tatham Mound.* This chapter is a tale adapted from the *Popol Vuh,* the sacred text of the Quiche Maya. My Indians are here in Florida, but there's a girl whose mother was a fugitive from the civilized Maya region (they wanted her to marry an Aztec chief, and the Aztecs were really into ritual human sacrifices), and so she brought her heritage with her. You say that's too farfetched; you can't imagine anyone's mother doing that? You can't fool me; I know you know of a case yourself. So we learn the tale, and it's a phenomenal one. There's this girl, Xquic, which I think is pronounced Shkeek, who goes to a tree where there is skull-like fruit and one real skull, and she talks with the skull, and it drips a drool of saliva into her hand, and she becomes pregnant with twins, who will go to avenge their father's death. No, that's *not* the way it's normally done, but the Mayas didn't use storks. It's a fascinating tale. When her father sees her pregnant he gets upset; in fact he orders her heart to be cut out and burned. Discipline was firmer in those days, you see. But she talks the men who are to sacrifice her into taking the blood-red sap of a tree and forming a heart-shape out of that, and they take that back and it fools the others. But her problems aren't over. So you can see that this is no dry treatise on Indian lore; I mean to do right by those Indians.

Tell your mother I took the brain-sides test she sent, and my score was Left = 76, R = 129 and I = 95, which makes me a right-brained person. The description fits—but so do the descriptions for left-brains and mixed-brains and integrated-brains, so it means nothing much. It reminds me of the Kuder Preference Test I took in college, that concluded I should be a writer of math textbooks. I could hardly think of anything I less wanted to do! I mean, would *you* like to write math textbooks? The problem with these tests is that they force unrealistic, nitpicking choices. You want to know what it's like? Okay, try this: Question One: would you like to eat a bug, or a worm, or either? If you try to say "Yuck! I wouldn't do any of those!" you are an uncooperative client, and maybe you should be put in reform school. If you say you would rather eat the bug, then the analysis will show that you have a morbid attraction for hairy-legged things. If the worm, then you like squiggling cold things. So you could wind up being a taster for a roach motel. This is one reason I don't do well on standardized tests; I always have too many objections that the test makers don't appreciate.

But some readers are pretty perceptive. Today I received a fat envelope from the National Institute of Dyslexia. The woman writing works there, and says she's noticed dyslexic aspects of my writing, and inquires whether I or any member of my family is dyslexic. Now that's interesting, because she doesn't mention my Incarnations Notes or *Bio of an Ogre*; apparently she picked it up from my Adept series and my would-be horror novel *Shade of the Tree*, wherein I have a hyperkinetic dyslexic boy. I don't think I'm dyslexic, but I did take three years to get out of first grade. Certainly my mind is different—oh, you had noticed?—but it's my wife who says "Go left!" while pointing right. A friend came to a screeching stop midway between the forks of a super-highway split once, when she did that. Still, we do have a dyslexic daughter. No I can't just dismiss the letter; she wants to nominate me for a dyslexic achievement award. I'll try to discourage her, because I think I'm ornery but not dyslexic.

We had a lot of rain this past week. We have a pool, and the water was up to 82°F, and I figured one more scorching hot day would bring it up to swimmable temperature—I freeze below bathwater level—and then the rains and clouds came and cooled it four degrees. Sigh. Those storms always sneak up on us, when my wife has laundry out drying. You hear plink, plink, and you think it's the eaves dripping. Then WHOOSH!! and it's a drenchpour. We dashed out anyway and scrambled in the laundry from the line. I'm sure your mother knows exactly how that's done. It reminds me of an old alarm clock I had when your age. It would go dink, dink-dink, dink, dink-dink gently for thirty seconds. If by that time you hadn't gotten up and turned it off, it would abruptly go **BBBBRRRRIIINGGGG!!** and send you up to clutch at the ceiling.

Are you asleep yet? I figure your folks use these letters to lull you to sleep. No? Oh. Well, it's Enclosure time. One

I won't enclose: a solicitation from the National Gardening Association for money, saying "Kids like Jenny are counting on *you*!" I didn't know you were working for them, but it does seem to make sense. They also say: "And from her wheelchair, young Jenny makes one of the most joyful discoveries of all: that gardening is really a nine-letter word for 'freedom.' " Well, I don't know; if four-letter words are bad, what about nine-letter words? I am enclosing a clipping telling of a man who is marrying a woman, and his son is dating her mother. You see what goes on in the outside world while you're in the hospital? And a picture and article about a miniature deer, and Curtis, and a couple I thought you might relate to: man unable to move well, and woman pushing a boulder up a hill. This business of getting your body back, bit by bit—I figure at times it feels like that.

Jejune 10—Now for my morning-after paragraph. I had done this letter, then last night your mother called me, telling me that it was Jenny Gildwarg rather than Jenny G. As long as I'm here again, let me fill in what I forgot yesterday. Despite the jokes and things, I don't take your situation lightly. When I walk in the forest—it's really more like a jungle—you are in my mind, and when I see interesting things I think "Jenny would like that," and I picture you trying to bump along across the forest floor in your wheelchair and I realize it's a foolish thought; you'd have to stick to the road, which fortunately goes by most of the magnolias and up Ogre Drive and past the bunny section and the heron section and the lines of pines. I think of you a lot, Jenny, and it lends meaning to what I see, whether it's a squirrel or a pretty flower others might call a weed. I understand how your mother feels, with the flowers, thinking of you. The truth is, it may seem dull and lonely in that hospital, but the thoughts of many of us are with you, if only this were the Elfquest world and you could receive those thoughts directly. When I mention you to correspondents, without details, they express concern and sympathy. Jenny, if you went to a fantasy convention with a name-tag saying Jenny Elf, you would discover how many friends you have, and how they care for you. I think one day that will happen.

Jejune 16, 1989

Dear Jenny,

I hope your day is good because mine is. What, because it's Jenny-letter day? Well, that too. But mainly it means that things have been falling into place for me, intellectually and physically. For example, this morning I was reading in a dull book about Florida history, because I need information on the Calusa Indians who lived in South Florida, and I wasn't finding much, but I plowed on—and then suddenly I encountered phenomenal stuff about their marriage and death customs. No, don't start scowling; this is neither dirty nor grim.

But first an interruption, because at this point my wife came home from a shopping spree with two recliner chairs, so naturally I had to dash out to unload and carry them into the house, and that was a job because I no longer have the muscle I used to before the tenonitis wiped out my arm exercises, but we struggled and heaved and shoved and managed to get them in before the storm that was trying to catch us in the act broke. They're nice chairs; they're soft and comfortable, and they swivel and rock, and they lean back to two levels, so you can relax for watching TV or go all the way back and snooze. If you think we're crazy to huff and puff to haul these into our family room, just wait till you see what your mother's hauling into your house: an elevator. Can you imagine your mother carrying an elevator? No wonder she gets tired!

I was about to tell you about the Calusa Indians. No, don't look like that; your mother gets all up in a heavel when you make that face, and she's already dis-heaveled from carrying that elevator. The Indians are interesting. You challenge me to prove it? All right, I will, but you have to listen. Nuh-uh—you have to keep your tongue in your mouth, too. (You thought I wouldn't see? Ha!)

First, it turns out that the Chief likes to keep things in the family, so he might marry his sister. When he got tired of her, he'd kick her out and take a younger, prettier wife. In one case he had his son marry her, after he was tired of her. Right; that was a mother and son marriage, and they had several children. I mean, just how close can a family get? But now the death customs: they believed that each person had three souls, one in the pupil of the eye, one in the shadow, and one in the reflection. When the person got sick, it was because he'd lost a soul, and they had to herd it back in the way you'd herd a wild animal, cornering it and forcing it back, until it reluctantly returned to the person, and he got well. When the person died, he lost two of his souls. But the one in the eye remained. That meant that if a living person went to the place of burial, he could talk with that third soul. The Spaniards who conquered Florida in the 16th century remarked that there must be something to it, because an Indian who had gone to talk with a dead relative came to know things he could not otherwise have known. Right—because the dead can see more than we can. I think this makes a lot of sense, and it explains some things that have perplexed me before. But it relates beautifully to my story in *Tatham Mound*, because there my protagonist (main character) has a bad experience, and spends a night by a burial mound, and communes with the chief spirit of that mound, Dead Eagle, who tells him that he must find the *Ulunsuti*, which is the terrible colorless diamond crystal, the most powerful talisman known; one look at it even in a person's sleep can bring death not to him but to his family. Think about that for a moment: that's one deadly stone! If he doesn't find it, his whole tribe will be wiped out. So he sets out to find it, and on the way he meets the nine year old girl whose mother was a Maya, and she tells him the story of "Little Blood" I told you about last week. But mainly he's checking in with all the burial mounds, to inquire of their spirits where to find the *Ulunsuti*, and of course some of those spirits refuse to tell him. Now he's passing through Calusa territory. So now I know how it is that he can speak with those spirits: because one of their three souls remains. Now admit it: wasn't that interesting? Oh—you already knew? Sigh.

So that was my morning research; soon I'll be writing that chapter, and it should be a good one. This isn't Xanth, but by the time it is written and published you'll be older, and you may even enjoy reading it. Who knows, you might get interested in the American Indians and become a world famous scholar.

But I was telling you about my day. It's a running day, and I needed a haircut, so my wife cut my hair just before I ran, and naturally in the middle of that a man came delivering 110 reams of computer paper. His little girl was with him, maybe five years old; we showed her the wren nest, and I told her how we once had little girls, but then they grew up and went to college. That's what they do, you know; you'll be doing it too, in due course. Don't shake your head at me; I tell you I know, because I've seen it before. You'll grow up and get educated and get married and move to Hawaii or somewhere and send your mother a postcard each Christmas, for which she will be duly grateful. Anyway, we got the paper in, then finished the haircut, and I trimmed my beard. Then I ran—and sure enough, with all the weight off my head, it was my fastest run of the year and the second fastest ever, on this track. (I used to run much faster, but I was younger then, still in my 40's). When I run I time it, and I sort of run a race with myself, against all my other runs. At the first quarter I was tied for fastest, but at the half I had dropped back to sixth place. But then I began overhauling those other selves, and by the three quarter mark I had passed three of them and was third. By the time I finished, I passed another, and so was second overall. But the thing is, those other fast runs were made in winter, when the temperature was about 70°F; today it was 90°. So I'm very pleased with this run.

The other nice thing that happened a few days ago was word from a man who had happened to be in a book store, waiting for his wife, and he saw people buying my novel *But What of Earth?*. That's a novel I wrote about fourteen years ago, but the copy-editors rewrote it and in my judgment destroyed it. So now I have had it republished, by a different publisher, with every word restored to the original version—plus 25,000 words of comment about what I thought of the editing. Your mother will have fiendish delight reading that one; it's a case where the worm turned and just about destroyed the wrongdoer. So I hope that that store was typical, and that all over the country people are buying it, and that they enjoy it when they read it.

Meanwhile, what else is new here? Well, our horses are doing fine; some day I'll tell you all about them, because they can be very nice when you get to know them. Last week I mowed the lawn, which was nervous business, because before I hadn't seen one of my wife's sets of plants in time and mowed it flat. Ouch! But several were day-lily bulbs and they put out new leaves without trouble, and the last one was the kind of plant you can grow from a single leaf, and now it has put out half a dozen new leaves from its decapitated stem, so it survived too. Phew! When I mowed, I encountered a big box turtle in the front, and another in back; I think they come to eat our grass, which is fine. There isn't much grass in the forest; in fact, we have about all of it. I also saw a toad, and mowed carefully to avoid it. Later I saw another turtle, just two inches long.

And a new color of dragonfly: deep black-blue, verging on purple, handsome creatures. I do like those dragonflies, because they're so pretty, being all shades of green, blue, brown and yellow, and because they eat the flies that would otherwise be chomping us and our horses. On my last run, not today's, I stopped at the magnolia tree—never mind why—and a deerfly sat on my leg to bite me, and a green dragonfly swooped in and grabbed it. You can't ask for better service than that! Then one evening we were watching TV, a James Bond movie *For Your Eyes Only*, which it turned out we hadn't seen before—I thought we had seen them all—and my wife went out to check something near the pool, and there was a four foot long rat snake. It had come in because the screen door hadn't quite closed. We know that rat snake; it circles the house in its quest for rats or whatever. But we were afraid it would fall in the pool and drown, so we had to get it out. Probably I just should have picked it up, as it's harmless. But four feet long? I was wary. So we just sort of herded it around and toward the open screen door, and finally it went out. Next morning there was an item in the newspaper about a harmless four foot snake loose on a jetliner. So that's where that snake went! You doubt? Okay, I'm enclosing the clipping. So you see, it's been an interesting week.

As usual, I have an envelope full of clippings for you. Is it true that you make your mother make copies of all of them? They really aren't that important, just things I think you'll like in passing. The Marmaduke comic on back of the Curtis is funny too. There's a Ziggy cartoon you may appreciate. There's a girl and horse picture that's so pretty I just had to share it with you. There's a Doonesbury comic, splatted with ink; all week long they had trouble with the careless cartoonist, and got pretty fed up about it. And there's a picture of a house in pine trees: I can take or leave the house, but oh, those pines! You'll have to let me know if you don't like getting deluged with these things; when I see something interesting, I say "Jenny would like that," and I save it for you. I'm also enclosing a more recent printout of the Author's Note in *Isle of View* for your mother. Once I knew how you wanted your name given, I went over it and naturally made four times as many changes as I expected—your mother's friend Andrea Alton can tell you how that is—and printed it out and shipped the novel off to my agent. I think it's a good novel, and not just because of Jenny Elf. I'm showing it also to Richard and Wendy Pini, so they can correct any errors I may have made in describing an Elfquest elf.

So let me know how you're doing. I write about myself mostly because there's not a lot to write about you. I mean, what's the point in inquiring about all the things you did, when I guess it's pretty routine therapy? But it's important even if it's dull. I hope you are still making progress out of that pit, inch by inch, and please do let me know when you break through to something new.

Know something? It's now 5:30 P.M., time to feed the horses, and it's raining. Hard. How do I get out to feed them? Pretty soon Blue will neigh to remind me, and I hate to get neighed at, because it makes me feel guilty. Those horses expect to be fed *on time*. Sigh.

Jejune 23, 1989

Dear Jenny,

Growr! Remember when I told you that the computer is out to get you? Well, it still is. Let me go back to a lot of ~~dull~~ relevant detail to clarify this. No, don't tune out. This is my letter and you have to listen to it, or you get magic itch-dust down your back. And on your tongue, if you stick it out. Ha, I thought that would make you behave! The secret in getting along with folk is knowing the right threat to make them do what you want.

You see, this week I got a program called QDos that

enables me to do mass file handling better. Your mother will tell you all about that sort of thing, if you give her a quarter of a chance. I like the program very well; in fact I discovered when I used it that my chapter about "Little Blood" was way too small, and I looked at it and found that only the first paragraph was there. I had the whole 15,000 word thing on my backup disk, so I could restore it, but that gave me a scare. If I had erased that backup disk, thinking I had it on the hard disk, I could have been in a week's worth of trouble, after calling your mother an idiot for doing similar. She would have done a dance of fiendish glee. So I'm glad to have QDos, that tells me the size of the files it lists, so I can see if anything is wrong. I installed it on my upstairs system, with the color monitor, and lo, it addresses color, and I had all manner of pretty colors of print and lines and such. Then I was showing someone how I could change the color in my word processor, Sprint, too, all except the actual page of print, when lo, I hit a different button and the page changed color. I *can* change that too! So I wasted an hour or more, foolishly, changing colors, finding out exactly what I liked best. Now I have yellow print on a red background, and **bold** shows up in bright white, and underline in dull black, and highlighting in white with a blue background, and so on. If you have a chance to get a color monitor, do it; you'll have endless fun playing with the colors, even without a paintbrush program. You could type a fiery red letter when something upsets you, for example.

Well. Now I'm downstairs on the backup system, no colors (sigh), but because QDos makes things so easy, I made a **JENNY** directory with 20 letters: 14 Jennys, 4 Mothers, and 2 Altons. This is the 21th letter for it. I used QD to move into it—with that program I can call up a "Tree" and travel along that tree by moving the cursor, and when I touch <return> I'm in the directory the cursor is on. It's like climbing a real tree, only easier, and fun. I can copy or move files the same way. So there I was in the JENNY Directory, with all the Jenny letters piled up around me. I set up for this one, and hit my "letter" glossary entry to get my address and the date and all in one swell foop—and it balked. It said there was no such entry. So I used QD to check the glossary file, and that entry was there. So I tried it again, and it still said it wasn't, and furthermore my "jenny" glossary entry wasn't either. I hauled in my wife and showed her. Apparently it couldn't read those entries from the subdirectory. So I went back to the parent directory, which is LETTERS, and tried again. Still no go. Growr! Finally I reset, and tried it, and all was working. I went back to the JENNY directory, and now everything works. Apparently the computer just decided to get me, for no reason. That's the way computers are, as I told you. Did your mother tell you how my disk-reading technique saved her hash, for no sensible reason? When you're dealing with nonsense, sometimes you can handle it by inputting nonsense.

Otherwise, how are things? Well, it's our anniversary today; my wife and I have been married 33 years. And I've been having good runs. Remember how my run last week was the fastest for this year? Well, the next run was faster yet, and broke my record on this track. The one after that was breaking that record through two miles, then pooped out and came in second. Today was slower again; these things don't last. It was a good series, anyway. So what's the moral? Oh, you thought you could get away without one? No such luck! Here I am, still knocking seconds off my runs for no good reason except that I do them, and I try as hard on the slow runs as I do on the fast ones. My body varies in performance, is all. I'll never come close to the seven minute miles I was running before I turned 50—soon I'll be turning 55, and I'll tell you my birthday if you'll tell me yours—but I still do the best I can. Okay, so there you are, in your boards and straps and things, and somehow it seems that you'll never get back to where you were before. But there's no certainty of that. You could stop where you are now, or you could keep on improving until it's as if you never were in any trouble. We don't know how it will turn out. But you can make a big difference. So just as I hope I am promoting my health by running, I hope you're promoting yours by doing those dull exercises. Even sessions that seem to be making no progress, or to be worse than before, may be improving you in ways that don't show, so that somewhere down the line you will improve a lot. Keep it in mind.

I've been meaning to tell you of some of the other songs I sing when I'm taking my shower after my run. Today I sang a couple I think you would like. I like forests, you see, and romance, and animals, and happiness, and music—am I boring you? Oh, you mean you like these things too. Sorry, I guess I misread the signal. So I like songs about these things, and I always did, because I memorized these songs back when I was your age, which was some time ago. One of them is titled "The Happy Plowman," and it goes: "Near a house near the wood, with a horse very good, a poor young farmer smiled as he stood. Looking down at his plow, in his heart was a glow, and he sang as he plowed the row: High-ho, my little Buttercup, we'll dance until the sun comes up! Thus he sang as he plowed, and he smiled as he sang, while the woods and the welkin rang." The second verse is about his helpmate in the house, who is lovely and good, and she echoes his song while the pots and the kettles ring. You know, I always thought Buttercup was the horse, but suddenly I realize that he may be thinking of his wife in the house. The other little song about the forest I like even better: "To the Woodland." It goes: "To the woodland longs my heart, longs my heart forever; there my heart will always be, this no man can sever; in the woodland far away there lives my darling loved one." Then the second verse: "Though the path is dark and long, rocky steep and narrow, though the wood is cold and dark, this brings me no sorrow; cares will vanish when I go to see her on the morrow." Now isn't that romantic? Well, you'd agree if you could hear it; it's a pretty melody, with a lot of feeling. Love in the woods—what could be better than that? We shall have to get together sometime and sing some songs.

So what else is new? Well, today I received a plaque for the Phoenix Award, which I won in 1980. Only nine years late. It was awarded at DeepSouthCon, and I never received the plaque. So finally I have it, and it's nice. I halfway agreed to go to a convention in Atlanta next Mayhem, so maybe they are encouraging me.

Meanwhile, I'm doing research for my novel *Tatham Mound.* You say you don't care about that, just Xanth? Sigh, okay. Yesterday I had a call from the editor at Avon; he had received *Isle of View* but hadn't read it yet. He was calling about a chapter of *For Love of Evil* that they will include in *Man From Mundania,* a teaser to encourage folk to buy the other novel and maybe increase my sales. But while I had him on the line, I asked whether Avon would be interested in having an Elfquest cover—that is, one done by Richard and Wendy Pini. I'm thinking of Jenny Elf with Che Centaur. I think it would be a cute cover. We're also pondering whether to do a limited hardcover edition of that one, for which the special cover might be nice. Avon will think about it. But I don't know yet whether the Elfquest folk would want to do such a cover. So this may come to nothing. But if it should work out, you just might wind up on the cover of the novel. Or did I say that before, too? Sigh again. Why didn't you stop me before I repeated myself?

Now may I talk about *Mound?* Okay, if I keep it short? Sigh. You know the girl is only nine years old at this point—oh, you're interested after all? You see, the main character is a fifteen year old Indian male who gets wounded by an arrow and is being pursued by the enemy. He hides and drags himself to an old burial mound, a sacred place, where he passes out. He has a vision, wherein he talks with Dead Eagle, the spirit of the mound, and the spirit tells him he must find the Ulunsuti, the—what? Oh, I told you about that last week? Sigh; I get so forgetful in my dotage. Everything I try to tell you, I've told you before! Anyway, the spirit also takes away his fear, and he heads off, looking for that magic crystal so he can save his people. On that trip he meets the little girl, called Wren because she's so small, but actually her name is Tzec and her mother was Mayan. A scene I thought I wrote two years ago, and evidently didn't, I put in today: they find a rattlesnake in the canoe, and he takes it in his good hand and helps it out, so it can slither off into the bushes on land. The Indians were more afraid of rattlers than we are, because they don't dare kill them, because the snakes' spirits would return to destroy them. So everyone is staring, and then he realizes that the spirit really *did* take away his fear. What he doesn't know is that he's going to marry that girl—in fifteen years, when they meet again. So it's a romance, but they don't know that at this point. The spirit of the mound knew, though. Now admit it: wasn't that interesting? There's more to life than Xanth, you know. Maybe not a lot more, but some more.

Would you believe: I received a letter from the National Institute of Dyslexia. Someone there had read some of my novels, and concluded that they had a dyslexic flavor about them. They want to nominate me for an award for doing well in life despite dyslexia. As it happens, I do have a dyslexic daughter, and I did take three years to get through first grade, and even my friends admit there is something strange about the way my mind works—but I don't think it's dyslexia. So I told them that I probably wasn't eligible. But it seems that dyslexics do succeed in life. Keep that in mind, in case you had any doubt.

Your mother's letter of the 12th reached me Saturday the 17th, after I had mailed my last letter. So I'll comment on it now. She enclosed two pictures, of you and your cat sweater. You do look like a clown, or like a butterfly, pinned to your board. When you get closer to walking—I realize you aren't there yet—I wonder whether they have those walkers the old folk use, that are like chairs that sort of plant themselves down, and you hold on to the top part and can't fall over? If your arms were strong enough, you could walk with one of those even if the rest of your body were made out of cooked noodles. She also enclosed a satiric column on hunting with semiautomatic weapons. In one of my Incarnations novels I arrange for magic so that the deer could shoot back; I have nothing but disgust and loathing for folk who like to gun down harmless creatures for the "sport" of it. Oh—and tell your mother I had a letter from Andrea Alton, and have answered it. She thought I had misunderstood parts of her novel, but I hadn't.

Some enclosures, some of which are for your mother. The ones for you are Curtis, and one about girls who broke into a home and wrote praises to God on paper there. The police probably won't put them in jail: they are ages four and six. Another is about a test—no, don't turn off your mind yet!—that a newspaper published. It was a statewide high school achievement test, and copies of the answer key had been stolen, and students were buying them. Now you know what that means: the cheaters would make high scores, and the honest ones would not do as well. That sort of bothers me. So the newspaper bought one of those stolen copies, then published it on its front page, so everybody would have the same advantage and the test would be fair. So what did the school authorities do? They canceled the test, and threatened to sue the newspaper. They weren't bothered by the cheaters, just the newspaper that stopped the cheating. Don't go to a school system like that! Which reminds me: I'm reading myself to sleep on a book about Scientology. If you haven't heard of that cult, you're lucky. Scientology was started by a science fiction writer, which goes to show that even science fiction writers can't always be trusted. Reading this book is like turning over rocks and watching the bugs underneath. So don't join any cults, either. Not even ones that promise to save the world.

Now I have to handle a couple of business letters and get back to the chore of checking and signing contracts. You never saw anything as complicated and messy as those contracts! It took so long to get them straightened out that I wrote the whole first novel meanwhile: that was *Isle of View*. So it's a pile of contracts for four books, four copies each, about eight pages each. What a mess. Of course there's a whole lot of money involved. Still, I'd rather just be writing. Maybe you better not grow up to be a novelist. You can be an artist instead, or a mathematician—not funny? Sorry. I've put my foot in it so many times in this letter that maybe one more doesn't matter.

Tomorrow your mother's next letter will arrive, as the Post Orifice takes four days to deliver it. The PO is nearly as bad as a computer when it comes to messing up connections. Meanwhile, have a halfway decent day, Jenny, and a better one if you can manage it.

Jejune 30, 1989

Dear Jenny,

I just finished a four page Family letter—I do one each month, and this time Family Letter Day and Jenny Letter day came together. No, you can't have four pages; I'm pooped out. No, that's not a bad word, so stop sniggering.

I understand you have a new roommate, called Cathy. Hi, Cathy! Just don't stay awake all night giggling, you two.

I remember when a neighbor had two daughters whom my daughter Penny liked, called June and Cathy. One day I went by and called "Hi, Juney! Hi, Cath!" Just wait till the nurses get confused and call you two Jenthy and Cathny. Don't tell her about the nitrogen—you say you already did? Ouch!

Okay, to business: sure enough, your mother's letter arrived just after I sent my last. Her next one arrived yesterday, but it didn't tell me what I wanted to know: when's your birthday? Somewhere recently she mentioned about doing something when you were 113 and she was 134; from that I suspect that if you haven't just turned 13, you are thinking of doing it pretty soon. I could probably even figure out your mother's age, if higher math weren't so difficult. Here, at any rate, is a birthday present from my wife. She has been slowly working on a cushion for you, with your name and a Xanth motif, and last month she completed the stitching, and this month she got it blocked out and assembled. Her initials are on it, XXX (we're in Mundania, remember; when she's with me at a convention, folks call her Mrs. Anthony, but there is no such person in Mundania), so you know who made it. Harpy Birthday, Jenny!

Something not really related: yesterday I got a half hour video tape called *Nothing But Zooms*, which is an animation of the Mandelbrot Set. Remember, I told you about it some time back? Your mother went crazy trying to find an illustration of it, but I don't think she succeeded. Well, this starts with the glowing original "Bug" (I don't know what they call it, but it looks like a tick to me) and slowly zooms in on its edge, so that you see finer and finer detail. It starts again, from another angle, and shows another aspect. It just keeps doing this, taking you through a wonderland of weird and lovely forms. Jenny, you don't need to do any math for this; all you have to do is appreciate beauty when you see it. Are you able to watch a video tape? Surely they can connect one to your TV set. I want to get another copy of this video and send it to you so you can watch it. If it bores you, then you don't have to watch it again, but I suspect you'll find it as fascinating as I do, and will want to watch it over and over. Then, when you're done with that, maybe your daddy will sneak in a video of *Indiana Jones* or something, and you and Cathy can watch it in secret, once you have the video cassette player in your room. Let's face it: you don't get a whole lot of fun, this year, and you might as well get what you can while you're recovering.

Tell your mother that that essay I wrote for THE WRITER, that mentions you, is now in print in the Aw-Ghost issue. But they typoed Elfquest, so now it reads Elquist. I see I had typoed it myself, leaving out the "f" but they worsened it. What will Richard and Wendy Pini say? Oh, dread.

Meanwhile, things have been interesting here. After we mailed my last letter to you, the power failed, and it was 21 hours before they got it restored so it stayed. It seems that lightning struck at the edge of our line, and blew out all the breakers so that the neighborhood for miles around was dark. The repairmen said they'd never seen such a blast before. Our most-of-a-mile-long underground line blew out in three places; they had to trace it down and use a giant backhoe to dig it out and repair it. We used oil lamps and candles. It was the day after our 33rd anniversary, so we went out to RAX to eat and called it a celebration of the occasion. Do they have RAX in your area? It's ideal for vegetarians, because they have everything in the salad bar, including wonderful cream of broccoli soup and bean stuff so you can make your own burritos, as well as all the vegetables. I always pig out on three kinds of pudding: chocolate, butterscotch and vanilla. Yes, I realize you can't go there just yet, and that you're not eating that way yet, but you're going to, right? Once you get back to regular eating, and you get to go home, then you can go out to a place like that and pig out on pudding. Anyway, such was our weekend, while we waited interminably for our power to return.

Yesterday someone called into a rock radio station and told them he was me. Growr! I don't even listen to rock music! A friend of my daughter's heard it, and inquired, and my daughter asked me. We tried to call in to tell them it wasn't so, but their line was continuously busy and we couldn't get through. Stop snickering. How would you like it if someone called in and told them it was you? It may happen, after *Isle of View* is published.

Remember how I changed the colors on my computer? I finally settled for yellow print on a brown background: vanilla and chocolate.

I was going to tell you about our horses. First let me tell you about the turtle: one of our big gopher tortoises was in the dog yard, banging the fence to get out. We don't want it to tunnel under the fence, because then the dogs might say "You can do that? We'll do it too!" So I picked it up and carried it out, its four legs scrambling. When I put it down, it headed off in the direction it was going without a word. They're like that. Today it or another walked by the front of our house, eating the grass. I went out to see where it was going, and a bunny bounded away. Do you think the tortoise and the hare . . . ?

Okay, now the horses. When Penny got old enough to know what's what, at about age six, she wanted a horse. "We can't have a horse here in town!" we protested. Then we moved to the country. "Well?" Penny demanded. Sigh. So we got into horses. Now I was required to ride horses in first grade at boarding school, and those monstrous animals went where they wanted, and it was a terrifying experience. For the next thirty years or so I stayed away from horses. But when we got one for Penny, I discovered I liked horses after all. We wanted the perfect horse: one who could teach Penny what she needed to know. So we got Sky Blue, who had been a harness racer in her youth, but was now an old hackney mare of twenty. She's a small horse, fourteen hands tall; below that they are classed as ponies. Blue had raised her former owner from age ten to age fifteen, and now was taking on Penny at age ten. Blue was an ideal horse, perfectly trained and gentle. She's registered, with papers, and is black, with white socks on her hind legs. She's thirty one years old now, having raised Penny up to college level, and her socks are falling down around her hooves, but she's still spry. She's a talking horse: she calls out to me "Fee-ee-ee-ee-eed!" and I'd better get to it. She served as the model for Mare Imbri the night mare, and also for Neysa the Unicorn in my Adept series.

Um, letter is ending. Blue just neighed at me, and I know what that means. To Be Continued.

---

*Author's Note:

Oops, the intended dedication got lost in the shuffle. Sigh.

July 1989

A little girl begins to eat semisolid food. A little girl's mother begins to eat semisolid food. Someone's finger signs improve. A bird. A plane. No, definitely a bird. An author pretends to be a reviewer. And the shortcomings of education are discussed.

Jewel-Lye 7, 1989

Dear Jenny,

You will not believe this. I spent two hours this morning writing a letter to someone about setting up a possible collaboration with Philip Jose Farmer. You haven't heard of him? Well, maybe your mother has. He's a fine writer, whose work I admired when I was in college. His first novel was called *The Lovers*, and it's a classic. A girl and I collaborated on an oil painting suggested by it; I painted the monstrous bug, and she painted the nude woman. We don't know where that painting is now; it disappeared into a men's dorm somewhere and hasn't been seen since. You say you believe that, and when am I going to get to something interesting? Give me time, girl; I've only started. So thirty years later I agreed to contribute to a ten-author collaborative novel. I wrote the first chapter, and Mr. Farmer wrote the second, but then it went wrong, because the later writers didn't relate well to the first two chapters, and the editor rejected it before it was finished. Now, over a year later, the editor who rejected it wants to see if it can be rescued by making it a Farmer-Anthony collaboration, starting with our two chapters and alternating between us until it is done. This intrigues me, because Farmer is one fine writer. If you ever get bored with Anthony, try Farmer. So I said okay, and now the editor will see if Farmer wants to do it. You say you believe that, and what's the point? Have patience, girl; you're a teenager now, and supposed to be interested in more interesting things. Well, the chapter I wrote to start off the book was adapted from a story I did about twenty five years ago, that never sold, about a thirteen year old girl who was blinded and maimed in a car accident, and is mute, and—you say you don't believe that? Look, I wrote it in 1963, when your mother was only eight years old, which was about the age of the girl when she was in the accident. The girl's name was Tappuah, Tappy for short, and she developed the ability to relate to animals in a way that ordinary folk could not. In fact they would come to her. You still don't believe? Well, I said you wouldn't. Oh, now you believe? You say you're a terrible teen young woman and you will change your mind as you please? Sigh. So anyway, if this project goes forward, in due course you can read about Tappy, who is your age now, and how she finds love and adventure in realms nobody can believe. Yes, she will learn to speak again; that was more psychological than physical. And I suspect she will see again, in due course.

So that was my morning, when I should have been working on *Tatham Mound*. In that novel, the nine year old girl Tzec has just been adopted as a daughter by the Trader, as she is an orphan. Fifteen years later she will meet the protagonist again, and marry him; she has a long memory. But first I have a lot of other adventures to figure out. Meanwhile, I wanted to mark the word "said" in the prior paragraph for **bold** printing, and this is the monochrome screen and doesn't show it, so I went to the color modifier and experimented, and discovered the darndest things. I put it on blink, and now it's blinking perpetually. No I'm not teasing you! Will you stop with that stuff! I tried putting the whole screen on blink, and it did it, but that's deafening, I mean blinding to watch, so I put it back. Two blinking words are enough.

Ongoing matters: As I write this I have your mother's letter, which says she hopes to go see you Friday—that's today, in my terms—when you will see the cushion my wife made for you. We had to guess at your birthday, but maybe we came close. You can have catnaps with it. She says you may be home before the house gets revised. No, you can't tell the house to hurry up. No, you won't be out of your teens before it's ready. Have patience. Your mother has little enough of that already.

Remember that power failure we had? No, it hasn't returned—I wonder where they go, in between times?—but we still have buckets of water we dipped out of the pool to flush the toilets. Maybe we'll have another power failure, so we can use up those buckets.

And horses: I had told you about Blue. Now I'll skim over two others, but I can't skip them entirely, so brace yourself, because it's sad business. We didn't want to have one horse alone, because they prefer company of their own kind, and also we had another daughter, so we got Cheryl a horse too. That was Misty, a white horse, fifteen and a half hands high. I represented her (with a sex change) as the Day Horse in *Night Mare*. She was sort of set in her ways, and preferred mooching food from people to giving them rides. She came down with foot problems, which is bad news with horses, and in the end couldn't walk, and we lost her.

The vet happened to have another mare, called Fantasy, who was a beautiful five year old with a perfect white shield on her brown forehead. She had had a serious illness when young, and looked fine now, but was not to be ridden; she was perfect for company for Blue. She loved people, because she had been raised among them. She would have been a twenty thousand dollar horse, but we got her for nothing, because she was now worthless as a show horse. Oh, she was a darling! I had an Astroturf mat by my study door, and she could not believe it wasn't edible, so every time I came to the study it was in a different place, where she had dropped it after tasting it. We have a mini barn we built for the horses—when we moved we built another just like it, so they would feel at home—and from the house we could see into the two stalls, but it did no good. Blue is black, and she faded into the shadow, night mare style, becoming invisible. Fantasy was brown, and she faded into the woodwork. But Fantasy was not as healthy as she seemed. When she began ailing, we called the vet, thinking it was something minor, but it was her heart, dating back from her fillyhood: it had a hole in it, so it couldn't circulate her blood well, and now it was catching up with her, and she was gone, only four months after we got her. She didn't deserve it.

The vet had a white pony, which someone had left for boarding and then never picked up. That's like dumping dogs and cats. But of course the vet didn't kick her out; he was just stuck for the unpaid board. So now we're boarding her, and if the owner ever comes to pick her up, he'll have to pay several times her value in boarding fees, so I don't think he will. We named her Snowflake, after a lost filly in *Blue Adept*, because the vet didn't know her name. She's a true pony, all white and the cutest thing, trained for children to ride. But we don't ride her, of course; no children here any more, and she's only for company for Blue. She's so fat that sometimes I call her roly-pony. We feed her only half a cup of grain at a feeding, but she forages well, and remains so fat we sometimes wonder if she's pregnant. She gets along perfectly with Blue. So it has been for two and a half years. When Blue—well, she is 31 years old, which is ancient for a horse—she's healthy, but eventually—well, then we'll give Snowflake back to the vet, who has a relative with a child who will by then be ready to learn to ride.

And I was telling you my songs. Today I had a good run, and I sang several to myself in the shower, and the one I want to share with you this time is *Rue*. I needed a song for *Mercenary*, the second novel in my Space Tyrant series—DON'T READ IT—you may be a teenager now but you're still below the age of consent and subject to the Adult Conspiracy—for a girl called Roulette, Rue for short, and none seemed suitable, and I looked through my daughter Penny's collection of song books—I turned her on to music, of course, along with the value of long hair (which reminds me: I had a terrible dream the other night, that my other daughter Cheryl had cut her hair short; what a horror!), and found that one, just right. I had it on a record, in fact. It's advice to young women, tending their gardens, and your mother will have to explain part of what makes it funny and sad because of the spellings. "Come all ye fair and tender maids, who flourish in your prime, prime; beware, beware, make your garden fair, let no man steal your thyme, thyme, let no man steal your thyme." Second verse: "For when your thyme is past and gone, he'll care no more for you, you; And every day that your garden is waste, it will spread all over with rue, rue . . ." And the third: "A woman is a branching tree, a man a sea wind, wind; And from her branches carelessly, he will take what he can find, find . . ." Keep that advice in mind, when.

Now our pool has crept up to a scant 84°F and is almost swimmable, for the first time this year; Cam and Cheryl are in it, and I must join them. So this letter must end, but there will be another in a week. Don't squander your teens all in one year, Jenny!

PS—Hi, Cathy! Same for you!

The Morning After: Here is a special bulletin: 84° is not warm enough! Brrrr! We swam for half an hour, missing a phone call in the process, and I think I turned blue. But while I'm here, some additional notes: I'm enclosing the usual clippings, such as an old one I found of a woman with hair ten feet long, some fun-sheets in a catalog with things like newsprint or handsome men on them—if you ever see ones with luscious young women, let me know—, an idealized map of the country, a math riddle your mother will delight torturing you with, a tall fish story, and illustrated headaches that describe your mother's worstest days.

And a final note: two days ago, as I rode my bicycle out to pick up the newspapers, I saw two clouds rising brightly out of the background smog, as if seeking their place in the sun. They were highlighted at the top, but their feet remained bogged down in glop. I think their names were Amorphous and Vagary. Remember them, next time you have a dull therapy session.

Jewel-Lye 14, 1989

Dear Jenny,

I consolidated the files and got all your letters together, here; this is the 20th Jenlet. Maybe we should celebrate with a cupcake with 20 candles on it. Well, you had something like that for your birthday, didn't you? So how come I can't—I *know* it's not a birthday, but—are you going to be a spoilsport about this? Growr!

What? Who's tugging on my sleeve? Oh, your mother. She says "Mmmph mmmph," and the rest is indistinguishable. Oh, that dental surgery! She's translating what you're saying, but somehow I'm not getting it. So how can I—Cathy, do *you* know what—?

Ah, there's your daddy. There's a law I made up: every family needs a man in it, to make sense of things. So what's the—

Ah, he explained it. You want to save that cupcake for when you can eat it. Well, why didn't you say so? You just lay there with your teeth in your mouth, and—

How did we get into this mess? I've already written today to a suicidal girl and a murderer, and now—What? You say I'm the one who's looking for the fight? How dare you! Just because the next thing I have to do is answer a letter in a fanzine that differs with me about whether there should be a Minimum Wage (I once had a job at a restaurant that paid 45 cents an hour because the minimum wage law didn't apply)—What? Oh, yes, I earn more than that now. I think. Now will you stop changing the subject? Hm, maybe we *should* change the subject; this one isn't getting anywhere.

Your mother's situation reminds me that when I first heard from her about you, at the end of FeBlueberry, I was recovering from dental surgery. The gum was getting low at the front of my mouth, pulled down by a tendon or something attached to my lip, so they took a little square of gum tissue from the roof of my mouth and spliced it into the front. The front recovered okay, but every time I tried to eat anything, that raw empty patch in the roof of my mouth said "Make My Day!" I had to stay on a liquid or mush diet for a couple of weeks. I guess you know what that's like. So does your mother. When the dogsled runners say "Mush! Mush!" they mean "Go faster!" but when we say it we mean "When the Censored will I be able to get off this diet?!"

Ouch—I started this letter this morning, and suddenly it's late afternoon. What happened? Well, I ran my run, and I remembered a wonderful song to tell you about—and forgot it right after. Sigh. The mail piled in, everything except your mother's letter she said wav on va vay. (No, she didn't sound quite that bad, but she did sound as if you had better hold her hand for a while.) You want to hear about my problems with the mail? No? Good, I'll tell you. Several fan letters to answer, and one from a former editor about that possible collaboration with Phil Farmer—remember, the one with the thirteen year old blind girl?—explaining that the other editor associated with that ten-author project might make trouble. I may have to buy him out, in order to recover the rights to my chapter, and Farmer's chapter. Could cost me twenty times as much as I was paid for that chapter. Oh, I can do it, but it's an aggravation; I only did that chapter as a favor to him. I'll be more careful about favors next time. If he gets too greedy, I'll point out that legally I don't have to pay him anything; the material has already reverted to me, because it's been two years since I delivered it. But this is nasty sort of business. Which reminds me: ask your mother whether she is pursuing a civil remedy. She'll know what I mean. Also in the mail arrived three books by Jack Woodford from his publisher. You never heard of the man? Small wonder; most of his books are decades out of print. He was an ornery cuss who got into trouble with publishers by speaking the ugly truth. You can see why I like him! It was one of his books about writing that gave me the information I needed to get going better as a writer, back in 1958. So now I'll return the favor and give a blurb—that's a favorable brief comment—for his books, though he's dead now. But that means my weekend will be gone, reading. Sigh. Would you like to read a book for me? No, huh? What kind of a friend are you? I can see it now: a blurb saying "This is a great book—Jenny" and everyone will wonder how Jack Woodford ever managed to get such an important person to comment. I still have in mind getting you to a fan convention, some year, where everyone will be amazed to meet you. But first let's see how far you progress; I don't think you're ready for it yet. Is it true you have prism spectacles, so you can look down without looking down? That sounds like fun.

Have I said anything yet in this letter? My head's spinning; I'm not sure what I've done and what I have yet to do. Well, let's go back to the beginning of the day: when I biked out to fetch the newspapers, I saw a raccoon on the way up and a bunny on the way back. We have an opossum on that section, too. I can tell the difference: the possum has a ratlike tail, while the coon has a ringed tail. Nearer the house I saw our Devil's Walking Stick. That's a plant. It's an ugly, thorny weed here, looking like a crooked cane, with thorns anywhere you might try to touch it. But it's distinctive. We went out to rescue a number of native plants in FeBlueberry, before the mower came to mow between the pines. We transplanted about eight rosemary plants, one ivy vine, and one little Devil's Walking Stick which was hardly more than a section of root. The rosemaries all died; I guess they didn't like the soil near the house. The ivy got chewed back several times, but survives. The Devil's Walking Stick survived and put out a new fernlike leaf—which a bunny must have chewed off. So I sprayed bug repellent on it, and then it was left alone. It put out another leaf, and another, and now it's about knee high with ten big leaves and beginning to come into its true ugliness. Wonderful; it's a success story. Maybe some day it will be tree-size. Say, do you think if they sprayed you with bug repellent, you'd grow strong and ugly? Maybe just strong and mad.

I guess I'd better get on to the enclosures, before you enclose me in a magic shield. I hate to throw things out, even when I can't use them, so I saved out a few of those magazine stamps: two about cats for you, one about Vegetarian Times, and one for SAVVY WOMAN for your mother. No, I couldn't find one saying GOOD NATURED MAN for your daddy. Also a clipping about V.C. Andrews, a writer currently on the bestseller list: she gets 20 fan letters a week, though she's dead. I know the feeling! What surprised me was to learn that she was quadraplegic—that is, she couldn't use her arms or legs. Shows you can become a highly successful writer regardless. No, you don't have to go that far, and I guess you don't want to be a writer anyway. But I think the same would be true for an artist. Maybe once you get home, if they ever finish fixing up your house, and you have room for a computer, you can use the time between therapy sessions to paint pictures on the screen and become a teenage artist. Which reminds me: do you have a radio? I listen to the radio all day while I'm working: popular songs, light classical music, the news, and interesting call-in programs. There's Dr. Joy Brown the psychologist, who addresses callers' most personal problems—um, the Adult Conspiracy might veto that. At 5:00 daily there's *All Things Considered*, an excellent program; you're a teen now, so you should be adult enough to appreciate it. There are violent liberal and conservative call-in hosts who can be fun to listen to even if you don't agree with them. The local liberal one is running a campaign to make the Orlando Blockbuster Video store carry *The Last Temptation of Christ*; he's even interviewing their customers, who say about two to one they want that video movie carried, but the store refuses. He's really putting it to them. I like that, because I'm an agnostic—that means I don't believe or disbelieve in God, and belong to no religion—and I support freedom of expression. I want to see that movie, which I understand is a thoughtful one, but I can't, because no store dares carry it locally. That's censorship, and I HATE CENSORSHIP!! (Sorry, didn't mean to yell.)

Where was I? Oh, the clippings. Why do you let me wander off the subject like that? There's one on a big maze called the Wooz (Zoom spelled upside down) that folk can wander through. Let's you and I walk through that one, some day. There's Curtis, with cheese flavored bubble gum. (Mozzarella is a cheese: we call it Monster-ella, just as Muenster is Monster cheese.) And my British mother sent a sheet for you: goofs English children made. "Noah's wife was called Joan of Arc." That sort of thing. So why isn't your mother laughing? Oh, those teef; I forgot. And a chain letter I received a year ago, and ignored; as a matter of principle I never forward chain letters. Don't send this one on to anyone; I just thought you'd like to see it. It claims you get good luck. Chain letters, in general, are a crock of—er, nitrogen; they are not legitimate. Many of them pretend to be thousands of years old, when they can't be, and to bring you money, which they won't. Any one involving money is illegal anyway. But let's pretend this one will bring you good luck, though we both know this is nonsense.

Jewel-Lye 21, 1989

Dear Jenny,

Wow! It's almost five, and I'm just starting this letter. I had hoped to have it finished by this time. My day has been—in fact my week has been—WILL YOU PAY ATTENTION, YOU DIFFICULT GIRL!? That's better. I've had piles of stuff to read, and piles of complicated letters to—nuh-uh, keep that tongue out of sight!—so it's just been a hassle, and I've gotten very little paying writing done since last week's letter.

I've been hearing from you folk! I have two letters from your mother—I'll get to them in a moment—and one from Sue Berres (before I thought it was Benes, but now those letters look like R's), and two from you. The first was a Birthday Card—um, I'd better discuss that. I offered to exchange information about birthdays with you, because I wanted to discover yours, so we could catch you in time with the Jenny/Xanth cushion. I figured we could just forget about mine, after that. The truth is, birthdays aren't nearly as much fun at my age as they are at your age, and I didn't want you to feel obliged to send anything. But since you have already sent a card, okay, I'll tell you. I'll be 55 on AwGhost 6. So thanks for the card, and I'll remember it when the ill-fated day finally strikes. The other was an Anniversary Card. I guess I mentioned our [power failure here—Ha! I had just Saved, so I didn't lose anything] 33rd anniversary because it fell on a Jenny-letter day. Otherwise I would not have bothered you. But thanks for that card too. I understand it's a real job for you to sign your name to these things. (That would seem like sarcasm, if we didn't know your situation. Folk outside don't realize—well, never mind.)

Now let me get a bit more serious. Last time I teased your mother about her supposed problem speaking. Then her letters arrived describing the progress of her jaw problem, and I wished I hadn't. Teasing is supposed to be a fun thing, and this isn't fun. I mean, if she had two days of discomfort, then was better than new, okay. But she's in real distress, and for all I know that complaint could have her in the hospital by the time you hear this letter. The chances of her being there to read it to you are next to nil. Since your mother has been my main inspiration for fun insults—well, this just isn't the time for that sort of thing. But I did want to say that even from this distance, I can see that her misery is composed of three parts. First, the actual discomfort of her mouth, which is physical and horrendous. Second, the inconvenience this malady causes, inhibiting her activity so she can't do all the things she wants to do. You know better than anybody what that's like. Third, it stops her from visiting you. I think that's the worst. She wants so much to be with you, Jenny, and everything keeps getting in the way so she can't have you home yet, and now she can't even get over there for visits. This tears her up. I guess you're not too pleased about this either, but I think at the moment that it's bothering her more than you.

So she is feeling worse than she might because of you, and you are feeling worse because of her. This does neither of you much good. Of course you can't just say "I don't care!" and not worry about each other, or not be concerned about your separation. But I hope some understanding helps. Send her an "Okay, I love you" through your daddy, and it will make her feel better. She might even send you one back. Meanwhile, in case she has to spend some time in bed and can't reach her computer, I'm sending her a bound galley that just arrived of my collaborative novel *Through the Ice*. That's the one I wrote with Robert Kornwise, who died in an auto accident just one year before your accident, with no more justice. It is as though I am fated to encounter one such tragedy a year, and his was the one for 1988. So this isn't a joyful association, but it's one you folk will understand rather better than most. When your mother gets better, maybe she'll read bits of it to you, as there is time. I hope there's not another case like this next year; there's already been twice as much misery as there should have been, for Robert Kornwise's family and yours.

Meanwhile, keep up with your dull mundane exercises. I know progress is slow, but it's possible to be slow and still get where you're going. I've always been slow—slow to speak, slow to read, slow to discover what girls were (stop sniggering!), and slow to make it as a writer. Remember the tortoise and the hare. One writer, younger than I, had already written and sold forty novels by the time I had sold my first, but today I think I have done more than he has, and certainly more successfully. So speed is not the essence; steady accomplishment is. You don't have to do everything in a month, or a year; you could take eight years, as I did to make my first story sale, and still go pretty far thereafter, as I did. Just don't quit trying.

On to incidental things: Today my wife may have seen a hummingbird. They flit by so fast it's hard to be sure. And on my run (yes, the little magnolia is fine), I saw tiny tadpoles in the tub we use for horse water in the pasture. We should have a whole flock of frogs! (Flock? Well, what *is* it called?) And yesterday I found a canoe. Well, not exactly. I was writing a chapter of *Tatham Mound*, and the southern Indians use dugout canoes, and my hero was traveling up to Tennessee, where the Cherokees lived, and I thought wouldn't it be nice if he could get a birchbark canoe there. But white birch trees don't grow in the south. I knew them up north, with their paperlike bark that you can actually write on. But maybe up high in the mountains—so I researched, and discovered that there is one variant of paper birch that grows in the south: high in the mountains of North Carolina. That's exactly where my hero is! So he can have a birchbark canoe, which is a great comfort to him, as well as a novelty, because he has one bad arm and paddling is hard. A light canoe makes all the difference. So that was a nice discovery, and now I have him and a friend in their birchbark canoe traveling down the Tennessee river, in the year 1516.

We had three power failures in a row, trying to wipe out this letter, so I had to quit for a while, and couldn't finish it today. Okay, hang on; I'll finish it tomorrow morning and still catch the mail, or else. Have a good night's sleep, Jenny. You too, Cathy.

Jewel-Lye 22, 1989—Okay, it's next morning. I was going to finish this quickly, so as to catch the mail, but I had to check on two things—and wouldn't you know it, that took me a #$%&*f!! hour. So now—what? No, those other items wouldn't interest you. So now I'll get on to the enclosures, which—what? No, those other things which delayed me are very dull, really; you don't want to know about them. So I have the Sunday Curtis, which Sue Berres tells me is the first thing you read in my letters; now I know what you like about my letters, the comics! And an item on cats, and one on big Florida mosquitoes, and—what? Will you get off that other business, girl? It's not interesting! You know something, you can be the stubbornest darn thing—now don't look that way, you know I don't like it—oh, all right, I'll tell you. Briefly. I had ten letters yesterday from fans, and I managed to pencil answers to nine of them yesterday during the power failures that were making this letter late. I scribble my answers on the backs of the envelopes, see, and every week the secretary types them up for me. You demand to know why you don't rate a secretarial letter? Because those take about an extra ten days, and—ah, now you understand. So this morning I tackled the last one, and the guy apologized for what he'd said in his last letter, and asked for my opinion of his marriage, so I thought I'd better reread his last letter, which I did not remember. One thing I'll say about you, Jenny: you don't ask my opinion about your marriage. Yes I know, you'll get to that a decade hence, when—let's get back to the subject, shall we? So I checked my correspondence, and couldn't find his last letter. Time wasted. So I turned on the computer and did a computer search of my letter record. Found it—for last OctOgre. Last week I filed all last year's letters in the attic. Sigh. So I unlocked it and headed off into the heat to delve through the voluminous files—what? Oh, "voluminous" means the way your mother's jaw is feeling these days. All blown up out of proportion, so that she looks like a—now stop that! You know I promised not to tease her about that. So finally I found the letter—and it bore no relation to anything the current letter said. Oh: different first name, different address. It wasn't the same person, after all. I could find no letter by the same person, and his present letter came through the publisher, so he didn't have my address. I don't think he wrote to me before. So why did he say he did? Beats me. Do *you* know? You're not much help, you know that? And keep that tongue in your mouth! And stop blinking at me. I'm on to all your tricks. No, don't you dare do your thing with the finger! And don't call me Nitrogen Face either! If you do, I'll tell Ray what you really called him, instead of the expurgated version. Ha—that finally got to you, didn't it! So the other thing was a letter from the fanzine I write to, where

I mentioned you, and the folk there send their good wishes to you. But this letter was about John Brewer, the prisoner I mentioned: the fanzine called the TV station near Brewer's prison, and the folk there say the man's not on death row but serving life imprisonment. Now the fanzine is upset, because I said he was on death row. Well, I sure thought he was. So I had to check his first letter to me, way back last AwGhost—right, in the attic files!—and when I ran it down, it said nothing about anything like that. So I went through more letters, and finally found it in his third letter to me: how he killed his fiancee and was sentenced to death for it. I'll quote that to the fanzine, so at least I won't be in trouble with them. You see, I had Brewer write to them, stating his case, and if you want to know what happens when you drop a nitrogen bomb into an outhouse—well, these folk can get righteous about law enforcement, so I thought I'd acquaint them with the reality and maybe jolt them out of their ivory towers. Your daddy will tell you what an ivory tower is. They aren't too pleased. You see, Brewer is trying to get them to execute him, because he says he's guilty and deserves to die. I suspect he's right. I only wish that drunk driver who hit you was next in line after him. Anyway, that's where my hour went, and I still have to write that letter—right after this one. Now aren't you sorry you brought it up? Stop looking so smug!

Let me conclude with a couple of minor things. I discovered last week that on this computer when I mark a word for bold printing, I can set it to blink. More fun. So now my bolds are blinking. Here, I'll show you: **Bold.** Isn't that something? Blink, blink, blink! Oh, you can't see it blink on the paper? Sigh. Well, take my word: it's a blinking bold word. And I remembered a song that seems suitable: the "Worried Man Blues." It starts out "It takes a worried man, to sing a worried song . . ." and I think your mother's humming it now.

Keep smiling, Jenny. I know it's not easy, now, but if

we concentrate this week on getting your mother better, then we can concentrate on you in a week or two. It's your turn to be strong.

Jewel-Lye 28, 1989

Dear Jenny,

Right—I'm on my upstairs system now. Alan, who is my daughter's boyfriend, is working for me this summer, and one of the things he does is figure out computer programs for me, so I don't have to use up my time for it. So he's working on the downstairs system, which is the one I usually use for letters. Okay—so you get a laser-printed missive; you'll survive. Oh—what program is he working on? Well, I needed a good mass file-handler, so I wouldn't erase good files and save bad ones—your mother will tell you all about that when she's back—and didn't have one, so when PC COMPUTING magazine offered me a disk with file handling if I'd subscribe, I decided to try it. It took them a month to send the disk, by which time I'd discovered QDos, which does a nice job. But now that the other program, DirMagic, is here, I'm having Alan put it through its paces, so he can tell me how it compares. So I'm working up here, in my novel-writing study, which is fine.

Yesterday we had the farrier over to trim our horses' hooves. A farrier is a blacksmith who can make shoes and such for horses, but mostly he just trims, because we don't ride our horses. It's like trimming your fingernails. Now Blue has been with us eleven years and she's okay, but Snowflake spooks at the sight of a halter. But we don't care to leave the halters on them regularly, because they're free in the forest, and a halter could get hung up on something. So we halter them only at need. So there was the farrier, and Blue got spooky, to my surprise; I did get the halter on her and let her go so I could do the same with Snowflake. Mistake! Blue headed into the forest, and the farrier couldn't do her. Meanwhile, I couldn't get Snowflake. Finally I did catch Blue, and Cam—that's my wife, who made you the Xanth pillow—took her to the farrier. I discovered I'd been trying to put the wrong halter on Snowflake, so I went back to the barn and fetched the right one, with the lead rope. Snowflake came up to inquire what I was doing, so I put the halter on her. Just like that. We got them both done. Yes, I was three times as lucky as I deserved to be. Getting the horses' hooves trimmed always makes me nervous, because I do have to catch them first. Once the halter is on and I have hold of it, they are no trouble at all, and behave perfectly. So that was my little adventure yesterday. If you ever have a pony, you'll have similar adventures. Monday we'll go through the same thing with the vet.

Let's see, I'm writing this letter in Jewel-Lye, but it will be two days into AwGhost before you hear it. So where is your mother? Well, it's the two-th of the month, so she's getting her tooths done. In fact she's getting the things yanked out. In fact she's so browned off about not being able to visit you that she looks like a baked potato. Especially in the face. She swears that she'll see you later in the month, though hell should bar the way. So relax; when she visits, you can lend her your talk-board (I forget what it's called) so she can wish you well despite not being able to open her mouth.

I have the usual enclosures, plus some oddments. There's *Nothing But Zooms*, which you can watch when you get home: that's the artistic animation of that formula I told you about, the Mandelbrot Set. It starts out looking like a bug, but the edges are amazingly complicated and beautiful, and the closer you look, the more intricate they are. So enjoy it when; this is your video. I'm also enclosing a block of 20 stamps for you or your mother; they were on a package I received, and I just couldn't throw them out, so here they are, and if you hate them, *you* can throw them out. And a cartoon about fire ants. And one about Florida politics, with our Governor Martinez as a frog. He's not a good governor, and this is becoming increasingly apparent. So there's this princess, kissing the frog—and he just doesn't turn into a prince. Right: she's browned off; you can see how brown she is. And a funny excerpt from *All I Really Need to Know I Learned in Kindergarten* that you should really enjoy. And a cartoon about the rare baby turtles here—a Kemp's Ridley sea turtle, one of the ten most endangered species and the rarest turtle known, laid her eggs on the St. Pete beach, so they're watching to make sure the eggs hatch, and maybe missing something else. Harpy reading!

Movie-review time. Yes, I know you haven't seen many original movies recently. But when you get home, you can watch video movies, and eventually everything will be available, so you can see it. I'm just giving you a notion what to watch for. You see, I don't see many movies myself; I'm too busy to get out. I hardly drive, in fact. The other day I had to move our microbus somewhere, and I'd never driven it before, and I couldn't figure out how to turn off the windshield wipers or even how to get the key out. There's a button you have to push, you see, but it just didn't do it. Right: wrong button; the real one was hidden around the steering wheel. Sigh. But my daughter the journalist—that's Cheryl, who is 19 now and in college, only she's working at the local newspaper this summer—no, Alan is not her boyfriend, he belongs to Penny, who is 21 now—yes, it does get complicated keeping track, but somehow they manage it—she has to review movies for the paper. Now I only go out to see a movie about once a year, and the one I saw this year was *Indiana Jones and the Last Crusade*, which is how I know you'd like it. But Cheryl had to review *Lethal Weapon II*, so we made it a family occasion. I mean, on my own I won't go out, but for a daughter

I will. There's something about daughters. So Cam and Cheryl and I went to see it. That's one slam-bang violent motion picture! But it does have some plugs for the environment, and some humor, and one nice sex sequence—oops, Adult Conspiracy! Okay, don't see that one.

Then Cheryl had to review *Dead Poets Society*. That's about boys at a conservative prep school. Yes, I know, it sounds dull as monotony. What? You say boys don't sound dull? Oh—you turned thirteen. Now you know what boys are. Ah, well. As it happens, I found this to be a profoundly moving picture. You see, it shows the kind of private high school I went to, and the kind at which I taught English. What a horror! Don't ever go to a school like that! But to this school comes a new teacher, who believes that poetry should be appreciated, not inflicted. I kept whispering the names of the authors to my daughter as lines from poems were quoted: Vachel Lindsay, Walt Whitman, Robert Frost, Beethoven's Ninth Symphony—as I said, I went to this type of school—(Oh, my, now there's a song by Crystal Gayle on the FM. I always think of her hair) only now they were being rendered with feeling and understanding. The boys began to catch on to the spirit of it, and formed their secret group, The Dead Poets Society. They would sneak out at night and smoke cigarettes—that's the adolescent notion of privilege, which you definitely don't need to emulate—and look at pictures of bare-breasted women—okay, you can do that if you want to—and recite poems with feeling. But later one of the boys, balked from anything meaningful by his stern father, committed suicide, and the school sort of framed the good teacher as responsible and fired him. So it's a sad ending, except that at the end the boys finally show their respect for him by standing defiantly on their desks. He had taught them to look at things in new ways, you see, such as from the height of their desks. You think that's stupid? No it isn't; that was a really feeling conclusion to the movie. Of course it hit me twice as hard, because I know the horror of the conformist education—my whole life since has been a muted protest to conformity—and I really appreciated it. Yes, I left teaching after one year because of similar frustration, and no, they didn't want me back anyway. I retired to full time writing and have never stopped. So yes, you should see this movie, because you will be moved by it, and it will help you to understand some of what I am made of, if you're interested. Good, competent, feeling teachers are a treasure, because the system discourages them. Penny brought home a paper with her teacher's marking on it, and all I can say is the man comes across like an illiterate ass. He writes "don't end a sentence with a proposition." No, that's not a typo, and yes, you can end a sentence with a preposition. Actually, his advice is good, in an unintended way; I'm trying to get Penny to send that example to Reader's Digest. But he's making up rules not to be found in Fowler's (that's the ultimate authority) and doesn't know the distinction between "to" and "too"—I mean, this is the ilk teaching a college course?! And if my daughter protests such ignorance—she happens to have been raised in a literate family—she'll just get penalized in her grade. So as you can see, I have some emotional involvement here. See that movie, when you get the chance.

Am I boring you yet? Not quite yet, but close? Okay, another movie. We live in a conservative Christian community, so naturally it banned *Last Temptation of Christ*, as I think I mentioned before. Well, this week Ron Lindahn, the artist in charge of the Xanth Calendar—yes, I'll send you one, when I get a copy—sent me a copy of it, so I finally got to see it. Actually I'm not terrifically interested in religion, but I keep an open mind. This was fairly dull, as I expected, but worthy; it's a more realistic picture of Jesus Christ than you generally see. When he is crucified he has a vision of being rescued, and getting married and having children: of being ordinary, in fact. But in the end he realizes that he can only deliver his message by being crucified, and he begs to go back. Then he is back on the cross, and the movie ends. I think it's a worthy movie, and that those who ban it are bigots.

Last night my wife and daughter were watching reruns—they seem to prefer them to new material—but during commercials Cheryl flicked through other channels. They say you can tell who is the boss of a household by who controls the remote control for the TV. I don't even know how to use it! One of the things on another channel was a movie about a man who got seduced by his best friend's sexy daughter. She was in a bikini and brother, did she have the stuff! Naturally that didn't interest my wife or daughter; they put it back on the reruns, then left the house for ten minutes. So I struggled with the controls and found the channel—which was now running continuous commercials. Finally it got back to the movie—and wife and daughter returned. Sigh. You say you don't understand why I should want to watch a girl in an overstuffed bikini? Well, naturally not; you're one of *them*. But the movie had degenerated into slapstick anyway, no more bikinis. Sigh.

Beautiful flute music on the FM. Life does have some compensations. Okay, next letter I won't talk about movies. Meanwhile, keep up with your exercises and practice your swallowing. And don't look at me slantwise through those right-angle-vision glasses! Is Cathy there? I understand you have a therapist named Cathy; how do you expect me to tell them apart? Well, say hit to roommate-Cathy. Did Sue read you "Dead and Breakfast" yet? She sent me a copy. Now she's in my Jenny Directory too; it's getting crowded in there with all you people jostling elbows!

August 1989

A young girl learns to finger-spell. A not-so-young man gets not-so-younger. The Tooth Fairy works overtime. And serendipity is discussed.

AwGhost 4, 1989

Dear Jenny,

Okay, I'm back on the downstairs system, with the conventional address macro. I had the day all planned out: In the morning I would answer the woman whose husband left her for the Other Woman after twenty years, and then answer the woman who is pondering leaving her alcoholic and abusive husband after a similar period, and then get on to this letter, and wrap everything up before horsefeeding time. Ha! I had two calls from my literary agent—he's talking to the folk who hope to make Xanth into video movies so you can see them (well, maybe some other folk will see them too, if that's okay with you), and I had to note some figures in my computer files because I got statements on seventeen fantasy novels yesterday—yes, Xanth novels are still selling well—, and we had a visit from relatives of the folk who own the property next to us, which acreage we would like to buy so that it can never be despoiled by encroaching houses, and the bunnies and possums and box turtles and all will never be disturbed, so of course we were polite to them but they aren't interested in selling the property, and well, here it is horsefeeding time and I'm only this far along in this letter. Ever thus! STOP SNIGGERING!

Stop it, or I'll stick my tongue out at you. I'm not bluffing. See? OPEN YOUR EYES! You think I can't make you do that? Just watch:

My first enclosure is a photograph of a painting of a cute little cat. I CAUGHT THAT! YOU PEEKED! On the back it says "This I did for one of Jenny's friends . . ." No, that's coincidence; this woman paints, and her daughter is named Jenny, but I'm showing you this—I can't give it to you, because it's a gift to me, and, well, you probably understand the ethics of that. But I thought you'd like seeing it. And your eyes are wide open now, aren't they! You keep trying to get the better of me, and you should know better.

Okay, I'm back from horsefeeding. I have to move this letter right along, because my daughters and wife mean to drag me off to eat out, because they won't all be here for my birthday, so I'll lose the last part of the day. So—what? What do you mean, what do the horses eat? Grain and hay, that's what. Oh, you mean what are *we* going to eat? Well, when I do go out, I take a little bit of everything edible (non-meat) from the salad bar. So let's get back to this letter—what? Oh, all right, I'll make a report when we get back. I'll have to do that tomorrow morning, because it'll be too late tonight.

Now to business: my daughter Cheryl found a baby turtle along the drive a couple of days ago. It was a water turtle, and it was far from water, so she brought it to the house—she was driving, and so it got a car ride—and I took it down to the lake. Then we went out and looked for more, in case they had hatched and were similarly lost, but didn't find any. Well, we saved one, anyway. This morning, or maybe yesterday morning, I saw another turtle, right by the barn door; I had to open the door over her shell. She was laying eggs there. That was a land turtle. Well, if some predator doesn't dig them out, we'll have more turtles in due course. Turtles are fun, and we encourage them.

Actually, my contacts with wildlife are fairly frequent.

Sometimes a bunny doesn't know which way to go to get off our drive when I'm pedaling my bicycle out to get the newspapers, and a couple days ago, during my run, I went full-face into a spider web. Remember that clipping I sent you? No, I got all of it except the spider, though I suspect the spider wasn't exactly pleased with the loss of her web. Stop smiling; it's not that funny. Meanwhile we have one magnolia tree that had a bloom on the first day of AwGhost last year. Guess what: not this year. But we have two azaleas, which normally bloom only in early spring, with flowers now. Maybe plants take turns.

Did you know that Neptune has three more moons? That makes six, now, though the new ones are all baby moons. In my novel *Macroscope*, which you don't have to read, I have Neptune's big moon Triton having a little moon of its own; I'm waiting to see if they spot that moon, in which maybe I'll be famous for having described it first. Maybe in a few million years those little moons'll grow up to be big moons. Which reminds me: there was an item about a couple who had a dwarf child. Something in the genetics. So they adopted a Korean child with similar dwarfism. I don't know those folk, but suspect I'd like to.

I had a call from your mother, right after they took her face apart. She informed me that my address of Twenty-Tooth Extraction Drive was wrong; they took out twenty-three teeth. Sigh. But it was the tooth of the month, just as I predicted. No, a drunk driver did *not* run his trailer-tractor rig over her face, it only looks that way. She'll be better any month now, and she means to come in and make you look at her face before it becomes uninteresting again. That way you'll know what kind of a glare to expect if you misbehave. She also warned me not to be too affrighted by the letter she had just mailed; it was written when she was mostly out of her mind. Today that letter arrived—and it was perfectly sensible and interesting. Maybe that's what she meant.

Next enclosure is for your roommate, Cathy: it's a

Cathy comic I thought she'd like, about how people train dogs and how dogs train people. You're a cat fan, so Cathy must be a dog fan.

Oops—I must have forgotten to clip out the Alligator Children's page last Sunday. Will you ever forgive me? Here's Curtis, anyway.

Today I received ten letters, a number of which were also birthday cards. I don't know how so many folk found out about my birthday. Are you sure you haven't squealed? Some even send gifts, which I'd prefer they didn't, because I'm not sending them gifts. One woman says she's madly in love with me, and no, she's not my wife, she's someone else's wife, but she keeps sending letters of adoration. Humorous ones, fortunately. I guess it's easier to love me from afar. STIFLE THAT SNIGGER! Once she wrote "I just turned forty, and I'm still mad about it!" Her last card showed a purple dragon, and said "I know how you like to fantasize. On your birthday, may all your dreams come true!" And a sign to hang on the doorknob: "DO NOT DISTURB—unless you're part of my fantasy!" This time she sent me a device you'd like: it's the Traffic Buster, which is a little box with an ON/OFF switch that turns on madly blinking lights, and four buttons marked Auto Machine Gun, Grenade Launcher, Death Ray, and Rifle Gun. The idea is to scare impolite drivers out of their wits, and of course that means just about every other car on the road. You want to listen to one? Okay here's the Grenade Launcher:——= =POW! Did you hear it? Tell your daddy to put the device on your Christmas list. Then you can visit the hospital and scare all the nurses with it.

I understand you're learning sign language now. Would you believe: there is sign language in Xanth #12, *Man From Mundania*. Because Ivy can't understand Mundane speech, but signs work okay. I also have sign language in my Indian novel, *Tatham Mound*. That's not quite the same, but similar. It's a universal language, really; with it you can talk to anyone who knows signs. My daughter Penny has done some work in signs. So I wish you well. All the same, if you can connect up one more nerve in your head so you can talk directly, that's okay too.

Which I guess brings me to a more serious item. Two days ago I had a good day's writing going, but in the afternoon it washed out because of phone calls and the mail. A letter asked me to send one of my dreams—the night kind—as they are collecting dreams of famous folk. Who, me? WATCH THAT SNIGGER!! Trouble is, the only really dramatic dream I can remember I already described, in *Bio of an Ogre*, and I don't like to repeat myself. Then the first call: from the guy who is working on the Xanth video movie. He said a studio is interested, and might send down a jet plane to bring me there and show off the first sample. I won't sign a contract, see, until I actually see a bit of it, to be sure it's of the quality I want. But they must be pretty sure it's good. So it's an exciting prospect; maybe Xanth really will be animated. Then, later, your mother's call, sounding as if they hadn't gotten quite all her teeth out, because she could still talk, and that reminded me that you still can't walk or talk or eat. It didn't seem fair that good things should be happening to me, when I really don't need them, while you are the one who really needs something good, like a burst of healing in the nerves. I mean, you have the brain and you have the body, you just don't quite have enough of a connection between them. That night I dreamed a sort of mixed-up melange that faded as soon as I woke and tried to remember it—you know how dreams are—but it was as if I took a jet plane and visited you and you couldn't talk to me. That didn't cheer me much either. So I described that dream, and its background, and maybe the dream-book folk will be satisfied. I penciled it out for my secretary, which means it'll be about ten days from now before it's actually typed up and ready to go, so if you or your mother object I can intercept it then.

8:30:40 P.M.—Well, I'm back tonight, to my surprise, so I'll tell you about it. We headed off at 7:00 to RAX, and I loaded up on a bit of everything. When I came to the broccoli soup I had a problem: they had forgotten to cut up the broccoli, and it was all in huge branches. I had stems sticking out over the edge of the bowl and dripping cream soup on the floor, and when I tried to tilt the bowl the other way the soup crept up to burn my fingers. (Was that a titter?) To eat it I had to pick it up by a soupy stem and chew off the ends, which tried to dangle like clam stomachs—I don't know how meat-eaters can stand to eat clams!—and though the ends I held were ice cold, the ends I was trying to eat remained ouch hot. (That sure sounded like a titter.) But the soup was good and so was the mixture of everything else I had on my plate. Do you like onions and hot pepper? No? Well I do, in moderation, so I had them, and of course finished with three flavors of pudding with peach and pear slices and apple sauce on top. We were a party of six—Wife and I, and our daughters Penny and Cheryl, and their two boyfriends—and naturally I was the last to finish. I always am. Everybody else in the world eats at hectic speed. I tried to hurry, but that just gives me gas—well, never mind. Just be glad you weren't there. We got to talking about how it was in school. In my day, when they served that kind of large-curd tapioca we called fish-eyes, folk would put a fish-eye in a spoon and use it as—you know what a mortar is? It shoots a shell up, so it loops down and hits someone else on the head? That's the idea. These big sticky fish-eyes, those innocent teachers . . . (now that sounded like a laugh!) More insidious was the butter. I had a pat of it once that was so cold it clinked as it hit my plate. But when it starts to soften, well, if you use a spoon to flip it up so it sticks to the ceiling, over someone else's head, and slowly melts—oh, that's old stuff to you? Ah, well. Maybe you should tell the nurse that you and Cathy want to practice eating, starting with butter and spoons. Maybe the nurse will be dull enough to fall for that.

Harpy therapy! Be a good girl, if you can't get any butter. (Hey—I think that's a pun! It was accidental.)

AwGhost 11, 1989

Dear Jenny,

Well, my days have been hectic again. Yesterday the phone started ringing, and I was calling New York and California and points between, and—but I guess you're not interested in that. So—what's that? You say yes, you're *not?* Oh. Well. Um. If you feel that way . . .

But one thing yesterday will interest you: we found a skink in the living room. A skink is a sleek local lizard. Nothing wrong with it, except that it won't find many bugs to eat in the living room. So we shooed it out, but it hid in a closet, and it was a job to shoo it out from there. We finally got it out the door, and closed the door—and later in the day there it was in the living room again. We pondered and concluded that either there had been two skinks, which seemed doubtful, or it had a secret entrance and had come in again. In which case it wasn't trapped and could find its own way out again. So we left it alone, and it disappeared. Okay. We don't mind it inside, we just didn't want it starving there.

Yes, I finally had my birthday, and no the world did not come to an end. My wife gave me a compact disk player, and my daughters and their friends gave me assorted disks to go with it. So I've been listening to Pete Seeger songs and Simon & Garfunkel and Tchaikovsky's 1812 overture—hey, on my stereo system, the cannon sound from different directions!—and his "Marche slave" whose marching beat I like. Funny thing, it seems that "slave" is not capitalized though it derives from "Slav"; he wrote it to help raise funds when the Russians were aiding the Slavs fighting the Turks. Anyway, having learned about compact disks, I find I like them. So we saw this ad to buy about 60 disks with most of the light classics cheap, and—ah, well, it's hard to resist a sale. Meanwhile I have also been listening to cassette tapes of Jim Reeves, about my favorite male popular singer, and Crystal Gayle, well, you know, that hair.

We were getting bit something awful by the chiggers. Those are a Florida phenomenon: tiny mites, so small you can't even see them. They are on the foliage outside, and when you walk by they brush off on your socks, and climb down into them and then burrow into your skin, and you get an itchy welt that can take a couple of weeks to clear, and some get infected. I got blisters from them on my ankles, which I had to puncture so I could run without a problem. My wife gets bitten more than I do, though she spends less time outside. Well, it's a fact that women taste better than men. So the past few days I'm been dousing my socks with bug spray or repellent, and that seems to be stopping it. So if you ever visit Florida, watch out for chiggers.

You know, I have some trouble with Carpal Tunnel Syndrome. No, that's not when you carp at tunnels. It's a problem with the hands. The nerves leading to them go through the Carpal Tunnel in the wrist, and if it's tight, your hands and fingers start getting numb. I wear my watch on my right wrist, though I'm right handed (well, what I was taught, I do right handed; what I learned myself I do left handed. Folk with ambiguous handedness are said to be confused mentally too. Now you know) because the slight pressure of the band on my wrist turns my hand numb. As it is, my left hand only tingles a little and perhaps is a bit weak, but I normally have no problem. Sometimes my right hand has trouble too, but not too much. Anyway, what I was thinking is that it is as if you have Carpal Tunnel Syndrome, only your whole body is affected. Now if only you could take off your watch and have everything better—

well, it was only a notion. Stick with the dull therapy. I keep hoping that you are about this far // from making a key nerve connection, and suddenly all circuits will light up and you'll be able to do everything. Well, it's a nice hope, isn't it?

While we're on the subject of you (how did that happen?): the Xanth Pinup Calendar is now getting published, and I'll send you a copy, maybe next week when I get my copies. Maybe I'll send one for your daddy too, so he doesn't get jealous. Men have a better notion what pinups are, for some reason. You will see that we have gotten a bunch of good artists together, and there are some nice pictures. But I'm only leading up to my subject. The artist who handled the project for me—you see, I did this calendar myself, paying for all the art, and then found a publisher for it, but I needed someone to actually do the job, who knew the artists and all—his name is Ron Lindahn, and he and his wife will be at a convention near you this NoRemember. I told him about you, and he said he and his wife Val might visit you and show you some more art. He knows you'll probably be in your wheelchair and not able to jump up and down and scream in typical teengirl fashion. In short, these are nice folk, and you will know them through their art in the Calendar, and if you would like to meet them, they will come to your house or the hospital or wherever you happen to be at the time. Now don't get the galloping shyness! I just thought that here's a chance for you to meet some artists—Xanth artists, really, and since you may some day be an artist yourself—well, think about it, and if you say you're not interested, I'll write you another paragraph about it.

I lost an hour here: phone call and horsefeeding. Oh, yes, the horses are fine, but a bit perturbed because the call made me about fifteen minutes late for their feeding. I got neighed at, and they had pushed the gate somewhat. The horses have firm rules about feeding time. As for the call—

now don't say you're not interested, how do you know that, until I tell you what it was? It was about the Xanth video movie. Yes it was; I'm not making this up. So a year or two from now, when you see it, you'll know what this was when it was getting going. We haven't signed a contract yet, but it looks good to me, and if the animation and integration of live and animation figures works well, I'll sign, and we'll be on our way. This isn't any big Hollywood outfit see; this is a guy way out in Washington state, who was cued in to Xanth by one of his children—I guess you know how that happens—and he's in the business of making video commercials, and he wanted to do something creative and fantastic and fun for a change, so he approached me about Xanth, and I like what he is showing me. Today it was about twenty-five artist's sketches of the things of *A Spell for Chameleon*, of the chameleon lizard at the beginning who assumes wild other forms, of Sabrina—she was Bink's first girlfriend, remember?—Justin Tree, Chester Centaur, Cherie Centaur, and so on. We were discussing important aspects at length over the phone, such as here is a full-busted lady centaur, and what happens to her front when she goes at full gallop? No, this is a legitimate question. A human woman that big in the bosom would have a real problem galloping naked, because, well, take my word for it. Also, we don't want to bring the censors down on our heads. So we concluded that lady centaurs are surely evolved to gallop bare-breasted without knocking themselves up, er, without flopping—well, anyway, they could probably handle it, and their firm flesh would move just a little. Remember that, when you see it, because I think we are going to make this video, and it may be the start of a great video series. Yes, I know he shouldn't have interrupted this letter for it, but he didn't know. Maybe you will grow up to be a fantasy video animator, drawing the original art for the computer to work on. Keep it in mind.

Meanwhile I'm still writing *Tatham Mound*, my archaeological/historical novel. My hero married two Cherokee women: a mother and her daughter. No, this sort of thing happened; men could marry sisters or mother/daughter or whatever, because they got along better. If they married two wives who were not related, they had to set up separate tipis for them so they wouldn't fight. Both of them gave him sons—and then the white man's plague came through and killed them. Don't read this novel; it will sadden you. What? Oh, the daughter was thirteen when he married her. No, that's coincidence; she's not like you at all.

This past week I saw a pure black dragonfly. In fact, it sat on the tap handle when I needed to turn on the water to refill the horses' drinking tub. It wasn't pleased when I put my hand on the tap, so it sat on my hand and told me so. What a handsome dragonfly!

We have a swimming pool, which we seldom use, mainly because we're busy and the water seldom gets up to 85°. It is paved all around, but in the winter a blade of grass decided to try its luck at the edge. We let it be. After all, if it is willing to try growing in such an inhospitable spot, who are we to interfere? Now it's about three feet across, dipping a stem into the pool—and another plant is starting at another corner. I guess the word spread that it could be done. We really don't want to take them out, but how far should we let this go?

Back in FeBlueberry when our tree farm was mowed and I first heard about you, we transplanted several wild rosemary plants to be around the house. They all died; apparently the soil or climate was wrong for them here, or maybe the shock of transplanting. But this past week I looked at one, and it had a single living sprig growing! It is recovering, when we thought it lost. That reminded me of you, because—

And we've been watching some movies on video. When they gave me the CD player and disks, one of the songs was "Mrs. Robinson," and I remarked that I'd always wanted to see the movie that was associated with. My wife and daughter said the movie was dull and we'd seen it before anyway, but since it was my birthday they humored me and rented *The Graduate*. No, I'd never seen it before; my memory for names and faces and dates may not be much, but I remember story lines very well, and know in a few seconds whether I've seen a movie before. No, it wasn't dull, either; it's about this twenty year old young man, who is seduced by this forty year old woman—am I running afoul of the Adult Conspiracy? Sigh. Anyway, she may have been forty, but she was one attractive woman. I guess my wife and daughter find such themes dull, but I found it fascinating. Actually, the age of forty may be considered old for a woman, but young for a man; President Kennedy was 43 when elected and they kept saying how young he was. But this business of assuming the older women can't be attractive—well, ask your daddy whether it's possible for any woman over thirty to be attractive. See? I told you. Another night we saw *The Accused*, which

****

Oops, that time the Adult Conspiracy censored me out. Sigh. Well, anyway, have a halfway decent day, Jenny, and blow your mother a kiss—it will reach her even if she is twenty miles away—and tell Cathy not to goof off on her exercises. Oh—I found out why I didn't have the Alligator page enclosed, because this time I looked for it and THEY DIDN'T HAVE IT. The wretches! I've half a mind to sic your mother on them. But here's "Curtis," anyway.

PS—now the skink is here in the study. Okay.

AwGhost 18, 1989

Dear Jenny,

I didn't expect to hear from your mother this week, because of her ongoing game of Tooth or Consequence—

she lost the first, so pays the second about 29 times over—but I had one last Saturday and another this Thursday. She returned the picture of the cat painting, which she says you enjoyed, and says your wheelchair and computer are still in the works, with varying degrees of frustration and progress.

Meanwhile, I got my Author's Copies of the Xanth PinUp Calendar, and am enclosing two. One is for you, because you like Xanth, and the other is for your daddy, because he likes—never mind, just shut up and let him look at the cover, okay? Men are the only ones who really understand pinup calendars, for some reason. I didn't want to unseal them in order to autograph them for you folk, so I'm enclosing autograph labels for each of you, hoping I got the names right. You can stick the labels somewhere safe, where they don't show. No, not on the toilet seat! On the Calendars. Anyway, if you read the credits on the back you can see that the Calendar's design is by Ron Lindahn, and that he and his wife Val painted the picture of Chex Centaur and the Xanth center-map. They're the ones I mentioned last time, who might visit you in NoRemember if you're interested. They are now assembling the one for 1991, the Question Calendar, featuring Grundy golem and Rapunzel. The deal is, I pay for it and they do the work. Well, I also develop the basic theme, and I approve the final pictures, but I'm not in there dealing with all the artists. Having set aside any hopes I had to be an artist myself, I now came at it as a sponsor. What? You want to do a Calendar picture? Well, first you have to get through the dull therapy, and learn to use your computer. If you get so you can make a really good picture—well, we'll see, when. Not this year, though. Which reminds me: they hired a model for Rapunzel, and photographed her so they could send copies to all the artists, because she'll be in the background of most of the Question Calendar pictures. She turned out to be a Xanth fan, who was thrilled with this assignment. Not the real Rapunzel, silly—the model. Wasn't that a nice coincidence! No, her hair wasn't that long naturally; she had to wear a wig. The truth is, very few girls have hair that long. Oh, you already knew that? Meanwhile, keep growing yours back.

My agent is working out a deal for a couple of hardcover editions of *Isle of View*, which may be published at the same time as the paperback edition, in OctOgre 1990. One would be a limited MORROW edition, for folk who just plain like hardcovers. The other would be a limited showcase edition, for folk who like beautiful books, with a cover painted by Wendy Pini showing Jenny Elf. No, don't go screaming the news all over the hospital; this is in the formative stage, and by no means certain yet. It's just what we're trying to set up if things work out. Richard Pini has expressed interest, but they are mighty busy folk, and we don't know what will happen. I just thought you'd like to know, since you're the one who made an Elfquest elf come to Xanth.

Meanwhile, how are things here? I've been going over my daughter Penny's college papers. She has this crazy professor who is grading off for things like having paragraph indentations of six spaces, when he thinks five are right. This is nonsense; the computer default settings establish such things—your mother will tell you all about that, in due course—so Penny was getting graded down from A level to D level because of things that were out of her control. So we have had to get into the programming and revamp the default setting on her computer, and we have corrected every possible syntax or spelling error or confusion, setting it up the professor's way even when it's wrong—as a pro writer and former English teacher, I do know what's right—so she can get through that course. But it does things to my blood pressure. So when you get to college—what do you mean, you're having second thoughts about that? You're afraid you won't be out of the wheelchair yet and folk will laugh at you? No they won't. Yes I know it's a long way away. So watch out for that kind of professor. I don't want to have to go over *your* papers like that.

Out at the horse stalls—we never shut them in there, we just feed them there—there were six and a half big spiders this summer. You know what I mean: one was small. Gradually they disappeared, until now there is only one and three-quarters spiders. No, I don't know where the others went; I didn't ask them.

I saw a listing for a fanzine—that's an amateur magazine in the SF genre—called PIRATE JENNY. No, I've never seen a copy of it. I suppose I could order one for you, but it probably doesn't relate well to your interests. I just thought it had a cute title.

Cat News: the newspaper says Miss Kitty of the old Gunsmoke program died. Too bad. I guess that program was before your time, and probably not to your interest either. Oh, well.

Did you know there was an eclipse of the moon this past week? Frightened the night mares something awful. We went out and looked, and there it was: the moon half eaten away. Fortunately it grew back again by morning.

Book Review time: I'm reading this one titled *New World, New Mind*. It's a serious book—deadly serious. You know how I don't like to see our global environment damaged, or animals rendered extinct. But Man is doing it at a horrendous rate, so that the greatest extinction is not the time of the end of the dinosaurs, but right now. Why is man so shortsighted? This book explains it. Man evolved to handle a more natural world, with reflexes to fight the sabre-tooth tiger and such, rather than to sweat the slow stuff like advancing glaciers. It was a matter of survival, and it worked. But now those slow things are becoming important, like ozone depletion, and Man needs to do something about them before our world is ruined. But he just ignores them, as he did the glaciers, figuring that if it isn't pouncing on him, it can't hurt him. So we need to retrain our thinking to match the needs of the day—but are we going to? I don't much like the answer I see. So when you have nothing better to do, you might ponder that, and see if you can work out a way to save our planet before it's too late.

Some other enclosures: some time back a fan sent me some play money he made up, and I thought it might amuse you. I wrote his name, Hellerstein, on the No Dollar bill, so I'd remember who made it. The guy has a fun imagination. Also a picture of a snow leopard plate; I didn't care to buy such expensive plates, but I thought you'd like the picture of those big cats. This time I cut out Calvin & Hobbes along with Curtis, because it's a cute one all about Hobbes, just in case your mother didn't send that one in for you.

Now I have to go back to my chapter about thirteen year old Tappy, the blind girl who is now in a strange science fiction adventure I'm collaborating on with Philip Jose Farmer, and to *Tatham Mound*, where my nine year old girl has grown up to age 24. Such things happen. Say Hi for me to Cathy; I hope she's doing okay. I hope *you're* doing okay; you're not slacking off on those therapy exercises, are you?

AwGhost 25, 1989

Dear Jenny,

Well, I've done it again: I have foolishly frittered away my time, and now am late writing to you. I was trying to figure out why my file handling program DirMagic would copy readily from Drive C to Drive D, but balk at copying from Drive D to Drive C. Over an hour gone, but I finally did figure it out. When I get hold of a puzzle, any type, grrr, I can't let go. I don't suppose you know anyone like that? More in a moment.

Several Big Events this week. One is that they are getting close pictures of the planet Neptune and its big moon Triton. Another is that I had to shovel a bag full of horse manure. But the most important is that I GOT YOUR LETTER!! Laurie sent it, together with a letter of her own. Rather than write to her directly (mainly because I frittered away that hour) I'll just tell you to tell her I got it. She says it took you five hours on your Scan Pac to do it. It says that you appreciate my writing to you, and are thrilled that Jenny Elf is in a novel, and you thank my wife Cam for the beautiful pillow. You also say you like the Elf Letter. I think that's a confusion; I didn't send you an Elf Letter, Richard Pini did. But next time I'm in touch with him, I'll relay the message. I may have mentioned that we hope to have a special hardcover edition of *Isle of View* with a Pini cover showing Jenny Elf. We'll see how that works out; it gets complicated because we have to negotiate with the publisher. Anyway, thanks for the letter, but next time you have five hours to spare I hope you'll spend them eating chocolate pudding; that's surely more fun for you. Laurie showed me your Scanning Boards too, with all the letters and words you can point to. Hey, I see my name is there! Right next to your cats. I like your messages "That's Not Fair" and "I Don't Like This."

Now I was going to tell you why I frittered away that hour. It started when I made a serendipitous discovery, and—what? Oh, you don't know that word? Okay, I'll tell you about Serendipity. Serendip is the old name for Ceylon, a big island off the south of India. The new name is Sri Lanka. There is a story that there were three princes of Serendip who were always finding good things that they weren't looking for. So they made it into the word serendipity. Yes, it's true—there really is such a story, and the word does derive from the name of that island. So when you look for a lost penny and find a dollar instead, that's serendipitous indeed. It's pronounced seren-DIP-ity; I know you'll like that word.

Okay, so this morning I made a serendipitous discovery when Alan finished typing the—what? Look, Jenny, how do you expect me to tell this if you keep interrupting me? Do you want me to touch the THAT'S NOT FAIR square? Oh, all right; what is it this time? Alan? You don't know Alan? Well, he is my daughter Penny's boyfriend. She stayed in St. Petersburg this summer, working, so we brought her boyfriend home instead. He is working for me, helping me with research for *Tatham Mound*. I'm a slow reader, and I'd never get this big novel written in the limited time I have otherwise. So when I need to know what was happening in Spain between the years 1500 and 1520, Alan reads the books and makes me a summary. It's been working very well. This time I found that a computer hard disk crash two years ago had wiped out my copy of the first chapter of the novel I'm doing with Philip Jose Farmer, the one with Tappy, the 13 year old girl who—oh, you remember. Okay. One day I may read that to you. Anyway, Alan nicely typed it back into the computer, and brought up the disk, and I copied it onto my hard disk. But I messed up; when I wanted to go to my directory on the D drive, I typed C: without realizing it, and got the wrong listing. So I typed \MO for the Mound directory, and it put me there, and I was on my way. But Alan, who had been watching, remarked that I had jumped from the C Drive to a directory on the D Drive without specifying the full path name. This was unusual, so we checked it out. Yes, the program really does that, though its manual doesn't say so; it can find a directory in a different drive, even when you don't specify the drive. So that was the serendipitous discovery: an easy way to go to other directories. But then in the afternoon I wasted the hour, because the effect was intermittent, and I wanted to know why. I finally ran it down: DirMagic zeros in on the default drive, and can go or copy to anywhere in it, but it can't do the same with other drives, and you have to use the full path name. Yes, I know this bores you, and you fell asleep three minutes ago, but at least your mother will understand it. In fact she probably figured out the answer long before I did.

By this time you should have your copy of the Xanth PinUp Calendar. I hope you like it. Your mother says she looks like Miss Mayhem the Ogress right now, because of her swollen face. I doubt it's quite that bad; after all, what about the rest of the Ogress? When you get a chance, you can go through the dates on the Calendar. There's a typo somewhere, where it says "Nymph's Mother Frightened by a Pun"—it leaves off the final N. Frightened by a PU? That must be a foul-smelling noise.

And why was I shoveling horse manure for Penny? It seems she's growing some plants and wants the best. So this is genuine Blue-horse manure, as similar to unicorn manure as Mundania gets. There's a song, "Sipping Cider," in which a man meets his wife-to-be when he joins her sipping cider through a straw. As I pitched that manure I thought of that song, but it didn't quite fit: "So cheek by cheek, and jaw by jaw, we both sipped manure through a straw." Ah, well.

Every so often I see those two clouds I mentioned way back when, Amorphous and Whathisname. Sometimes they have lovely bright fringes at dawn, when they are sunning themselves. Once they followed me home. They must have, because when I looked east from the house, there they were on the horizon.

I have some other readers—you didn't know that?—and one of them has named her dog after me, "Piers." Actually it's a fake dog, that she puts around her house; when she takes a picture, it looks real. That reminds me of a novelty item called "Dog-Done-It" that looks exactly like dog poop. You put it on someone's bed, and it's almost as much fun as a Whoopee Cushion. A variant looks like fresh vomit. Think of all the fun you can have, once you get home!

So have you been keeping up with the news on Neptune? Neptune is about my favorite planet, because back in the 1960's when I wrote *Macroscope* I had my characters go there and stop at its big moon Triton, and they discovered that Triton had its own little ice-moon which they named Shön. So if Voyager II finds such a moon—well, I was there first. So far they have discovered blue clouds on Neptune, with white cloudlets that cast shadows on the lower clouds (lower clouds don't like that), and rings and ring fragments (somebody must have blundered through and messed them up), and on Triton are pretty pinks and blues. But no moon-of-moon. Yet. Nevertheless, this all goes to show how much information can come through how small an aperture; the radio that is sending all this has the power of a refrigerator bulb. I bet you think I'm about to make some sort of point here. Well . . .

Not as many enclosures this time, because last time Cam was taking Cheryl back to college and there was no one to mail the letter until Sunday, so I included the Sunday Curtis. However, today there were pictures of cats, so you can have those, and I cut out Calvin and Peanuts a few days ago for you because I thought they were cute and just in case you didn't get to see them, here they are. And ditto for a Dear Abby column you should enjoy, especially when you get carsick.

So say hello to Cathy and the Therapists for me, and hang in there for another week. Who knows, something good might happen.

PS—this is my 132th (hundred and thirty-tooth) letter so far this month, on the way to over 160. I have too many readers!

September 1989

Chocolate pudding gets augmented by pureed pizza. A new wheelchair cushion appears. A blowhard passes through. A possibility is mentioned. And the world most likely does not end as predicted.

SapTimber 1, 1989

Dear Jenny,

Yes, Alan is typing research notes for me on the downstairs system so I'm up here in color and laser printing. Did I mention that my background is chocolate and my print is vanilla? I've gotten to like having a color monitor.

Yesterday we had to take the dogs in to the vet for shots and such. Oh, they were satisfied to go; Lucky is a big dog—he weighed in at 73 pounds this time, and he's old now; in his prime, who knows what he weighed. It's just that they get too excited, and it's hard keeping them under control. I managed to skin a shin—what do you mean, what am I complaining about? You're thirteen; you're *supposed* to skin your shins, but I'm too old for that—and today I have a sore back, so I must have pulled a muscle without knowing it. Then today I went on my run, and went full-face through a spider web. I was trying to claw it off without stopping my run when I hit a second one. Fortunately I saw it, and only clipped part of it. Then I encountered a third, and managed to duck most of it. They all had those big orb-weaver spiders. I have nothing against them, but I wouldn't want one on my face. Then I stopped for the pump and the horse's pasture water, and the small black biting flies swarmed around me. I swatted a dozen or so—I prefer to live and let live, but those flies don't share that philosophy—and then pulled off the cap of spiderweb that remained on my hair. I discovered six black flies caught in it. They had buzzed my head and been caught! Served them right. I was sorry I couldn't take them back to the spider. I don't like spider web on my face, but I also don't like ruining all those hours' work by the spider. We have webs around here with lines that extend up ten feet, to the branches of trees; they can go to phenomenal lengths to anchor their webs properly, and I admire the industry and architecture of it. The other day a mosquito came to bite me—there's another thing I swat—so I swatted it and took it outside, but at the screen door I saw a little running spider—do you remember Jumper in Xanth #3?—so I put the mosquito down next to it, and blew on the mosquito so that it moved a bit, and that little spider pounced on it and took it away. There was my good deed for that day, maybe. So I like spiders, who are sort of the cats of the bug world. Except when they catch dragonflies. Last year I found a dragonfly caught by a bit of web, and I managed to free it. If you are ever down here, I'll show you how to get a dragonfly to sit on your hand. I finished my run, stopping every so often to comb out the sandspurs clustered in my socks—sandspurs are the mundane version of curse burrs, and I've found that a hair-comb works as well as anything to get them out. Anyway, you can see I've been busy.

I just checked today's incoming batch of mail. Now I dictate my answers into the cassette recorder and the secretary types from that. The trouble is, I tend to ramble and lose coherence when I'm speaking, and the secretary doesn't know what a run-on sentence is, so I have a mess of correcting to do when the letters come back. Sigh. But today the last letter I read was in reaction to the Author's

Notes in the Incarnations series. She lives near the giant redwoods, and says the last of those lovely trees is being cut down for furniture. Ouch! Mankind is such a destructive slob, with so little sense of the art and significance of natural things. She said her world seemed to be coming to an end, because her husband deserted her after 8 years and two children, and then she was riding with a friend, and didn't know the friend had been drinking, and drove the VW into a pole, and she—the letter-writer—was on the passenger side that hit. Ouch! I know about that sort of thing; ask your mother to tell you about Robert Kornwise, any week now when she recovers so she's slightly more mobile than you are without your wheelchair. She's so cheesed off about not getting in to see you that the cats are looking strangely at her, wondering whether she's a mouse. Anyway, this woman was injured in the heart, and it stopped beating twice while she was on the operating table. She had a vision that she sat up and looked around, realizing that she was leaving her body, and a man said "You can go back, you know." She thought about it, and didn't want to leave her children without a mother, and the fact was that there was a new man she thought might be worth marrying, so she decided to go back. Four days later she woke in this world, and a year later she married the man. Now she's reading my Incarnations books, which relate to things like this, and wanted to let me know. So you see, there's no telling whom you might have met, back when you were 85% in the next realm.

Which brings me to the next subject: there's a prediction that the world is coming to an end today: Friday Saptimber Oneth. So if you don't get this letter, you'll know why. Maybe if you hold your breath, it will happen sooner. Which reminds me deviously of an old song. I think it was titled "Brighten the Corner," and its essence was that you should brighten the corner where you are—that is, don't worry about going far away to have a good time, have it right here. But the version I learned was a parody: "When you gotta go, and the toilet's too far—right in the corner where you are." So what has this to do with the end of the world? Well, it was the idea of making things happen sooner, whether meeting God or something a bit lower.

Yesterday I had two letters from your mother. One was postmarked AwGhost 25, so it took only six days to get here, and the other was postmarked the 29th, so it took all of two days. She evidently sneaked a peek at one of my letters to you, and was snapping at "Tooth or Consequences." She said they gave you some tests, and that you read well (those right-angle lenses must help!) but don't spell well, and you still don't like math. You sound just like my dyslexic daughter Penny! I didn't learn to spell until I became an English teacher, and had to grade spelling tests. There is no relation between spelling ability and intelligence, because spelling in the English language doesn't make any sense. But when you get set up with your computer, you can have a spelling checker program. They highlight the misspelled word, and offer several suggestions for the word you're looking for. So it becomes a game of multiple choice, which should be easy enough for you. So make a note: SPELLEN CHEKKER. Anyway, she hopes she has a mouth with teeth in it soon. That was the letter where she announced your Pudding Triumph. What happens if anyone calls you Puddinghead? Right: splat in the face.

Her second letter contained her penciled picture of you, drawn from memory. And here I thought *you* were the one in the family who was interested in art! She says her jawbone surgery is doing much better than they thought. I can explain that: when everyone and sundry got into mischief, she let fire with such heated words that any remaining infection was burned right out of her jaw. Fire-breathing dragons don't have much trouble with infection either, for the same reason. So maybe she'll have teeth again on schedule. She says you went on to eat more real food, not merely pudding. She says that if you can manage to eat again, that should help you to talk too, because the same tongue you eat with is used in speech. Well, keep eating, then!

She also tells me that I have the "Serendipity" explanation in my big novel *Tarot* just the way I gave it to you. Oh? I don't remember, and now can't find the place. *Tarot* is the kind of novel your mother shouldn't be reading. Anyone who reads it without being affronted at some point doesn't understand it. I regard it as my best work, but it's way beyond the competence of my average Xanth reader. So don't you try to read it, even with your right-angle lenses. I note, on rechecking the one-volume edition, that it says "the classic fantasy adventure trilogy," though it is science fiction rather than fantasy, and it's a single novel. My contract even says it shall never be referred to as a trilogy. So much for contracts. So don't become a writer, Jenny; there's too much aggravation. And she says Ray tried to order *Bio of an Ogre* at Waldenbooks, and first they tried to make it *Ogre Ogre*, then the Bio of a Space Tyrant series. But for all that, at least Waldenbooks carried it; Dalton did not. Tell Ray that in about two weeks it will appear in paperback; he should have saved his money. I really didn't mean to bring so much aggravation to your friends.

She also says you have one of those special effect sounds devices like the one I described, only with different sounds. Well, have fun! I remember when I was in high school, and someone played a joke on an instructor. When the man started his car, it went WHEEEEEE-BOOM, and then thick black smoke poured out from under the hood. I really shouldn't laugh. . . .

And she says you already know about dog-done-it and plastic vomit. Ah, well. I believe in education, and I made sure to educate my daughters. That meant that they learned early what a whoopee cushion was, and bouncy imitation snakes and the like. What schools think is education is something else.

So you see, your mother had a mouthful to say. Actually she said even more than that, but rather than boring you with it I'll write her a separate note. Your mother says a lot! Oh, you already knew?

How is Cathy, your roommate, doing these days? I remember when she moved in with you, but I haven't heard since. You girls didn't quarrel, did you?

I have some enclosures. Curtis and Alligator Express are back, and a couple of Far Side cartoon reruns I thought you might like if you didn't see them before. Also a picture for a computer ad, with RAM being rendered as male sheep.

Keep going, Jenny; life may get more interesting soon.

SapTimber 8, 1989

Dear Jenny,

I wash my hair each Friday, because that's when I take my weekly shower whether I need it or not (stop sniggering; I do wash up every morning and after every run; I just don't take a full shower), and noticed that I was running low on shampoo. I need to keep changing brands, because any one brand stops working and in three days I'm all over dandruff. So my wife bought what looks like a bottle of bleach called Selsun Blue. Next week I'll try that, but I'm afraid this stuff is really laundry bluing and I'll turn bleached or bright blue. What do *you* use? Oh, you don't get dandruff? Well I didn't either, when I was your age. But one of the disgusting things about growing up is that you get dandruff. Just wait; you'll see. So there. Anyway, I had my fastest run in two months, and yes I stopped at the little magnolia tree. The sandspurs stuck in my socks, and when I stopped to take them out (ouch!) the flies swarmed in to bite me. Par for the course.

I have to get on with this letter, because I have a couple of others to follow. A fan in Texas says the folk in his class have to choose an author to study, so that next month they can *be* that author before the class. He chose me, so he wants to learn something about me. I'll tell him to get the paperback *Bio of an Ogre* which will appear in paperback soon after he gets my letter; that will tell him more about me than he cares to know. Why he should want to be 55 years old with a receding hairline I don't know. I also have to write a note to Richard Pini (what do you mean, Richard Who? Richard Elfquest Pini, that's who) because he sent me three copies of *The Blood of Ten Chiefs* and one of its sequel, *Wolfsong*, out of the blue. You know, in *Isle of View* (What do you mean, is that part of a series?!) I have Jenny Elf mention part of the past history of the elves of her land, which is not Xanth (oh, you'd caught on to that?), and the part she mentioned related to the story I did about Prey-Pacer, who was mostly known as Prunepit. I wonder what Jenny Elf will be doing in the future? Even the Muses can't say for sure, because she's not really part of their frame.

I am now in the last chapter of *Tatham Mound*. It's depressing. I do get depressed sometimes when a novel ends, because for months I have been in the thick of it, living and breathing with my characters (yes, they do breathe, especially the buxom young women) and it is finally over, and that part of my life is done. Normally I get right on into the next novel, to ease the unease. But this one is worse, because it's a bigger novel than most—it should be about 180,000 words when finished—and sadder. All the characters die. I knew that before I started, of course, because we found their bones in the Mound. Still, now I know those folk, and I hate the way they died of smallpox. Tale Teller's daughter Wren had just married and had a baby when the plague killed them both, for example, and her beautiful bones (even the archaeologists marveled) and those of her baby are there together. I made up the story, but a beautiful young woman and her baby really did die then, and who is to say it wasn't Wren? This morning I got the bodies buried—what a job that was, covering over 77 bodies using baskets of sand hauled by hand!—but there's still the ceremony of the Black Drink to go, to be sure the spirits of the dead are satisfied and don't get mad at the living. It is bad business when the spirits get angry! Then I'll have to do the Author's Note, with all the dry discussion about population statistics and plagues and excavation of mounds. So this letter is a kind of relief, because we aren't going to bury you in a mound and dig you out over 400 years later to look at your bones. We're not going to bury you at all; we're going to get you up and about and out of Cumbersome hospital.

What's that? No, don't tell me you didn't mutter anything; I heard it. What was it? Something about getting out—you mean to say you're nervous about going out, after all this time there? Well, sure, that's understandable, but Jenny, you surely don't want to stay there forever! There are things to do outside, like school and homework and chores—let's start this sentence over; I don't like the way you're nodding agreement. There are things to do outside, like petting cats and shopping for pretty things and watching VCR movies and using your computer to paint pictures and staying up late and sleeping late and all that. Besides, your mother's getting lonely; she says there are too many stupid males and not enough smart females at home.

You don't want to leave your friends there? You don't have to. You can come back to visit them. You'll probably be seeing some of them anyway, because you'll have to report for therapy sessions and such. You can go to the Five and Ten Cent Store (yes, I know, now they are five and ten dollar stores, but in my day they were priced right) and buy them little presents. Or just go out to the garden, where your flowers are languishing for lack of your presence; they feel so inadequate when you aren't there to smell them. Pick a pretty flower for someone, or a pretty seed. No, don't laugh; seeds can be pretty. Here, I'll prove it: I stopped by the big magnolia tree that had three flowers on the one little branch that extends onto our property, and none anywhere else—I tell you, the magnolias like me!—and took some of the seeds from its seed-ball. They are bright red, some with two sides or three sides, like grapefruit seeds. Here are two of them: one for you and one for Cathy. Hi, Cathy! (I discovered this past week that one of my earlier letters told you to say "hit" to Cathy for me; that was a typo. It should have been "hi." I hope you didn't hit her!) Maybe if you get little pots you can plant them and they'll grow. Then you can return fifty years later and see this giant magnolia tree growing out of the hospital window, providing pretty white flowers and pretty red seeds for all the patients.

Meanwhile, how are things here? It has been a dull week, except for a couple of things. One was a power failure last Saturday: lightning hit our line and blew out our transformer and our pump. It took them five hours to replace the transformer. I read *John Dollar* by candlelight. That's a novel by the wife of Salmon Rushdie, the man the Ayatollah threatened to kill. It's the kind of book the critics like, which means that real people don't like it. It's about girls your age, but don't you read it; it is truly ugly and shocking in places. But what could I do? It was night without power, so I read. Now I'm reading Stephen King's *The Gunslinger.* You don't want to read that one either. Anyway, it was Sunday afternoon by the time we got the pump replaced; it actually worked on Saturday, so we didn't know, but then it started glitching. The lightning had glitched it up at several places. Because it was Sunday—and the following day a holiday—that's always when these things happen, as your mother well knows—we had to pay double time. It came to $761. All because the lightning arrester didn't work. I would make a pithy comment, but your delicate shell-pink ears would turn an indelicate color.

Then on Tuesday I started out by cleaning the algae from the pool, then putting Dvorak letters on my downstairs computer keyboard so I wouldn't have to keep carrying my upstairs keyboard down and maybe dropping it. See, the big letters are all red now, with the old QWERTY letters in small black. Do you notice the difference in this letter? (You're supposed to say yes, you do, in a very calm voice.) Then I wrote to my current Ligeia girl, who I think is gradually becoming less suicidal. And I had a visit by two English girls. One was the daughter of my British agent, visiting this country. She remarked how odd it was to be driving on roads where all the cars are on the wrong side. Right. I don't normally entertain visitors, but there are some few exceptions, and the daughters of my agents are one of them. That agent just sold my novelization for the movie *Total Recall* in Japan. Of course it wasn't my name that did it; it was that it's a Schwarzenegger movie, and the Japanese are big on such movies. And I'll only get some of the money, eventually; the publisher and the movie company get most of it. Still, I'd better stay on that agent's good side. She stays on my good side too, because the reason she is handling the foreign rights for this book is that I asked for my own agents, American and Foreign, on it, and the motion picture company agreed. The company didn't have to, because it owns the rights, but it humored me. It's a sixty million dollar movie, probably next year's big blockbuster. Yes, I'm sure your daddy will take you to it, humoring you, though there isn't anything in it that would interest him apart from unremitting action and violence and a slew of luscious bare girls. Unless he likes science fiction; then he can enjoy the planet Mars scenes, and the phenomenal alien nuclear plant there. Remember, I didn't write the movie, I just adapted the script to make it a novel. But I did add some significant material, if they care to use it. So I talked with my agent's daughter, who is an environmentalist, and her friend, and they had lunch with us, and I showed them our deep forest and horses and lake with the water lilies on it. If you ever want to visit, Jenny, I'll do the same for you. So it was three and a half hours in all. Then in the afternoon your mother called. What? How many pages did she talk this time? I lost count. A dozen, at least. She told me that they measured you this way and that, and that you've grown two inches, and that, uh (blush), you're giving up childhood and trying young ladyhood. Next thing we know, you'll be joining the Adult Conspiracy. Ah, well. At any rate, you are much on your mother's mind, Jenny. I suspect you already knew that. My daughter Penny also visited from college, bringing her latest papers for me to copy-edit. That took me half a day, most of it Wednesday. Anyway, that was my Tuesday; as you can see, it was duller than yours.

Say—I looked out the window, and there's one of our big box turtles—actually a gopher tortoise—walking along our drive, past our house. We have a number of them here, and we like them. Elsewhere in Florida they are trying to protect them, but development keeps encroaching, and they have to catch them and move them to safer regions—which are in turn encroached on by development. Bad business. But *our* turtles will remain unencroached on.

Slew of enclosures this time, maybe a slew and a half. A page on kids and the news, with several kids who have pets; one has 14 cats and wants a white rabbit. I guess you know about that. Article on insect metamorphosis, surely old stuff to you, but pretty anyway. One on a man whose legs are paralyzed, but he hopes to walk with magic boots. Article on questions kids ask, such as whether cats really have nine lives. One on the other wildlife of Citrus County—that's where I live—and how development is disturbing it. Alligator Express. Curtis. Picture of butterfly with flowers. And one of a drum that sounds liquid; is that how you play the drum? And of course the two magnolia seeds. No, don't eat them!

SapTimber 15, 1989

Dear Jenny,

Growl! Things have been aggravating me at the rate of about one a day, and just now another. No, it wasn't having to write to you; this one was because last week—the same day I last wrote to you—I wrote to a fan in Texas who is supposed to be me for a day. I sent him my "Author" sheet and recommended *Bio of an Ogre* for more, as it is coming out in paperback momentarily. So today I get a letter from him saying he needs just a few more bits of information, and has a list of 17 questions, most of which can be answered by the references I already gave him. He'd rather waste my time than bother following my advice. Well, he is about to learn something about the way I respond to those who ignore what I tell them, and perhaps it will help him personify the Ogre.

What else has been aggravating me? Why do you want to know? Maybe you should tell me what's been aggravating you. Come on, you can tell me! Oh—the wheelchair chafes what part of your body? Maybe you're right; it's not a fit subject to get to the bottom of.

Okay, what aggravates me is that last Sunday I had to take two hours to go out and sweat myself to death hacking out sandspurs from my running path. Sandspurs are the Mundane equivalent of curse burrs; they stick in my socks and ouch me with every step, so I have to stop and take them out, and then they stick in my thumb. Ouch! By the time I hacked them all out, swatting swarms of biting flies at the same time—the burrs and flies are in cahoots—I was so soaked in sweat that I had to change all my clothes. Next day my legs were tired and I had a slow run—and some more sandspurs reached in from just beyond where I'd hacked and *still* got me. Today it was worse, and I had to stop several times to dig the #$%&*!! things out, sticking my thumb several times. Then yesterday morning I was eating my breakfast, which consists of a bowl of cereal, rolled oats, brewer's yeast, wheat germ, nuts and milk—the rolled oats swell up later and keep me from getting hungry before lunch, see—and reading the newspaper (which I tend to pronounce nudes-paper, but there aren't any nudes in it), when my hand came down and just caught the edge when I wasn't looking. Flip! The thing landed upside down in my lap. WHAT'S SO FUNNY!? I had to change my shorts. Another morning they were to have Arnold muscleman Schwarzenegger on the morning TV program, and I wanted to see that because he'd probably say something about *Total Recall*, which movie I novelized and is just now in print in hardcover, so a mention might help sales. But I forgot. I never turn on the TV myself, you see; I just don't tune it in. My wife came down after an hour and turned it on, but wouldn't you know, they must have run it in the first hour of the show, and we missed it and now will never know. Growr! And the publisher forwarded reviews of *Man From Mundania* with comments such as "junk-food fantasy" and "loose ends" (by that they mean it's part of a series) and "another Xanth potboiler." A literary potboiler is material a writer just grinds out because he needs the money. I never write that way. You don't see why I'm so touchy? Well, just wait until they review *Isle of View* and say that Jenny Elf is the stupidest character ever and the Author's Note is too boring to read. Then let's see who is touchy! So you see, it's been exactly the beastly kind of week your mother specializes in.

Speaking of whom, I got two entire letters from her this week, which I'll have to answer. Don't let me forget. So

I'll have to keep this letter reasonably short, so I can get everything done, because there's also a collaborator to answer, and that fan, and another woman who wants my comment on a chapter of her novel and won't be pleased when I tell her what's wrong with it. Sigh.

Meanwhile I completed the first draft of *Tatham Mound* and now am adding in ceremonies and legends. This morning I did the one about how tobacco came to be and am part way through the one about how the world was made. Do you want to know about that? The world is a flat island suspended from the sky by four ropes anchored at the four directions—North, East, South and West—and if they ever break, it will sink into the ocean and everyone will drown. Aren't you glad you found that out in time? Yesterday I did the one about the rolling heads. No, I can't retell that here; it's 4000 words long! Let's just say that in Indian mythology, when someone's head is cut off, it may roll back and tell off the one who did the foul deed.

We got an ad for about an 18 volume series of field guides, starting with *Peterson's Field Guide to the Birds.* We're not buying, partly because they are leather-bound and partly because we already have the volumes we want and don't need to pay $35 for duplicate volumes. My experience with Peterson's goes way back. When I was in high school I knew how to identify only one bird, the cardinal, because it was red. My roommate, a birdwatcher, taught me the slate colored junco, and I still know that one today. My great aunt gave me the field guide, and the summer after I graduated I used it to identify every bird I saw in the Vermont Green Mountains. It was about fifty birds. Today I know all those fifty, and almost no others. Fortunately some of those are here in Florida too, like the wrens and woodpeckers, though the species differ slightly.

When I took my shower today I sang "It's a long time, girl, may never see you, come let me hold your hand." That song has a long history for me, including serious trouble with a publisher. So if I ever see you, I'll tell you all about it, and sing it to you, and maybe hold your hand. Don't wrinkle your nose; how do you know you won't like it until you hear it? Oh, you mean the hand business? Oh.

I saw some fashion items on TV. I know I said I don't turn it on; my wife does. Fashion designers know nothing about decent dressing. These ones all thought that women's hair should be boyishly short. Yes, I do wonder about the sexual preferences of that ilk. Meanwhile, you can just ignore them and concentrate on growing your hair back long.

I read an item about the poor way history is taught. Amen! I'm interested in history, but I nearly flunked the high school course in American history. I took the text home for the summer before, read it, and loved it. Then I took the course. It did not address the dynamics of what the white man did to the natives, or the significance of things as I saw them. I still remember the first question on the first test: "Name the man who made the maps that influenced Columbus." Notice it doesn't ask about the concept of the round world that motivated Columbus to try to find a shorter passage to India by sailing around the other side of the globe when others thought he would fall off the edge of the world; it wants a name, as if that's what counts. Names and dates—that's what they think history is. Gah!

My wife brought home rental video tapes the past two nights. The first was *Rain Man*, which is a quality story involving a partially autistic man, well worth seeing. The second was *Her Alibi*, which is straight entertainment about a writer and a beautiful girl. See it when you can; you'll love it. But the critics rate it mediocre and call it "witless." Well, "critic" is a six letter word for a four letter concept. Critics seem to think entertainment is sinful.

Here's another magnolia seed or two; I hope they aren't crushed by the thought of traveling.

The computer said my letter was 122 lines long, which fits on two pages, then later said 124 lines, which won't. I deleted my address.

SapTimber 22, 1989

Dear Jenny,

Did I ever tell you how I set up for your letters? I have you on the glossary, so that I just type "jenny" and control-F4 and it puts your address on. Well, I was checking something for my daughter Penny, and it pretended there was no such. So I checked the list of glossary entries, and Penny was there. Don't tell *me* these programs can't get whimsical! Now it agrees that Penny is there, along with Jenny.

We've been getting rain. It's a tag-end of the outflow from Hurricane Hugo. Let me tell you about hurricanes. Right, here comes one of those patented Anthony explanations; let go of your nose. It's this way: every hurricane forms in the warm tropical ocean and takes aim at Florida. It's like a pinball game: there are all these barriers in the way, like Haiti and the Antilles and Cuba, and the trick is to get by them unscathed and into the Gulf of Mexico, then curve back and catch my house. One hundred points if any succeed in blowing off our roof. We are hidden where it's just about impossible for a storm to find us, but every summer season they just have to try. So here was Hugo, and he set out well, but then drifted off-target and saw he couldn't make it to the Gulf. Also, he had lost some power. So he said "If I can't huff and puff and blow Piers' house down, I'll go for Jenny's hospital instead." So he veered north, which had the advantage of restoring some power over the open water, so he got back up to top winds of 135 miles per hour. That's respectable. But again he misjudged it, and wound up crashing into land halfway between us, at

Charlotte, South Carolina. That was a secondary target; I know an editor at TOR BOOKS who lives there, Harriet MacDougal, former senior editor. Her husband is Robert Jordan, author of several Tarzan novels, but don't judge him by that; he's about to get into major fantasy, and will be one of the leading figures in the genre. I know. What do you mean, *how* do I know? Can't you take it on faith? I read his first huge fantasy epic in manuscript; it hasn't been published yet. Now shut up and let me continue: she came down to see me here several years ago, and we discussed my novel *Shade of the Tree*, and I revised it and TOR published it and has done well enough with it, and your mother will no doubt read it in due course if she hasn't already. So that's why Charlotte was on the list. Hugo scored directly on it, and just about leveled it. Poor Harriet! Next hurricane begins with I, and then there will be J. Just wait until next year, or whenever, when Hurricane Jenny comes. I don't know whether you ever quite understood my pun about Spinning Jenny; it's an early form of sewing machine. But it may also be that hurricane, when. So remember.

Yesterday we went to our old house, because storms had brought branches down on the roof and punched a couple of holes. We went up and put big spoonfuls of tar on them—it looked like chocolate pudding—and of course it got on our hands. No we didn't touch it; it just magically jumps from the can to your skin, and then won't come off. We used pieces of roofing shingles over the tar, and that should do it; we've done it before. Just as well, because we've had over an inch of rain today. While we were there, I checked my old study in the pasture, looking for my notes on the sixth martial arts novel, because TOR is interested in republishing the first five if I do one more. No, they aren't for you to read; it just explains why Hurricane Hugo marked the TOR editor down as a target. I was struck by the way the property was overgrown, and how the little cedar trees we planted by hand are bigger now. There's just so much nostalgia; after all, about eleven years of our lives are in that property. When you go home—I have it on good authority that eventually that will happen—you'll probably discover it is smaller than it was when you left it, and some of the cats don't remember you, and there are rooms it has sprouted since you left, and it will be terribly reassuring and saddening at the same time. That's just the way it is, Jenny.

I remembered another one of those trick math-type riddles. Get your fingers out of your ears—I'll give you the answer too. (How come you're so ornery?) If a hen and a half lays an egg and a half in a day and a half, how many eggs will three hens lay in five days? Now here's how you tackle it: first you simplify it. If a hen and a half lays an egg and a half in a given period, then one hen would lay one egg in that time. Doesn't that make sense? So it's one hen, one egg, in that day and a half. That means two thirds of an egg in a day. Okay so far? Now it's just a matter of multiplication. Three hens, each laying two thirds of an egg in a day, would lay six thirds, or two full eggs in a day. So we have a production of two eggs a day. In five days it would be ten eggs. That's your answer. Now you can adapt it: if a girl and a half eats a chocolate pudding and a half in a day and a half, how many puddings will Jenny and Cathy and a therapist eat in five days?

Sigh. I don't eat many puddings, because they have too much sugar, and I stay clear of extra sugar. This week I read an article in SCIENCE NEWS about a syndrome related to diabetes they have discovered, and it seems to be what I've got. You see, most diabetics are fat, but I'm not. Sure I watch what I eat, and I exercise, but I never did put on weight even when it was otherwise. Well, now they call it Syndrome X, which is obviously an abbreviation of Xanth: thin diabetics. It seems we have high blood sugar, but also high levels of insulin in the blood, because our body cells just don't use insulin very well and it piles up. Now they think we are at risk for heart attacks, because that extra insulin causes trouble in the blood vessels. Then they clog, and blood pressure rises, leading to—Oops, I don't like that! But don't worry; not only am I thin, I have low blood pressure. I think my exercise keeps my blood vessels clear, so I shouldn't have any problem. But it was a disturbing article, and I think I'll continue to stay clear of sugar and to exercise vigorously, if it's all the same to you.

Today when my wife came back from town she reported half a dozen baby water turtles trying to cross our drive. They hatch out, and are supposed to find their own way to water, but sometimes they do get lost, and of course evolution never prepared them for fences and asphalt roads. So we went out to help them, but found only two: one alive, one dead. Apparently the ones my wife helped across the road had gone on toward the lake. I took the one down to the lake, and it was plowing through the thick weeds toward the water when I left. It's nice living in the wilderness, and we plan to keep it this way forever.

I received my first copy of Xanth #12, *Man From Mundania*. The next one is yours, *Isle of View*, in a year. Can you keep a secret? Okay, don't tell anyone: Richard Pini of Elfquest is considering whether to make *View* into a graphic novel. You see, he has expertise exactly where it is needed: in the elf aspect. We hope to get together one of these months and work it out, and if it seems feasible, we'll sign contracts and things and get the project rolling. What's that? You want to be there when we work it out? Now look, Jenny, it isn't that easy to—I mean, it's really pretty dull stuff, deciding whether to do small black/white comics first, or jump immediately into a massive expensive color edition, and what artist to use, and what it will cost, and my agent Kirby McCauley, who by coincidence is also Richard Pini's agent, would have to figure out what terms are appropriate, you know, who gets what when the thing goes on sale and the money starts coming in, so it's all pretty technical, and—I mean, you want us all to pile into your hospital room and lay out charts and things across your bed? It would never work; your room's too small. So—will you stop that? I just explained how impractical it is. Just because it's Jenny Elf we're talking about, you don't have to—Sigh, okay, I'll see what I can do. No promises, though. (You can be as bad as your mother, when you get set on something unreasonable, you know that?)

Remember when we had to replace our pump, after the lightning strike? The new one has more power, though it's supposed to be the same one-horsepower. Now when I turn on the water full force to refill the horse water tub, it arcs right over the tub and splashes on the ground. Stop laughing! I have to choke it down and fill the tub slower. Yes, the big spider is still out there, and there's a little brown toad, too. I found it in the barn a couple of times and thought it was lost, and guided it outside, but it kept reappearing inside. I don't know how it got in, but if it finds flies there, okay.

I read a novel, *She Who Remembers*, that my wife picked up in town. It's historical, set in southwest North America before its discovery by the white man. I read it for comparison with my *Tatham Mound*, which I have now completed in first draft, 180,000 words (that's big) and am about to spend a month editing. *She Who etc.* turns out to be a romance, with men forever yearning for women and women yearning for men, but it does move along well and is more interesting to read than some historicals. My novel is quite different, though it is mostly pre-white American Indian and in the same general genre, and told from the Indians' point of view, as is *She etc.*

Oh—when we came home yesterday, and went to turn off our alarm system, it alarmed instead. It malfunctioned, which annoys us; we'll have to have it checked. And one of the things we picked up at the other house was a small collection of candles, which are useful when there is a power failure. Two of them are scented: they smell of raspberry jam and apple butter. I like them; they have personality.

Today I spent some time reading an eight page missive from a woman with a daughter named Jenny. No, it's not your mother; this is Toni-Kay. She's five feet tall and likes to paint—you saw a picture of one of her cat paintings—and every so often she sends me a nice original painting, and I can't pay for a gift though I hate to have her use her money to buy the canvas when she has to scrimp just to survive. She wants to buy my novel *Balook* when it comes out, though it will probably cost $30 in hardcover. She saved the money, then saw a big book on cats for sale at that price and got that instead. You can see how foolish some folk would call her, but you know why I don't see it that way. Well, when *Balook* is finally published, I'll send her a gift copy; that much I can do. She tells how she had a strange dream-vision of a man stabbing a woman of her general description to death, and the next day there it was in the newspaper: a grisly stabbing murder of a woman that a girl of twelve discovered. It's eerie, and it reminds me how desperate the lives of others can be. What joy of life she has is achieved through her painting. Jenny, do you happen to know where the wand is, that I can take and wave and fix everything that is wrong with the world? So you can just get up and walk out of the hospital, and Toni-Kay can walk away from her situation? I need that wand.

SapTimber 29, 1989

Dear Jenny,

You know, I hadn't heard from your mother in a couple of weeks, and I was getting worried, so I called her. She had just arrived back from the ~~torture chamber~~ dentist, who had been ~~ripping out~~ working on her jaw, and she felt horrible. But I made her laugh, because she mentioned ~~needing~~ kneading dough, and I told how my sister used to form it into the shape of someone's bare bottom and spank it. Who said it can't be fun to make bread? Anyway, the dentist seems determined to keep your mother from visiting you or writing to me, but I think she will outlast him and finally tell him to get out of her face. It was a relief to learn she was only in physical pain; I was afraid she was mad at me.

So how's my week been? Maybe like yours. Every time I run now, I get spiderwebs plastered across my face and sandspurs in my socks and biting flies all over; they bang into my face and even fly into my mouth as I run. I have to plow through dog fennel that reach across my path from either side, and avoid thorny blackberry vines. Sometimes it's wet and I have to avoid puddles. Sometimes it's dry and the sand skids under my feet. In short, running is getting to be a real challenge. Last Monday I went out again to chop out sandspurs—have you ever been stuck by one of them? They are little balls of hooked spikes, so they hurt when they stick you and hurt when you pull them out—and there were so many that I saw it was hopeless; I'd have to spend as much time keeping them out of the path as I do running on it. Now it galls me something awful to give up my running path and let the confounded sandspurs and biting flies be victorious, but I just can't afford the time. So I came back and told Cam (my wife—she was Carol Ann Marble before she married me, so her initials were CAM) to order exercising machines, and I'd try exercising inside the house. She can't exercise outside at all, because she's allergic to those fly bites. So she ordered an exercycle and a treadmill.

Now you see what I'm getting at. I don't know what those therapists make you do, but if they could they'd put you on machines like these, so it's probably somewhat like your workouts. Naturally the treadmill was back-ordered until next month—someone at Sears always knows what you want, and takes it out of stock so you can't have it soon—but we did get the cycle. It's pretty good: you pedal, but it also has hand-bars that move with the pedals, so you can push-pull with your arms at the same time and exercise them too. You can do it all with the pedals or all with the hands, or anywhere in between. It keeps track of how many miles you go, and how long you do it, and your pulse rate and all. So I tried it for twenty five minutes and went six miles, which is twice what I'd do running, so now I know: divide the mileage by two to get a comparable level. My pulse rate varied from 140 to 160, which is slower than when I run, but I don't have all the muscles for this type of exercise yet. So if you ever get so you can pedal and pull, you'll probably be on a device like this, traveling miles without getting anywhere. Maybe we'll buy some of those video tapes that show you riding through the Yellowstone Park or somewhere while you exercise. In a year or two I'll be writing a novel, *Killobyte*, about a man who is paralyzed and depends on a computer for his life-support, and watches a program, and discovers too late that it's a suicide program, intended to kill him when he loses the game. I signed the contract for that earlier this year, but haven't had time to write it yet. No, don't worry; it can't happen to you; you're not on life support. The travel-programs business reminded me of that, is all. So if your therapists ask you whether you get bored during therapy, tell them you'd like to watch one of those programs, but don't ask for *Killobyte!*

Speaking of cycling: this week I got on my bicycle to ride out to pick up the newspapers—it's a mile and a half round trip—and the rear tire was almost flat. Sigh. It was a sandspur. That's right, they even make tires hurt! I went to patch it—and our full tube of rubber cement turned out to be empty. It had all evaporated away in the tube. Growr! We had to buy a whole new kit to get more cement, because of the conspiracy of the manufacturers. I normally have low blood-pressure, but that sort of thing surely raises it. Why can't they make tubes that are tight, and why not sell you only what you need? Because they can make more money this way. Tell your mother to curse them for me.

But I did see something interesting out there. A pine tree. What do you mean, so what? I know we have thirty acres of pine trees here. I know it's a tree farm. But this is one we hadn't planted, and it's different. It's not a slash pine or a longleaf pine; it may be a sand pine, which means it seeded in naturally, on the other side of our drive. That makes it special. It's a baby pine, about waist high. Yes, we'll keep an eye on it. No, you can't have a pine cone from it; it's too young to make pine cones. Make them give you an ice cream cone instead. Do they have pine flavored ice cream? Ah, well; don't pine.

Another thing that depressed me this week, almost as much as the notion that your mother might be mad at me, was a fanzine. A fanzine is an amateur magazine about science fiction and fantasy. I write each month to one where I can interact with fans and other professional writers. No it's not always polite; it can get mean at times. I am politically liberal, and most of the folk there are politically conservative, and I delight in making them look like asses when they try to argue their ridiculous views. But they really annoyed me this time. You see, I had that death-row prisoner write in to them, because I thought the interaction would do everyone good. He stated what he had done, and went on to other things that interest him, such as flying saucers. No, not the kind that fly when your mother gets mad! I mean the ones with little green men from Mars in them. But some folk approached the editors at the World Science Fiction Convention recently and asked them to cut him out, and the editors have now censored him out of the magazine, though the majority of the letter-writers said he should be allowed to have his say. He is a murderer, true, and his crime was detestable, but to censor him out because of anonymous complaints—that is just plain wrong, and it disturbs me so much that I may stop writing to them. Just so you know my attitude, so you can copy it if you like it: in a society of laws and decency, even murderers have certain rights. You don't censor those you don't like, you just avoid them. That's not because of their standards, but because of yours.

Doctor Edell on the radio just now: a girl called in with a sore tongue, and he said "Hold the phone up to your face and say 'Ah.' "

I am now editing *Tatham Mound*, and it keeps nudging up longer as I keep adding in things. I wasted time trying to find out what the pattern was on Pasco Plain pottery, because the little girl named Wren was making her first clay pot. Know what I finally learned: there isn't any design on it. That's why it's called "plain." Yes, I realize that was obvious. I just wish I'd realized it before I wasted that research time. Now the novel is 185,000 words long, and by the time I finish it should be over 190,000 words. That will be about 500 pages in published form. It's an emotional experience, because whenever I get done with a novel, I feel as if I am losing part of my life. Also, there is so much tragedy in this one. Remember, my protagonist marries two wives among the Cherokee—they called themselves the Principal People—who were later killed by smallpox. He returned home to Florida and married again—and smallpox wiped out his family again. It was one of the diseases the white man brought to America. I get all choked up when I read about it, even though I wrote it. So why didn't I write a happier story? Because the bones of his second family are buried in Tatham Mound. That's where the novel started; I knew it would be a tragedy at the outset, because I was animating those who were buried there. But it still hurts. Your mother is threatening to read that novel; fortunately it should be 1992, the 500th anniversary of

Columbus' discovery of America, before it is published. Maybe by then she will have forgotten about it. I haven't even sold it yet. Yes, I hope to make a lot of money from it. No, I didn't write it for money; it was just something I had to do. You know, like therapy. But I'd like to make money from it too. What do you mean, how much? What business is it of yours? Oh, stop looking like that! Ask again after my agent has sold it, and maybe then I'll tell you.

Today I received a package from Richard Pini: several comic books, ranging from small black and white to a 180 page full color amended edition of ELFQUEST 1. It has some pages the original didn't; I compared it to my daughter Cheryl's copy. Another is an elegant slick comic version of a BEAUTY AND THE BEAST episode. Stop drooling; these are mine, not yours! I have to go over these and come to a conclusion what type of treatment I would like for the Xanth comic version. Remember, we are pondering doing Jenny Elf, who will surely look a bit like you. It would be fast to do a small comic, and slow to do a big fancy one. But I like the big fancy one! Sigh. It can be hard to form a conclusion. I also received four martial arts novels from a writer named Steve Perry, who would like to collaborate with me on the reworking of my out-of-print martial arts novels and on a new one. The trouble is that my time is so valuable and my reading rate so slow that the value of the time it would take just to read them would be more than I would be paid for them. No joke. So how fast do *you* read, Jenny? That fast? Well, I don't. So what do I do? I want those old novels back into print, as they are the only ones of mine out of print, but I don't want to use that time. I mean, I could be writing another Xanth novel instead! Well, let me know if you have any advice, Jenny.

I have some different enclosures for you this time. One is a little page of stickers to put on credit cards; I thought you could stick them to plates, armrests, your wheelchair—are you in it yet?—books and whatever else amuses you. If it doesn't amuse you, throw away the labels; they are just junk mail. No, don't stick one to Cathy! There's a clipping about a kid supposedly stolen at Disney World; that wasn't you, was it? An article titled "How To Get Out Of Your Own Way" whose first statement is "My life seems to be out of my control." Do you ever feel that way? One about dinosaur stamps; they claim a brontosaur isn't a brontosaur. That's like saying "There ain't no such word as ain't!" A plan for a private little garden; I think your mother is already setting that up for you. One about hand-feeding a pet praying-mantis named Claws. A Brain Boggler puzzle from DISCOVER magazine, along with the answer, so you don't have to sweat it. I had another of those, but can't find it now. Curtis. Alligator Express. I understand you use these enclosures to delay therapy; well, these should delay it right out of existence!

Well, keep skidding along, Jenny; I have confidence that your life will get more interesting soon, and I'm hardly ever wrong.

---

*Author's Note:

When these letters were written I was making plans to go to a convention near Jenny, and meet her there. But I couldn't say so directly, because her family was not sure whether the hospital would allow her to attend. So I just hinted.

October 1989

Feeding tubes disappear. A convention is mentioned. A visit occurs. And twelve cats and a mother purr in unison.

OctOgre 6, 1989

Dear Jenny,

Five days after my treadmill arrived at the local Sears store, they got around to letting us know, and we picked it up and assembled it, and today I tried it for the first time. Last week I tried the exercycle. Stop yawning! I tell you, they will put you on similar devices, in the name of therapy, the moment you start walking. The cycle enables you to use your arms too, which is good, but the treadmill seems to be more intense exercise. I set it at five to six miles an hour, which is slower than I normally run—I do about seven and a half mph—but that was enough, because I found that a level limited treadmill, where I couldn't swing my arms, was different from running out under the sky. I feel it more in the upper thighs and less in the calves. So I "ran" 2.62 miles in 30 minutes, instead of 2.9 in 24 minutes, but at least I got no sandspurs or fly bites or spiderwebs in the face. Now my wife is concerned, because for the first time in twelve years she actually saw how hard I exercise and she says I'd better slow down—wives are like that—and she's also afraid my flying sweat will stink up the house. Anyway, when they put you on one of these machines, remember I told you so. Tell them you'd rather take a walk outside. It won't do any good, but you might as well tell them anyway, just to make them feel guilty.

I received your letter, dictated to Laurie, I think—she didn't give her name. In that you say it is fun to think about going home soon. Well, if my information is correct, you are home right now as I write this, because it is Friday. I hope you are having a good time, meeting all the cats again. I hope your mother survives the experience. She thought she would go visit you, and instead you went to visit her. Her nose will be browned off about that; you're one up on her now. (Oops, I'm in trouble; your daddy is laughing about that "browned off nose" comment, and your mother doesn't know why.)

I also got a cute little letter from your roommate Kathy. All this time I thought it was Cathy, with a C, but it seems to be with a K. So I sent her my reply by way of Sue, and she may get that before you get this. So if she's been smirking, that's why.

Your mother says the Post Orifice is chewing up all the red magnolia seeds I send you. I'll get one to you somehow; it takes a lot of intelligence to figure out how to get around something as stupid as the P.O., but I'm sure it can be done.

Let me tell you about a trip I made this week. I hate to travel, but this was set up by my daughter Penny: a visit to her boyfriend's grandparents. It is almost impossible for a father to say no to a daughter. Oh, you had noticed? So on Sunday the Oneth of OctOgre we drove down to St. Petersburg, and it started out well: before we even got off our tree farm, we saw three deer. One was small; maybe they were Daddy Deer, Mommy Deer, and Baby Deer. But none had horns, so we aren't sure. Now we know we have at least three on our property, because we saw them all at once. Good enough; we'll do our best to see that they are never hunted.

Where was I? I just got interrupted for half an hour by

a call from a publisher. How can I concentrate on something important like this letter, when these sniveling other things interfere? What? What do you care, which publisher, about what? It wouldn't interest you. You say you'll be the judge of that? Okay, it was from Susan Allison of BERKLEY, letting me know that they printed 175,000 copies of the paperback *Bio of an Ogre.* Yes, I know that conversation wouldn't have taken half an hour. But while I had her on the line, I told her about how the ELFQUEST folk and I may do *Isle of View* in comic format. You see, BERKLEY distributes the Quest folk's books, so are interested. So you see, it didn't interest you—oh, it *did?* Well, you're perverse. If it wasn't for Jenny Elf you wouldn't be interested, admit it.

But I was telling you about our trip. It turned out that Alan's grandmother—Alan is Penny's boyfriend's name; he worked for me this summer, doing research, so I could get ahead of schedule on *Tatham Mound*—had a stroke two years ago, and that caused her to be unable to speak, and to lose the sight of one eye, and she can't walk very well. Now she has recovered the ability to speak, and is about to get special glasses that will enable her to read again. So I mentioned you, because you have similar complaints. It's funny how different things can cause similar problems. A stroke is when there's a problem with the blood circulation in the brain, and it causes part of the brain to suffer, and the parts of the body relating to that part of the brain can malfunction. So she and I got along fine. She has a rock collection she has given me: stones she picked up from around the world, each with its history. I have the stones, but I have to get the histories from her, or they don't mean much. We all went out to eat at a restaurant, and the waiter came to tell us we had parked in a handicapped zone, but it was legitimate: Grandma McCulla is indeed handicapped, and has a handicapped car sticker. We talked about problems with restaurants, because my two daughters and my wife and I are vegetarians. I guess you know about that sort of thing. If you and I are ever eating in a restaurant, we'll have the same problem. It's a challenge. I told of the time I first encountered whipped cream in a squirt-can, back about 1953. It wouldn't work, because I didn't know how to push the top. Then suddenly it did work, and the cream shot out and bounced off my gingerbread dessert and across two and a half other people. No, don't get ideas! Your mother would Not Approve. But it's sort of fun to remember.

Am I boring you yet? Oh, you mean that dreamy look is just because you are thinking about what you could do with a squirt can of whipped cream? Don't you dare!

Something I heard on the radio: the toilet paper habits of families are different, according to their income. If they make over $50,000 a year, they have the toilet paper unroll from the top; if they make under $20,000, from the bottom. Can you figure that out? I think it must be a status or class thing; upper-class unrolls from the upper side, and the underclass from the underside.

Have you been keeping up with Calvin and Hobbes? This past week he locked the poor baby-sitter out of the house. She's a nice girl, but Calvin isn't a nice kid. Why do we enjoy reading about such a brat so much? Well, maybe you can skip being a baby-sitter, Jenny.

Remember when our alarm system fouled up? It did it again, after being fixed. What's the point in having a high class system if it just malfunctions? Maybe they finally have it straight now. What bothers me more than our setting the siren off when we are punching the code to deactivate it is that the automatic dialing of the police doesn't seem to be getting through. We called to tell them it was a false alarm, and they said that they had received no alarm, and anyway our number wasn't valid. So we checked with the folk who installed the system, and they said our number *was* valid. Hm. I wonder if Calvin and Hobbes did something to it?

Tuesday morning I went out to feed the horses, and they weren't there. Worried, I trotted out to the tree farm part, but they weren't there either, and my flip-flops kept flip-flopping off my feet as I tried to run. When I came back to the barn, there was Snowflake but not Blue. So I went in the other direction, down to the lake, and there was Blue, browsing on the water plants. "Feeeeed!" I neighed, and she followed me back to the barn. So all was well, but I was worried for a while. This week I also met a cute little green frog in our newspapers two mornings, and a midnight black spider, and a crow on the top of our closest power pole. I thought its head and beak should be bigger, but I was led astray by cartoon crows, you know, like Heckle and Jeckle, which are not realistic at all. Someone is waxing sarcastic at my expense in a fanzine now because I said it was inhumane of him to routinely squish spiders; he wants to know how humanity can relate to spiders. How can it not? But I doubt anything I say can educate that sort. Meanwhile we have two azalea bushes still making lovely red flowers. They're supposed to bloom in early spring, maybe FeBlueberry, and these did—and never stopped. Which reminds me of all the trees we saw in the section of St. Petersburg we visited: you could hardly see the houses among them. That's nice; maybe houses don't *have* to displace trees.

Am I boring you yet? You're so silent. Kathy asked whether I ever phoned you, and I said no, because I don't think you can talk well enough yet, and I couldn't hear the talk-board if you pointed to words on it. With horses you can't tell what they're thinking unless you watch their ears, which move freely. But I can't see your ears, either.

Well, let me tell you one more thing. This week we had a water filter system installed, because we have sulfur and iron in the water. The one smells bad and the other stains my teeth. The man warned us that for a couple of weeks the deposits in our pipes from the water would be flaking off, now that it's pure, so we shouldn't worry if we see things in it. Well, just so long as I don't see big hairy things in it that look back at me! They had to cut off our water for several hours to install it, so when I brushed my teeth I had to take a cup of cold water from the refrigerator to rinse my mouth, and I carefully poured the rest over the toothbrush to clean it. I never turned on the tap at all. Then I learned that the water had been reconnected. Sigh. Does that sort of thing ever happen to you? Not recently? Ah, well.

Okay, let me know what was boring about this letter, and I'll cut out those parts next time. Meanwhile, have a harpy therapy session, Jenny. I hope you enjoyed your visit home. I hope your mother survived it.

OctOgre 13, 1989

Dear Jenny,

You have the privilege of being the second person to receive my new-format window-address type letter. I'll pause a moment while you catch your breath; I know the news overwhelms you. What's that? What do you mean, it underwhelms you? Didn't you see the window in the envelope—no? Well, make your daddy fold the letter back into the envelope so he can show you! The thing about this is that it enables me to avoid typing the envelope; if I have the address right in the letter—and I do, because that's put on from my glossary file—it's also right on the envelope. I'm doing this so I can answer fan letters faster, and handle the job myself again, as I did before I got the secretary. For various reasons I'll be phasing out the secretary, one of them being that it can take me two weeks to answer a letter that way, and sometimes I'm in more of a hurry than that. So—what? That wasn't what you were asking? Well then, girl, what *were* you asking? Who the first person to receive my window letter was? You mean you're jealous that you weren't the first? For shame! Do you think I would test such a dangerous new procedure on *you?* No, I tested it on my collaborator Robert E. Margroff. We do the *Dragon's Gold* series novels together, and are about to do the fourth one, *Orc's Opal*. When it worked on his letter, I knew it was safe for yours. Now aren't you sorry you made all that fuss? No? Did I ever tell you how difficult you are? Yes? I thought so.

Brother! I just heard the radio mention casually that the stock market had dropped 190 points today, and I dashed through the house to check with my wife, and cracked my left shoulder into the door frame and scraped my elbow and wrist. Ouch! Why? We have some stocks, is why; I hate it when they plummet. In the old days when I had nothing to invest, I rooted for the stock market to set new lows, but now I don't. Oh, you mean the door frame? It seems to have survived. For a minute I thought maybe you cared about my bashed shoulder—Ha! I see that smile! You were teasing me! And you say I shouldn't go dashing around the house between paragraphs? Well, maybe you have a point.

However, just in case there's a smirk still in you, let's talk about arithmetic. Yes, I thought that would sober you up. But it can be fun the way I do it now. Unblink your eyes; I tell you it's true. You see now I have this program that can cut and paste the numbers and do the math for me, so I don't even have to type them in. If you did your math that way, you'd never make a mistake. That way you might even learn not to detest it too much. Maybe. Possibly. Conceivably.

Meanwhile, how are things here? This morning I saw the sunrise as I biked back from fetching the newspaper. The sun was under the clouds, so they were red underneath. But there were a couple of clouds sitting on the horizon, like mountains, having nowhere else to go without falling off the edge of the world, and they cast shadows. So there were these two radiating bands of gray shadow crossing the red. I never saw the effect before. And last time I mentioned the little green frog in the newspaper box; yesterday I brushed what I thought was a green leaf from my pocket, and it jumped: it was the frog, hitching a ride on me. I was going to take it home, but it jumped off halfway there. So I shooed it off the drive, to be sure no one would run over it; I hope it finds good flies there.

Today was a scary day. It's Friday the Thirteenth, and there's a computer virus that's supposed to wipe out systems on this date. So yesterday I backed up everything, just in case. But there was no problem; evidently my systems are not infected. Say—maybe that virus got into the stock exchange computers, and that's why the horrendous drop! But the investors are like chickens, spooking at anything, so probably when they learned it was Friday the Thirteenth, there it went.

I ran on the treadmill again today. I set it at seven miles an hour, which is comfortable for me, and it kept slowing, then speeding up again, and in half an hour it showed 2.99 miles. So it was averaging six miles an hour instead of seven. It's malfunctioning, and I want to complain—after all, it cost $900—but my wife says that's just the way it is. The world's a pretty sorry place when equipment is expected not to function properly, even when new. I like the exercycle better, but my knees bend too far and start hurting, so I can't go as hard as I want. So that's not ideal either. Sigh.

I'm seeing more articles about the tragedy of the forests. In Brazil they are destroying one of the last great rain forests, and ruining the world's climate in the process. But we're no better here, as special logging interests cut down the Alaskan Tongass forest, with the few remaining virgin stands we have. A TV program was going to expose it, but the logging interests threatened to boycott the sponsors, and most of them dropped out. So the forest keeps getting cut, so someone can make a dollar today, though the world go into terminal funk tomorrow. I am disgusted. So are you, I think.

Meanwhile on a more positive local note: this week a TV station decided to see whether Duracell or Eveready batteries were better. They put them into two toy piggies, and the piggies oinked, wiggled their noses and walked. Which one would go longer? They thought it would be over within three hours, but when the time came for the evening program both piggies were still snuffling along. Next day they were still doing it. Finally today, just in time for this letter, after thirty hours running time, the Duracell piggy gave out. The Eveready was still going, the winner. Actually, both types of battery were impressive; in my day it seemed that a battery would last ten minutes and poop out. Those were certainly cute piggy toys, though!

Bunch of enclosures this time, mostly comics and cartoons I thought were fun; you may have seen some already. The No Cent man sent me more "money," so here are his "one world" and "hug" coins. I liked the picture on the Business section, with its treacherous path; try cruising your wheelchair along that one at speed! And ALLIGATOR EXPRESS. Most of the contributors are younger than you, so I thought I wouldn't send it, but I liked the "Tropical Depression" cartoon with its sad cloud, so here it is.

Have a harpy day, Jenny, and say "Hi" to Kathy for me. Your mother tells me you folk are calling me "Uncle Xanth." I must be writing uncley letters! Oh—you say you want a purple dinosaur on your letter, because I put a blue one on Kathy's letter? Okay, this time.

OctOgre 20, 1989

Dear Jenny,

You would not believe my day! Here it is quarter to seven in the evening, when I had nothing to do today except your letter and one other. Now I'll have to scramble to get yours done. Let me tell you about it—what? You're not interested? Okay, then, you tell me about your day.

. . . .

Jenny, you'll have to speak up! All I heard was a row of dots.

****

Well, that's louder, but now it sounds like a row of asterisks. Did I tell you the poem about the asterisk? I don't remember. I don't think I have. Okay, here it is now: Mary had a pair of skates/ With which she loved to frisk/ Now wasn't she a foolish girl/ Her little *

You don't get it? Well, don't have your mother read it, idiot! Have your daddy read it, and make sure he pronounces the * (asterisk) at the end. Oh, now you get it!

Here's something I heard on the radio this week: "A theologian is one who answers questions no one is asking." You don't think that's funny? Well, how about this one—what? Oh, you've decided to listen to my day after all? Are you sure? How sweet of you!

It started at 5:30 A.M., when all was dark. I woke to the sound of a faint beep-beep-beep. That's what my power-supply box says when the current is off. Was the power off? So I got up and barefooted it down to the study wing of the house—and the lights were on. They hadn't been on before. My daughter Cheryl was home overnight, visiting from college; was she there? No, the room was empty—and no beep-beep. Not there, anyway; now I heard it behind me. From the bedroom I had just left? I padded back, but it wasn't from the bedroom either. It was from downstairs. Was it the security alarm system? But that doesn't go beep-beep, it goes WHOOO-WHOOO-WHOOO!! earsplittingly. Maybe it *wasn't* a burglar in the house. So I went downstairs. It was coming from the kitchen. I turned on the light.

Are you bored yet? Well, I thought that since you

weren't too keen on hearing about my day—oh, all right, I'll continue. (I'm just getting you back for saying you weren't interested.)

I turned on the light, and the beep was coming from the phone answering machine. A light was flashing, and the beeping was continuous. But that's not the way it usually works. I peered at it, but couldn't make out which button was glowing without my glasses. So I went back upstairs to the bedroom, fetched my glasses, came back down, peered again, and it said RECORDING. Recording? I lifted the phone: dial tone. What was it recording—a message from Mars? I didn't dare fool with the machine, because it tends to erase automatically. On Tuesday when we were away, all hell broke loose—uh, rephrase that: your mother called, and then, well, let's leave that until a later paragraph. So I went up and woke my wife. I didn't like to do it, because her natural hours are midnight until noon for sleeping, or would be if I didn't drag her up at 8:30 to face the day, but if there was something important on that machine, such as news of the San Francisco earthquake headed this way, we'd better find out. She came down and checked it out: no message. The thing was malfunctioning. But it did finally produce a message: the one your mother had left, which had disappeared after one playing. Time travel, maybe? The message jumped from Tuesday to Friday without passing GO or collecting $200—oops, wrong game.

But how about that light turned on in the study? All the outer doors were locked; no one was prowling. How could something turn on the light and leave an un-message on the machine? We concluded that there must have been a power surge. That light switch is a touch-type: you just tap it to turn it on or off, rather than switching it. A surge might have had the same effect as tapping. And might have bollixed the answering machine. All our computers and things are protected by surge suppressors, but not that answering machine. Yes, sad to say, a prosaic answer; no Martians. Sorry about that.

But of course I was sound awake by this time. My wife went back to sleep, but I fixed breakfast and went back to the study—with its lights conveniently on—and made notes in my P file (that's P for Piers, where I record my passing thoughts on things) and edited 500 more words of *Tatham Mound*, about how de Soto met the lovely Indian Lady of Cofitachequi who lived not all that far from where you live now, who gave him a string of pearls that wound three times around her lovely body. Yes, that's historical; it really happened. Then de Soto took the Lady captive and forced her to come with his army. Yeah, some hero! The factual parts of this novel will open some eyes, I trust. Then on with horsefeeding, newspaper—our temperature had plunged to 43.5° Fahrenheit, having had lows of about 70° before—yes, I *know* it gets colder than that without even trying, in Virginia, but this is Florida. One newspaper was on the ground instead of in its paper-box, and scattered across the landscape; the new deliverer is a mess. I gathered six parts and thought I had it all, but a major section was missing.

Then on to that other letter: after two months I was writing to that libertarian-style fanzine that decided to practice censorship when I introduced the fan who is a murderer to it. I had pondered in the interim, and, like your mother, decided to do the right thing: that is, to let them have it in the face with both barrels. I can be eloquently cutting when annoyed. Then I went through to comment on what others had said about other things, including one sap who accused me of using my vegetarianism as "a highly specious platform from which to air [my] sense of superiority." No, I hadn't mentioned vegetarianism; it's just one of those things I don't make a secret about, but to each his own life-style. He just wanted to pick a fight with me, because he had said he considered it humane to squish innocent spiders, and I said we evidently differed on what was humane. So as you can see, this character needed special treatment, and I think he will not forget what I said to him, which relates to sociopathic behavior. But it took a bit of time to say it just right.

Now it's quarter to six, tomorrow, OctOgre twenty-oneth. I couldn't finish this letter on the same day, after that late start, and then I woke up early, so I thought, well, Jenny's waiting, so here I am. Do you see how dark it is outside?

Where were we? Sociopathic behavior—you haven't encountered that term? Of course you haven't, Jenny; you're a nice girl. It's a fancy term for folk without conscience, really mean people, like the drunk who hit you with his car. People the world would be better off without.

I was mostly through that letter by noon, but then had to quit to exercise, because my wife and daughter—Cam and Cheryl—had to drive back to New College and I didn't want to make them late. You see, I never ran my three miles when my wife was away (well, there was a time, when her mother was dying, and she was away for most of a month, but apart from that, no) just in case I took a fall and needed help, and now that I'm using the cycle or treadmill—the cycle seems better—it's the same. So I cranked up on the cycle, moving at 18 miles an hour according to its reckoning, and was nine and a half minutes through my half hour, when the phone rang. It was my agent in New York. So I stopped and talked to him, and that took about 45 minutes, and then the girls had to leave, so I never did finish my exercise and take my shower. Sigh. Now my beard is all itchy; I'll take that shower today.

What's that? What did the agent say? Jenny, that's none of your business! Now back to this letter.

. . . .

. . . .

You mean you didn't listen to my last two lines? Why not?

. . . .

Will you stop giving me the silent treatment! What use is it to type this letter if you just tune it out?

* * * * * * * * * * * * * * * * * * * *

Oh. Sigh. Okay, I apologize for saying it was none of your business. He talked mostly about how *Man From Mundania* was on the bestseller lists, so the publisher is pleased, and how we will market *Tatham Mound* when I finish it later this month, because that one has the potential to be a major mainstream bestseller. We hope. And about setting up a contract with Richard Pini for turning *Isle of View* into comic form. Yes, you'll get to see the first copy! Are you satisfied? Then why aren't you smiling? Ah, there's that smile!

So then I had lunch and read my incoming mail and went back to the letter, because it was time to begin *your* letter. And the men came to work on our front gate: they have to install a radio transmitter that can signal the gate to open, because it's about half a mile away as the crow flies, and longer as the car drives. Naturally this happens when my wife is away, because she's the one who knows about these things. So I showed the man our attic where he thought some wiring might be, and what he needed wasn't there, and things were all complicated, because that's what happens when my wife is away, much the same as what happens to you when your mother is away. Complications wouldn't dare happen to your mother, but when she's off having her face mangled then the complications come right after you; isn't that the way it is?

Speak of the—let me rephrase that. At this point, your mother called, with several pages on her mind. She was furious. No, she hadn't been reading this letter! At least, I don't think so. No, she wasn't mad at me. Someone at Cumbersome Hospital did something phenomenally stupid, and—ah, now you understand. She was fit to be tied—no, what I mean is, she had a mind to tie someone else up in concrete and throw him in the deep deep sea and run a submarine over him. Twice. No, I didn't succeed in calming her; she succeeded in riling *me* up. Next time you talk to her, you can ask her about what happened, and then hunker down for the storm. I mean, if you want to know what it was like in Charleston when Hurricane Hugo hit . . . However, it wasn't all bad. She told me that the Navy has learned about your case: how you were sort of nothing until I sent you a letter—what do you mean, what letter? The *first* letter! The interesting one.—and then you turned around and faced back toward this world instead of the abyss. I think they want to mention that in their publicity somewhere. Okay, Jenny, if you don't mind, I don't. Do you think they'll give us a ride on a ship? Oh, you get seasick? So do I. Cancel that.

So finally I finished that letter, and started on yours, and that was my day. Wasn't that fascinating?

. . . .

Sigh. Well, let me tell you about Tuesday. No, wipe that look of disgust off your face; I don't mean the whole day. Just the afternoon. My wife wanted to go see the movie *When Harry Met Sally* so I reluctantly dragged myself away from the computer and went with her. No, of course I don't like relaxing; I'm a workaholic. So we went—and naturally that's when all the phone calls came in: your mother, Franklin Mint, and Morrow the publisher. Somehow they knew when I would be out. What's that? What did Franklin Mint want? Well, they hadn't heard of *Man From Mundania* and were confused when I mentioned it. I got a bit disgusted, but by the time they called back again they had read the novel and appreciated the "Frankinmint" pun in it. That's a plant which gives access to the Magic Mountain the Franklin Mint folk made for their Xanth figures, to be put on the market soon. "You must have thought me a perfect idiot," the woman said, and I did not demur too strenuously. Oh, you weren't asking about that, but about Morrow? They wanted to know whether I would autograph books at a Waldenbooks store near a convention I'm going to. Yeah, I guess I will, grumble. But the movie was fun. No, I'm not sure it's suitable for you; you'll have to ask your mother about that. She said you listened to *With A Tangled Skein* on the talking books tape; did you survive that? You did? Okay, then maybe the movie is okay for you; it has less violence. It's about a young man and young woman who drive together from Chicago to New York, sharing costs and taking turns driving, and they really don't get along all that well. He eats grapes and spits the seeds out the window, only the window isn't open. Splat! But ten or more years later they become friends, and finally fall in love; it just took time to develop.

Speaking of movies: someone sent me a copy of the Dr. Who episode that was never broadcast or finished, because of a strike in England when they were making it. My daughter Cheryl is a Dr. Who freak, so I saved it until she was home so we could watch it together—and it turned out to be a copy of a copy, visually and sonically garbled so we really couldn't follow it. Ah, well. Next night we watched one my wife bought, because the price had come way down cheap: *Who Framed Roger Rabbit?* Now there's a movie I can recommend to you (so you can let your mother read this part of this letter). It's a mixture of live actors and cartoons, which sounds pretty hokey, but it does come together, and I know you'll like it. The bouncer at a bar really is a monstrous gorilla, and there are other jokes, and Roger's cartoon wife is impossibly sexy, but you do get to care about Roger Rabbit and what the mean folk are trying to do to him. Yes, the meanest is a sociopath.

So I'd better wrap this up. Sorry if I bored you.

. . . .

Jenny, you're supposed to protest sincerely that oh, no, you weren't bored at all! You're not supposed to make a silent agreement. That's called social awareness. It's one of the forms of lying which society approves. Everyone knows that. Ask Kathy. See? Shall we try it again?

Sorry if I bored you . . . Oh, thank you so much for saying that!

OctOgre 27, 1989

Dear Jenny,

Sigh. Remember when I was way late starting my letter to you last Friday? This time it's later. The time is 7:24:06 P.M.—that's right from my time button on the computer—and supper is at 8:00. Well, I'll continue tomorrow morning. So what happened? Well, I have stopped with the secretary—what do you mean, stopped *what?* Stopped using her. Will you stop tittering?! For my mail. What did you think? The letters were running as high as ten errors per page, and it excruciated me to send them out with all those corrections. So now I'm doing it myself again, on the computer; that's why I set up with these letter macros. So I started in on three days' accumulated mail, and then more came in today, so I've done twenty letters today, and that's why I'm so late. But I'm almost caught up, except for one to your mother and the other Jenny's mother. I'll keep plowing through and try to get everything in tomorrow's mail.

What's that? No, I *wasn't* frittering away my time! That pile of 20 letters contained things like a contract on the reprint of a story, and one to my collaborator Robert E. Margroff about the fourth novel in our fantasy series, *Orc's Opal*, which I'm about to start revising, and one to Philip José Farmer about my collaboration with him. You see, I was editing the first chapter, which is my 26 year old story about Tappy, the girl who—ah, I see you remember. But I couldn't leave well enough alone, and now it's about a thousand words longer than it was. No, I improved it. Oh, you don't believe it? You don't think I can write better now than I could twenty six years ago? Well, maybe I can't, but I can still revise something. Anyway, I do like that story and I mean to read it to you, Jenny. Sometime, somewhere, someway. You just have to promise to remain 13 years old until I do. Then you can judge whether it's improved. Anyway, so some of those letters were complicated and took time. The only other thing I did was exercise on the cycle. How far did I go this time? What does that have to do with it? I mean, I cycle for half an hour regardless. So let's get back to business—you still want to know? Jenny, have I told you how aggravating you can be when—oh, last week? And the week before? Sigh. Okay, 9.6 miles. That would translate into about 3.2 miles on the treadmill, but the treadmill now just grinds and staggers even when I'm not on it; it's definitely a bum machine. I like the cycle better anyway. So will you take my word, I wasn't wasting time? What's that? Why did I leave your letter until last? Well, I can answer that, Jenny: because I wanted to do your letter, and I didn't want to do the others, so I did the chores first so that they would be out of the way. Now aren't you sorry about your suspicion? You're pretty quiet, all of a sudden!

You know, it was a job completing *Mound!* It's 815 pages in manuscript, about 204,000 words. But the emotional aspect is wearing, too. I care about the characters in it, and now I'm through with them. There's Tale Teller, of course, but also Tzec, whose mother was Mayan but sold into slavery in barbarian Florida. Tzec was nine winters old when Tale Teller met her; then he met her again fifteen winters later and she married him. She had had it in mind all the time. She was forty-four winters old when the small pox evil spirits killed her and she was buried in Tatham Mound. If the white man hadn't come, bringing his deadly diseases, which may have killed nineteen of every twenty Indians in the western hemisphere, and then had the gall to claim the land was unpopulated—well, I have mixed emotions.

So how are things with you, Jenny? Well, yes, I know the routine gets dull. But apart from that? Well, if I told you I know how to break that routine, would you believe me? No? Ah, well.

Meanwhile, back here, things continue. I received a call from the man who was going to clear another dozen or so acres for us, to put in more pine trees. But in the intervening year since we made that plan, I have slowly changed my mind. I have seen how the bunnies live in the palmetto and small brush, not the pines. That's the natural wilderness, while the pines are planted, and the local wildlife isn't adapted to them. I don't want to cut the habitat of that wildlife. So I told him I was sorry, but no: I no longer wanted to clear those acres. And do you know what? No, he didn't throw a fit because of lost business. He said he likes wildlife too, and prefers to keep land natural when he can. He clears land when he is hired to handle that, but he doesn't like it. So he was glad I had changed my mind. That brightened my day.

What else? Well, it is getting closer to the time when we'll see about making that video movie of *A Spell for Chameleon*. I learned that they will start with live actors, then remake them into animation. I guess they go over the film, and the live actors become models for drawing over—Jenny, you must understand this sort of thing better than I do! I've been out of art a long time. But it should result in extremely realistic animation, and that's what I want: animation so real that you can't be sure it *is* animation. What's that? What about the Elfquest folk and their project? Well, that seems pretty firm, now; they'll do Xanth

#13, *Isle of View* in comic format. Oh—that's right, I said you could be there to help negotiate the contract. You *would* remember that! As I recall, you pulled one of your fits, and—no, don't pull another! It's bad enough when your mother does it, without you proving whose daughter you are. We'll see, we'll see; with Xanth magic, you can never tell what may happen.

Speaking of Xanth, I may have to write two Xanths next year. One a year is comfortable; two may be a bit much. No, they won't be as good as the one Jenny Elf is in. Unless she's in one. I don't know yet. You see, at the end of *View* her future is in doubt; for all we knew she might go back to Elfquest. But with the Elfquest folk handling her in Xanth, maybe she'll like Xanth well enough to stay. Sammy's with her, remember. Xanth #14, *Question Quest*, is pretty well locked in; Jenny Elf might appear in a bit part, but no more than that. But if I have to do *The Color of Her Panties* the same year—what? You want to know why I may do two in one year? Because this is a paperback series, but we might want it to go hardcover, and the way to do that would be to do two so that they could publish the hardcover edition of #15 the same time as the paperback of #14 and the paperback readers would still have one a year, same schedule, instead of having to wait an extra year for the hardcover edition to clear. We're thinking of the readers, see. What do you think? Should I write *Panties* next year too?

OctOgre 28, 1989—Yes, it's next morning now; I zoomed as far as I could, but I couldn't finish this letter last night. So have you thought about whether I should write two Xanths next year? I mean, you've had a whole night to ponder the matter. Don't tell *me* you haven't; there's one date at the top of this letter, and another just now, so I know a day has passed!

Well, on to the enclosures. Do they show you "Garfield" each day? I can't be sure they are taking proper care of you, so I cut out this week's adventure. I mean, Garfield is a brown cat, so he's in your department. He was snoozing, and he dreamed, and this is his dream: of the far future when everyone else is gone. It concludes with a message about imagination. So here are the strips for your collection, and your homework is to think about that business of imagination.

Other items: how to magically figure out someone's age using math. Little color map showing the path of Hurricane Jerry, back when. Another year when it's Hurricane Jenny, it'll be much worse. A chart showing how the stock market plunged, that day. You know, when I banged my shoulder into the doorframe. If you think of the stock market as a landscape, this is a mountain that became a cliff. Wheeee—crash! A picture of a house. It's an ad, and I couldn't cut out all the ugly print, but the house is nice enough. Your mother has something like this in mind for you, with an elevator in the center and a pony out back. And inside is your room with a computer and a light fixture which looks like a rocket ship crashing through the ceiling. An ad for a toaster made in the shape of two pieces of toast. A cartoon about how a witch turned her publisher into a frog. That's simple justice. Clipping about a killer whale making friends with a Norwegian ferry. "Curtis." And one I don't generally send, "Sally Forth," about you and your mother. Plus three for your mother relating to computers and such, including definitions of common computer terms such as "End User: one born every minute." If you don't see what's funny, ask your daddy to explain about Barnum the circus man.

Okay, Jenny, that's it for this week. I want you to promise to be in a better mood next week, and to figure out whether I should do two Xanths next year instead of one. Wave "Hello" to Kathy for me. No, not with one finger; use the whole hand, dummy! That's better.

November 1989

A new roommate. A plane takes off. A plane lands. A little girl goes for a ride. And a happy coincidence.

NoRemember 3, 1989

Dear Jenny,

I just got off the phone with your mother, and she says she finally told you something, I forget what, and—what's that? Well, how do you expect me to remember everything your mother says? Something about her jawbone growing back the wrong way, and—that's not it? I think she also said I needn't bother to write you a letter next week. Oh, are you getting tired of them? Well, I can't think what else—OUCH! Why did you run your wheelchair over my foot?!

Oh, that's right, now I remember: we'll finally get to meet! I'm going to Sci-Con 11, and by an odd coincidence you're going there too (I'm sure they'll let us in, even if we're not 11), and we can meet all the artists. They already have me jammed in with things, like autographing at Waldenbooks Saturday morning, so I probably won't see you when you arrive, but Saturday afternoon will be open. I will want to talk to you, and sing you a song, and hold your hand—you mean you thought that was an empty threat? Ha! You'll have just a few hours to do the whole convention, thanks to that man your mother is running the submarine over. But you should find it interesting. Then on Sunday I'll visit you at the hospital, so I can read "Tappy" to you (provided you're still 13), and to Kathy also if she's interested. I gather she graduated to another ward, but you still keep in touch.

Meanwhile, it's the usual mouse-race here. A college magazine wanted to interview me, and by the time the publisher forwarded their request, it was a day past their deadline, so I phoned them, and they interviewed me by phone from 9 to 10 last night. About the only other thing of note was a good review in PUBLISHERS WEEKLY. No, that was astonishing; they *never* give me good reviews, only thinly veiled sneers. Must be a new reviewer who didn't get the word, and he'll be fired when the chief editor finds out. I mailed out the copies of *Tatham Mound*, and now I'm typing *Orc's Opal*—except that 22 letters piled in yesterday, after I answered 160 last month, and 10 more today. Sigh. I don't suppose you take dictation? Only in your off hours, I'm sure. Ah, well, I have found out how to assign more functions to my computer keys, and these facilitate my letters, so I'll just have to wrap this one up and get on into that pile of 30 letters. I don't think I need to write you a long missive this time; I'll save up whatever I have to tell you until next week, and save the postage. I hope you will have half an hour or so to talk to me, before the teeming masses of fans come charging in demanding your attention. Maybe I'll hide behind your wheelchair so they won't find me.

CONVENTION

We started Friday morning, driving down to the Tampa Airport, and Cam (my wife) put me on the airplane to Charlotte, North Carolina. The plane left late, and I worried that it would arrive too late to make its connection, stranding me; that happened to me with buses, and

I'm sure the plane companies have picked up and improved on all the old bus and train tricks. They served a snack, consisting of a ham and turkey sandwich. That's one of the reasons I don't like to travel: airlines hardly know what a vegetarian is. I took out the meat and ate the rest without joy; the meat would only be thrown away, so my gesture accomplished nothing. Oh, we could have ordered a vegetarian meal, ahead; but when we did that before, they gave us some kind of Oriental dish that was so fiery hot it was impossible to eat. They do have ways to make you regret making such demands. At Charlotte I found the connecting flight; it was supposed to take off from one gate, but they had changed gates and I had to go searching for the new one. That's another reason I don't like to travel. The plane left the terminal on time, but waited twenty minutes in the queue for the ten preceding planes to take off. It was listed as "on time" but was actually twenty minutes late, which suggests that since airlines may be penalized for running late, they find ways to conceal rather than correct their lateness. When it comes to travel paranoia, I yield to none.

I was met by Jenny's parents, and the ten-minute drive to the hotel took an hour: the lateness of the plane had put us deep into rush hour, and the road patterning was abysmal. Why I don't like to travel: let me count the ways . . .

Jenny's folks had taken out three rooms at the Holiday Inn Executive Center, which was the convention hotel for Sci-Con 11. Two were for their use, and one for mine. They had put mine directly across the hall from theirs, but that one was the Con Suite, open and crowded all hours; I'm glad they bumped mine down the hall a bit, as I don't think I could have slept very well in the Con Suite. As it was, my room was quiet; I never even turned on the TV set the whole time I was there. The convention folk were glad to see me; I had turned down their invitation, months ago, then changed my mind when I saw how close it was to where Jenny was. I had said I would go to the convention if Jenny did, and though Jenny was limited to one day because of a late reversal of policy by a doctor, she definitely would be there on Saturday. I met Debbie, the Con Chairman, and Cathy, programming. Along with my con badge I got a button: DEBBIE DOES SCI-CON. Well . . .

I attended the Opening Ceremony, so that the fans could see which professionals had arrived. Laurence Watt-Evans officiated, and we each said a few words. I asked folk not to take my ogre reputation too seriously: "You only need to talk with me five seconds to know that I'm no threat to you." It happened that five artists who had worked with Xanth were attending, and Richard Pini of Elfquest also drove down from New York state at my behest: he too will be working with Xanth, setting up the graphic version of #13, *Isle of View*, which features Jenny Elf from the Elfquest world. Richard and I have been interested in doing a project like this since we met at the American Booksellers Association convention in Dallas in 1983, but it never quite jelled until Jenny came on the scene.

At 9 P.M. I talked with folk in the Con Suite, which was so noisy that I could not distinguish anyone's words from more than three feet away, and was in danger of wearing out my voice before my reading came up. I was surrounded by eager fans. I can take conventions or leave them; my pride is such that I already know I can write well, even if this is news to critics, and I am not driven to hear it personally from fans. But I can survive adulation too, though I would rather be home writing my next novel. It is my policy to make myself available to fans when I go to conventions, and to avoid them at other times. I had a green ice cream sandwich there, which served for supper.

My reading was at 9:30, from *Isle of View*, introducing Jenny Elf, and then in the Author's Note introducing Jenny herself. I explained that she would be there, and that though she would understand what was said to her, she was paralyzed and would not be able to respond readily. I felt that with this caution, the folk at the convention would treat her well. I was not disappointed; they made her more than welcome.

Saturday was the big day. I had breakfast at 6:30 with Richard Pini, and we discussed the prospects for the graphic novel. It should be published in three parts, the first part preceding the text novel and the third part following it. We hope that this combination will introduce Xanth readers to Elfquest, and Elfquest readers to Xanth, and be a success. Wendy Pini will not be drawing it; she has other commitments. But they have a good artist in mind, and it should be an impressive volume, and a ground-breaking one: the first cross between these two fantasy realms, unified by Jenny Elf.

I met Toni-Kay, here at my behest, and her friend Barbara, from New Jersey. I have corresponded with Toni-Kay for years, and have several nice paintings of hers—duck, rabbit, horse, piliated woodpecker, alien creature—generally naturalistic, rounded and soft, like Toni-Kay herself. She credits me with turning her back into painting; she may be too generous, but certainly art is in her nature. I had commissioned a painting of cats from her, for me to give to Jenny, and prevailed on her to bring it herself. Because Jenny could not stay the night, the room was available for Toni-Kay and Barbara to use without charge, and Jenny's family welcomed them. I understand they were most compatible—four Avon Ladies, they said—and perhaps that will be a lasting friendship. Things just seemed to come together in special ways for this occasion.

Jenny arrived at midmorning, and after she had gotten settled—travel is difficult for her, because she gets carsick in addition to her paralysis—I went in to meet her. I have no trouble facing audiences of any size, having long since abolished stage fright along with writer's block, but I felt a bit of nervousness at that moment. I was finally going to meet *Jenny!* There she was in her wheelchair and her big spectacles, looking just like Jenny Elf only with rounded ears. She can move her limbs somewhat, but has real control only in her right hand, so she is able to finger-spell, slowly. She can turn her head and move her eyes, and will blink to say yes. She suffered multiple injuries and fractures in the accident, but apparently it is damage to the brain stem that is responsible for the paralysis. I think of it as being like a cable that has been mostly severed; only a few strands connect, and it is problematic whether others can be reconnected because the doctors don't know what is supposed to go where, and might make things even worse if they messed in. She was twelve when it happened, and is now thirteen, becoming a young woman. She can move her jaw, but not enough to close her mouth completely. She can not speak, but can laugh. I sat before her, and took her hand, and tuned out the rest of the world. [What I said to her is a personal report, "Let Me Hold Your Hand," personal and intense.]

Let Me Hold Your Hand

On Saturday, NoRemember 11, 1989, I met Jenny in her hotel room at the Sci-Con 11 science fiction convention. She was in her wheelchair, wearing her big glasses (Mundane spectacles), unmoving, expressionless—or, as her family later described it, rapt. This is what I said to her, from memory—or perhaps what I meant to say, as I may have garbled words or sentences and gotten things out of order. I tuned out the others present; it was Jenny and me in the foreground, and the rest of the world in the background. There was an interruption at one point, and I lost my thread and skipped part of what is here. So this written version may be more complete and precisely worded, though the emphasis and feeling are muted here; the essence is the same.

* * *

Jenny, I have to do things my own way, and I don't always go directly to the point. So bear with me while I say some things which may seem irrelevant; I will get to the subject in due course.

When I was in college I learned a folk song, "Come Let Me Hold Your Hand." The refrain referred to Peel and John Crow, and at first I thought it was racist. But it isn't; it is Jim Crow who is the symbol of racism in the south. As far as I know, these are real crows: Peel and John, who sit in the treetop and watch what's going on below.

When I wrote the first Incarnations novel, *On A Pale Horse*, I incorporated a line from that song. It was in a scene with a woman who had just had her father die. She loved him and missed him, and all she could think of was this song. This happens to people suffering grief; they have to block out the big thing, and focus on some little thing that is not so closely connected. So she thought of the way he had held her hand, and that bit of the song kept going through her mind. "It's a long time, girl, may never see you; come let me hold your hand."

But when I got the galley proofs, I discovered that the song was missing. In fact the whole scene was missing. It turned out that the editor thought I was borrowing from a Beatles song, and was afraid of copyright infringement. Now that song wasn't from the Beatles; it was before the Beatles existed. Their song is "I Wanna Hold Your Hand." But the editor would not relent, and though I got the scene put back, I had to make up other words in lieu of the song that weren't as good. I regret that, and I am getting more difficult about editorial interference in my novels.

When I got in touch with you, I remembered that song. Now I will sing it to you, as I said I would in my letter:

> *It's a long time, girl, may never see you; come let me hold your hand.*

> *It's a long time, girl, may never see you; come let me hold your hand.* [At this point I reached forward and took her right hand with my left hand; the remainder of the song and monologue was with our hands held.]
>
> *Peel and John Crow sit in the treetop; pick up the blossom; let me hold your hand, girl, let me hold your hand.*
>
> *It's a long time, girl, may never see you; come let me wheel and turn.* [Repeat line, and refrain: Peel and John Crow.]
>
> *It's a long time, girl, may never see you; we all shall wheel and turn.*
>
> [Repeat first verse. It's not that I'm a great singer, but that this song now relates to my feeling for Jenny, and to the theme of this discussion.]

It's been a long time, girl, since I met you, and longer since you met me, because you knew me through my novels, while I learned of you only when I received your mother's first letter. Now we have met personally, for the first time.

It is said that a person who saves the life of another person is thereafter responsible for that other person. I didn't understand that, at first; it seemed to me that it was the one who was saved who owed the debt. But as time passed I came to appreciate the meaning of it. A person who is dying will not have much concern with this world. Whether he goes to Heaven or to Hell or to nothingness, he is finished here. But if someone else interferes with his life—his death—and brings him back to this world, then he may not be ready for it. He may have had reason to leave this world, and be ill prepared to handle it. So the one who brings him back should at least see that the life he returns to is worthwhile, and that he can cope with it.

When I wrote to you while you were in the coma I

wasn't sure that my letter would bring you out of it, but I gave it the best try I could. Now it may be that you had decided to wake up on your own, the day my letter arrived. That you said to yourself "Well, I've had a good sleep, and it's time to get up. Oh, there's a letter from Piers Anthony? How nice. What's for lunch?"

Was it that way? [Here was the first reaction from Jenny: a trace of a smile, and perhaps a slight squeeze of her hand. Humorous negation: it wasn't that way.]

But maybe you were walking through the valley of the shadow of death, and you faced resolutely toward that other world. Until my hand caught your hand, and held you, and turned you back toward this world.

Now understand, I did not do this alone. When my hand caught yours, my other hand was holding your mother's hand, and her other hand was holding your daddy's hand, and there was a line of therapists and friends extending from our world toward you. [At this point I reached back and put my hand on the arm of the next closest person, Jenny's father, illustrating the chain.] But they could not quite reach you, until I came and added one more link, and finally caught your hand.

So I do feel responsible. The chain needed every link, and I was the last link. I helped bring you back to this world. Then I thought about it, and wondered whether it was right to have done this. If I had brought you back only to a life of paralysis, to a life of no joy—then maybe I had done you no favor. Maybe I should have left well enough alone.

But it was too late. I could not undo what I had done, and I think I would not have changed it if I could have. So I had to justify it.

When I was your age, I was not happy. I had not suffered as you have, yet I reviewed my life, and realized that if I could have the choice of living it over exactly as it had been, or of never existing at all, I would choose not to exist. But that was early in my life. As I lived longer, my life improved, not steadily—it was two steps forward and one step backward—until today I have what is by any standard a very good life. If I had to live it all over now, I would do so.

I realized that I had to do what I could to make your life worth living, so that twenty years from now you can look back and say "Yes, yes, it was worth it, taken as a whole, the bad with the good, and I would do it again." So I wrote to you, and encouraged you, and tried to help you in whatever way I could.

This convention is part of that. I think your salvation lies in art, in your drawing and painting. With the assistance of the computer you may be able to paint as well as you could with full use of your body. There are several good artists here, and they will talk to you. There are many other things to see here, and I think you will enjoy it.

And Richard Pini of Elfquest is here, and he has something for you. [Jenny broke into a great smile.] I will fetch him now.

Then I introduced Richard Pini, and got an immense smile from her. Richard gave her a color portrait of Jenny Elf, painted by Wendy Pini, looking just like Jenny but with pointed ears. He treated her like a little princess, and I could see how thrilled she was. Her two favorite realms are Xanth and Elfquest, and representatives of both were here to be with her. It was my hope that she could have a really good day, and it was coming true.

Then Jenny had to rest, and I went with Toni-Kay to look at the art exhibit. There were many beautiful and strange paintings, my favorite kind. After that I had to go autograph books at a Waldenbooks. They were supposed to have Sci-Con flyers there, but didn't; par for the course. They limited it to hardcovers, so it was not pressed; indeed it was quite slack in the middle of the two hours they had scheduled. But it evidently sold a number of *Total Recalls*, my version of the big Arnold Schwarzenegger movie for next year. I had not had a chance to eat lunch, but they dug up some chocolate doughnuts for me, and I munched on them while signing copies. One of the fans gave me a package of whole wheat crackers and smoked cheese. This business of eating: I am a creature of regular habits, but forget the notion of regular meals during such excursions. Why I don't like to travel, # whatever.

Back at the hotel, I met Jenny in her convention dress: purple satin (I'm a dunce about such things, but that's what it looked like to me) with matching high-heeled shoes: her first pair. She was like a doll. She had a corsage of artificial roses, and she gave me one. I wore it for the rest of the convention, and took it home: my memento of Jenny. Toni-Kay presented the painting she had brought: "Cats in the Window." It showed a cluster of the softest, furriest cats sitting in a boarded cobwebbed window frame. Jenny collects cats; there are twelve at her home, because no stray can be allowed to go unrescued. By one of those supernatural coincidences, the wrapping paper Toni-Kay had chosen matched the shade of Jenny's fancy dress.

Then Richard Pini and I took Jenny to the art exhibit, along with her parents and the therapists from the hospital and Toni-Kay and Barbara, so it was a party of nine or ten. Jenny indicated which paintings she liked, and Jenny's mother entered bids for them. Jenny was really quite choosy; her mind is all there, and only the connections between it and her body are weak. Ron Lindahn gave her his personal tour of his art on display, which art was most impressive; he and his wife Val were the Art Guests of Honor for this convention. I have associated with him for two years, since meeting him at the World Fantasy Con in Nashville and making the compact to produce the Xanth Calendars. Kelly Freas, the dean of genre artists, came to say hello; Jenny met him at a convention years ago, as a child long before the accident, and he remembered her.

We emerged to the main hall, and the folk of the

convention came to meet Jenny. She was the center of attention, surrounded by people, while Richard Pini and I stood back and watched, ignored. That was exactly the way we wanted it. It was Jenny's hour. There was a small woman in an Elfquest costume, and three huge Klingons from *Star Trek* who kissed Jenny's cheek and posed with her for photographs. Jenny has on occasion been treated by other children at the hospital as if she is retarded; she is not, and it was infuriating. She just can't talk or move well. Here at the convention there was none of that; no one talked down to her. They even presented her with an award for best costume.

Finally she had to retire to her room, because she can't remain sitting for long. She was very tired, but also very happy. She hoped to come out again after resting, but couldn't make it. It was unfortunate that everything had to be jammed into a single day; originally she was to stay for the whole convention, so that her excursions could be properly spaced. But the convention folk had done everything I hoped for, and made it a phenomenal experience for her. Jenny was like Cinderella at the Ball, the center of attention for the occasion.

I signed autographs at 5 P.M. After forty-five minutes someone came up and reported "You'll be glad to know that the end of the line is now in the building." It's a good thing we limited it to one title per person! Someone gave me some homemade chocolate chip cookies; I was amidst signing and didn't catch the name, to my regret.

Then we saw Jenny off. They tucked her Xanth cushion behind her head—my wife made that for her, and she keeps it with her—, loaded her into her wheelchair, and the wheelchair into the van and she was gone. She was tired, and I understand was falling asleep already, and that was surely best. But for me, and I think for many others, it was like the lights going down; the main event was over. She had been queen for a day, but now it was done.

In the early evening Richard Pini and I met with Kirby McCauley, who represents both of us, to discuss details of the graphic adaptation of *Isle of View*. Normally an agent represents the writer against the publisher, but this is a special project I'm into for love rather than money; my only concern was that the contract be fair to all parties. I hope the adaptation is a wild success and sells millions of copies and makes everyone rich—but I'll settle for Jenny Elf coming to life in pictures as Jenny's fantasy self.

I went to the Green Room, reserved for guests (as opposed to fans), and inquired what leftovers there were, as I had not had time for supper, and lunch had been those doughnuts. They dug up tofu salad, bagels and hot chocolate, being most accommodating. In fact the convention proprietors were good throughout; I told them how much I appreciated the way they treated Jenny. They knew that I had attended only for Jenny; in fact the program book lists me as the guest of Jennifer Elf, and they donated the proceeds of their Sketch-A-Thon to the Ronald McDonald House in Jenny's name. I think that came to something like $900. I don't have much use for McDonald's, but I certainly approve of their House, which serves the families of those in distress, as it did for Jenny's family when the accident was new and it was uncertain whether Jenny would live, let alone recover.

There were other programs, such as the Costume Dance, but that started at 11 P.M., past my bedtime. I would have stayed up for it if I could have gone with Jenny. As it was, I read myself to sleep on *Conan the Defiant* by Steve Perry; it was one of several books he sent me, when we were setting up for a collaborative project which I then scuttled for reasons unrelated to his merit as a writer. (I turned out six novels—almost 700,000 words—in 1988, and it will be only four in 1989—but one is the 200,000-word historical *Tatham Mound*, perhaps the major novel of my career. My schedule for 1990 stands at five, and I was simply getting overextended.) They say that Robert Jordan is the best Conan writer, but I liked this Perry Conan better than the Jordan Conan I read. Which is not to disparage Jordan; I am highly impressed by his major fantasy.

Sunday morning I discovered what had been there all the time: a big basket of flowers and fruit sent by Jenny's family. I am a professional writer, an experienced observer who notes the nuances as well as the larger picture in all things. So how come I can't see what's under my nose? Had my wife been with me, she would have noticed the basket as we entered the room. But she had to stay home to feed the horses, because both our daughters are now in college and can't do it. This was the first time I had traveled alone since the 1966 Milford Conference. Why I don't like to travel—oh, never mind.

So my meals thereafter consisted of wheat crackers, chocolate chip cookies, bananas, apples and grapes, all provided as gifts from those attending the convention. The pears, unfortunately, were like rocks, being unripe, and the apples were borderline; apparently the folk who provide these items are more interested in appearance than consumption. Thus the best intentions of those who pay for these things are diverted by those who assemble them. I did not dare touch the oranges; the acid sensitizes my teeth, so that I can't even brush them without pain. But the rest helped, and I got through, despite getting sensitive on the left side. Well, a week or so would see that fade. Why I don't like to—forget it.

Ron Lindahn showed me eight of the pictures for the 1991 Xanth Calendar, and they were phenomenal; the artists are outdoing themselves, and it should be an even better calendar than the 1990 edition. I suspect that the existing one is already just about the best calendar in the genre. (I know, I know; let's just leave the critics out of this. They *always* have another opinion. I should mention, however, that there is also an Elfquest Wolfriders Calendar for

1990, and yes, Jenny has one of those too.) I am the sponsor of the Xanth Calendars; I pay for them, Ron Lindahn makes them up, and then we sell the package to the publisher for printing and distribution. That way there is no editorial interference, and we can do the best job for the calendar and the artists. Now if only we can get better distribution . . .

At 10 A.M. I joined Guest of Honor Todd Hamilton for autographing the *Visual Guide to Xanth* only. We were ready, the fans were ready—but it seemed that every copy of the book in eastern Virginia had sold out and neither stores nor distributor had any more. Now this might be taken as an indication of really hot selling—but the truth was unfortunately mundane. The publisher and distributor had simply not provided enough copies. There is nothing like a self-fulfilling prophecy: decide which books will not sell, and distribute few enough copies to guarantee it, never mind how many folk actually want to buy them. It is not the first time I have been rendered from a best-selling author to a low-selling author by the carelessness of others. I had not even received my author's copies, though the book had been on sale for several weeks; Ricia Mainhardt had gotten some from the publisher, and she gave me one for myself and one I could take, suitably autographed, to Jenny. Thus it was that I discovered significant errors in the volume. Sigh. I had gone over the text, but hadn't seen the late charts and illustrations. Most of the fans simply could not get copies, so the signing was a fair flop. This is unfortunately typical. When writers take over the world, things will be run better. Why I don't like to travel to autograph: begin a list. At any rate, I took advantage of the slack to introduce Toni-Kay to Todd, who gave her advice on marketing her art and passed her on to Ron Lindahn, who gave her more that I hope will enable her to move forward in a career in art. In art, as in writing, there are folk who have talent but who aren't into the swing of marketing; the right advice can make a significant difference. You need everything to make it: talent, persistence, good advice, luck and compromise.

At noon I went to the panel on *Marketing Your Writing* which I shared with my agent Kirby McCauley and Ricia Mainhardt, also an agent. My name was underlined, which meant I was the moderator. Ha! I grabbed the mike and started joking about agents. But I think we did manage to provide some solid comment and advice for hopeful writers, and I think it was a good panel.

As soon as it was over, we bugged out. I had a date with Jenny at the hospital. Her father drove me up there; it was about seventy-five miles through lovely autumn-turning forest. It was a nice place, in a parklike setting, with a number of separate buildings. Jenny's ward was much like a nursery school, only with children of all ages. All of them are there for rehabilitation; their degree of incapacity differs. I suspect that two with the greatest body limitation and most alert minds are Jenny and her former roommate Kathy.

I asked whether Kathy could join us, and she came in her powered wheelchair, which she can control with her right hand on a button. Her range of motion seems almost as limited as Jenny's, but she can control the wheelchair and also use her little computer to activate preprogrammed sentences. Her ailment has drawn her mouth up so that her upper teeth and gums show, and she is smaller than Jenny though about six years older. What she lacks in appearance she makes up in personality; she is a sweet girl. It is a fault of our species that we tend to judge by physical appearance rather than inner nature, and folk like Jenny and Kathy suffer unfairly. I had the impression that Kathy was thrilled to have been invited.

I showed Jenny the original drawing from *Visual Guide to Xanth* that Todd Hamilton gave her. I gave her the copy of the *Visual Guide* which Todd and I had autographed for her. Then I presented a little gift of my own: a "magic" quartz crystal, set with a small purple amethyst, on a silver chain. "You expected a *red* amethyst?" Jenny finger-spelled archly to her father. I put it on her, fumbling with the tiny catch. I gave another to Kathy, with a red garnet inset, surely surprising her. Then we went into Jenny's room so I could read to them in private.

What I read was "Tappy," a story I wrote twenty-six years ago and wasn't able to sell. I regard it as the most sensitive one I have done. Two years ago I placed it as the first chapter of the ten-author *Light Years* novel, but when that project foundered I bought it back (actually I'm buying the entire project) and converted it to a collaboration with Philip José Farmer, in which we alternate chapters. Why go to all this trouble for a story? Well, it's a special one, and who would pass up a chance to collaborate with Farmer, one of the remarkable authors of the genre?

So I read it to the two girls, and I believe they liked it. It is an adult story about Tappy, a thirteen-year-old mute girl who was maimed and blinded in the accident that killed her father, orphaning her as a child. The protagonist is a twenty-two-year-old hopeful artist hired to drive her to a clinic in another state. As he comes to know Tappy, his doubts about the nature of his job increase; he fears she is to be incarcerated in an institution so she won't be an embarrassment to her guardians. He stops at a motel in the Green Mountains of Vermont, reads to her from *The Little Prince*, takes her hiking to a mountaintop that seems to fascinate her, and treats her like the human being she is. But he is too feeling; when he attempts to comfort her, he is swept by emotion and makes love to her. He is horrified, well understanding the law on statutory rape. But Tappy gains confidence as he loses it, and leads him up the mountain again at night. At dawn she draws him into a large rock which had been solid by day; it is a portal to elsewhere. Neither of them has reason to remain in our world, and this is their escape. Phil Farmer, in the second chapter, describes the alien world they emerge in, with strange creatures and plants, and an enormous space ship. The novel is on its way.

I read this story because aspects of it are similar to Jenny's situation: Jenny is thirteen, and severely hurt in an accident. Tappy is blind; Jenny is paralyzed. Both are mostly mute, but can hear and understand perfectly. The story's protagonist is a hopeful artist; so is Jenny. Tappy faced the cruelty of indifference or censure by others, because of her condition; so does Jenny. It was a calculated risk, reading a story involving statutory rape to Jenny, but I felt that it is not appropriate to censor adult material that relates so nicely to her situation. The "safe" course would be to read Xanth, with its puns and simple elements, but how long can a person exist on only that level? "Tappy" relates to what is real, despite being the lead-in to what is fantastic. So I risked it, and hope that what I did was right.

Jenny said she liked the story, and I saw Kathy's flash of pleasure when I described the phenomenal new world to which Tappy went. So perhaps the reading was a success. I have read to audiences of hundreds with less trepidation than this! I came to the convention to meet and talk to Jenny, and to read to her, and all the rest of the convention was less important to me than my interaction with Jenny. I never concealed this from the folk of the convention. Instead of being annoyed, they applauded my attitude.

Kathy touched a button on her computer, and it said "Please sign my point sheet." They get points for good behavior and progress, and can use these points somewhat like money for privileges. It's an incentive system that seems to work. The therapists have to sign the sheets, documenting the points earned in each session. What she wanted was an autograph, so I autographed the margin of her point sheet. Then of course Jenny wanted hers autographed too.

As I was leaving, Jenny spelled out something. Her father translated: I had called her Kathy instead of Jenny. Sigh; I do make such slips, and she had caught me.

On the drive back we saw a deer, a stag, standing by the side of the highway. He finally bounded back into the forest. Then we saw a cat who threatened to dash in front of the car, but finally got off the road. Jenny and her mother are vegetarians, as I am; nobody in her family runs over animals.

Back at the convention I talked with Jenny's family, and we went to the late show: we had missed the Lindahns' slide show, but they were rerunning it for the convention personnel. I had not attended a single convention function other than those where I was onstage; I had been busy with autographings, Jenny, and meetings with professionals. Sometime I would like to go to a convention and see the sights and attend the programs, as ordinary fans do, but I fear that is not feasible. The slide show was of Ron and Val Lindahn's paintings, with a musical background, and it was impressive and evocative. They are great artists and great people; I respected Richard Pini and Ron Lindahn before, but after seeing how they treated Jenny, I respect them more. I was also impressed with the convention itself, for similar reason; they all worked together to make this perhaps the greatest experience of Jenny's life since the accident.

Ron Lindahn had me sign his autograph book, in which each person addresses the subject of the Meaning of Life. I pondered, and wrote: "Honor Compassion Realism" and signed it. Each of these words bespeaks volumes in my philosophy.

Monday morning I checked out, using my MasterCard for the first time; it actually worked! I had half expected it to malfunction, because that's the nature of things when I try to handle them. I remember the one time I tried to make the ATM cash vending machine work; it kept giving me error messages, until my wife explained that it was registering cents instead of dollars, and it didn't give out cents. Then why was it registering them? I was just supposed to know without being told that a machine that handled only dollars nevertheless registered numbers in cents. Evidently that makes sense (or cents) to the rest of the world. At any rate my bill was in order, except that they had charged me two dollars more for my restaurant breakfast than the bill had showed at the time. I had left a two-dollar tip on the table; maybe they added it to my bill. I don't claim to comprehend the logic of the world. That two dollars for the tip was the only cash I spent on the trip, which perhaps suggests how I handle money.

Jenny's father drove me to the airport, and this time it really was a ten-minute drive. Everything was going suspiciously well. Could my curse of traveling be giving out? After he left, they canceled my flight. Why I don't like to travel—sigh. They don't do that sort of thing when my wife is along, which is why I hate traveling alone even worse. I wound up on a plane bound north to Baltimore. I was just in time; I think I was the last person to board, and got the last seat available, and it took off right after. Jenny's rose, pinned to my carried jacket, was taking a beating as I bundled in. I know it's artificial; that still bothered me. It was as if Jenny herself was getting battered. I heard that three of us were being routed that way to Tampa. I heard the girl in the seat ahead of me mention Tampa, so I inquired whether she was one of the others. No; she turned out to be a stewardess. Ouch; I found such an innocent confusion acutely embarrassing. Then at Baltimore I inquired and found the gate for the plane to Tampa. They were in the throes of rerouting passengers for a canceled flight to Albany. USAir seemed to be canceling flights all over! I phoned Cam, and after several attempts with the newfangled computer-screened phone managed to get my collect call through to her. Phones don't like me. I caught her about forty-five minutes before she was due to start out to meet the plane I wasn't on. I don't know how we would have connected otherwise. In short, this was normal traveling, for me. I'd rather stay home.

I read during the flights and delays, and managed to finish the Conan novel, and look at two fanzines I had been given along the way. One was *The Knarley Knews*, a small personal production, and the other was *Anvil*, its fiftieth issue, put out by Charlotte Proctor. That's a solid production, but it runs the addresses of those who write it letters, so I won't.

The new plane served a good meal for me. The flight started on time and arrived early. I had an aisle seat near the front; I got out fast and spied Cam studying the schedule to spot my plane, not realizing that it was already in. We hurried to the car and skimmed through the beginning of rush hour; that surely saved us a good chunk of time. That's why I don't check any baggage; not only would they lose it, because of my curse, I would suffer critical delay. As it was, we were an hour late feeding the horses; fortunately they were nice about it. Cam had during my absence put a new picture up in the family room, and set up and filled four new filing cabinets with my year's correspondence. Twenty letters had piled up, and ten more came in the next day, and a dozen more the following day. It was evident that I would get little if any paying work done this week. Sigh; I was back in Mundania.

NoRemember 17, 1989

Dear Jenny,

Well, here I am safely back at home. Your folks probably told you how USAir canceled my plane flight after your daddy left me at the airport. That's why I don't like to travel. They wouldn't do that to my wife, or to your folks, but there I was alone, so they did it. I had to go home by way of Baltimore: that is, I flew north, and then south. I was an hour late feeding the horses. Sigh. But I don't need to go into all that here; I have written up a report on everything that I will send to my family at the end of the month. Yes, you get a copy. I just like to get things written down, before I forget the details. So if you want to know about the convention from my point of view, tell your daddy to read it to you. No, you don't have to! I *know* you were there! Oh—that's not it? I don't know how to read your finger-signs. Do them again slowly. D O E S I T I N C L U D E—oh, yes, it includes what I said to you when we met. That's a separate report, more private, titled "Let Me Hold Your Hand." But why should you care about that? You already know what I said. Oh—you want to make sure I wrote it down right. It really doesn't read as I said it; things that were important just look like dull words, and more time is taken on the trivia than on the essentials. But here's a copy.

Yes, that's what I meant: a copy. I printed one copy on the laser printer, and then took it down to the copy machine we bought yesterday. It's a Mita DC 1205; I think the number means that it makes 12 copies a minute, or five seconds per copy. It does; I timed it. We realized that we have to do a lot of copying, and it's a pain to go into town and feed money into the machine, so we shopped for a copier we could use at home, and this is it. It's so simple to operate that even I feel at ease with it. So your Convention Report is a copy which looks just like the original. Sure, I could have run off more copies on the laser printer, but this is twice as fast, and anyway, I wanted to make sure it worked. The same day we got it, I received a letter from Philip José Farmer asking for a copy of his Chapter 2, which he no longer has; now I'll be able to make it for him. That's the second chapter of our collaborative novel; I read the first chapter to you and Kathy, remember? You don't? When I visited you at the hospital, and accidentally called you Kathy—yes, *that* time. And you are never going to let me hear the end of it, are you! Farmer will now do the fourth chapter, because I've already done the third, and we'll give it to my agent to sell to a publisher. My agent is Kirby McCauley, whom you also met; yes, I know you don't remember, because it was only a few seconds, but he was there. So you see, you are involved, one way or another, in more than one of my projects. When we finish that novel I'll send you a copy, so you can see how it turns out, if you're interested.

Meanwhile, my nose is fauceting; another allergenic front came through, and antiallergy pills for me are like anti-motion-sickness pills for you: they make me sleepy without stopping the allergy. Sigh. Tomorrow McCauley and a man named Wil Nelson will be here, so I can see the five minute sample of the first Xanth video movie and decide whether it's good enough to proceed with. No, that's not the graphic version of *Isle of View*, silly; that's what Richard Pini is doing. This is *A Spell For Chameleon* on video tape. If we do it. If things fall into place. And I'll have a sore nose. This is what my life is like. Yes, I realize that it's not your nose that's sore! It's still a nuisance and a pain.

Let's see: you told me not to write two Xanth novels next year. Was that because you're tired of Xanth? Oh—because you figured I'd be working too hard. Jenny, it's not like that. I'm a workaholic; I'm always working. If I don't do another Xanth novel, I'll be working on something harder, like my novel about the sociopaths. You know, folk like the one who ran you down with his car. It would be more pleasant to be in Xanth. So I may do it, if the publisher really wants it.

Meanwhile, I have some accumulated clippings for you: comics and such. I'll dump them in with the Convention Report. It's not that I'm trying to get rid of you, Jenny, but my dripping nose is making my face hurt, and I just have to lie down somewhere and read something. Otherwise I have to wipe my nose constantly, or it will drip into the computer keyboard, and that's really not best.

Have a good week, and let me know how you liked the convention. What do you mean, *what* convention? The one that came into existence just for you, Jenny, so you could be princess for a day.

NoRemember 24, 1989

Dear Jenny,

Harpy Thanksgiving! Yes, I know it's over for you, but we're in the throes of it here as I write this. No we didn't eat any turkey! We didn't eat any harpy either. We're a family that serves the stuffing without the bird. My two daughters came home from their separate colleges, and we ordered new computers for each of them, and today the man brought them and set them up and the girls are figuring them out. You see, we wanted to get them aligned with us, so they can do homework when they visit home, and so the computers have to be compatible. We got them nice printers, too: they are dot matrix with 24 pins (that's good—ask your mother) that can print regular or script so well it doesn't look like dots at all. Penny grumped because it wasn't a laser printer. Sorry; I don't trust something that expensive in a college situation. All we need is someone spilling iced tea into it. Meanwhile, Cheryl is using my stereo system to transcribe music from her CD disk to her cassette tape, because she has a tape player but no CD player. And I showed the girls how to set underlined words on the screen in blink. Now I've set my own "Bold" in highlighted blink mode. See? **BOLD** Well, I know my screen isn't there; you can just imagine it. Innocent fun. Anyway, we've been busy; how has it been with you?

Your mother was asking for Kelly Freas' address, having thrown it away before. Okay, I'll tell you, and you tell her. If she loses it again, tell her again.

Speaking of your mother: she was naughty. I gave your daddy a copy of *Pornucopia,* which is my Super Adult Conspiracy XXX-rated close-your-eyes-while-reading Not For Women And Children censored novel—*and she read it!* Naturally her brain now looks like rotten eggs on drugs. So if she visits you, and she seems to have swallowed all her teeth and suffered a foul-smelling jawbone infection, that's why. What's that? **NO, YOU MAYN'T READ IT TOO!!** Haven't you been paying attention, girl? Stick to Xanth, where stuff like this is banned.

It was nice getting to see you and Kathy at the hospital. I understand you have a new roommate now, named—wait, that's *your* name! You mean she's Jenny too? How will you tell each other apart?

I forgot to give you the two magnolia seeds I brought along. I saved those from way back, when they kept getting crushed in the Post Orifice, so finally I had to bring them myself. That's why I came, after all. I remembered them Monday morning, so I gave them to your daddy. You mean he forgot too? Well, demand them; he has them somewhere. If they sprout in his shirt pocket he'll look like a walking magnolia tree.

Some tag-ends about that hospital visit: I thought of the quartz crystals I gave you and Kathy because they are in *Tatham Mound.* The Indians believed they had healing properties, and could be used to tell the future. So if you recover more of your powers, you'll know why. I hope Kathy liked hers; she didn't want to put it on, but maybe she was just too shy. I wonder if she really didn't receive that letter I sent her over a month ago. I have it on the computer; I can send it again if I need to. And about that song I sang you: "The Eddystone Light": it's a funny song about the sea, and I thought it would make you laugh, but it didn't. Sigh. These things don't always work out. Actually it wasn't easy to get much of a reaction from you on anything. I worried that you were falling asleep when I read "Tappy." Kathy was awake, but you were getting uncomfortable. And I never got to meet that boy you mentioned—I can't remember his name now, which is par for the course; I can't remember any names without rehearsing them. Oh, well; the way we picture things is seldom the way they happen. It's a nice hospital, and I'm glad to be able to picture you there.

Which means you'll be moving soon, so my picture won't count. This is in the nature of things.

Meanwhile we have progress on that project to make a video tape from the first Xanth novel. The man who is working on it came to visit me last week and showed us his five minute sample. It's okay but not phenomenal; he said it costs $9000 a second to make such animations, and he doesn't have that kind of money, so had to fill in with still pictures. Yes, nine thousand dollars a second! That's more money than your mother makes, even when her teeth aren't bothering her. But it seems like a good project, and we'll probably go ahead with it.

Did you hear the news about Kimberly Mays? She's the girl who turned out to have been baby-swapped in the hospital ten years ago. The Mays family got her, and the Twiggs family got the other girl, and only now have genetic tests confirmed it. So Kimberly was in effect adopted. No one knew, except whoever swapped the babies, way back when. Imagine what it would be like if you turned out to have been swapped: then someone else could be in the hospital and you could go home to strangers. I don't know; that might not be that much fun. I understand Kimberly is upset about it. Strange things happen on occasion!

Well, Jenny, say hello to Jenny for me. I only have one

enclosure for you this time: "Curtis." Yes, you may show it to Jenny too. Have a harpy week!

NoRemember 30, 1989

Dear Jenny,

Friday is my Jenny-letter day, but I'm doing this on Thursday, because I'm wrapping up much of my correspondence for the month now and want to keep the first of next month free for paying work. If I can get in four more good days, I can finish *Orc's Opal* except for the editing, and be just about on schedule for the next novel, *Virtual Mode*, which features the suicidal fourteen year old girl. What would happen to the world if you turned fourteen and I didn't have that novel done, so I couldn't read you a chapter from it? (Would you believe: I typed control-O instead of control U to underline *Orc*, and it jumped me to the top of the paragraph, inserted a ruler, and started typing there. Apparently control O followed by O does that; it's part of the "O" roster of commands which Sprint has but doesn't list; they are there to emulate one of the other stupid word processors that do things in peculiar ways. Remember what I told you about how computers are always out to get you? Believe it!) *Mode* should be published in 1991, and maybe catch your Last Days of Fourteen. See, there is order in the universe. You'll like Colene; she's not at all like Tappy, but she's all girl. You might get the notion from all this that I like girls. Right; I've been tuned in to girls ever since my first surviving daughter was born, and maybe even a bit before then. A correspondent recently wrote me to tell me that she had just had a son (she appeared in Xanth as EmJay, who married the Ass who helped her compile the Lexicon of Xanth). I wrote back that she should keep trying, and maybe next time she'd have a daughter.

Meanwhile, what's doing here? Well, on Tuesday we had our thickest fog yet. It made the morning forest quiet, a wonderland of only close things, no distant ones. It's probably easiest to reach Xanth from here on such mornings, because the magic trails have proper concealment. I think it was such a morning that Jenny Elf crossed over into Xanth from the World of Two Moons, starting a complication that the Muses still haven't quite resolved. Which reminds me: I tell them not to do it, but I have had experience with my fans, and they'll do it anyway. They will write letters to you, sending them to me through the publisher. I'll have to send them on to your mother, who will have to read them to you, and then you'll have to answer them. So be prepared for your fan mail, Jenny, after *Isle of View* is published. Because I know you will intrigue the readers the way Ligeia did.

Which somehow has led to my next subject: much as I'd like to see you recover the full use of your body, and become a marathon gymnast, and live happily ever after, I have this nagging little suspicion that you will have to settle for something less. But I feel that the computer can bring you a great deal of joy, once you get around its out-to-get-you syndrome. All you need is a way to input it, and it doesn't really matter whether you use a finger or your head or your big toe. (No joke; if you have good control over that toe, they can set you up with a toe button to operate it.) Then you can have sentences programmed, such as "Thank you for writing to me. I still can't walk or type, but with the help of this computer I can answer you. I'm sorry to learn that you also got hit by a car. Doom to all careless drivers!" You can have a signature block made up, even. Your mother could program that sort of thing, I'm sure. Did I ever show you my Xanth stamp? No? Okay, here is one; don't try to use it in Mundania, though.

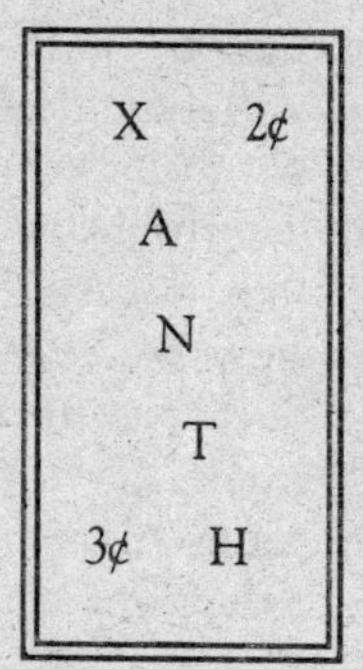

So you see, much can be done with the computer, and not just sentences. You'll have a ball with a drawing program. First get a good way to direct the machine—maybe a little "Thinking Cap" that is attuned to the small motions of your head—then enter the wonderful world of increasingly proficient control. It really is like a magic realm. I was dragged kicking and screaming into computers; I wouldn't have changed over from pencil and manual typewriter if they hadn't stopped making good manual typewriters. But once I really got into the computer it was wonderful, and I really wouldn't trade it. Those little talk-box computers you and Kathy have are fine, but I'm thinking of the heavy stuff, that has the potential to tune you in to the larger world so well that others would not know your situation unless you told them.

Say, maybe we can make a Jenny stamp! Let's try it:

J 12¢
E
N
N
13¢ Y

Anyway, I now have a nice mental picture of you at the hospital, though I guess you won't be there much longer. I also have one of you in your fancy go-to-the-ball gown, with your matching shoes. Actually, I thought your little bare feet were cute, too. I have your rose by my computer; I see it sitting there and I think of you, between paragraphs.

Meanwhile, back here, we had another visit by the cows. They were suddenly grazing right by our house: Elsie Bored, HowNow Brown, Bossie, and one whose name I didn't catch. We phoned the sheriff, and that afternoon he came and shooed them back onto his property and patched his fence. Air-boaters on the lake keep breaking it down, and then the cows get out. I guess those boaters don't know whose fence they are so cavalierly violating. One of these days they may find out the hard way. Which reminds me: we have deer on our property, and there's another deer who joins the sheriff's horses, grazing in the field right in sight of passing hunters, leading a charmed life, because everyone knows whose horses they are and how he feels about his horses' friends. I wrote that into *Firefly*: a true story folk will think is fiction. But that deer hasn't been seen for a couple of months. We hope some hunter didn't—or some reckless driver. Maybe that deer got to know our deer, and is with them now. But we're worried. Deer are so innocent, and hunters are such ||**CENSORED BY ADULT CONSPIRACY**||!

Which reminds me: I have played with the typestyle modes on this mono-mode system, and find there are seven ways to show print on the screen: plain, underlined, HIGHLIGHTED, Blink, invisible, blink/underlined and blink\HIGHLIGHTED. You can't see several of those in the printed version, of course. But let's try the invisible, and see whether it does or does not print: *Invisible*. On the screen that word does not show; if it doesn't show when printed out, it's truly invisible. Yes, it's really there; I can see it when I go into Codes Mode: ^WInvisible.^N Yes, I know, here I am wasting time instead of getting on with the letter. It's my way. Meanwhile right now my wife Cam is wasting her time trying to make our DEC printer print from her IBM-clone computer; it's supposed to be possible, but a new cable and several codes later it still won't do it. We bought new computers for both our daughters, which are fine except that they insist on stopping after every page. We'll get that ironed out in due course. Maybe you can find the setting on your computer that makes *you* invisible, Jenny.

A year and a half after we moved here, we still can't open and close our front gate from the house. The radio signal can't get through the jungle. This one is guaranteed for five miles, but we said "prove it" and they couldn't. So now they are setting up a tall tower by the gate, which will transmit to our TV antenna, and it finally should work. The thing is, if I ever get famous and crowds of fans are trying to get in, I'll want that gate closed—but we need to be able to buzz it open for deliveries and such.

And we received four boxes of fresh fruits from HOUSE OF ONYX. Sixty fruits in all. Brother! We have made it through the pears and are working on the apples. No, ONYX is a gem dealer, not a fruit dealer; it's just their way of saying thanks for doing business with them. But four boxes?!

Do you keep up with Calvin and Hobbes? This past week has been fun. Calvin kept getting larger until he stepped right off the world and found a door deep in the universe, leading back to his room. Calvin has my kind of imagination.

You know, Jenny, when I was your age I used to imagine that maybe my life was all a bad dream, and I would wake and find myself back in England where I was happy. I suspect you have similar dreams. But my life has improved so much that now when I think of waking I fear it; my real life might be as an unsuccessful writer, and all my best-selling novels might have been a wish-fulfillment dream. So I'd rather stay with it. But if one day you disappear, I'll know that *you* woke up and everything since the accident was your bad dream. Then you'll read *Isle of View*, and wonder.

I'll wait to print this out tomorrow, in case your mother has a last moment phone call saying "Don't send it; Jenny just woke up!"

December 1989

A holiday passes. Progress is made. A stay is extended. Three new words are spoken. And one new word is defined.

Dismember 8, 1989

Dear Jenny,

Well, while I was struggling through a letter to a British publisher, your mother was talking with my wife on the phone. So my report is secondhand, but I gather that they are extending your stay at Cumbersome, because you are improving. Isn't it odd, when the better you do, the longer you have to stay, instead of the other way around! Maybe it's because you went to the convention, and saw how many folk care about you, so it's just natural to respond. So—what? The British publisher? No, you wouldn't be interested in that. Oops, every time I tell you you aren't interested, you say you *are!* Just to be ornery. Okay, then, briefly: this publisher was demanding four hardcover copies of my novels, to tear up and use for typesetting and promotion and such. Such as four hardcover copies of *With a Tangled Skein* to destroy. Poor Niobe, getting ripped apart and laid out in pieces! So I finally told them no, make your own copies from the original one. They agreed, but then in the next contract demanded *six* copies to destroy. So I said—well, never mind; just poke a finger in the air and you'll have a notion. I don't need that publisher. Well, now they have a new editor, who came there hoping to edit my books, and he discovered I wasn't there any more. So he wrote to ask what the problem was. Okay, I'm telling him. Picture your mother receiving a letter from that doctor, saying: "I understand you are the one who sent that submarine to run over me. What seems to be the problem?" So she would respond: "The problem was that I couldn't get my hands on a tank, you **CENSORED BY ORDER OF THE ADULT CONSPIRACY!!"** Then she would reconsider, and instead write him an oh-so-polite but nevertheless extremely-cutting missive telling him exactly how his blank would be blanked if he did it again. And if he had the sense God gave an idiot gnat, he would apologize and guarantee it wouldn't happen again. So that's the sort of polite but cutting missive I was writing, while your mother was telling my daughters' mother how you could now speak three (3) whole new words and were graduating from pudding to solider food like casseroles and overcooked green beans. Um, don't overdo it on those beans, because—well, never mind.

So meanwhile, back here at the tree farm, we—what? How did I actually politely cut up that British publisher? That's really pretty dull, out of context. So let's—sigh, you want to know anyway? Have I told you in the last five minutes how difficult you are when your beady little mind locks on to something irrelevant? I have? Sigh. Really, it's just highfalutin' language you wouldn't—oh, all *right*, here's a quote: "It was obvious that [this publisher] placed no great value on my novels. My response is similarly obvious: I must go where my work *is* valued." That translates to that finger I mentioned above. So as I said, it's dull material for you. The editor will no doubt express dismay that such a misunderstanding could have arisen, and will see to it that things improve, and I'll sell him some novels, as a favor. You see, there's this series of collaborative fantasy novels that hasn't yet found a British publisher, and this editor is even interested in *Pornucopia*, which gives a hint just how far he will go. I can do business with a publisher, once it is established just who is the master. Your mother understands perfectly; she gets along with people the same way. Too bad her dentist hasn't caught on yet; he thinks she's just another patient.

Now may I get back to my regular letter? I may? Oh, thank you Jenny! We had one more loose cow turn up; a neighbor told us (who happened to be the girl who delivers flowers; we invited her in so she could see how well the four poinsettias she delivered last Christmas—a gift from Putnam Books—were doing; we transplanted them outside and now they are big bushes. No, we didn't tell her about my secret nitrogen fertilizer), and we called the sheriff, and he came out, spied the cow, and the cow saw him and took off for the forest and he couldn't catch her. I think her name is Delia, as in the song "Delia's Gone." And we had a cold front come through. Yes, I know, it's not supposed to happen in Florida, but sometimes things slip up. So there it was, just under 30°F, with five beautiful red flowers on our azalea (remember, the one that didn't get the word that it was supposed to limit its blooming to spring); those flowers survived nicely, but we suffered frost damage to our poinsettias. They are just turning their top leaves bright red, too, having taken it on good faith that freezing wouldn't happen here.

Do they keep you up properly with the comics? I have this nagging suspicion that they get careless on some of these important details. For instance, in "Curtis," Gunk, the vegetarian and token white in a black comic strip, has a chameleon from Flyspeck Island; it adapts to any background and becomes completely invisible. Now it has escaped, and they are having a terrible time finding it. It just gulped down Curtis' sandwich, invisibly.

Meanwhile, here's a news item that should make you squirm. You have an affinity for the Navy, right? And you're an environmentalist, right? Well Greenpeace is a militant environmentalist organization; I belong to it, along with a number of other environmental groups. It focuses mainly on the sea, and sends folk out to interfere with whaling ships and such so they can't kill the whales. This time the Navy was running a submarine missile-launch test, and Greenpeace doesn't like nuclear weapons in the sea, so got in the way, and a Navy ship stove a hole in the Greenpeace ship and shoved it out of the way so the test could be run. So here is the $64 question: which side are you on? Isn't that mean of me, to get you into an argument with your daddy!

On public radio they had another fund-raising week. We sent in our money, but they keep going until they make their target, and it's dull as anything, listening to their constant guilt-inducing appeals for money. But in the middle of it this time they had something clever: young, bright, idealistic woman applies for work, because she really believes in what public radio is doing. Then this vampire-voice says "You are young and beautiful; you will make an excellent Fund Raiser!" Which is the one thing she can't stand. So there she is, reading in a dull monotone "We know you will want to help this effort and contribute generously" etc., obviously hating it, while the vampire watches her throat as she talks. I think I've asked before: do you listen to the radio? There are some good programs there, such as *All Things Considered,* and you can get songs to your taste. I listen all day. My taste runs to the softer songs of the 50's, 60's and 70's. There's this one I heard in 1957, "Dark Moon" and never since, and they never play it now, but maybe some day they will. So if you have a radio, you can practice coordination on the dial or digital buttons.

This week I'm proofreading my novel *Phaze Doubt,* and I discovered a typo that may amuse you: I have a reference to a mythological character Hermia. It came out Hernia. Now that intrigues me: a girl named Hernia. That suggests all kinds of Adult Conspiracy notions. This week

I also got into revamping my computer setup. You see, we bought these hard plastic keyboard covers, and the cover flips up and becomes a paper holder, so I can type from a vertical sheet. I was doing just that, but had trouble finding my place, with no marker. So I tackled the problem head-on, as is my wont, and my wife got into it, and we finally fashioned a foam-plastic cutout in the shape of a fat L: vertically it reaches four fifths up, and horizontally three fifths, and the two inside sides of the L reach to two fifths and one fifth. So I can mark my place to within five lines of text, simply by turning over my L. It works perfectly; I wonder if I can patent the notion and make a fortune? We also added some macros on particular keys, such as my three dot ellipsis with hard spaces. That looks like this: . . . It's on Alt-Period, and the thing about it is that those hard spaces prevent it from being broken up. I don't like it when I have two dots at the end of the line, and the third at the beginning of the next line. But it takes me some coordinated fingerwork to do it with hard spaces, which is a nuisance, so now I can do it readily. Want another ellipsis? . . . There—see how it refused to split across lines?

So what else is happening here? Fun in court, would you believe it. There's a judge here in Citrus County (Citrus County is a lot like Flyspeck Island, I think) who objects to strong language. When he overheard a lawyer say "B*lls**t!" he fined him and I think put him in jail. Now someone has written a song: "The Ballad of Gary Graham," all about the silly things this judge is doing, and it's being played on the local radio station and is very popular.

Your mother says—no, horrors, it can't be!—that you lost your Magic Crystal. How could you? For shame! For sh—oh, you found it again? Well, okay this time, but don't let it happen again. That magic is supposed to be helping you to get better. You know, you'll get to speak one word per facet, and then you can start over.

So have a nice week, Jenny, and say "Hi" to Jenny for me.

Dismember 15, 1989

Dear Jenny,

The big news is that three days ago, Tuesday, I saw a two foot long coral snake. Do you know about them? They are just about the prettiest snakes, and they have the most deadly poison. But they aren't dangerous. A coral snake's teeth are small, and it can't really bite a person unless he sticks his finger in its mouth. The snake is mild tempered and just wants to avoid trouble. So I called to Cam (my wife—remember the Xanth cushion?) and she brought out her camera and took pictures. Of course the snake just wanted to hide. It was right along the side of the swimming pool enclosure. She got a picture, we think. No, we didn't hurt it; we just went back inside, and it must have wandered back into the forest. I'm glad to have it around.

Other news? Well today as I was typing letters—I did 13 before getting to this one. What do you mean, why? Because you're 13, why else? Oh, why before yours? Because I always wait until afternoon, in case your mother calls to tell me that you're tired of my letters, and not to write another. Where was I, before getting into this interminable dash? Oh, yes, I was typing letters—I looked out the window and saw a phoebe. What do you mean, how did I know? If I tell you it was a phoebe, believe it. Because it's a flycatcher that wags its tail; that distinguishes it instantly. No, I don't know why they do, but they definitely do. I even named a character Phoebe, in the Adept series; she was a harpy with a sore tail, so she kept twitching it about.

What else? Nothing as significant, I'm afraid. Tomorrow I start writing *Virtual Mode*, which novel I conceived on OctOgre 14, 1987—yes, I have my computer printout notes with that date, and in 1988 I signed a contract to write it for PUTNAM/BERKLEY Books—and I have a problem. That wouldn't interest you. What? You say you'll decide what interests you? Sigh. Must we go through this every single letter? I have all these heavy significant things to say, and here you are demanding to hear about—oh, all right, all *right!*

I have this vision of the very beginning of the novel. Fourteen year old Colene is coming home from school—will you stop interrupting, girl?! What do you mean, that's misspelled? I just changed the spelling, is all. I looked it up to see whether it had two L's or one, and discovered that either will do, but that there's a third variant with "ene," so I decided I liked that better. So it's correct because I'm writing this novel and what I say goes. That's just the way it is. And don't bring up that business about my calling you Kathy again; I've been trying to forget that for a month. You're acting just the way Cheryl does when I call her Penny. You girls are all alike. Any little inconsequential thing, and you—no, don't you dare start calling *me* by the wrong name! Anyway, Colene is coming home from school with her armful of books, and she's an absolutely typical ninth grade girl, sort of cute and popular and happy with many friends and an active imagination. Then something happens to change her life forever. No, there's no reckless driver. Only in real life does it get that bad. She sees something, and investigates, and it's a man in a ditch. He's face down, in funny clothing, and just sort of groaning. Now she knows she should go on home and call the police or something; her house is the next one down. He's probably a drunk. But instead she does something almost suicidally crazy: she puts down her books and hauls the man into her sort of dollhouse cabin in the back yard. You know, her place, where she can shut the world out and listen to records or read fantasy novels or whatever. It's all she can do to get him there, because she weighs something like a hundred pounds, and the man is at least 150 pounds. But she drags him in and shuts the door, so he's hidden. Then she gets water and some food and takes care of him.

So why did she do this? Is she really crazy or suicidal?

Yes she is. The truth is, her happy normalcy is but a front; underneath she is a deeply unhappy girl, and when alone her favorite pursuit is to slice open her wrists. She would have committed suicide before this, but her nerve always fails when she sees the blood flowing. Both her wrists are bound in cloth; others think this is just an innocent style she affects, but it's really to cover the scars. So it is entirely in character for her to haul this dangerous man in here. He may recover and rape her or kill her; she knows she is flirting with this. The edge of such danger fascinates her. She's not like you. What? Did I say that? Where? Back at the foot of page one? Oops, I see it now: "You girls are all alike." So how can she be not like you, if—okay, okay, I apologize. You girls are *not* all alike! Now are you satisfied? (Brother!)

Actually, this is no drunken bum. He is Darius, Cyng of Hlahtar, from a far different realm where magic works and science doesn't. No, this is not the Adept series; you haven't read that, have you? This is a different setup. Anyway, he got separated from his native land, and here in this realm where magic doesn't work he is pretty much helpless, because science is not something he understands. He normally conjures food, for example; the idea of buying it in a store for money is beyond his grasp. So he is starving. Colene fetches him food, and blankets to sleep under, and yes, she warms him by embracing him, because this place doesn't have heat and he has the chills. She is taking a phenomenal risk. But look, I can't do the whole novel here; that's for tomorrow. I'll just say that Colene nurses him back to health, and begins to learn his alien language, and he begins to learn hers, so they start to communicate. He is a good and decent man, just different. He tells her of his world, where he is the—loosely translated—King of Laughter, and though she hardly believes about the magic, he is good at making her laugh. He appreciates her help; she did after all save his life. She helps him figure out how to get home. She's smart with things like computers, and it is a computer analogy that accounts for the title. So in the course of maybe a couple of weeks, not only is he well enough to travel, but he knows how to get home.

Now here is the problem: From the time Colene meets Darius, she never slashes her wrists. He absorbs her whole attention. In fact, she falls in love with him; it's very fast, but she was sort of in love with death already, and this is a much better alternative. By day she's in school, unchanged to external appearances, but now her private moments are spent thinking of him rather than in slicing her wrists. But you see, I wanted to show her slicing her wrists. I wanted that stark contrast: happy girl, suicidal girl. How can I show that if she never slashes her wrists? Well, I could go back a few hours, before she finds Darius. But then I couldn't begin with this typical ninth-grader (or so she seems) discovering the body in the ditch. It seems I can't have it both ways. D*mn! I *want* it both ways! So how do I begin this novel, Jenny? Don't answer that; by the time you get this letter, I'll have begun the novel; in fact I'll have begun it by the time this letter gets mailed out. I guess I'll just have to go back those few hours, growr.

So now on to the main letter. What? You want more of the novel? Look, I can't tell you the whole thing! I haven't even figured it out yet! Okay, I'll tell you just about this section. Darius gets interested in Colene, then realizes how young she is. No, this isn't "Tappy"; Darius immediately backs off, being an honorable man. Colene is heartbroken, but helps him complete his return to his fantasy frame. He goes, and she remains behind, though she would have given anything to go with him. Her thoughts of suicide return with doubled force.

Once home, Darius thinks things over, and realizes that he has made a mistake. He owes his life to Colene, and now realizes that he loves her. She's not too young by his realm's standards. But he doesn't know how to find her.

Travel between realms is extremely tricky; he can't just go back. What is he to do? Meanwhile Colene realizes that her choice is between Darius and death; she will either find him and be with him, or she will kill herself. She can suppress the almost overpowering urge to commit suicide only by fashioning a desperate plan to follow Darius to his home. And—the rest of the novel concerns this effort on the part of the two of them to get back together. There's a telepathic horse named Seqiro, and an alien super-science conqueror, and a woman who remembers the future instead of the past, and—but why bore you with all that? On with this letter.

Hm—I have notes for all manner of significant things, but here you kept me talking about the novel for two pages, and I can't afford to do a six page letter. You'd just fall asleep. Okay, I'd better postpone the book reports until next time. No, don't you dare sigh with relief! I have some books about trees and nature and the reclassification of the Burgess Shale, and if you think that's dull, you'll have to listen anyway. I'm worried about your education; I'm afraid they aren't covering things of importance, such as the Burgess Shale and the daily comics. So here are a couple of Hagar the Horrible and Bent Offerings, and an item about a person being charged $35 for not eating any food at the hospital—you say you're on that diet too?—and a dingus to help folk like you walk, and Curtis and Alligator Express with a fantasy princess story. I tried to copy a couple of atheist folk songs, but it was black on red and I guess God wouldn't let it be copied. They are part of an atheist Christmas card a correspondent sent me, with songs like "O Come Ye unfaithful" and "Bad King Wenceslas." I'm agnostic, which means I don't choose to make an issue of my lack of belief in the supernatural, but the truth is my private belief is essentially atheistic. Well, here, I'll quote some: "Bad King Wenceslas looked out/ On the Christmas season/ Where the peasants lay about/ Hungry, poor and freezin'." I like both the original song and this bitter parody. I also like the old Pogo parody: "Good King Sauerkraut looked out/ On his feets uneven/ Where the snow lay round about/ Gee, his feets was freezin'!"

Through the Ice has now been published, and I am receiving letters of appreciation from the friends and family of Robert Kornwise. What does this have to do with you? Robert Kornwise was killed just about a year before you were hit, by another reckless driver. I completed his unfinished novel, that his memory might live to that extent. You and he are linked in my mind. He died, you survived, and I became involved. I think you would have liked each other. Your mother will read you the novel, when you get home, if you ask her. More next week, Jenny—

Dismember 22, 1989

Dear Jenny,

The big news this week is Penny's cat. Penny, my elder daughter, adopts stray animals. Do you know anyone like that? Yes, I thought you did. Well, there was this stray cat in her neighborhood a couple months ago, and then it disappeared, and then in the past month it reappeared and she adopted it, took it to the vet for shots, and brought it into her apartment. Now he is named O Neku Sama, which is Japanese for Honorable Mister Cat. He is nine months old, brown/orange with tiger stripes, and fairly lively. Yes I know: up until that last, you thought I was describing a relative of Sammy's. Well, maybe a distant relative.

So Penny drove up two days ago, and Neku has been exploring our premises. We can't let him out, because he might get lost in the forest and perish, but he's had a ball exploring the house. The first evening Cam and Penny went off to a cocktail party put on by the local bank—we do a lot of business with the bank, so we're on their list, but I don't have a lot of use for either cocktails or parties, while Penny, now 22, can drink if she chooses, and maybe she just wanted to demonstrate she could do it, though I don't think she has much taste for it either—and Neku remained here with me. He disappeared. I looked all over the house, fearing what my daughter would say if her cat had vanished forever when in my charge. I mean, what would you say to your daddy if—yes, that's why daddies are careful. When Penny returned, Neku reappeared. Where had he been? That bugged me. So I kept an eye out thereafter, and I believe I know, because he's there now: in the living room there's a TV set in the corner, and there's some space behind it, right *in* the corner, and that space is in shadow. But if you look carefully, you can see that some of the shadow has tiger stripes. Neku sleeps when Penny is away, so as to have plenty of energy for her return. Yes, I see you nodding your head; you knew it all the time.

Yesterday I was typing Chapter 3 of *Virtual Mode* and Neku was up with me in the study when they left. Women are always off shopping, especially at this time of year. What interests a man is the sight of a beautiful young woman without much clothing; what interests a woman is the sight of a big department store without much limit on the credit card. If department stores had nude young women as clerks, men would get more interested in shopping. But cats aren't much interested in shopping. So Neku explored the study. He came to sit on the desk beside the computer monitor, near your Rose, and then went down behind to play with the wiring. I was a little worried about that, but I did manage to have a good day, typing 4,000 words. Colene, the heroine, is trying to recover the key to alternate realities, that muggers took from Darius. If she can get it back, he can return, and maybe take her with him. But getting anything back from gang-type punks is tricky, especially when you're a fourteen year old girl without much money. But Neku wasn't much interested in this, and wandered away. I think he finds me sort of boring. What, you do too? Oh, you want to know exactly how Colene gets that signal back? I don't know; the Adult Conspiracy—how old did you say you were? If your mother found out I told you—Okay, you promise not to tell her? Remember, Colene is a gutsy girl, and suicidal. So she makes a deal: she'll play the punk who has the key a game, and if she wins, she gets the key, and if he wins, he gets her. No, of course this isn't a legal deal, but she's desperate, and he's a tough fence—that is, someone who makes illegal deals for cash, or whatever. He likes the idea of whatever, with a young, clean, non-addicted girl. So he agrees to play the game, provided that his friends are the judge of who wins. And her game turns out to be a contest to see who can bleed the most before fainting. She starts, slicing open her arm with a big knife. She's suicidal, remember. Now he realizes that he has more blood than she does, and can probably outbleed her, but he's about to faint even before cutting himself, and he decides to forfeit, and she wins. Never get into a bleeding contest with a suicidal girl! His tough friends think it's a great ploy; they admire her for it, and honor the deal. So that's the scene I'm in upstairs. But today, downstairs, I've got to type letters to confounded fans—oops, no, I didn't mean you! Why do you have to jump to conclusions? Then who *did* I mean? Well, there was this girl who hasn't read any of my books, but she wrote me an angry letter, calling me ignorant and sarcastic, because one of her friends had asked me how I felt about fan letters, and I said I'd rather be typing my novel. So I—no, I didn't burn her letter. I wrote her a thoughtful missive asking her to consider how she would feel if she was required to answer 100–160 letters a month, squeezing out all her free time and some of her working time, and someone asked her how she felt about it, and she said she'd rather have more time for herself, so then she was accused of being ignorant and sarcastic? In short, I wrote her a pretty nice, sensible letter, that will make her feel like last months' uncleaned litterbox. Moral: don't take off on a writer unless you are awful sure of your point. So anyway, this morning Neku wanted something to eat, so I poured him some milk, and he wouldn't touch it. Only he and I were up at 6:15 A.M., you see. Sigh. Now he's back behind the TV set, and I'm typing this letter.

Meanwhile, what else is new? Well, the fanzine I write to published an edited-down version of my Convention Report, cutting out some of the detail about traveling and such, which makes sense. So now those readers know what it's like to meet you. Unfortunately, it may be the last thing I send them, because I just can't abide this business of censorship. I told them how I felt, and others have too—another writer even called me last month to tell me how emphatically he agreed with me, and that he was writing a strong letter to them—but no such letter has been published, and in the latest issue they published a snide remark by someone they favor—the one I implied was a sociopath, for taking pride in squishing spiders—about my being "testy" and taking my marbles home because of not having my way. In short, someone who will practice censorship is not about to admit that it's wrong. So I will indeed take my marbles home, and I may not be the only one. They can ponder that at leisure. I don't know whether you consider it an honor to be featured in my last report to a magazine, but I assure you that many of their more decent readers will be glad to know about you. I may write up the matter in the Author's Note for *Virtual Mode*, as it is my custom to comment on what happens to me while I'm writing particular novels. Meanwhile, with a certain irony, the one who set this off, the prisoner on death row, feels very guilty about causing such mischief. He didn't cause it; I caused it, by having him participate in what was supposedly a forum open to all. He asked what I thought of what he did to get sentenced to death, and I have written to tell him in unmincing words: he had no more business killing that girl than the fanzine had censoring him. I don't like what he did any better than I like what that reckless driver did to you. But what I like and what I do may be different things, because what I do relates to principle, not pleasure.

All of which is pretty heavy discussion to hit you with, at this season. And I still haven't tackled those heavy subjects that got squeezed out last week. Well let's tackle one of them: the reclassification of the Burgess Shale. I know, I know, you couldn't think of a more boring topic if you concentrated for a week, and your daddy's rolling his eyes as he reads this letter to you, wondering if maybe I didn't just take my marbles home, I lost them entirely. Well, shut up and listen, girl, and if you're still bored at the end, okay, you win. You see, a scientist recently said that the two most significant things to happen in the past decade or so in paleontology—that's the science of the earth's history, which includes dinosaurs—were the discovery of the periodicity of extinctions and the reclassification of the Burgess Shale. The extinctions of dinosaurs and other creatures turns out to follow a pattern of about twenty six million years; every time that period passes, boom! more extinctions. Because, it seems, severe meteor showers hit the earth, blasting things to smithereens. That's how come the dinosaurs departed, so we mammals could take over the world; you owe your existence to a meteorite from space. So okay, you understand about that, but what's this business about stupid shale? Well, the Burgess Shale was a fossil-bearing section in Canada about a city block in size and ten feet thick. It's in the Canadian Rockies, 8,000 feet up. But the fossils are of sea creatures, so you know something strange must have happened. The fact is, back about 530 million years ago that region was under the sea; since then the mountains have formed and lifted it up. Remember in "Tappy" the bit about how history lives in the decline of the mountains? Well, it lives in their uplifting, too. Our earth is dynamic, and if you could watch fast-motion pictures of it, one frame every hundred thousand years or so, you would see how it wrinkles and the continents slide about. But that's not the point.

You see, there's a lot of life in our world, and much of it is in the ocean. But there is a greater diversification of life forms in that one little sample of the Burgess Shale than in all today's oceans. And it's different. There are creatures there never seen before or since. And this makes no sense, according to the conventional theory of evolution. It's supposed to be that simple forms evolve into more complicated forms, and split off into new species, so that the more time passes, the more species there are. But here at the beginning there were more species than there are now. What happened? Can evolution be wrong? Well, not exactly; we aren't about to return to the Biblical version, saying that God created everything in one week. But it does suggest that everything existed a lot sooner than we thought, in that "Cambrian explosion," and that the pattern since has not been one of increasing diversity of species, but of the elimination of most of the original species. Maybe by those meteor blasts every twenty six million years. We're just lucky that it was our branch of life that survived; had one of those meteors hit a bit to the side, it might have abolished our ancestor and spared something else, and today's life would be quite different. Instead of you in Cumbersome Hospital, it would be an invertebrate with a squintillion legs. You don't find that interesting? Well, I do, and I think maybe I'll use such a world as the setting for Mode #3, *Chaos Mode*, and we'll just see what Colene, my suicidal protagonist, thinks of it. She's into that sort of thing—extinctions. Forty years ago, when the Shale was discovered, they tried to classify it conventionally, and it just didn't work; now they have done the job over, and scientists' jaws have been dropping. So admit it,

Jenny—don't you find the reclassification of the Burgess Shale a bit interesting after all?

Okay, I hope you have been having a harpy Christmas. This letter should arrive about two days after Christmas, when you're sinking into Post-Holiday Depression, and really weight you down. Don't be mad at me for making you think when you wanted to laugh; you were the one who made me tell you all about Colene in *Virtual Mode* last week, so that I had to postpone the Shale. Christmas doesn't mean a lot to me; I just keep plowing on with my work and my thoughts. Christmas day my family will drag me away for a couple of hours for opening presents and having a big dinner and such, but I think I'd be about as happy celebrating with the Grinch. Do you ever find holidays depressing? Some folk do. I just find them sort of neutral.

Speaking of depressing: I had to exercise on the cycle today with it raining (it's on the pool enclosure, outside but under cover) and the temperature mucking about between 39° and 41°. I wore a shirt and warm body vest and got through okay, cycling just over ten miles in half an hour, but I'd rather have it warmer. Tonight it's supposed to get colder, and tomorrow colder yet. We worry about our plants, that may suffer freeze damage, and our dogs, who are not young any more. It's not supposed to get this cold in Florida!

Well, have a good holiday, Jenny. I'm sorry I didn't have things to make you laugh this time, but maybe you can enjoy thinking instead.

Dismember 29, 1989

Dear Jenny,

So I started out doing eleven fan letters, bringing my total for the month to 145, with about 15 more in my "unrush" pile. Then came the mail: 18 more. No, I won't have to answer them all; several can be done with just Ogre Cards. But I'm just barely holding even. Well, I'll catch up on some more on Sunday, after I write to my family; that Family letter now goes out to ten members of the wider family, and some of those ten recirculate their copies to others. Your mother knows exactly how it is done. Today, ironically, my parents, both of whom have one or more PhD's, are known less for their credits than for mine. "Oh, you're related to *him?!*" You will have some of that experience, Jenny, when *Isle of View* is published next year and your relatives start being known through you. "You're related to *that* Jenny? I don't believe it!" Some will recognize you from the graphic edition the Elfquest folk will publish. "That's Jenny Elf!" So brace yourself; you have some interesting times coming, in due course.

No, I didn't send you any gift for Christmas. My mind works in obscure ways. Neither Christmas nor gifts mean a lot to me; what counts is personal contact and understanding. I have been receiving gifts from fans, and it's awkward, because I don't send any in return. I want to discourage it. For one thing, they tend to be from female admirers, which makes it awkward at the outset. Three more arrived today. One from a female admirer, another from her husband. I think he caught on that (A) I was giving her a polite no time of day, and (B) I'm a useful contact for a hopeful writer. And he's a hopeful writer. Now I have to explain to him how I do superior dialogue, when the truth is, I'm not sure how I do it. Critics think my dialogue is bad. Sigh.

So how did you say you were doing? Eating more pudding? Speaking more words? Somewhere in the pile is a letter from Sue Berres, who gives an unpronounceable term for how you have to learn to speak again. No wonder you have trouble! Think how much easier it would be, if they had an easy term for it. Well, keep plugging away at it.

So how am I doing? I've got a nuisance cold. Oh, you could tell? By my attitude? Usually I stave off colds with vitamin C, and I don't care how many doctors say it doesn't work; I am right and they are wrong. No, I don't think vitamin C will make you recover faster, though I wouldn't say it's impossible. But this cold snuck up on me while I was on a long phone call with my agent, getting ready to market *Tatham Mound*. I went into the sneezes, and thought it was an allergy to something in the air. Hours later I realized it was a cold, but by then it was late. You have to use vitamin C right away, or it can't do much. So I'm feeling generally about the way your mother feels after the dentist has entertained himself fishing for another elusive bone fragment (wouldn't be sporting to catch them all at once!) and blowing out my sore nose every ten or fifteen minutes. No, the commercial pills don't seem to work on me; my daughter got me a couple of kinds, and my nose laughed at them. Well, "laugh" isn't quite the proper term; "snot" is. Finally yesterday I tore up tissue and stuffed it into my nose so it couldn't drip on the keyboard; that gave me an hour to work in peace.

Oh, we had a decent Christmas, and I trust you did. My daughters came home from all over; one had been visiting in Michigan, and our roads got frozen over and closed, so we weren't sure we could get her back. She was visiting the family of a Jewish friend. But she made it back, bringing her friend, so he had the privilege of participating in our Christmas. I think he paid more attention to it than I did. But I did receive a Sony Walkman "Outback" radio/cassette player, so that I can listen to music in stereo while exercising. It looks like a little waffle iron when opened for the cassette. A daughter dragged me out to shop the day before Christmas, and among other things I got my wife a box of chocolates. In 33 years of marriage I have learned something, after all. But overall I'm exactly as klutzy about such things as the average man. That's why God made women, after all.

We had a cold wave. Oh, you had it too? But we aren't used to such things in Florida. We're on a kind of wooded peninsula in Lake Tsoda Popka, and our temperature doesn't go to the extremes it does elsewhere; even so it hit 16°F and all our decorative poinsettias and such were wiped out. We had snow flurries, the first I've seen in thirty years in Florida. Cheryl went to Michigan to see snow—and during her absence it snowed on her car, here. We had hundreds of icicles on the eaves. When it warmed, they fell one by one, crashing; it was several hours before I figured out where the crashes were coming from. I hate cold weather!

Toni-Kay Dye sent cookies in many shapes; a number are dinosaurs, including a Xanthasauras. You remember her; she painted "Cats in a Window" for you. I sent her a copy of my Sci-Con report. And no, you can't have one of those cookies; wait till you can chew better.

What's that? You say you're getting tired of this depressive letter? Sigh. Sometimes it's as hard for me to be bright and cheery as it is for you to goose someone left-handed. It's not that you don't want to, just that—well, never mind. Let me tell you about one of the newspaper clippings I'm enclosing: here in Florida they raised the taxes and the tolls on a bridge, and drivers got mad. So they "shot toll machines, hurled plums at toll collectors and filled toll baskets with cherry bombs, razor blades, liquid soap, guns, bras, panties, shrimp and chicken dinner left-overs." Ha! You laughed! I heard you. You know it isn't funny; that's what makes it so funny. So admit it: depressive humor can be fun too.

Meanwhile I have now written 28,500 words of the 30,000 I hoped to do this month on *Virtual Mode*, and will write the rest tomorrow. After Colene won the key by freaking out the thug who had it—you know, that bleeding contest—she gave it to Darius, who is from the fantasy realm. But two things happened: she just couldn't believe him, and thought he was deluded, and he learned that she was suicidal. He needed a woman full of joy to be with him, because where he lives emotions can be transferred directly from one to the other. A woman full of depression would wipe them both out. So he used the key and disappeared—at which point she realized that he *wasn't* crazy and she had just missed out on what could have been the best thing of her life. And he, too late, realized that his effort to save them both was in vain; she would die anyway, alone. He should have taken her with him and loved her even if he couldn't marry her. Thus is set the stage for the main adventure of this novel: how they get together again. Soon she will be meeting a friend along the way: Seqiro, the telepathic horse. Stay tuned.

Naturally other things piled in to take my time from my writing. I had to judge the winner of the story contest Morrow/Avon had at a New York book fair. I wrote the beginning, about an ambitious female reporter who wants an important assignment but is put on an adoption story instead. Then she discovers that all the babies though of different races and sexes, are practically carbon copies of each other. What can account for this? The contestants, ages 15–17, had to finish the story. I got to see the four finalists. One was unfinished, another was full of blood and guts and alien monsters, one was close but not quite, and one was in proper proportion, and I declared that the winner. Yes, it was by a girl; they seem to have better taste in this area. So she'll win the $50 prize. Yes, of course I used up more than $50 worth of my time judging the entries; that's not the point. Yes, you can enter such a contest some year, if you get to handle the computer well enough to write. Or maybe an art contest.

I finally talked with the publisher about whether I should write two Xanth novels in one year so they could do a hardcover edition. We conclude that since I already have two hardcovers a year, this would just be crowding the field and maybe taking sales away from my other hardcovers, so it's better to leave it alone. So I'll just write one Xanth novel next year. Yes, I know; you already decided that; you told me. Maybe I'll use the time to work out a Xanth computer game. My notion is to have the Player start by selecting a Companion: a character who knows his or her way around Xanth and the rules of the game. Then the Player won't have to fumble around figuring out how to play it; he can get good advice from his Companion. The problem is, suppose a virile male Player chooses a sweet innocent nymph for Companion, and starts to get fresh? Maybe she'll call her friend the ogre, who will stuff the Player through a knothole in the nearest beerbarrel tree. End of game. But maybe if he approached her with more respect, she would be more receptive. So this game could have aspects other than just winning through to the golden castle or whatever. Maybe the Player has to learn some courtesy along the way. You can see that this would be quite a job to program; your mother is already shaking her head. She likes the idea, but says it would be easier to program a balky printer to sing "Joy to the world." But with the potential of the 386 computer . . .

I have to wrap this up. I had other books to comment on: *The End of Nature* and *A Forest Journey*, just as I commented on the one about the Burgess Shale last time, but they'll have to wait another week. STOP SMIRKING! It won't hurt you to get a bit of education along the way, you know. Not very much, anyway. Anyway, admit it: you got interested in the Burgess Shale despite yourself last time, didn't you?

Yesterday I heard on the Paul Harvey News that the Rush Limbaugh (No, I'm just guessing about the spelling) radio show had been dropped because of bad words. Then Rush came on, talking about why women should not be farding while driving. Women were calling in and saying, "Well, I fard while driving, and it's okay." I finally looked up the word: F A R D, meaning to apply makeup. Oh. That guy's a conceited conservative, but it's hard not to like him, sometimes. So remember, Jenny: no farding during therapy.

January 1990

A mother comes to visit. And a daughter goes home.

Jamboree 5, 1990

Dear Jenny,

Yet once again I'm starting this letter late. I had nine other letters to buzz out, and those kept being interrupted by phone calls from my agent and a conference call with Morrow Books. They have read *Tatham Mound* and wanted to make a pre-emptive offer so we wouldn't send copies of the novel out to half a dozen other publishers. You know what pre-emptive means? You do? Okay. So they told me how important I was to them, and how they would be making my work into a major hardcover best-seller. Then they made a lowball offer. No, get that finger down! We shall be more polite than that. We shall simply show the novel elsewhere. If we get a better bid, Morrow will have the chance to match it. We're calling their bluff. It isn't that I am greedy, but that publishers show how much they value an author, and how committed they are to a novel, by how much they pay for it. So, with reluctance, I have entered the big-advance arena. It's like a story Colene will tell in *Virtual Mode:* there are two horses in a pasture. One is Maresy Doats, to whom Colene writes private letters in her Journal; Maresy is the only one who knows Colene is suicidal. Colene always wanted a horse, but lives in the suburbs. So Maresy is imaginary. But a good and sensible friend. But this particular problem is Maresy's: she sees that they are grazing their pasture at such a rate that it will be exhausted before spring, and it is all they have. So she talks to the other horse, saying "We had better slow down, so our pasture will last, and we won't starve in the winter." But the other horse goes right on grazing at top speed. What should Maresy do? If she eats less, to conserve the pasture, she will grow lean and the other horse will get more, and the grass will still run out. Then Maresy will be in a worse position to survive than the other horse, who has eaten better. But if she eats more, the pasture will be exhausted even faster. It's a real problem. If Maresy sacrifices herself, only the greedy and insensitive horse will survive. So in the end Maresy has to eat fast too, giving herself the best chance though she knows it is not a good way. Well, that's how it is with me and the marketing of my books. If I settle for low advances, publishers, who are like the insensitive horse, will give my novels indifferent treatment, and I will be bypassed by other writers who go for big advances. It has been happening. So I have to compete, though I don't need the money. I don't want to lose the race to the greedy and/or insensitive writers.

Meanwhile, back at *Isle of View*: The copy-edited manuscript arrived here yesterday. I had not received your mother's corrections, so I phoned her—did she tell you about that? No?—and got them directly. She also said you had sent me a bushel of peanuts. A *bushel?!!* They have not arrived either. Maybe God diverted them to Squeedunk, because I didn't send you anything. Sigh; life does get complicated. Anyway, I have marked in her corrections, and added a three page Jenny-Con supplement to the Author's note. Yes, you can have a copy; here it is. And don't complain about the streaks down the margin; my laser printer is doing it, and won't stop. I think it's leaking toner. We'll use up this batch of toner, and then if it continues with the next one, we'll have to call in the repair man. One problem I anticipate is that readers will want to write to you, and some may even want to send some money to help with your treatment. I got two addresses from your mother, one for letters and one for money. I pondered, considered, cogitated, and thought about it, and the more I did that, the more it seemed to me that the address I should give is the one for letters. If someone wants to send money, and puts it in with a letter, your mother can forward that to the money account. But I think most will be girls about your age who send letters of sympathy and hope.

The novel itself looks good. I haven't told you a lot about it, because that would take 124,000 words or so, but Jenny Elf acquits herself well enough. Someone will surely read you the Jenny Elf sections when it is published. Maybe also about the way the Demoness Metria, whom you met in *Vole*, comes to tease young Prince Dolph. She even offers to assume the form of his fiancée Nada Naga, wearing only panties. He's been trying to see Nada's panties for years, without success. He has no shame. In the end, it is not Nada's panties he sees, but Electra's, which are not nearly as exciting for some reason, and—but I see I am boring you, so I'd better move on.

What? Well, of *course* Jenny Elf wears panties, and no, no one sees them. You have a suspicious mind!

And I was going to do that Book Report on *A Forest Journey*. No, I haven't read it yet. I haven't read the one about the Burgess Shale either; I've been too busy to read. I hate that; I want more time to read. Anyway, this one is about the role of wood in civilization. Stop getting bored—I tell you this is interesting, or else! It tells how wood is vital to civilization. For example, in 2000 BC the isle of Crete in the Mediterranean was a forested wilderness. Then it was colonized, and soon was a center of civilization, with a great fleet of ships made from that excellent wood. Then it exhausted the trees, and declined. I'm not sure whether this book mentions a small matter of a volcano named Thera which blew up and blasted the Cretan civilization to smithereens. But it's probably right about the wood. I know from my research for *Tatham Mound* that some American Indians did similar—no, not setting off volcanoes, dummy!—using up all the wood and collapsing. Wood is important! When England used up its trees it shifted to coal, and that started pollution. So now you know why I'm into tree farms. Trees are wonderful things, and much better alive than dead. If you don't like trees, you're—oh, you *do* like trees? Well, I knew that.

I have to talk with someone about a Xanth computer game I may try to devise, with Companions the Player can choose to help him. I told you about that last time. You want to know whether Jenny Elf can be a Companion? Hm; I hadn't thought of that. Does she know enough about Xanth yet?

Have a harpy week, Jenny! I understand the time is drawing nigh for you to come home. Then you can see that your mother gets some rest, instead of rushing madly after old monias and catching a new monia.

Jamboree 12, 1990

Dear Jenny,

Sigh. Our poinsettias and hibiscus are dead on their stems. We knew the cold snap at Christmas killed them, but it took a while for it to show so clearly. They were getting so pretty, and—you say you don't want to hear about it? Well, there's also the local news. A man was starting out on a bicycle ride for the homeless, to publicize their plight, and he got mugged and his bicycle stolen before he had hardly gotten underway. A young woman was dragged into a nine foot deep pit, held captive for several hours, then taken out and, um, the Adult Conspiracy warning light is beeping at me. Let's just say that something she didn't like happened to her. Another woman was squished by the dump truck she drove. They renamed a Tampa street the Martin Luther King Jr. Boulevard, and the new signs keep getting vandalized, sprayed over, ripped out. Racism is rampant here. What do you mean, you don't like that news any better than the business about the plants? I'm just telling you what life is like in sunny Florida. How come you're so hard to satisfy?

What's that finger-signing you're making? I think it translates to BIRD. I don't understand. Well, I do have some news about a bird. There's this correspondent I call the Bird Maiden, because she used to rescue injured raptors—that is, birds of prey—and nurse them back to health and set them free again. When I got my novel *Hasan* republished, I mentioned the Bird Maiden in the Author's Note. That novel is an adaptation of an Arabian Nights tale, "Hasan and the Bird Maiden." You'd probably like it. The Bird Maiden in the story is one who could put on a bird suit and fly away. Sure enough, the mundane Bird Maiden took off for Germany after that, found a man there, and now she's married and with an 18 month old daughter named Alessandra. That's close enough to the story. Good things happen to my readers.

What? You mean that wasn't what you were asking about? Let me see that finger again. Oh—*that* kind of bird! Very well, I'll tell you the story about that. You see, about three months ago one of the also-ran FM radio stations decided to change its program and its image and go all-out for glory. It became the "Power Pig." Its manager painted his car shocking pink with splotches and announced that the proper signal of respect was one middle finger thrust into the air. He called it "Flipping the Pig." Now he drives around town and everybody gives him that signal of affinity. Meanwhile the radio station quadrupled its market share and became #1 in the area, overall. That Pig is really flying!

So now let's get on to—what, you aren't through with the Power Pig? Okay. The leading station had been Q-105. Power Pig said the Q stood for "queers." No, I won't tell you what that means. Then the local gay group got on the case, and the Pig had to apologize. Then the Pig put out T-shirts with the Q-105 logo, with a screw superimposed on it. That means—no, I'd better not explain about that. Q didn't find that very funny. In fact, Q is now suing for trademark infringement.

Okay, enough of that, before you get bored. Oh? Not yet? Sometimes I'm not sure about your mind, Jenny. Well, all right, a bit more. The Pig urged women to send in nude pictures of themselves in another promotion. No, you can't join that one! The Pig also said on the air that the only safe way to listen to it was "with a condom over your head." No, I won't tell you what that means; I'm already in trouble as it is. And the Pig went to the St. Petersburg high school and issued fake hall passes during a student protest.

So now you know what local FM radio is like. You should listen to the radio, Jenny; it can be a lot of fun. If they can get you one of the ones with "Seek" buttons, so you just turn it on and touch the button and it finds the next good station. The radio can be good company when everyone else is too busy to bother with you. Oh, no one would ever say that, but you know there are times. I listen to it all the time while I'm working, FM and AM.

I had to refill the can with a 40 pound bag of bran for the horses. I just managed to make it all fit—then remembered that the cup I use to serve the bran was in the bottom. Yes, I know: your mother does that all the time. Fortunately I was able to reach down through it with my bare arm and hook the cup out; bran is light stuff.

This week would have been Elvis Presley's 55th birthday, except that he died over a decade ago. He was five months younger than I. What do you mean, who is Elvis? Brother, do times change!

This summer they will have a solar car race starting in Florida. It will pass near here. Each car is worth half a million dollars. When they get the price down, we'll be interested. I'd love to see the world get off fossil fuels, because—oh, that's right, you know why.

Elsie the Bored Cow showed up again. At least it may be her; all we saw was her manure in our road. The sheriff never caught the one cow left over. So we called him, and today heard sirens all over, and a helicopter circled overhead. No, I suppose it's possible it wasn't searching for the cow, now that you mention it.

So how has life been with you, Jenny? That ordinary? Well, maybe it will perk up when you go home. Then you can snooze, buried in cats.

I'm enclosing more comics. As I said, I have this nagging suspicion that they aren't taking proper care of you, so that you miss some of these comics, so I'm enclosing the best ones. There was a block of four good ones associated with Curtis, Sunday, so I'm sending the block. Plus some daily ones. Marvin's mother is named Jenny; I figure she represents what your life could be like when you grow up, etc. Cartoon of a writer's life; they could have based it on mine. Picture of girl with horse, sort of like Colene and Seqiro, the telepathic horse in *Virtual Mode*. And a golden one hundred dollar bill I pasted together from an investment ad, with pictures of sailing ships on it; I thought maybe you'd like this kind of money.

Now, about that next book report I was going to do—what do you mean, there's no room left for that? I might almost get the impression you weren't interested, and I know that's not true. Is it? Uh, Jenny, did you hear the question? Sigh. Well, then, maybe next week.

Say hello to the other Jenny for me, if she's still there.

Jamboree 19, 1990

Dear Jenny,

Hey, it's Friday again (Wednesday for you; you run half a week behind me), and time for the JenLet. I hope things have been less hectic for you than they have been for us. I've been writing *Virtual Mode*, the novel featuring the suicidal fourteen year old girl. All I get are twenty working days a month; the rest goes to correspondence and such. So I try to write 3000 words of text a day in whatever novel I'm in, and in the first month of *Mode*, Dismember 16–Jamboree 15, I succeeded, completing over 60,000 words. Then things started going wrong. Yesterday I only got 800 words done; the rest of the day went to accounting, business letters and I can't remember what else, just that it wasn't my novel. Oh, now I remember: my laser printer went on the blink on Monday. It flashed the smug message 27 OPC-1 and refused to print. Aggravating time with the manual, whose perfectly clear instructions nevertheless manage to be perfectly unclear, indicated that the something-or-other magazine needed replacement. No, it didn't want ANALOG SCIENCE FICTION MAGAZINE replaced with PEOPLE; this was a complicated dingus deep in the works. So we ordered one and replaced it—and the error message was unchanged. We called in the guy who handles the computers, and it mooned him with the same message. So we called the repair service. That's in Tampa. It turns out that a repair man costs $115 an hour whether he's driving here or working on the printer, and it's a four hour round trip drive in addition to the time he's here. Plus 31¢ a mile, and parts. So it will be a $600 repair bill for a balky printer, and the amount of paying work I haven't gotten done in this period is a good deal more expensive than that. In short, it isn't only your mother who gets aggravated about things. Especially about balky printers. Growr!

Remember last week I told you how we reported some cow manure on our driveway, and next day a helicopter was circling our tree farm? Well, it *was* the sheriff! He drove by a few days later to let us know, with his horse in a van behind. No, he didn't find that cow. Man is supposed to be a smart species, but he's not as smart as a cow in the wilderness.

Meanwhile my wife asked me whether I'd refilled the pasture water. Ouch! I'd forgotten it for over a month. That's not the only water the horses have; I fill the tub at the barn every day, and they can drink from the lake if they want. But I like to keep the pasture water full too, to encourage them to be out there. I went out, and sure enough, that old bathtub was down to about one inch deep. So I dumped it out, because the bottom was solid with leaves and sludge, rinsed it, and then pumped it up again. Took 450 strokes with the red handpump. Ever thus, with mundane life. But if we ever have a weeklong power failure, we'll still be able to pump water with that handpump, so it's worth maintaining.

Plans proceed with Richard Pini and the graphic edition of *Isle of View*. The three parts of the adaptation are to be titled *Return to Centaur* or "What Kind of Foal Am I?" and *Nada Worry in the World* or "A Serpent Teen Exposition" and *Morning Becalms Electra* or "All the Snooze Befits the Prince." You see, Che is the lost five year old winged centaur foal at the beginning, and in the middle we have the problem with Nada Naga, the princess who can become a serpent, betrothed to Prince Dolph, and at the end we have the problem with Electra, who must marry Dolph before she turns eighteen or she will die. But Dolph is smitten with Nada, not Electra, and the judgment of a teenage boy is—well, would *you* trust that? Anyway, publication of the first part is scheduled for JeJune, which means it won't be all that long before you get to see Jenny Elf in person, as it were.

Which reminds me: you will be getting fan mail, Jenny. A reader has already asked for your address, so I gave him the box number your mother gave me, c/o Jenny Elf. By this time maybe he has written to you, and you've heard the letter. There will be more when the novel is published in OctOgre. Just don't get a helled swead about it.

60 Minutes on TV had a feature about a girl with muscular dystrophy, the wasting away of her muscles. She's your age, and uses a powered wheelchair to get around. I thought of you when I saw that. There was also an item on the news: they have discovered something that encourages nerve regrowth. Tell your mother to run that down, if she hasn't already, because the only thing between you and the use of your body, Jenny, is some nerves that could use some regrowth. It could make a significant difference.

Meanwhile I received an envelope from Sierra. Well, I'm an environmentalist, so that wasn't surprising. But this turned out to be Sierra Games, a different outfit. There was a letter thanking me for my suggestions, but saying they wouldn't be using them. Interesting for two reasons: First, I never wrote to them; I didn't even know they existed. Second, I had just heard about a computer game called *Hero's Quest*, with good graphics. I'm considering making a Xanth computer game with some special features, and have been pondering whether to allocate time to it. So I want to look at that Sierra game, and several others they have, to see how they are; then I'll make a better one. What was that sound? Were you sniggering? You doubt that I, with no prior experience, can improve what others have spent a lifetime doing? Oh, you don't doubt? Okay. So this was a very timely arrival. Who sent in my name I don't know, but—hey! I heard it again! You definitely made a sound! I caught you this time. Oh—you want to know whether Jenny Elf will be in my game. Well, do you want her to be?

Okay, I can put her in. And you want to know what's different and superior about my game? Well, as I see it, most role-playing games get all complicated with things like hit points and closely defined levels of proficiency on a number of levels and they lack any genuine human interaction. Computer role playing games seem to share such problems, as well as requiring endless lists of supplies and things, and if you forget one, boom, you're dead. This is not appealing to any but a game freak. I want to pull in ordinary folk like you, who don't want to have to memorize a manual to play, but also don't want something stupidly simplistic. So I plan on having Companions, and—what's that? You mean I've already told you about that? More than once? Why didn't you stop me, then?! Anyway, I have now discussed this with the experts—that is, my daughters and their friends—and I conclude that what I want to do is technically feasible. Whether I will do it I don't know; probably I'll get some of those games and see how they are, and then decide. Once you get home, Jenny, you should be able to start playing computer games, maybe some of the high-graphic action ones, and if they're as interesting as they are supposed to be, you'll have a lot of entertainment there. Tell your folks that it's good digital therapy.

Meanwhile I have been exploring FM radio stations. The newspaper lists some, but some of the best it doesn't list, which annoys me, so I finally wasted some time charting them myself. There are about fifty I can get well, and some seem promising. For example there's one that plays nothing but mellow vocal oldies. Once I know where all the stations are, I'll be able to listen to what I want continuously while I work, changing stations whenever commercials hit. I heard an ad for a dance on one, and at the end it said "Improper dress required." Hm.

Meanwhile I still ride my bicycle out each morning to fetch the newspapers, and it's always interesting in its fashion. The architecture of dawn moves me. The clouds form such spectacular and always different formations, with orange or red as the sun arrives, and the low clouds form thin sheets about ten feet above the ground. The bunnies run off the road. No, they don't seem to hop much. The men are working on our front gate again; it's been out of commission ever since the bad lightning strike some months back. Now they have set up two tall towers to transmit signals between house and gate, so maybe we can open and close the gate from the house, as was always intended. I want to be able to shut out those hordes of fans, in case I ever get famous. They got the signal working from the house, but not from the gate. But it's getting close. Maybe.

I suffered a minor revelation this morning: accounts are like sex. Don't laugh; I mean it. You see, I added up my earnings for last year, using my account book, and my wife added them up using her accounts. They didn't match. That's par for the course. She had more money than I did. So I gave her my calculator tape, and she found half a dozen errors. So I corrected those—and now I had more money than she did. So she corrected hers, and now we agree to within two dollars, which is pretty good. So how does this relate to sex? No, we didn't decide that sex was more fun than accounting, and quit accounting. It *is* more fun, but that's another story. But I realized that though each of our lists of figures had errors, those errors didn't match, so we were able to cancel out all the errors by cross-matching. Well, that's what sex does. If living creatures reproduced parthenogenically (that is, without sex), any errors in the genetic blueprint would continue. But with sex, there are two blueprints, and the errors in them cancel out. So it's a good system. If those who hate sex were able to abolish it, they would soon enough breed themselves into extinction, because there would be no good way to correct for deleterious mutations. Serves them right.

And tomorrow we must get up at 5 A.M., so we can

drive to Ocala and meet my mother on the train. Then two days later we'll take her back to the same train, same hour. I don't see my parents often, because they live in Pennsylvania.

Okay, I still have a book report in mind—what, you say we're out of time? Just what do you have against book reports? Oh, well, maybe next week. Just let me know when you get home. Actually I may know it anyway, when you stop answering my letters.

Jamboree 26, 1990

Dear Jenny,

All right. Your mother phoned Sunday and said you had been home almost a week! I hope your dad didn't take my last letter out to the hospital on Wednesday, only to discover that you weren't there.

So let's discuss important things, like comics. I've been enclosing some because I've had a suspicion that you weren't getting to see enough of them. But now you're home, so you probably see them all. So maybe I'd better cut down on those, except for the Sunday Curtis, which your mother forgot to make the local newspaper run. So I'll enclose what I have this time, and then cut down. This week's Curtis features Gunk, and the only problem is that Gunk wouldn't have picked up a sausage pizza; he's a vegetarian. As it was, he was right to step on it.

I'm also enclosing a big fake $20 bill which you can use to pay off your mother next time she reads you the comics, and a clipping of a poem about a cow.

Now about last Sunday. Did your mother tell you about that? My mother was visiting us, for the first time since 1988; she was here for two days. We picked her up at the train station at 6:30 Saturday morning in Ocala, which is about an hour's drive from here, and put her back on it Monday morning. So I put my mother on the phone with your mother so they could analyze their children. It seemed to work out okay.

One thing I learned in the course of this visit. My mother had hair so long she could sit on it—but she cut it short when she was twelve years old. She says there is a picture of *her* mother in tears, with all this beautiful hair from her daughter on the floor. It seems my mother looked just like the picture of Alice at the Mad Hatter's tea party or whatever—they drink tea in England, you know—but she didn't like it. There seems to be something about age twelve that's bad for long hair. Do you think some evil creature put a curse on long-haired twelve year old girls? Then again, my daughter Penny never cut her hair; I was there to protect her from that, and it's still beautiful today, now that she's 22. Well, keep growing yours back, Jenny; you know what a difference hair makes. I may have details slightly garbled, but it seems to me that you lost all your strength about the time they cut your hair, and are gaining it back only at the rate your hair grows back. Remember Samson in the Bible.

I hope your mother is able to get help for you and her. Maybe the folk at Cumbersome Hospital figured she could take over and do everything that the 24 hour shifts of assorted personnel did, in addition to earning her living. I may be wrong, but I'm not quite sure that's the case. If the right person could come in and help, it could be very good. I remember how good the Nanny was in England, when I was young; if I had had a choice, I would have stayed with her and not bothered with my family. Of course they don't have such folk in America; closest we come here is the movie with Mary Poppins. Ah, well.

Meanwhile I had a letter from the Bird Maiden. Did I tell you about her? Yes, my Computer Find says I did, a couple of letters ago. Well, she sent a whole package of

Christmas cards and letters to her mother in America, for remailing at local rates—25¢ instead of 90¢ overseas from Germany—and they ran it through one of their Patented Post Orifice Cruncher machines and burst it apart and most of the letters were lost. But I got mine, with 90¢ postage-due from Germany, and then another letter from her explaining what had happened, thinking her letter had not arrived. Mundane mails are like that; they have no respect even for bird maidens. (Come to think of it, the way you use that finger, I should call *you* the Bird Maiden!) Anyway, she told me how her cute 18 month old daughter Alessandra did a Cute Thing: locking her mother outside the glass door on the upper-story balcony in Dismember while she was washing it. It was an automatic latching door, sort of. So there was mother outside in temperature in the 30° range in her housecoat, and there was cute daughter inside alone, with the apartment locked. The neighbors below had to toss up an overcoat and shoes, and Bird Maiden had to keep Daughter entertained and occupied for an hour so she wouldn't do something like turning on the oven and climbing in for a snooze. So they played pantomime games through the glass, while the locksmiths came and drilled out the lock and opened the door so they could rescue Bird Maiden before she froze. And you thought that only *your* mother had adventures like that!

And how is my dull life doing, you inquire? Well, after a year and a half they finally got our gate buzzer done. Sort of. Had to build a tower to get the radio signal over the trees, and at this point it has cost us over $3,500—just to be able to open our front gate from the house. Yes, yes, I know—your mother encounters such problems on an hourly basis. But she's used to it. So we tested it, and it worked. And next day it didn't. So my wife and I took the gate buzzer and she drove out to the gate—it's three quarters of a mile by the road, remember—and signaled me to buzz it open, and I tried it in all different parts of the house.

The buzzer buzzes the radio unit in the attic, which in turn buzzes the gate to open. But the hand buzzer turned out to work only in the parts of the house closest to the attic unit. Sigh. So we finally mounted buzzers on the walls, upstairs and downstairs, where we know they work, and we run to buzz them when someone pushes the button at the gate. It worked when the lady editors from Putnam and Berkley came to see me yesterday, anyway.

Oh, what were they here for? Just visiting. They were at a sales meeting in Orlando, and they're reading *Tatham Mound*, and *Unicorn Point* is on the New York Times best-seller list, so they came over. We went to eat at a restaurant where they have a fine what-do-you-call-it, where you take plates and serve yourself to whatever you want in the way of anything, all you can eat. There was even an ice cream vending machine, which the ladies delighted in using, then pouring on chocolate syrup and nuts and all. I stuffed myself with onions and mashed potato and three kinds of pudding. You'd have loved it. No, you would not have to take onions! I still feel stuffed, a day later.

So keep struggling through, Jenny. People do care about you. You should already be receiving fan mail; two readers asked for your address. So if you get letters "care of Jenny Elf" you'll know.

February 1990

A symmetry is achieved. A story continues.

FeBlueberry 1, 1990

Dear Jenny,

I'm starting this letter a day early. It is my 30th letter of the month, after 160 last month. What happened was that yesterday 39 letters arrived in the mail, 31 of them in a package from DEL REY BOOKS, about a dozen of them dating back to Apull 1989. Right, not long after I started writing to you. Someone must have cleaned out the cobwebby recesses of his desk. If your mother had sent her letter through that publisher, and it had taken nine months for it to be forwarded—well, if I said what needs to be said about those bloatbottomed noodlebrained functionaries at publishing houses, my mouth would catch fire. You see enough of that with your mother already. I think her teeth had nuclear meltdowns. So anyway, I have now answered all those letters, doing them at the rate of up to seven letters per hour cold—that is, from first reading to proofreading—starting last night, and as long as I'm doing letters, it's your turn. So if this arrives a day early, don't worry; it won't happen again. The Post Orifice would never allow it.

What's that? You want to know how I answered letters so fast, when it takes me five minutes just to type the address and ten minutes to read the letter? Well, I made up an apologetic paragraph for the glossary, and invoked that at the beginning of each letter. That gave me about half the letter right off. Then I touched on personal points, answering questions and such. I have some other standard paragraphs in the glossary, such as for the question "What's the next Xanth novel, when's it due, and what's it about?" which help.

Oh, you want to see one of those paragraphs? Why? To make sure it isn't the same as the first paragraph of *this* letter? Jenny, have I mentioned your suspicious mind?! Okay, here it is; I just type the word "late" and then CTRL-F4, and it magically transforms it to this:

I received your letter on Jamboree 31, along with 30 others in a package from DEL REY BOOKS, some dating back nine months. I feel mixed pain and anger with this inordinate delay, and only hope at this point that you have not long since given up reading my books in disgust. It seems pointless to answer you in any great detail, since I can not even be sure your address remains valid. My apology for the long non-response, and if you write again directly to this address, you will receive a faster answer. Which is not to say that I'm trying to encourage more mail; far from it. But ordinarily you should have had a reply within a month or so.

Okay, satisfied? It *isn't* quite the same as the lead-off for this letter. So now let's get on to—what? I can't quite make that out, Jenny; you know I can't read those hand signals as fast as you can make them. In fact I can't read them at all. Just the "Thank You" signal, and these definitely aren't that. X A N T H —you want the Xanth stamp? Ouch! No need to make a curse-face at me! Oh, you mean the next Xanth novel glossary paragraph? Sigh. Okay.

Xanth #14, *Isle of View*, should be published in Oct-Ogre. It's about Prince Dolph's choice of which girl to marry, and also about Jenny Elf from the Elfquest graphic novel realm, who is visiting Xanth and finds it odd. There will be a graphic (comics) edition as well, from the Elfquest folk.

Now are you satisfied? You thought Jenny Elf would not be in there? O Ye of Little Faith!

I'm enclosing Curtis, with Calvin/Hobbes on the back—I'm rather pleased with the way I work that—and a special Hagar the Horrible sent me by another correspondent. She modified it a bit, see, to make it fit me. Yes, I thought you'd like it. I get the darndest things from my fans. I have a dancing flower, and an hourglass that has green bloblets in clear liquid instead of sand, and a letter opener in the form of a thirteen inch Samurai sword. Another thing a reader sent me just a few days ago was a thirty page History of Xanth with dates from the time man arrived there right up through the present, complete with charts and genealogies. It's amazing, and just in time for the writing of *Question Quest*, about the long life of Good Magician Humfrey. Now I won't have to guess about things; I'll use that as my reference. I'll try to get it published as an appendix, with due credit to the reader who made it. He seems to have worked independently of the Lexicon and *Visual Guide*, because he doesn't have their errors. What a nice surprise!

What's that? No, Jenny Elf isn't in it, because he hasn't seen that novel yet. But yes, I told him about her.

Meanwhile, how are things here? Our poor dead bushes remain dead; we hope they will sprout new growth from the stems, but so far those stems are shriveling. Maybe from the roots. We hope. The grass is sending up new shoots, at least. We now have a big yellow Gerber Daisy flowering in the last two days; it looks almost like a sunflower. And the azaleas—remember how I said they are supposed to flower only in early spring, but kept it up through summer and fall, until the DisMember Freeze? Well, they lost some leaves, but now are back flowering again, managing not to miss a month. So there is some joy in Florida.

What else? Well, no more visitors. Chapter 4 of *Tappy*

(working title) arrived from Phil Farmer, and yesterday I was going to make a note for Chapter 5—and suddenly had a thousand words, summarizing the whole chapter. Just before every old letter in the world landed on me. So tomorrow I'll start in writing that chapter. I had Jack and Tappy fleeing in a small aircraft, but others were pursuing and gaining. Farmer got them out of that, then they were headed into a strange glowing cloud that kills the minions of the Gaol empire, but Tappy blithely forges ahead while Jack is about to pass out—which is where Farmer turned it back to me. But he did tell me how to get into the phase-traveling ship in that cloud. I'm going to have them do futuristic medicine on Tappy and fix it so she can see and talk again—except that she doesn't. It's as if she doesn't want to. So Jack has to work with her, and try to get her to—while the Empire forces are closing in. Because Tappy is the Imago, the one power that can stop the Empire, if only—what do you mean, you've read that before?

Meanwhile I'm progressing on *Virtual Mode* too, in which Colene and Seqiro, the telepathic horse, reach the region of the evil Ddwng of the DoOon—you've read that too? Jenny, you're impossible!

Well, keep going, Jenny. I understand you'll be going to school, too, with folk who know how to do it. Harpy learning!

FeBlueberry 9, 1990

Dear Jenny,

Let's start with the Book Report—what's that? The comics? You want to start with the comics? I really can't understand why, Jenny.

Okay, this time I'm enclosing a whole week of Curtis. This is because I just couldn't risk having you miss it. Your mother might be having an attack of the purple grue and not read it to you. You see this is about Curtis' vegetarian friend Gunk, the comic strip's token white, who is running away with the action. It is frog dissection time at school, and I remember when we hit that at college. They were going to dissect a live worm. I made a cutting (uh, no pun) remark about how I hadn't gone to college to participate in vivisection, and other students began to get uneasy, and finally the instructor backed down. "Well, if I *had* cut open this worm, you would have seen thus and so," he said, and went on with the class. I'm sure you can picture the scene well enough. So now you know what to expect from Gunk. Did you notice what happens to the teacher's skirt in the third comic? Then he puts the curse on her, and—say, Jenny, why don't we go visit Flyspeck Island some time? I think we'd like it.

I'm also enclosing a picture of your mother eating an apple with her new false teeth. The local newspaper ran it. You probably didn't realize how widely known she is.

Okay, now that Book Report. I'll—what? Pictures? You want to talk about the pictures first? Well, okay. This week I received a big bunch of pictures from Toni-Kay Dye. She's the lady who painted "Cats in a Window" for you, with the purple wrapping that matched your Cinderella Gown. Do you watch junk TV? She reminds me of the policewoman in *Hunter*. No, not in personality. She took pictures at Sci-Con 11, and you were in many of them, Jenny. These give me a solid evocative memory of the occasion. She'll be sending pictures to you and your mother too, if she hasn't already, so you can see what I mean. One of them I didn't keep; instead I sent it on to Richard Pini. I told him it was coming, on the phone, and now he's teasing his wife about this incriminating picture of him kissing another woman. Yes, that's you, Jenny. Aren't you ashamed? How come you don't *look* ashamed?

There's more on pictures, of another nature. When

my wife's father, my daughters' grandfather, died, about three months before you almost did, there was a big job of estate and house cleaning up to do. My wife handled it, and now the house has been sold and the estate liquidated and the money distributed to his three children. Assorted items came to us, and among them was a set of pictures of my wife Cam as she was at age two, with her father. She was the cutest little thing, much like our daughter Penny, when. Sometimes I just stop and look at those pictures of that bygone day when my wife was fifty years younger than she is now, feeling nostalgia for what I was never part of. Life, even in its ordinary course, can be cruel; it proceeds inevitably from cuteness and novelty to age and death. Then I resumed work, typing my novel about a cute girl who is obsessed with death, Colene in *Virtual Mode*, and the radio played "Scarlet Ribbons." You know that song, Jenny? Surely you do! Cute little girls and scarlet ribbons—it just made me feel so sad for the moment. We can't hold on to the precious aspects of life, we can only remember as we see them fading.

Well, on to the Book Report; I know you've had enough of nostalgia. You say you haven't? Sigh; okay, I'll tell about another song. Back a couple of weeks ago when my mother visited—you remember that, when I put my mother on the phone with your mother? You don't? Ha—I saw that bit of a smile! You *do* remember! Well, we had to get up at 5 A.M. to be sure of catching her train, so Monday morning our house intercoms came on with the radio blaring out news, commercials, and then a song, "Eternal Flame." I had heard that song before, but only in the background of my mind. This time in the hassle of getting dressed and all, that song in its sudden beauty was like a bit of Heaven being heard in Hell. "Does he feel her heart beating . . . ?" There's an evocative half-note in there that does something to me. Then it was cut off; Cam had to turn off the intercom so she could phone the train station and learn that the train was 38 minutes late, so we could have slept another half hour. Sigh. Well, we got my mother to the train in time, and now she's back in Pencil-vania. She's pushing 80, so we like to be sure things are okay. Then this past week I heard that song again, and this time I got to listen to the whole of it. It's not the most elegant song, but instead seems sort of wistful and amateur, as if this young woman is just awakening to love and this is her song of expression. I made a note of the FM stations on which I heard that song, and now I have them zeroed in on my instant-station keys, so they'll be there to play the song again. Have you heard that one? Well, make your mother set up an FM radio so you can listen to such songs. I'm sure you'll like it when you hear it.

Now that Book Report. (Pause) What, no objection? You've finally given up changing the subject? Okay, onward. This is the third of those three books I was telling you about. This is *The End of Nature*, and I hope to read it when I read the other two. Its thesis is that man has just about destroyed nature, so we no longer live in a natural environment. We are cutting down the last of the forests, we are polluting the land, sea and air, we are killing the wildlife, and we have made of the world the equivalent of an enormous heated room. If we don't change our ways in one hell of a hurry, we shall pay one hell of a consequence. And, the author fears and I fear, we are not going to change. So life as we know it now is doomed. Unless the warning signals become so strong that even the ignorant, self-interested man on the street realizes that it is time to act, because it's his own ox being gored to death. Let's hope!

On to something less significant. Last Sunday I went out to pump up the bathtub full of water for the horses in the pasture, and the water was way down, and the pump just wasn't pumping right and finally pooped out entirely. It was coming apart, so that air was leaking in. So Tuesday I went out with a vice-grip wrench—and couldn't fix it. So

Wednesday I went out again, with three vice-grips, and this time I managed to tighten the almost inaccessible nuts and make the pump tight so it could pump again. Victory at last, I think. Such is my life.

So I hope you are doing well, Jenny, and wowing them at school, and I hope your mother is getting some sleep. Till next week—

FeBlueberry 16, 1990

Dear Jenny,

This time I'll start with the enclosures again, because there's one that shouldn't be here. That's because it's a Valentine cardlet sent to me, but I thought you'd find it cute, so I'm sending it along. This person always includes little cutouts he makes, and this is a man on a horse, sort of. Now admit it: isn't this your sort of cutout? I'm also sending a picture of manatees, the ugliest and gentlest of sea creatures; they like to have swimmers rub their tummies, as dogs do. And a cartoon showing the Gettysburg Address copy-edited; maybe that isn't painful and hilarious to you, but it is to me, because it is exactly the sort of editing I receive. If it doesn't amuse you, give it to your mother. And "Curtis" of course, and "The Far Side" because I love that notion of the La Brea Carpets. And "Calvin"—don't show that one to your mother, because then she won't let *you* do that for school. And a cutout quote: "Life is what happens to you while you're making other plans." That can be painfully true, as you know. And a little graph showing a formula for P/E Plus Inflation. Now you may wonder what P/E stands for. Well, at school it's Physical Education. In some circles it's Penis Envy. Here I think it means Price/Earnings ratio. Take your pick; I think the graph will work for any of them.

What's that? I violated the Adult Conspiracy? Sigh; it's hard to avoid it, if I don't want a hopelessly dull letter. Which is the point of the Adult Conspiracy: it is to see that folk never get to see or do anything interesting. Especially young folk like you.

And a fax of a page from a news fanzine that evidently picked up the Jenny story from the Sci-Con report published in that other fanzine I keep telling you about. Just so you know the news about you. That was the last thing I sent to them; I have dropped them. Yes, they are now printing comments about my supposed attack on another person and my name-calling, while the other person is accusing me of all the crimes he can think of without regard to accuracy: he says I suffer from PMS (your mother will define that for you), that I don't know what a logarithm is (I taught logarithms when in the Army), that I have amazing arrogance, and so on. This is because I criticized him for squishing spiders just because they were there, and when he attacked me in a barrage, I said that needless cruelty to animals is an early sign of sociopathic behavior. I think he is pretty well proving my case. Anyway, that's what's being published about me now that I can't respond because I stopped writing because of their censorship. Par for the course, apparently.

But you're not interested in my aggravations. Oops, you mean you *are*? But Jenny, these are supposed to be nice sweet positive uplifting letters to cheer you up. You mean you're sick of that stuff, and want something nasty to chew on? You're getting more like your mother every day! Okay, I'll tell you my latest aggravation. Do you remember the Xanth Calendar? The one with the Siren on the cover, in her bare skin? No? How about the picture of Miss Mayhem, the ogress? Ha! I caught you remembering! Well, because I wanted it done right, I financed that calendar myself. I paid for everything, and every artist was paid immediately when the picture came in, instead of having to wait months the way publishers do it. Then I signed a contract with Ballantine to print and distribute it. The deal was that they would pay 6% royalties on each calendar sold, which means that I get about 59¢, and if they sell more than 25,000 of them, I start getting repaid for my expenses in making up the Calendar. The idea was that if they printed 100,000 copies or so and sold most of them, we'd all be well ahead. Well, Ballantine kept being out of the office when we called to inquire how the calendar was selling. Meanwhile I got letters from fans complaining that they couldn't find it on sale. One even suggested that I do a Xanth Calendar; not only had he not seen it on sale, he didn't know it existed. So much for their publicity and distribution. So I put the matter in the hands of my agent, and he got the information: they only printed 33,000 copies. That guarantees that I lose half my money, and unless they sell almost all of those, which isn't to be expected—there are always some returns—they won't have to repay *any* of my initial costs. Apparently they deliberately printed too few, so as to stick me with the loss. It doesn't hurt them; they had no initial costs, because I paid the artists. So they make extra money by avoiding what should have been their costs. It's a great deal for them, but for some reason I find that annoying. So don't be surprised if you see someone else publishing the next Xanth Calendar. As the saying goes, "If my friend cheat me once, shame on him; if he cheat me twice, shame on me." No, I can afford the loss—but if they ever want to deal with me again, they are apt to discover it more expensive than they expected, because I don't forget.

So let's get to something more positive. I got a new file handling program called XTreeProGold, and it turns out to be everything I ever wanted in computer housekeeping. Yes, I realize this interests your mother more than you, so I'll keep it brief. With it I can set up two windows, one showing the directory I'm in, the other showing the directory I want to copy files to. So I can see exactly what needs copying, and I can see it happening. That stops those disastrous errors right there; in fact I've already caught some out-of-date versions of files. When you get into word processing, and have dozens of files to watch, then you'll appreciate the delight of a program like this.

This is my 112th letter so far this month, and yes, I have dozens more waiting. So what? you inquire? Well, this does concern you, because one of the letters I answered this morning was from a young man of about 18 who was hit about a year ago by a drunk driver and smashed up something awful. They are now taking some of the pins out of his bones so that he can start bending a knee again. He's had a bad year, but is recovering. He would like to be a writer. So I gave him advice on marketing his novel, and I gave him your address, the Box # c/o Jenny Elf. So if you hear from him, listen politely; he has a notion what it is like.

Meanwhile our blooming dogwoods are—let me rephrase that; our dogwoods are blooming. Bunnies are showing up on the drive again, when I go out to fetch the newspapers on the bike and sneak a peak at the sunrise. So things are normal. Have a decent week, Jenny.

FeBlueberry 23, 1990

Dear Jenny,

Ouch! It's after 7 P.M.! Where did the day go? Well, I typed 16 letters, and my wife's brother and his family visited for five hours, and I had a call from my British agent. She called with the news that there is a Spanish offer for *Pornucopia.* They made the offer, then made a better one before the agent could respond. Apparently another publisher was getting interested. I told my agent not to read it;

she sent it to the publisher still sealed in its plastic wrapping. You know how that book boiled your mother's brain. She's hardly had a good night's sleep since. So yes, I suppose you could say that my letter to you was delayed by a dirty book. So maybe it does entitle you to give me a dirty look. If you feel that way. But if you do, I won't tell you about the next paragraph.

You see, this is sort of an anniversary. My first letter to you was written FeBlueberry 27, 1989, and this is the 23rd. Maybe I should have waited four more days on this one, so—no? Ah, well. In that letter I told you how I had heard about you from your mother, and how we had just had our tree farm mowed between the rows of pine trees, and I went out there and regretted the cutting down of the blueberry bushes and thought of you, also cut down. I mentioned Robert Kornwise, who was killed by another reckless driver, whose novel I completed; your mother has a copy of that. I told you to pet the Monster under the Bed, who had gotten lonely without you and come to join you at the hospital. And I told you how I would put a Jenny character in *Isle of View*, an elf or an ogre girl, and you chose the ogre.

What's that? Oh—I was just checking to make sure you were listening. You chose the elf, and after that one thing led to another, and in a few more months you'll see Jenny Elf in person in the graphic edition. After that you won't dare show your face on the street, because someone might recognize you. Then the regular novel will appear, with its Author's Note, and you'll start getting letters. I don't know how many, but there could be a dozen or so at first, and then the pace would slow down. Do they have Show and Tell at your school? You can take a pile of letters in.

So a lot has happened in the intervening year. You went to a convention—what do you mean, what convention?! Sci-Con 11, where—ha! I heard that peep. You just couldn't hold in that laugh any longer, could you! Then you came home, and now you're going to school, and who knows what you'll be up to tomorrow. Your mother phoned last night and reported that you were doing very well, and that you have a little signature stamp with a unicorn so you can answer letters. She said you got the Salad Bar Botanist of the Week Award. What were you doing—throwing salad around? And that you went to the circus. How come you get to do all these things when I can't? But that you still get tummy pains in the night. Well, maybe if they stop feeding you beans—

So how come you're glaring at me? How can I finish a paragraph when you act like that?

Meanwhile, how are things here? Well, yesterday we saw rain approaching on the radar: a big patch of it, all sparkling with color to show where it was most intense, looking like a double fried egg or an interior configuration of the Mandelbrot Set. Have you seen *Nothing But Zooms* yet? You haven't? Well, get on it, girl! And I have finished the first draft of *Virtual Mode*, all but the Author's Note. Yes, you get mentioned there, in a paragraph, but it's mostly about the Ligeia girls, because of Colene, the suicidal protagonist. You'll learn more about her when you're her age, fourteen.

Meanwhile some enclosures. Remember when Penny was here with her adopted cat? Well, here's a picture of him pretending he's Sammy, snoozing on the VCR. And here's Curtis, and Mother Goose & Grimm, because, well, see for yourself. And The Far Side, because I just don't get it, and thought maybe you could figure it out. And a horse card drawn by another correspondent. Folk think that the pencil isn't an artistic medium, but they're wrong, as this card shows. And finally an article for your mother, from a British newsmagazine: they are learning how to make the nerves of the brain and spinal cord grow back. This may be a number of years away for human beings, but it could be very significant for you one day, if it works. And a current biblio for your mother.

So keep perking along, Jenny, and we'll see what the next year has in store.

Author's Note

It was an arbitrary decision, cutting this collection off at the end of one year, but there was too much for one volume. I continued to write to Jenny every week, about a thousand words a letter, so that as this is published there is another volume's worth of material, continuing to grow. I did not write to Jenny with the intention of publishing it; that was a later thought. Perhaps I would have been more circumspect about certain matters, had I realized. This was essentially a closed correspondence, one on one, though of course there were always others in the circuit. Part of the humor of it is in my cautioning "Don't tell your mother," when it might be her mother reading Jenny the letter. Fortunately Jenny's mother was happy to be teased, if it made Jenny smile. Now there will be thousands of others reading these letters. Well, all of you can help keep our secrets. At this writing I do not know whether more of these letters will be published; that may depend on the nature of the response.

No letters from Jenny are included here. This is because there really weren't any. Jenny simply could not write well, even with her good hand. Now, as she is computerized, she can do better, but her energy is taken up with school work and therapy and the hassle of simply surviving with her paralysis. So this is really a one-way correspondence, with a phantom Jenny reacting as I go along. However, her mother does call periodically, updating me on Jenny events and letting me know how she reacts. My guess is that she responds in much the way I suggest she does in the letters, laughing, being mad, getting bored, and in general enjoying it. That is after all the point: to see that she continues to make progress toward life and satisfaction.

Jenny's progress continues. Every so often she returns to Cumbersome Hospital for more therapy; she goes there not because of problems but to improve her performance. Thus hospitalization is good news, not bad news. She had further surgery on her jaw to facilitate speech, though her verbal vocabulary remains quite limited, and surgery on her legs to enable her to stand and even walk, with a walker. Once a young man lifted her so she could actually dance with him. But such events are exceptional; she still has miles to go. She is getting better using her right hand, but her left side lags. So she is bed- and wheelchair-bound, and largely dependent on the help of others, though she is doing more for herself, such as taking her own showers.

Meanwhile, the drunken driver who hit her paid no meaningful penalty I know of, not even remorse. He was given a suspended sentence in criminal court, and the state of Virginia has a "one per cent" rule that effectively prevents a civil settlement unless the victim can prove she was not even one per cent at fault—something virtually impossible to do. Fortunately Jenny's family has excellent insurance, so that it was possible for her to survive and recover to what extent the fates decree. I have a harsh opinion of the leniency with which drunken drivers are treated, and of the way the system seems designed to protect them at the expense of their victims.

When I ran Jenny's address in *Isle of View* the mail poured in. Her mother lost count after reporting about two thousand letters. There was no promise to answer them, but they did try, and many did get answered. Certainly that tremendous outpouring of support—as far as I know, there were no negative letters—buoyed Jenny, showing her how much how many of you cared. Some led to remarkable things, such as the naming of an Iris after Jenny Elf. Some were touching; one woman reported that she laughed through the novel, and cried through the Author's Note. We have heard from some who had similar experience to Jenny's, even to the impunity of the reckless drivers.

Now I am running her address again, not to solicit more mail, but because I've had a good deal of experience with fan letters, these days answering about a hundred and fifty a month myself, and I know that if folk can't reach Jenny directly, they will simply write to her in care of me, requiring me to forward them. So I remind you that neither Jenny nor I guarantee to answer letters, though we do read them, and if you wish to reach Jenny, her address is JENNY ELF, PO BOX 8152, HAMPTON VA 23666-8152. The easiest way to reach me is to call my "troll-free" hotline, 1-800 HI PIERS. This is a marketing service for all my titles and my personal newsletter, and they will forward letters to me, though this can take time. But I encourage you simply to appreciate this book in your fashion and go on to the next; you have no obligation to write.

Jenny Elf continues as a character in Xanth, appearing in *Isle of View, The Color of Her Panties, Demons Don't Dream,* and perhaps future novels. Her likeness is in the graphic adaptation of *Isle of View,* "Return To Centaur," which had difficulties with distribution so is hard to find, but remains available via HI PIERS. She also appears in a Xanth calendar, but this series too had distribution problems, and the one with her has not yet been published. And—oh, yes—Jenny and I share the cover of this book. Jenny, we have to stop meeting this way!

I had to make an ethical decision about this volume. Most of it I wrote, and normally it is the writer who gets the royalties from published books. I could have written a book in the time I diverted to write to Jenny; indeed, this book is the proof of it. But the letters would not have been written without Jenny's misfortune, and would not have been published without the agreement of her family. It did not seem right to keep all the money myself, but neither did I want to establish a principle of giving away what I earn. So I pondered, and compromised: I take most of it, but some goes to Jenny. I'm tithing it: sending one tenth to Jenny, just as the publisher is tithing the cover price of the book for my royalty. So for each dollar you pay for the book, a penny will go to my literary agent, a penny to Jenny, and eight cents to me. The rest goes to the booksellers, distributors, publishers, printers and so on: the complicated machine that is Parnassus. Should the book be wildly successful, those could become significant figures. But that was never the point. I simply did what I had to do, and that was to follow up and make sure that the life I helped recover was worthwhile. As I said when I met Jenny at the convention, a person who saves the life of another may thereafter be responsible for that other. Perhaps this falls under the heading of "Compassion."

This is an unusual book, even for me. It tells somewhat more about me than I ordinarily prefer to let my readers know, because I thought it was just between Jenny and me. Parts of it may prove to be embarrassing, and parts may anger some readers. But it is as it had to be.